A 2021 Vivian Award finali
in the romance industry, **La**
stylish and sensational roma
emotionally epic tales that a
by reality's paintbrush. This Brooklyn native writes
unapologetically bold, character-driven stories.
Her novels feature diverse ensemble casts who
are confident in their right to appear on the page.
Contact: dot.cards/laquette.

Carol Marinelli recently filled in a form asking
for her job title. Thrilled to be able to put down her
answer, she put 'writer'. Then it asked what Carol
did for relaxation, and she put down the truth—
'writing'. The third question asked for her hobbies.
Well, not wanting to look obsessed, she crossed her
fingers and answered 'swimming'—but, given that
the chlorine in the pool does terrible things to her
highlights, I'm sure you can guess the real answer!

This is **LaQuette**'s debut book
for Mills & Boon Modern.

We hope that you enjoy it!

Also by Carol Marinelli

Midnight Surrender to the Spaniard
Virgin's Stolen Nights with the Boss

Wed into a Billionaire's World miniseries

Bride Under Contract
She Will Be Queen

Rival Italian Brothers miniseries

Italian's Pregnant Waitress

Discover more at millsandboon.co.uk.

PALACES
AND PALAZZOS

LaQUETTE

CAROL MARINELLI

MILLS & BOON

First published in Great Britain 2025
by Mills & Boon, an imprint of HarperCollins*Publishers* Ltd,
1 London Bridge Street, London, SE1 9GF

www.harpercollins.co.uk

HarperCollins*Publishers*, Macken House, 39/40 Mayor Street Upper, Dublin 1, D01 C9W8, Ireland

Palaces and Palazzos © 2025 Harlequin Enterprises ULC

Royal Bride Demand © 2025 Laquette R. Holmes

Italian's Cinderella Temptation © 2025 Carol Marinelli

ISBN: 978-0-263-34461-5

04/25

This book contains FSC™ certified paper and other controlled sources to ensure responsible forest management.

For more information visit www.harpercollins.co.uk/green.

Printed and Bound in the UK using 100% Renewable Electricity at CPI Group (UK) Ltd, Croydon, CR0 4YY

ROYAL BRIDE DEMAND

LaQUETTE

MILLS & BOON

To sixteen-year-old LaQuette, who never thought she'd see herself, a curvy Black Brooklyn diva, in the pages of a Mills & Boon Modern royal romance, and to curvy Black divas, all divas, across the globe.

Reigna and Jasiri's story proves that epic love and beauty comes in all shapes, sizes, colors, cultures, and geographical locations.

CHAPTER ONE

"I DON'T CARE who he's meeting with or how many guards you have at this consulate. I want to see him right now!"

Prince Jasiri smiled as the familiar sharp tones of an angry woman pierced the heavy walls of the consulate. Reigna Devereaux was finally here, a full day earlier than he'd expected too.

From the moment Sherard informed him of Ace's death yesterday, he'd known Reigna would end up on his doorstep. Ace Devereaux was Reigna's beloved great-uncle who had swooped in when things were at their worst with her parents and protected Reigna and her identical twin sister, Regina. He'd doted on them, given them the parental support and love their parents failed to provide, and according to Reigna, he was the only reason the twin girls grew up with any joy in their childhood. As a result, Reigna and her sister were devoted to Ace.

Considering how much the man meant to her, Jasiri wagered it would take her a few days to process this enormous loss. Despite her grief, however, she was apparently ready to wage war if her loud bellow in the hall was any indication.

"I guess the show begins now."

He readjusted his big body in the large office chair before pressing the button on the intercom on his desk.

"Bring her to my office" was all he said before ending the connection. When you were a man with as much power as he, there was no need to explain yourself. Those in your service simply did what you said without question. Something the woman currently yelling at his staff had never learned to do.

He took a calming breath as he anticipated how this impromptu meeting would unfold. Reigna might not have learned how to listen in the past. But now that he had something she wanted, thanks to Ace Devereaux, he was certain she'd submit the same way everyone else around Jasiri did: completely and without question.

The carpeted flooring couldn't stop the echo of her heavy footfalls as she walked toward his office. Knowing she was angry, knowing why she was angry made his heart thump hard against his chest with the sweet taste of revenge on the tip of his tongue.

Two years ago, it had been him who was marching to her office, mad as hell and seeking answers. Today... well, today, the spoiled society princess Reigna Devereaux would finally get what was coming to her, and he couldn't wait. He hadn't planned it this way. He'd not spent the last two years planning Reigna's destruction. Holding on to a grudge this long wasn't his usual way. But his father's life was hanging in the balance, and if that meant inconveniencing Reigna, even for a little bit, he would do what he had to do to keep his father healthy and alive. He'd do whatever he must to keep his country safe from the likes of Pili.

His adjutant, Sherard, was only able to get the door open halfway before Reigna pushed her way through, heading directly for his desk. Sherard followed her inside of the room and waited for Jasiri to give a soft nod before he exited, leaving the two of them alone for the first time in two years.

"You arrogant prick. You did this."

Her sharp words drew his gaze and instantly his sight was filled with her lovely form. Reigna was a beautiful plus-size woman, with plentiful curves, and deep brown skin. Curves and skin he'd spent hours admiring with his eyes, his hands, and his body. After two years of separation, he'd hoped the only thing the sight of her physical attributes did was remind him that she was off-limits, tainted by the memory of their failed past. Unfortunately, the straining muscles of his body and his racing heart made it apparent her effect on him wasn't as benign as he'd hoped.

"I've done a lot of things, Reigna. Many that would get me labeled much worse things than an *arrogant prick*. So you'll need to be a bit more specific if you want me to understand what you're referring to."

Her jaw tightened as she glared at him, and the spectacle of her standing in his office, thrumming with anger, made his lips bend into a smile. The first rule of conquering an enemy was to let them see just how little they meant to you. And after turning down his marriage proposal and rejecting him, Reigna meant less than nothing to him. His body might disagree, but his head knew the truth. She was simply a means to an end.

"You got Uncle Ace to leave you half of the house that was supposed to be mine alone."

"Supposed to be?" he quipped. "If that were the case, wouldn't it have worked out that way?"

"Listen, I don't know what you did to get Ace to do this, but I am going to fight to overturn it." She huffed, pointing her finger at him as she geared up for what he assumed would be more vitriol. "I knew you were a piece of work, but I never thought you'd stoop so low as to steal my childhood home just to get back at me for the great sin of turning your proposal down. It's been two years already, Jasiri. Get the hell over it."

"It *has* been two years," he countered, his speech slow but intentional. "And trust me, I *am* well over *it* and *you*. But I haven't forgotten a thing about your betrayal, Reigna. Our history notwithstanding, I didn't do anything to make Ace give me half ownership of that house. He called me into his office two years ago and gave it to me. He said I would need it one day, and it appears he was right, because here we are."

He could see the question folding into her pinched brow before she uttered it. "Then, why would Ace do this?"

He shrugged, relaxing even more as her anger bled into bewilderment. "I wouldn't know."

She narrowed her gaze as she leaned over his desk, placing her hands flat on its surface. "Then, if you didn't ask Ace for the house, does that mean you'd be willing to sell me your half of the ownership?"

There it was, the selfish, spoiled brat she'd always been, climbing up to see how she could make a situation beneficial for herself first and foremost.

"Reigna," he said with amusement in his tone as he tilted his head to the side. "I didn't ask Ace for this gift, but you should know I have no intention of parting with it."

He could see the tightness in her features return as her ire burned a deep red beneath her skin. "Why the hell not? The place holds no significance to you. It's my childhood home, the place I…"

"Felt the most love. The place where your life was the most perfect after your parents' divorce? I know."

She'd said those exact words to him time and time again over their two-year courtship. He'd admired her emotional attachment to the place then. Now he was counting on that very same attachment to give him the power over her he needed to wield if he was going to save his father.

"You're doing this just to hurt me." Her words were spoken on a soft breath, but they were heavy and impactful all the same.

In her eyes, he could see the cloud of hurt mixed with grief and part of him, a tiny sliver, wanted to pull her in his arms and tell her it would be all right. Damn this woman and the hold she'd always had over him. He shook his head, refusing to give in. She might have fooled him before, but now he knew better. Reigna didn't want him. And no matter how good her body made his feel, he could not let those memories make him vulnerable to her. If he was to protect his father and his nation, he had to do what was necessary.

"Reigna, I'd have to care about you to be concerned with hurting you." He could see the involuntary flinch she tried hard to hide. Good. He needed her to know exactly where they stood with one another if his plan was going to work. "Spite is the last thing on my mind." She might not believe him, but it was the truth. He wasn't doing this just to anger her. That was a bonus. He was doing this because he had to, because all would be lost if he didn't.

"Then, why do you want it?"

He stood up from his chair, walking around it until he stood close enough to her that he could smell the spicy fragrance she was wearing floating up from her skin.

"You, Reigna. I need you. And owning half of this house gets me exactly that."

"What the hell could you possibly want from me?"

"That's simple," he smiled. "I need you to marry me."

* * *

"What the hell?"

That was all she could manage after Jasiri's unexpected declaration. Two years ago, he'd been spitting mad when he'd stormed from her office after she'd told him she wasn't ready to be a wife.

"Jasiri, you made it very clear two years ago that you didn't want me if I didn't accept your proposal. Why would you want me now?"

He sat on the front of his desk, stretching his long legs out as he casually crossed one ankle over the other. Her breath caught as she marveled at the sexy picture he made. In or out of clothes, Jasiri had the most tempting body she'd ever known. A fact that hadn't changed in the last two years since they'd broken up.

She could feel the blood rushing through her as memories of how he once used that strong, broad body of his to keep her writhing in pleasure. And even though she was livid that he'd stolen her family home from her, she couldn't shake the need being this near to him caused.

"I didn't say I wanted you, Reigna." His mouth hitched in a sinister smile. "I said I needed you. There is a difference, and you'd do well to appreciate that."

She could tell from the cold glare in his eyes that his pointing out that distinction was meant to cut her, and it certainly did. Who wouldn't be offended if the man they'd once loved with all their heart plainly laid out that he couldn't give a damn about them?

But Reigna was a Devereaux, and she'd be damned if she let this pompous man with his proper diction and his oversize ego see she was the slightest bit bothered by his lack of feeling for her or the time they'd shared together.

"Fine, then," she huffed, trying her best to present a bored affect. "Why do you *need* me to marry you?"

The answer to her question really didn't matter. It was just curiosity that was driving her to ask it. No matter what he said, once again, the answer would be no. Before, it was because she was building Gemini Queens cosmetics with Regina. Now, it was because he was an arrogant, entitled jerk who, from the confidence swimming in his dark eyes, thought he had her where he wanted her.

"My father is ill, Reigna."

He folded his arms, his body tensing before her as a dark shadow fell over his dark brown skin. She could almost feel the tension emanating from his being. Instantly, she could feel a chink in the brick wall she'd erected from the moment she'd entered the consulate.

Without realizing it, she stepped closer to him, laying a hand on his. Purely running on instinct, she sat next to him and said, "I'm so sorry to hear that, Jasiri. The few times I video-called with your parents, they were both always so kind and gracious to me."

"Thank you for that." He whispered softly. "He always did and still does hold you in the highest esteem."

Her fingers wrapped tighter around his and warmth flowed through her. She wasn't sure why it mattered that his father still thought of her kindly, but it did.

"While I regret to hear of his poor health, that still doesn't explain what you need from me."

His jaw flexed, the muscle there jerking as he prepared to continue. "The office he holds back home has put a great deal of pressure and stress on his health. His doctors say if he doesn't relinquish his duties, he could die. I won't let that happen, so I'm stepping into the role. Unfortunately, there's an archaic law on the books that forbids me from succeeding my father unless I'm married. Since this is a pressing matter and I don't have time to find a wife in the usual manner, I need you to fulfill the role."

Amusement bubbled up in her chest, spilling through her lips in a loud laugh until she nearly doubled over.

"I'm glad you find my father's failing health amusing."

His words cut her laughter short, and she leaned closer to him, closer than good sense warranted. Now she could smell that perfect mix of cool, sultry sweetness and him that she'd always loved to inhale whenever he'd held her.

"You know damn well I'm not laughing about your father's health."

Her rising anger should've pushed back the flashes of their past where her sense memory of that smell was taking her. Instantly she remembered long nights of their bodies pressing together until they were blissfully exhausted and damp with sweat. She tried to brace herself against them, but moments of them enveloped in each other's arms attacked her senses, forcing her to shake her head.

She didn't need to remember that. That was past, they were two different people, and currently he was holding her family home hostage. Forgetting that would put her at a disadvantage in these weird negotiations they were broaching.

She'd come here to get her family home back. Taking a trip down memory lane wasn't part of that.

"Since we both know this can't possibly be a real proposition, how about we begin the real negotiations. I'm willing to buy you out with a generous offer that's well above market value. Name your price, and I'll cut you a check."

"This is not a joke, Reigna."

She inhaled deeply, trying hard to gather her thoughts and keep her focus. Being around Jasiri had always mesmerized her. But falling into that old habit now would cost her too much.

"Why me, Jasiri? We both know as a fancy ambassador, there have got to be a bunch of women back home who would jump at the chance to marry you."

"There are," he agreed. "But my father doesn't want me to marry just to take on his duties. He's a romantic and wants me to marry for love. You're the only woman I've been romantically involved with that my father has more than passing knowledge of." He folded his arms, casting his soft gaze down to her, making her want to pull him into her arms. "If I marry you, he won't be stressed, and he'll let me take over his duties without further worry. My only goal is to protect my father, Reigna. Can you understand that?"

She definitely could. Especially after losing Ace, she understood more than most what happened when you lost someone you loved. But this? This couldn't be the answer.

"Jasiri, my heart goes out to your father. You're mistaken if you think this is the solution, though. Come on, let's get down to the real negotiations because we both know me marrying you isn't going to happen."

He tilted his head, considering her for a moment before he stood, stepping in front of her, filling up her senses as his hard gaze bore down on her.

"You misunderstand the situation, Reigna." He brought his large hand to her face, gently cupping her cheek. The feel of his skin against hers made need explode inside her. Her pulse ticked up and her breath lodged in her throat of anticipation of what his next move would be.

When they were together, him cupping her cheek was always followed by his full lips pressing against hers. She should be angered by that idea; she should be pushing him away. But as his eyes bore down into hers, her body decided—without her permission—that it would stay in this exact spot waiting for Jasiri to put her out of her misery and finally kiss her.

He was so close to her, all she had to do was lean in and their lips would touch. But she was frozen, too afraid to press forward and too hurt to walk away.

"There are no negotiations." His voice was strong but quiet, lulling her into an almost trancelike state. "These are my terms. If you want full ownership of that house, you'll have to marry me and live in my country as my devoted wife for two years. Refuse, and I will keep Ace Devereaux's very generous gift, and you'll just have to deal with me…"

He leaned down, the heat of his nearness scorching her, as the deep rumble of his voice caressed the shell of her ear.

"Forever."

She was slightly dizzy, and her pulse was elevated, reactions that could come from anger and desire. But the problem was she couldn't tell which was causing her to feel this way. Anger she could deal with. But desire…that was a totally different matter altogether and so very dangerous to her well-being. Because wanting Jasiri Adebesi was a weakness she couldn't afford to succumb to if she was going to get her family's home back.

"So what's your answer, Reigna? Do you accept my terms?"

She stepped back, needing to get her bearings because there was no way she could think clearly with him sucking up all the oxygen in her personal space.

Once she'd put a safe amount of distance between them, she straightened her shoulders and stiffened her spine. Jasiri might be a powerful ambassador for his country, but she was determined that he would have no power over her.

He raised a brow, showing her he was still waiting for her answer. She wouldn't make him wait, not because she was submitting to his demands but because she couldn't wait to wipe the smug look sitting on his face off.

"My answer is simple." She bent her lips into the broadest smile she could manage. "Go to hell."

CHAPTER TWO

"I DON'T KNOW why you went over there. You should've known Jasiri wasn't going to just give you his stake in the house."

Reigna narrowed her gaze, sending a stiff glare in her identical twin's direction. She had come to her sister's austere office that looked more like a lab with its white walls and furniture, not an ounce of color to be found except the identical brown beauty herself.

"What I should've known is that my twin was going to point out my flaws instead of supporting me in my anger against my trifling ex."

Regina, born two minutes after Reigna, with the exact same face and a completely opposite personality, was all logic, process, numbers, chemicals, and equations. Where Reigna was all fire and emotion, Regina was the twin that didn't let herself get led around by her finicky heart. It was a trait Reigna wished she possessed, especially after her meeting with Jasiri yesterday.

"Reigna, stop being dramatic. All I'm saying is you know how Jasiri is, how he always has been. Hell, I wasn't the sister sleeping with him and even I knew he wasn't going to honor your request after the way you threw dirt on his proposal."

Reigna glared harder, but just like before, her sister

stared at her with not even the slightest bit of concern or compassion for her.

"Regina, I didn't throw dirt on his proposal. I told him I wasn't ready to get married."

"No," Regina shook her head as she pointed an accusing finger at Reigna. "You told him you didn't want to marry *him*."

Reigna huffed at her sister's penchant for remembering the slightest detail for everything.

"I was nervous, Regina. He surprised me in front of the entire Devereaux family, and with all those expectant eyes on me I just froze up. He never gave me a chance to explain that what I meant was that I wasn't ready to get married to anyone, not specifically him."

Reigna remembered that day as if it had happened mere moments ago. After two years of dating, Jasiri knelt with his bright smile, holding the largest diamond she'd ever seen, waiting expectantly for her yes. When it never came, he prodded her for an answer. Feeling trapped, she blurted out that she didn't want to marry him and ran from the room.

If there was any day she could take back, it would've been that one. Not that she would've changed her mind about the proposal, she wouldn't have. But she would've made sure Jasiri understood it had nothing to do with him and everything to do with the horrible example of marriage her parents gave her.

Backbiting, cheating, and physical, emotional, and verbal abuse, those were the relationship tools her parents had gifted her with. No matter how much she wanted to accept his proposal, she couldn't trap him in the vicious prison she knew marriage to be, not when she loved him so much.

Her sister rose from her desk, taking the open space next to Reigna on the couch.

"I know that, sister. But he doesn't. Jasiri is a proud man. You hurt his pride. Until you make that right, you'll never get him to sell you his share of the house."

Regina took her hand, lacing their fingers together. It was something they'd both done for as long as either of them could remember. Even though her sister rarely held pretty words for Regina's antics, she always knew how to make her feel protected and safe.

"Is the house worth all of this, Reigna? We both know you can afford to buy a home anywhere. Why do you have to own this one?"

Reigna slid down on the cushions, placing her head on her sister's shoulder. "Because we were happy in that house. We walked around Mom and Dad on pins and nee-dles for so long. When she left, we were still afraid to even breathe the wrong way for fear she'd come back, and the nightmare would start all over again. It wasn't until we moved into that house after the divorce that Ace prom-ised us we'd have nothing but happiness there. That we'd be safe."

"I know," Regina squeezed her hand lightly. "But is past happiness worth giving Jasiri what he wants? I love that house and all the memories we had there. But I couldn't make the sacrifice Jasiri is asking of you. Is this truly about how happy we were there?"

Reigna took in a shaky breath, and it was as if the dam of pain she'd been holding inside for nearly a week since they'd learned of their uncle's death began to crumble.

"I just miss Ace so much, Regina. He promised me that he wouldn't leave me before I was ready."

"I know, sister. He promised me the same. I wasn't ready either."

Reigna curled into her sister's embrace, needing her strength to keep it together.

"We have to say goodbye to him today, Regina. The closer we get to the funeral, the more I just need to hold on to something that I shared with Uncle Ace. Is that so wrong?"

Regina placed a sweet kiss on her head and patted her cheek. "No, Reigna, there's nothing wrong with that at all. But you know what you're going to have to do to get it. You're either going to fight Jasiri in court, and our cousin Amara has already said it would be a fruitless pursuit. Or, you're going to have to become Mrs. Jasiri Adebesi for the next two years. So again, I must ask you if the house is worth that."

It was a fair question, and if she'd witnessed anyone else going through this situation, she'd probably ask the same. But she couldn't walk away from this house. It was the house where their uncle had brought love and stability into their lives. It was the house where Ace found her in her bedroom after her mother had left them, and when she asked if Ace was going to leave her too, he'd said, "I'll always be here for my babies. I'll fight the good Lord himself if he tries to take me before you're ready."

She'd held him to that promise, and he'd been there through all the ups and downs of her life. The only thing he'd ever asked her in return was that she would someday make the house a home again and fill it with joy and laughter the way it once had been.

She'd gladly agreed to that promise then. And as much as she wished like hell Ace hadn't put her in this situation, a promise was a promise, and she would keep it, no matter what she had to do to accomplish it.

"It's the only thing I have left of the man who loved us

through some of the toughest times of our lives. I can't just walk away from this, Regina."

Her twin separated from their embrace and looked at her with clear eyes. "Then, I guess you have your answer."

Reigna managed a weak smile before she nodded. "I guess I do."

"Baba, how are you?"

Jasiri sat in his diplomatic limousine adorned with the flag of his nation and his princely coat of arms as he watched mourners filter into the large Baptist church on the corner.

"Mwana," King Omari crooned in the loving way he'd always done when he used the Swahili word for *son*. Jasiri's heart swelled at the sight of his father's smile and the clear sound of his voice. "I miss you, my boy."

The last time he'd seen the man in person, Omari had been lying in a hospital bed connected to tubes and machines as doctors worked tirelessly to bring his blood pressure down from near stroke levels.

Determined to keep his father alive and in good health, Jasiri had promised the ancestors right then and there that if they protected his father, he'd do everything in his power to remove the burden of the mantle of king from his head and simultaneously protect their descendants, the people of Nyeusi.

Jasiri shared a warm smile with the man. "Baba, things are moving along as expected."

It was the closest thing to the truth Jasiri could come up with. His father would not have sanctioned Jasiri's tactics into strong-arming Reigna into marrying him to make him eligible for the throne. No, he would not approve at all. That was yet another reason Jasiri was intentionally keeping the truth from his father.

"I was so happy when you told me you and Reigna had reconciled and she'd agreed to be your queen."

Agreed to be his queen? That was laughable. She'd have to first know Jasiri was royalty to know marrying him would make her queen of Nyeusi. A truth he had no intention of sharing until they were either in Nyeusian airspace or land for fear she'd run off. Jasiri was born into this life, and the thought of bearing such great responsibility on his shoulders nearly toppled him. He couldn't risk Reigna deciding it wasn't worth the bargain he was certain he could get her to make.

Even during their courtship, he had struggled with the secret of his birthright. The only way to survive the viciousness attached to royalty was to quickly discern who was with you for you or simply for what you could do for them.

He'd wanted to tell Reigna who he was from the first moment they met. But Sherard reminded him how unwise that was.

"People will use you and, by extension, the royal family to get what they want. Unchecked greed and desire will inevitably lead to scandal. Royal scandals are harmful, not just to the royals but the nation too. Look at how the paparazzi are always dogging the Windsors. You cannot be the cause of such shame and mockery being thrust upon the Nyeusian monarchy. Now some British people question whether they even need a monarchy. As the heir to the throne, you cannot give your people an opportunity to question if the monarchy is needed or not. Unless you are absolutely sure this person will protect you and protect the monarchy, you cannot risk sharing your identity with her."

Jasiri had heeded Sherard's wise counsel. He'd used the two years he'd spent with Reigna to prove to himself and his adviser that she could be trusted. They were in love, and he'd never felt safer than in her arms. He planned to tell her the truth after she'd accepted his proposal. But when Reigna refused his proposal, as outraged as he was that she'd turned him down, he'd never been more relieved that he'd followed Sherard's advice about revealing his identity. Now it was essential she remain unaware until he'd set every part of his plan in motion. He couldn't be seen as weak right now. To do so would amount to him handing the monarchy over to his uncle who only sought the throne to benefit himself, not the people.

"Is Reigna with you?"

"No," Jasiri answered honestly for the first time since he'd answered the video call. "She's with her family right now."

His father nodded. "Please give Reigna and the Devereauxs my sympathy on the passing of Ace. He was always a great friend to me, and if my doctors would allow me to travel, I'd be right there with you among the rest of her family to support her. She was very close to Ace. Every time I talked to the man, he'd go on and on about his babies. And Reigna was certainly included in that number. It tore him up to keep the secret of your royal status from her. Fortunately, as a man of great power, he understood the need for you to walk in the world as a normal man to get the sense of what the real world was like. He protected my son, and I will always be grateful to him for that."

The King dropped his eyes in reverence to his late friend before clearing his throat of the thickness of grief. There were few people in the world that his father held so dear, his expression of pain and loss was clear proof of that.

"This is a significant loss for her. You make sure to take good care of her during this difficult time."

Jasiri knew his father spoke the truth. Reigna and her sister Regina had been extremely close to Ace. He could only imagine how painful this day must be for her.

"Mwana," his father sat straighter, leaning toward the camera of his device. "You lost this woman once. Don't let inattention be the reason you lose her again. I'm serious when I say take good care of her. She will need you to get through this."

"Baba, I will be everything Reigna needs me to be right now."

His father's pride in him as a son and a man shone through the screen. Knowing he was lying to his father about the state of his relationship with Reigna and his position among the many mourners who would pay tribute to Ace should have made Jasiri feel lower than a snake's belly slithering on the ground.

But if lying to his king and father was the only way to keep the man alive, then Jasiri would spin as many tales as necessary to keep King Omari happy and safe. Doing what needed to be done for the greater good was the responsibility of any king. And since Jasiri would be next to rule, he considered this charade practice for the sovereign he was about to become.

Marrying Reigna was the best thing he could do for his father, his country, and himself. Yes, marrying her would help him protect his father's health, stabilize the monarchy, and keep his father's line as the rightful monarchs of the nation. More importantly, however, marrying her meant he wouldn't be so distracted by love that he'd let his relationship rule him the way it had when he'd loved her.

Reigna's dismissal of him and his proposal had twisted

him in knots for months. He'd barely been able to function, and his work as crown prince and ambassador of Nyeusi had suffered greatly. He'd been fortunate that Sherard had been there to cover for him, ensuring no harm resulted from the dereliction of Jasiri's duties. As king, he could not take that risk. That meant that the safest bet was for him to marry the woman who'd crushed his heart and make certain he'd never love anyone else again, not even her.

The sight of an elegant woman dressed in black with large black sunglasses headed toward his car caught his attention, making him brace for battle.

"Baba, Reigna's here. I must go."

"Very well, son." With a brief nod, his father ended the call, and his phone screen went dark. Before his security detail could knock on the glass and ask his permission to let her near the car, Jasiri opened the window just far enough to give the guard an affirmative wave of his hand.

Soon, the door opened, and Reigna was sliding inside, pulling her sunglasses off before locking gazes with him.

"Hello, Reigna. You have my deepest sympathy."

She held up a hand, her eyes narrowing into sharp slits as she glared at him.

"Spare me the platitudes, Jasiri. I know they're not genuine."

His body tensed at her words. He wasn't sure why, but it almost bothered him that she didn't believe him.

"Well, if it's to be that way, let me get straight to it, then. Why are you in my car, Reigna?"

He waited patiently, refusing to push her. Reigna tended to bolt when she was cornered, and he needed her thinking clearly if his plan had a prayer of working.

"I'm here to accept your terms, Jasiri." Her words were as sharp as her glare. "I'll marry you and live in your country for two years so you can take over your father's office. But the moment two years is up I will be on the first thing smoking back to New York with the deed that declares me the only owner of my family's home."

Jasiri sat back in the soft leather of his seat, lifting an eyebrow in acknowledgment.

"You've made a wise decision, Reigna."

"I've made the only decision that you've given me."

"True," he replied. "And as long as you remember that, this will work out perfectly."

She watched Jasiri as he leaned forward, as if he were making sure she could see his face clearly. He took hold of her hand, sliding the same large diamond onto her ring finger that he'd offered her two years ago when he'd proposed. The heft of it, both physically and emotionally, caused her to flex her fingers. It was proof of their agreement. She was getting exactly what she wanted and keeping her promise to her late uncle while simultaneously helping Jasiri protect his father. It was a simple business transaction. But as her chest tightened as she stared at this outward sign of their engagement, she couldn't escape the fact that the ring felt more like a shackle than a piece of expensive jewelry.

"If you try to double-cross me, Reigna," he said in a deep, low grumble, "I promise you will live to regret the day you laid eyes on me." It was a warning. One she knew she couldn't ignore.

"Too late for that, Jasiri." She swallowed, trying hard to push her visible anger down. "I already do."

CHAPTER THREE

REIGNA LOOKED AROUND the hallowed walls of Brown Memorial Baptist Church. The service had been going on for an hour, and she'd refused to look directly at Ace's casket the entire time she'd been there.

This place had always been filled with joy and exuberance as people, including the Devereaux family, had worshipped and communed in both brotherly love and their faith.

Funerals were no exception to this. They were celebrations of life, home-going services where those that remained worked through their grief with uplifting songs that told of going up yonder to be with their creator, and spiritual dances that seemed to electrify everyone in attendance.

Inside this sacred place, even in pain, the masses could find momentary joy.

Reigna tried her hardest to remember that. To remember those memories where love and joy flowed so easily from Ace to her and to her sister. To sing along with the choir in joy as the church jubilantly celebrated Ace's life and contributions to this community. To not let the grief welling up inside her smother her.

She sat bookended between Jasiri and Regina on the long wooden pew. Her cousin Stephan sat in the same position on the other side of the pew with his husband Carter holding him up on one side and their daughter Naveah stroking his large hand with her small one on the other.

What she wouldn't give to have what those two men shared, a family, a built-in comforter for when the world was on your shoulders. Would she have had that by now if she'd accepted Jasiri's proposal? Would he have been her shelter in this tumultuous storm?

She knew what the comfort of a loved one felt like. Her entire childhood, Ace had been that person. Her mind traveled back to the day her sister, their father, and Reigna moved into the beautiful brownstone house around the corner from the Devereaux Manor mansion Ace resided in.

Her father and mother's divorce was finalized, and Ace allowed her father Johnathan to move in with his eight-year-old twin daughters.

Regina, of course, had found a way to bury her pain in her schoolwork. Reigna, on the other hand, could hardly function with this new existence she was being forced to live. She could still remember sitting on the bench by the back windows, looking out into the concrete backyard of their new Brooklyn home when the warm voice of her favorite uncle had surrounded her.

"Hey, little one. Why so sad?"

Reigna hadn't been able to bring herself to turn around. At least if she kept her eyes fixed on the cold concrete, no one could see her tears.

Her young mind hadn't been able to articulate all the big feelings she was experiencing, so she'd shrugged her shoulders, then turned to her great-uncle and said, *"Because we don't have a family anymore. Mommy's gone and Daddy's at work all the time. It's just people Daddy hired to take care of us."*

Those words had ushered in another round of jagged crying, but this time, instead of leaving her crying alone, Ace had wrapped her up in his arms and said, *"As long as you have me, you'll have family, little one."*

He must've seen the doubt creeping into her little furrowed brow because he'd pulled back to make sure she could see the sincerity in his eyes.

"I promise I'll come see about you and your sister regularly. We'll make as many happy memories as you can stand in this place."

Her tears had stopped as his words fostered hope to bloom inside of her.

"You promise, Uncle Ace?"

"I sure do, baby. But I need you to make me a promise too."

Hungry for the attention and affection of a father figure, Reigna had nodded.

"First, I need you to dry your tears. Because when I come to see my girls, all I wanna see is them happy."

Reigna had quickly wiped her face with the backs of her hands and did her best to hold a shaky smile in place.

"Second..." His eyes had sparkled with the love and joy only an elder could manage to muster for the younger generations in their family. *"I need you to promise me that when you're all grown-up, you will pour joy and laughter into this house too, so the next generation of Devereauxs can be happy."*

Reigna hadn't understood what that meant, really. She hadn't exactly been sure how she was gonna put joy and laughter into a bag and then pour it all over this fancy new house Uncle Ace let them live in. But she figured that must be something she could learn how to do as a grown-up, right?

She'd nodded enthusiastically, ready to promise this man anything, including her favorite Kenya and Kiana dolls, if it meant having someone who cared about her because of her and not because they were getting paid to.

He had smiled down at her, calming every insecurity that had been sewn inside of her by her parents.

"Do we have a deal, little one?"

She'd tilted her head as she looked up at him before speaking again.

"Almost."

Ace had chuckled, his shoulders shaking as his laughter filled the room. She hadn't been quite sure what he was laughing at, she'd just known that she wanted to hear more of it. Because she didn't feel so alone when the grown-ups around her laughed.

"You gotta promise that you're never gonna leave us like Mommy and Daddy."

He'd grabbed her to him, hugging her so tight she'd thought he might squeeze the air out of her like a balloon.

"I'll always be here for my babies as long as they need me. I'll fight the good Lord himself if he tries to take me before you're ready."

The feel of Jasiri's arm sliding across the back of the pew pulled her from her living memory, tearing away the one reprieve from the pain of Ace's loss since she'd learned of his passing.

"Are you holding up okay? Would you like me to have one of my men bring you a bottle of water?"

His voice in her ear and the inevitable way he had to lean into her in her current position felt like relief and warmth, and pain and sorrow all at the same time. If he were anyone else offering her this small kindness, she would've graciously accepted. But Jasiri wasn't anyone else. He was the man who was blackmailing her to keep the one piece of Ace she had left.

For that reason alone, she wouldn't be weak in front of him, not for any reason. Not even to grieve Ace.

"No, thank you." She managed to whisper those words, even as the thicket of emotion from glimpsing the black lacquered casket at the front of the church that held her beloved uncle's earthly form.

"I just need to get through the rest of this service, and I'll be fine."

His knowing gaze said he didn't believe a word of what she'd just said. But he nodded in acknowledgment, keeping whatever he was thinking behind those warm brown eyes that seemed to call to her.

"Reigna, it's okay to not be okay tonight."

His words sounded so sincere. She couldn't shake the feeling, though, that this was all an act. Yes, he'd held Ace in great esteem, but was that regard enough to have him put down his battlements for a time just to comfort her?

She refused to risk it and make a fool of herself yet again when it came to this man that was sitting all too close for her comfort.

Between the renewed ache covering her heart after her mind had brought her to the present and the anger Jasiri's mere presence invoked, those same mix of confused emotions that filled her up when she was eight seemed to resurface with a vengeance.

Her thoughts clattered around her head, and her chest tightened making it difficult to breathe.

"I bet you'd love that." Her teeth were clenched, and her mouth was flat. She was leaning into him while the choir sang the upbeat "When We All Get to Heaven" and, with the hand-clapping that accompanied them, no one could hear her but Jasiri.

"Wouldn't you? To see me broken and weak?" She struggled to take a deep breath before she spoke again. "I won't give you the satisfaction."

She returned her vision to the front of the church and watched as the choir, all decked out in white robes, began to sway to the slower transition notes the organist played. As the choir sang the heartfelt lyrics of "Order My Steps in Your Word," Reigna could feel what little resolve she'd managed to hold on to splinter as her chest tightened and her heart began to beat like a loud drum in her chest.

Not now. Oh, God, not now. Not in front of all these people, not in front of Jasiri.

She held her hand to her chest, trying to anchor herself in the moment and not the overwhelming grief suffocating her or the icy panic she could feel tightening her muscles and spiraling up her spine.

She stood up quickly. When her sister stood with her, she shook her head. Yes, they were twins. But this, these moments where her body and mind refused to work in harmony, Reigna wouldn't allow even the one she'd shared a womb with to witness her like this.

Her body trembled with fear, and as much as she told her legs to move, they refused to listen.

She grabbed the back of the pew, hoping to borrow its strength to keep herself upright.

"Reigna?"

Jasiri's voice broke through the raucous noise ringing in her head, disrupting her tumultuous thoughts.

She opened her mouth, but no words came out. Something flashed across his eyes that she couldn't recognize. Was it fear, panic, concern? She didn't know. Her own senses were overstimulated, making it hard for her to make sense of the world around her.

She closed her eyes, taking in a slow shaky breath and fighting to push all the racket out of her head. Goodness, she was so angry. She was angry at Jasiri for putting her in this position. She was angry at Ace for leaving her. But most of all, she was furious at herself for forfeiting this round to Jasiri so easily.

She tried so hard to be quiet. To not draw attention to herself, to be strong in her pain, to bind the ache that demanded to be set free. She didn't want to let the enemy sitting next to her see her so destroyed.

The problem, however, was that she *was* destroyed. She was wrecked.

She tried to take another breath, but her lungs seized, and then she knew she'd either have to swallow her pride or die where should stood.

And wouldn't that be the story running through the gossip rags? *Heiress and Great-niece of the Brooklyn Mogul Ace Devereaux Collapses Dead at His Funeral.*

She locked eyes with Jasiri, and he stood immediately. He asked no questions. He wrapped a strong arm around her waist that made her feel anchored and safe.

Before she could grab on to his arm like the lifeline it was, she felt herself being lifted.

"I've got you," he whispered in her ear and the tightness in her chest seemed to ease just a bit. "Just hold on."

She buried her face in his chest, hoping to preserve even a sliver of her dignity. But her traitorous heart just wouldn't let her hold it all in.

By the time she felt solid wood beneath her again, her body was a trembling mess and her fight for air was making her dizzy.

She felt a familiar hand at the center of chest pressing hard enough that she focused on it but not hard enough to bring harm.

"Breathe with me, Reigna."

Jasiri placed one of her hands atop his on her chest and took her remaining hand and cradled it against his chest.

"Let's do it together. Slow, deep breath in."

He began calmly, and she tried her best to follow.

"Slow, deep breath out."

Again, she tried to follow him. She tried to close her eyes and the panic began to strengthen like a powerful storm out on the water.

"Eyes on me, Reigna. Eyes on me."

He'd said those words before. Usually when she was so blissed out from their lovemaking that she could hardly see straight. He would utter those words, demanding she be present for every moment of pleasure they gave to each other.

She obediently opened her eyes and continued to follow his commands to take slow, deep breaths in and out.

When her head stopped spinning and his strong features came into sharpened view, she looked around to find them in the near-empty vestibule where he had her huddled in a corner while his security team stood by the entrances and windows. He knelt before her, pulling a silk black handkerchief from his front pocket and tentatively handed it to her.

"Reigna." He said her name with such care, as if it were something delicate he needed to protect. "I know that you despise me, hate me even for what I'm making you do."

He wasn't wrong; there was no denying it.

"But tonight, let us call a ceasefire to our personal battle. For tonight and tomorrow, while you must bear your grief publicly, just let it go. Let me pay my respects to a great man by helping you carry this burden."

She trembled with the need to both fight and acquiesce simultaneously. How she ached to let him take this away from her, even for a second.

She shook her head. "Jasiri, I…"

He cupped her cheek, softly stroking the wet skin beneath his thumb, and in this moment of despair, it felt like a life raft.

"Just for tonight and tomorrow, Reigna. Just for tonight and tomorrow. When these services end, you can go right back to hating me… I promise."

The soft timbre of his voice had her nodding, and before her next tear could fall, he sat beside her, pulling her into his warm embrace, and she let go just like she had all those years ago when Ace had comforted her in an almost identical way.

She knew she would come to regret this. She knew her momentary weakness would cost her in the end. But for tonight and tomorrow, she would use the shoulder he was offering and just let go.

As he held her tightly against him as her body shook with hurt, a small voice whispered in her ear.

Maybe he's not the devil incarnate. Maybe there's a tiny bit of the old Jasiri still in there somewhere.

Jasiri watched Reigna as she circulated through the room tending to guests and family at Ace's repast. He'd been at her side for both the private and public services, and he'd done what any loving fiancé would do for the woman he loved in her time of need.

But he didn't love Reigna, not anymore.

This fact made it even harder for him to understand

why it was so easy for him to slip back into his old role as her protector, her rock.

In their time together, he'd seen Reigna angry, happy, passionate, and so many other loud emotions that she never tried to hide. But in that sanctuary, he had seen absolute panic in her eyes.

How had he not known? They'd been so close. Shouldn't he have known if this was a problem for her before? Or was this just grief-induced? Had the funeral and the pressure Jasiri was placing on her just been too much?

He reconciled his warring thoughts by telling himself he was just doing what any other human being would do. Although his position in life sometimes meant he had to be calculating, he wasn't heartless. He didn't revel in her pain. Well, he reveled in annoying her and getting under her skin. Call him juvenile, but her frustration with him, especially when he outmaneuvered her, it felt glorious. He was a petty prince, so sue him.

But even his pettiness had its limits. There was no way he could sit next to her, immovable as stone, and watch her crumble under the weight of her pain. Besides, his mother would've had his hide if he had. There was no way a son of hers would be anything but a gentleman in that situation. Not if he knew what was good for him.

"Jasiri."

At the sound of his name, he turned to find Regina Devereaux coming toward him. His protection detail was all around the room, blending in with the other mourners but giving him just enough space to interact with others. He tipped his head to the head of his security, and the man moved seamlessly, letting Regina slip through.

"Regina, I'm sorry for your loss."

Regina took a steadying breath, gently smoothing the sleek hair she had pulled into a severe bun.

Jasiri had never had trouble telling the two sisters apart. Yes, they were identical down to the placement of their beauty marks right above their lip. But to him, Regina's cool logic and Reigna's fire and passion had always distinguished one woman from the other.

"Thanks, Jasiri. I really appreciate you coming. Especially considering all that's going on between you and my sister right now."

"So you know about our arrangement?"

Regina scoffed as if his question were the most ridiculous thing she'd ever heard.

"Of course I know about it. She's my twin. We don't keep secrets from each other."

The corners of his mouth curled into a genuine smile. He'd missed Regina's no-nonsense attitude. Unlike most of the people Jasiri had to engage with in his official capacity, Regina never pulled any punches. What you saw was most definitely what you got. You never had to worry about where you stood with her. She would tell you.

"I guess this is the point where you voice your disapproval."

She folded her arms across her chest and leveled her gaze at him.

"The only thing I disapprove of is the way you went about enlisting her help. You didn't have to threaten her with the thing she needs most…especially now."

"I had no choice, Regina. My father's life depends on her agreement."

"I understand that." He could see a glimpse of pain cascade over her face, but before he could acknowledge it, it was gone. Where Reigna wore her pain outwardly, Regina kept everything inside. He almost felt sorry for her in that moment.

"After losing the man who was a father figure to us, I understand your fear of losing your father. I would've moved heaven and earth to keep Ace here if I could've."

She dipped her head for a moment before clearing her throat and continuing.

"If I understand your plight, Reigna does too. You didn't have to blackmail her. She would've done it because it's the right thing to do. She would never want anyone else to bear this pain like we are. All you had to do was ask."

He glanced over to where Reigna was standing, needing to know where she was in the room.

"I did ask, and she refused."

Regina shook her head matter-of-factly.

"No, you demanded. Just because you phrased that demand as a request doesn't mean it was one."

She had him there. In his defense, he was the next ruler of a nation. The ability to command had been drilled into him from his childhood.

"You've always been a decent man who treated my sister well. Make sure that remains the case when you take her to your homeland."

She plastered a broad smile on her face before she picked an imaginary piece of lint off his lapel.

"Because I might be too pretty to go to jail for busting a diplomat's head to the white meat. But if you hurt my sister, there's not a military or government official alive that will keep me off you."

She said it in jest, but Jasiri believed every word she spoke. Knowing how determined and capable the Devereaux sisters were, he was certain she could get away with it too.

"I know Reigna hurt you by turning down your proposal. But if you spend less time digging into your pride and more time talking to her instead, I think this little deal the two of you have could be beneficial to you both in ways neither of you have considered."

Regina gave him a reassuring smile before she stepped away from him, leaving him to realize how much he'd missed out on in having her as a sister-in-law.

Was she right? Could he really have avoided this tension if he'd just genuinely asked for Reigna's help?

It was too late to worry about that now. The die was cast, and there was just too much to lose to risk it to chance. But perhaps Regina was right. Perhaps he could relax his manner around her. Make things less formal and rigid between them.

At just that moment, Reigna's cold gaze met his from across the room, and her disapproving glare halted any idea he had of relaxing his demeanor around her. Reigna was a woman out for blood, and he'd be damned if it was his father's that spilled as a result of his inability to make Reigna live up to her end of their unorthodox bargain.

"All right, then." He tipped his head toward her. "I guess the truce is off."

CHAPTER FOUR

HER LANDLINE RANG, which signaled it was probably her doorman calling. Anyone else knew to call her on her cell.

"Hello, Ms. Devereaux. This is Ralph at the front desk."

She'd called it.

"Hi, Ralph. How may I help you?"

"There's a Mr. Sherard and he's here with four rather large men accompanying him. He's asking for permission to come up. Should I buzz them in?"

Reigna pictured Sherard and who she imagined must be part of Jasiri's security detail standing in front of the poor, elderly man who'd stood at the front of her building since it was erected decades ago, terrifying him with their mean faces and serious body language.

"I know who he is, Ralph. Please let the five gentlemen up. They'll probably be another set of people following them. If one of them is a Jasiri Adebesi, please send them up."

Reigna stepped away from the mountain of clothing strewn across her bed. Relieved to ignore the pile, if only for a few moments. She made her way to the front door of her penthouse to let Sherard and his goons in.

As soon as she opened the door, Sherard and two of his four men filled the space while the remaining two stood vigil on either side of the entryway.

"Sherard, it's a bit early for your secret-agent-man routine. What do you want?"

"The ambassador is waiting to come upstairs. Before he can, his team will need to do a security sweep of your abode."

When they'd first begun dating, this routine rattled her. She'd never dated a diplomat before. She'd had no idea they required so much security, especially from a little island most people hadn't heard of. Now she was seasoned and knew what to expect, so she stepped aside, standing at the door with Sherard as he and the men started the sweep.

When they'd finished, Sherard directed the two security specialists at the door to remain while he instructed the other men to retrieve Jasiri.

"Did you put him up to this, Sherard?"

He turned around, meeting her gaze for the first time since he'd arrived at her apartment.

Sherard was a tall, solid man. An elder statesman that moved with grace and exuded cool detachment almost as well as her sister Regina.

His posture was perfect, and his manners impeccable. Even when he was being glib, it was so polite you couldn't tell if you wanted to curse him out or curtsy in response.

His skin was a deep brown. High cheekbones and full lips with a smooth clean-shaven face, and only gray patches at his temples to hint at the decades he had on her and Jasiri.

He was Jasiri's Alfred Pennyworth, always in the background, always taking care of Jasiri, and always working out a plan to protect the young diplomat.

"That is a safe assumption, Ms. Devereaux. It is of the utmost importance that the young Adebesi fulfill this requirement to spare his father and our country."

"Is one ambassador really so important to a nation?"

He straightened his shoulders, as if they weren't already straight enough to rest a platter of wineglasses safely on them.

"Yes, Ms. Devereaux. *This* ambassador is."

His words were straightforward, but there was something about his delivery, about the way he stressed the word *this* that raised the baby hairs on the back Reigna's neck. She ignored the prickles of trepidation crawling over her skin and chalked it up to the annoyance this man and his stiff and unapproachable demeanor had always stirred in her. Even when she and Jasiri were dating, she'd always had to resist the urge to roll her eyes whenever she came in contact with this pretentious traveling butler.

Before she could respond, her front door was opened by one of the men standing outside, and Jasiri entered.

"Reigna." He took her in slowly as if he were assessing her, making sure she was all right.

She fought not to shrink under his gaze. She'd been weak enough in front of him. She wouldn't embarrass herself any further.

"Sherard, I wish to speak to my bride alone."

"Sir, that's not protocol."

"Sherard, I do not—"

"It's okay, Jasiri. We can go to my home office to speak in private. Your men can remain inside the apartment."

If Jasiri was as important as Sherard seemed to think he was, Reigna thought it better to be safe than sorry, even though she couldn't imagine someone entering her fourteenth-floor penthouse.

Jasiri nodded, and she led the way to her office. She hadn't changed anything about her apartment since he'd last been here two years ago. So, she wasn't surprised to see him follow her easily along the corridors in the spacious apartment.

Her office was a monochrome ivory dream. Her walls, her desk and chair, the thick, plush rug, all the technological accessories, and furniture were ivory. Everything looked like heaven had exploded in this one room. There were splashes of beiges and browns throughout to bring just a pop of color to it, including the large beige-and-brown rendering of President Nelson Mandela, President Barack Obama, Dr. Martin Luther King Jr., and El-Hajj Malik El-Shabazz, better known as Malcolm X, sitting comfortably, smiling and conversing as joy and respect spread between the four of them.

"What a time it would've been if those four great men had been gifted the chance to sit and talk about the greatness of our people across the diaspora."

Warmth spread through her, making her lips curve into an involuntary smile.

"Ace used to say the same thing."

Jasiri gave a brief tip of his head in acknowledgment. "I know. I've heard him say it multiple times. He had great admiration for those pillars in our community."

Admiration was a mild word to describe the limitless pride and esteem Ace had had for those four men. He was in awe of their brilliance, their courage, and their commitment to the diaspora.

"You know," Reigna smiled as she remembered and then spoke the very words Ace had spoken to her several times over, "he supported all of them during their individual movements. He walked with Malcolm and Martin during the sixties Civil Rights Movement. Malcolm and Martin might not have agreed with each other's methods, but they both respected Ace and his respective love for each of them."

Jasiri kept his eyes on the painting as if he was committing each stroke to memory. She didn't blame him: the power the imagined moment captured was enough to captivate anyone who had a passable understanding of who these four leaders were and what they meant to Black people.

She walked closer to the wall, running a gingerly finger across the canvas as if touching it somehow allowed her to touch the greatness of the history depicted in the artist's strokes.

"He visited Mandela frequently while he was imprisoned," she continued. "He was there when he was released. And when Obama ran for president, Ace was so proud of him. He stood on the stage for President Obama's victory speech, crying like a newborn baby. Barrack Obama was the one miracle he'd never thought he'd live to see."

He stepped across the room until he was standing shoulder to shoulder with her.

"If you ask me," Jasiri offered, "the painting is missing one illustrious man. Ace should've been included in this imagined meeting of the greats too."

Reigna closed her eyes, not because grief was threatening to overwhelm her right now. No, it was because hearing someone else talk about Ace, painting him in the exact same greatness she'd always seen him cloaked in, felt warm and inviting.

She turned around, ready to share a smile with Jasiri when she remembered why he was there. As much as they both admired Ace, she couldn't let that be the reason she let down her guard when it came to this man.

"So I assume you came to bring details of our trip to Nyeusi."

She could tell her cool words had broken whatever spell reminiscing about her uncle had surrounded them. Part of her wished she could take her words back and just stay in that moment of kinship and peace between them. Jasiri may have been Ace's friend, but he wasn't hers. If she were going to survive this ordeal unscathed, she would have to remember that.

"I came to check up on you. To see how you are doing."

She could see the concern marring the smooth skin of his forehead.

"I'm fine, Jasiri. It was noth—"

"How long have you suffered from panic attacks?"

"Jasiri, you're imagin—"

He waved his hand, cutting off the lie she was gearing up to tell.

"I know what I saw, Reigna. You knew what was happening to you, even if you couldn't stop it. That tells me the funeral wasn't the first time this occurred. How long?"

Her heavy sigh filled the silence of the room. She didn't know if it was resignation to admit to his observations or relief to be able to speak the words to someone else.

"I haven't had one since I was a child." Her voice was soft as she met his gaze. "Ace was the only one who knew."

"Your parents and your sister didn't know?"

She pulled her bottom lip between her teeth, her tell that she was feeling out of her depth.

"I hid them. I'd lock myself in my room, run to my en suite bathroom and run the shower while I worked through them. They only ever flared up when my parents were fighting. Regina and I always ran to our own separate corners when that happened. Like neither of us wanted to acknowledge the hell that was being raised in our home."

She sat down on her large ivory couch and waved her hand, silently inviting Jasiri to sit.

"Ace was visiting for dinner when my parents started going at it. Both Regina and I took off to our respective rooms. He must have gone to Regina's room first, because it took him a few minutes before he knocked on my door. But when I didn't answer, he panicked and used his pocketknife to unlock it."

She twiddled with the hem of her dress, needing something to do with her shaky hands. She cleared her throat and continued in the same matter-of-fact tone she'd been using since he'd brought the topic up.

"He found me in the throes of an attack. Without the slightest bit of hesitation, he sat on the floor next to me, pulled me into his arms, and cradled me until my heart stopped racing and I could breathe again. The next day, he made my parents an offer. If they'd divorce and my father agreed to the three of us moving into one of Ace's houses, Ace would pay them five million dollars each and allow my dad to live in luxury rent-free."

"And your attacks?"

The gentle, yet firm tone of his voice was generously seasoned with expectation. She should've revolted against it. None of this was his business, especially now when he was forcing her into a marriage that neither of them wanted to be in.

But beneath his calm, she could see his entire attention focused on her, and in some strange way, she felt almost comforted. He was listening to her with concern.

"Once Ace became our de facto parent and removed us from all that turmoil, they never came back. Not until..."

"Ace's funeral."

She didn't have to reply. They both knew he was right. She looked up at him expecting to see pity or glee staring back at her. What she wasn't prepared to see was compassion.

"I can't imagine what my own response to that kind of trauma would've been. Thank God for Ace's care. Reigna, I—"

"Jasiri," she held up her hand to stop him. Whatever he was about to say wouldn't change what they each needed from each other in that moment. At this point, they were only a means to an end. That's all they could be.

"I don't need you feeling sorry for me. You care too much about your father to let me out of this ridiculous deal, so save whatever pretty words you think would make me feel better, and let's get on with this. What did you come here to tell me?"

He straightened his shoulders before he spoke again, tucking whatever concern she'd seen in his eyes safely away.

"We need to marry on Nyeusian soil. It must happen quickly, as in a matter of days. Can you be packed and ready to leave by the end of the week? Will you be able to scrounge up a witness by then? If not, I can just appoint someone."

"Regina would be my obvious choice as a witness." She answered coolly as if she were just talking about something unimportant. Even though this marriage was fake, it had very real consequences. That made it feel like they shouldn't be talking about it so casually.

"I know this isn't a real marriage. But it kind of feels wrong to get married without my family beside me. At the very least, I feel like I should have my sister present."

"Good," he responded. "We'll bring her along, then."

If only her life were that simple. She fell back into the cushions of her sofa and sighed.

"I'm not sure that will be possible. She has a lot on her plate, now that I'm leaving. I don't know if she'll be able to leave the country right now just to watch me get fake-married."

"Reigna," he said as he stood and walked to her office door, "our relationship may be a lie, but this marriage will be very real, legal, and binding."

The intensity in his voice made her spine stiffen, forcing her to stand as if she were preparing for an attack. What exactly did he mean by *real, legal, and binding*?

As if he were reading her thoughts, he lifted a brow as he let his gaze sweep from her head to feet and back again. "I've never had a woman in my bed who didn't expressly agree to be there, so you can wipe that worried look off your face. My expectation of this marriage is this. There will only be two people in this partnership, you and me. Infidelity is not an option on either of our parts. Are we clear, Reigna?"

Those words poured over her like fire on ice, melting something inside of her.

"Was that some sort of an accusation?"

He pushed his hands inside of his dress paints, creating a more imposing figure in front of her office door.

"It's been two years since we've been together, Reigna. I don't assume you've been living like a nun since then. Whoever may have been in your life up until this moment is irrelevant to me. Just know that whether we consummate this marriage or not, there will be no other men in your life until we are divorced. Are we clear?"

The chill his words had filled her with was giving way

to her rising anger. She hated this version of Jasiri, the man who expected to have his orders followed when he spoke. He'd never shown his head while they were together. But from the moment she'd rejected his proposal, he always seemed to be present.

"Please don't talk to me like I'm one of your little minions. Remember, I'm helping you get what you want too."

His jaw ticked, and the immature child in her did a little victory dance in her head. If he wanted to act like a dictator, she'd check him every chance she could.

Whatever was running through his head, he must've decided to forgo speaking it because he reached inside of his jacket pocket and pulled out what looked like folded legal papers instead.

"I've had our prenuptial agreement drawn up. Have your lawyers check it over. Seeing as this marriage is happening so quickly, my lawyers suggest that we both film a declaration that neither of us is signing the document under duress. I've already filmed mine and signed the document. All that awaits is your signature, and we can get married."

Efficient and direct. That was always Jasiri. It shouldn't surprise her that he would carry out the process of their marriage the same way.

"I'll try to figure out our dilemma of having your sister present. I'll call when I have everything set up."

With a brief nod, he opened her office door. She stayed rooted to her spot as she listened to his footsteps, joined by those of his entourage, clicked on her hardwood floors in the halls and living room before she heard her front door close with a resolute click.

This was really happening. She was marrying her ex, Jasiri Adebesi. All it had taken was Ace dying and Jasiri's father nearly dying to bring it about.

CHAPTER FIVE

REIGNA WATCHED AS the limousine rolled through the gates of the Nyeusian embassy, and her chest tightened with just the slightest bit of concern. While she'd been at the consulate in Brooklyn many times throughout the course of their relationship and recently when she'd barged into Jasiri's office to call him out on his BS the moment she'd learned that Ace had willed him half of her family home, she realized now that she'd never been *here*.

The wide and high iron gates reminded her that this place was beyond her power and her privilege as an American citizen. Knowing what she was here to do made the hairs at the back of her neck stand at attention, as if someone were walking over her grave.

She was marrying the ambassador of Nyeusi beyond these gates and for all intents and purposes had stepped onto Nyeusi soil to do so.

Is past happiness worth giving Jasiri what he wants?

Her sister's words echoed in her head, each reverberation of her voice shaking Reigna's confidence in the wisdom of her accepting Jasiri's terms.

What the absolute hell had she been thinking to do this? Regina was right: she could buy any house she wanted. It didn't have to be that one. She didn't have to essentially sell herself to Jasiri to gain ownership of a home. She could just walk away.

But then the memory of Ace's black casket being lowered into the cold ground played behind her eyes as if she were standing there again, reliving the horror and the pain, and she knew she couldn't just walk away. It wasn't about having a house. It was about having a piece of the father figure she'd loved and lost. A piece she could keep with her forever, despite him being gone.

"Madam," the detached voice interrupted the troubling train of her thoughts, forcing her to remember where she was and what she was here to do. She met the gaze of the driver looking at her through the lowered privacy glass. "They're waiting for you inside. Are you ready?"

Reigna sat straight in her seat, making sure to still herself. She might question her own sanity in doing this, but no one in this embassy, including Jasiri himself, would know she was anything but strong and confident. It didn't matter if her insides felt like a bowl of wobbly jelly. It didn't matter if her mind kept asking her if it was wise to get this deeply involved with a man who'd caused so much havoc in her life. She would not let Jasiri be the thing that stopped her from honoring her promise to Ace and to herself. This was her heritage, and as she'd told her sister, Regina, it was well worth the cost.

Meeting the questioning gaze of the driver, she put on her Gemini Queens CEO smile and said, "I was born ready."

She watched as people she assumed were embassy staff lined up on the stairs leading to the front doors. When the driver opened her door, she placed one sleek Louboutin heel on the pavement and then the other, standing to her full height with her shoulders back, removing any doubt from anyone who looked at her that she was a self-made woman who owned every place she stepped inside of.

She shoved the last bit of uncertainty she had to the pit of her stomach and focused on each step, smiling along the way up the stairs until she was met by Sherard in the foyer.

"Welcome, Ms. Devereaux. Let me take you to your quarters."

As always, Sherard's words were short and to the point. She followed him, taking in the large spacious foyer adorned with dark wood paneling that screamed luxury and understated opulence. The upstairs was much of the same. Thick, plush carpeting that silenced her stiletto heels covered the expansive hall. When they reached the end of it, Sherard opened the door and ushered her in.

When she stepped inside, there were two women and a man dressed in black with their hands positioned behind their backs. "Jenna, Asha, and Deshawn are here to get you ready," Sherard informed her. "The ceremony starts in exactly two hours. I will return for you and bring you downstairs for the ceremony. Should you need anything, pick up any telephone and dial one to call me. Everything you need should be here in your suite."

She gave him a brief nod to acknowledge him before he exited the room. When she turned around and saw the strange faces staring back at her, she doubted very seriously everything she needed was here as Sherard had said. How could that be true when her sister wasn't standing in front of her with her signature, no-nonsense scowl she always donned whenever they both knew Reigna was about to do something reckless that was going to land her in hot water?

"Are you having second thoughts? Because if you are,

I've already figured out an escape route through the basement."

Reigna's heart thudded against her chest as she followed the sound of the familiar voice to a doorway she hadn't seen when she'd walked in. There, in all her surly glory was Regina, her identical twin, standing with her arms folded across her chest.

Reigna ignored the three strangers, walking over to her sister and grabbing her into a fierce hug that nearly made the woman stumble back into the room. Happy to see her sister but aware they weren't alone, Reigna closed the door to what a quick glance told her was a bedroom before turning back to her sister.

"What are you doing here, Regina?"

"The question isn't why am I here," Regina replied, "but why didn't you tell me this was going down today? I had to get a call from that blowhard of a fiancé of yours telling me my sister needed me to stand up for her at her wedding."

Shame forced Reigna to drop her eyes from her sister's gaze. It was one of the difficulties of having an identical twin. When the same eyes you saw in the mirror were taking you to task, it made you feel even worse about yourself.

"Regina," Reigna huffed, "because of me, everything at work is being thrown in your lap. That, and I know you don't necessarily agree with my decision. I didn't feel right asking you to take part in this knowing why all this is happening. Besides, the original plan was for the wedding to take place on Nyeusi. I didn't think you could get away for that."

"That was your first mistake," Regina responded. "Thinking."

Reigna smiled, knowing whatever came next out of her

matter-of-fact twin's mouth was either going to burn her britches or make her laugh. Probably some combination of the two if she knew her sister. And she did.

"I'm the brainy twin. How about you leave all the thinking to me? You're the twin with all the heart. Your heart is telling you this is the right thing to do. Your heart has never led you wrong, Reigna. Trust it. Trust *me* when I tell you nobody has your back ten toes down like I do. I don't care about the circumstances. My sister is getting married today. There isn't a devil in hell that could keep me from standing by her side. Not even a foreign dignitary with all his diplomatic powers."

For the first time since all of this began, Reigna felt reassured. Her nerves stopped shaking as her sister's words soothed her. Regina was right. All Reigna had to do to make this work was trust her heart.

"I love you, sister," Reigna crooned as she pulled Regina into another hug.

"Of course you do," Reigna answered. "I'm the best."

Reigna stared down at the large diamond engagement ring, now accompanied by an eternity band, on her finger. Three hours ago, she'd married Jasiri in a small ceremony in the foyer of the embassy with an officiant and with her sister and Sherard as witnesses. After the businesslike ceremony where they'd answered in the affirmative in all the right places, they'd had a lovely brunch with her sister, and then they were off to a private airport and heading for Nyeusi.

"Why did you do it?"

Reigna said the words as she kept looking down at the wedding ring Jasiri had placed there.

"Why did I do what?" His voice was strong but soft,

reminding her of the many times they'd been in a room alone talking without looking at one another.

Back then, it was because they were so in tune, they didn't need to see each other to know what the other was thinking or saying. Now...now she wasn't so sure why she refused to bring her eyes to his.

"Why did you bring my sister to the embassy? That was uncharacteristically kind of you."

The plane cabin was quiet. They were alone inside this section of it, but she knew there were guards beyond the closed doors of where they sat now.

"I know you think me a monster, Reigna. The truth is, when I need to be, I am. But I'm not unnecessarily cruel either. I'm taking you away from your entire life for the next two years. The least I could do is have your closest family member there before I take you."

A knock on the door prevented her from saying anything else. Not that she had anything to say. She was too busy mulling over his words to want to speak any of her own. Had Jasiri ever been cruel to her? No. But the moment she'd rejected him, he'd shut down on her so quickly she'd had a hard time believing anyone who could freeze her out so completely had ever cared for her in the first place.

But this...this was an act of care. Even if he didn't want to acknowledge it and even if she didn't want to believe it. She just didn't know what to do with that.

"Sir," Sherard nodded before stepping into the room and standing next to Jasiri's seat. "We will land in ten minutes. Might we prepare Mrs. Adebesi for what she should expect?"

Reigna stiffened at the sound of that name. She knew Sherard was referring to her, but it felt so strange and disconnected from her, it forced her to draw her eyes across the table to watch the two men.

There was something silent happening between them. Sherard's expression was expectant, and Jasiri's was cold and unyielding.

Sherard cleared his throat before saying, "Fine, sir. I'll leave it to you."

She waited for Sherard to leave before she locked gazes with Jasiri.

"What was all that about? What do I need to be pre-pared for?"

"My position on Nyeusi is a lot more complicated than you know, and I need to bring you up to speed on some pertinent details you need to be aware of before we step off the plane and encounter what waits for us."

"If you mean your constant entourage, Jasiri, I figured it would probably be bigger in your own country."

"More than you can imagine."

She crossed one leg over the other and grabbed both armrests. It was something her sister called her *bad news posture*. Whenever one of her executives had something bad to tell her, she adopted this pose to maintain her calm and keep the WTF resting on the tip of her tongue from leaping out into the air.

"Jasiri, what's that supposed to mean?"

"It means that when we get off this plane, I need you to follow my lead. You are the wife of a very visible man. From the moment we touch down, all eyes will be on you. Just smile, stay close to me, and look like you're thrilled to be in my country. If you do this for me, I promise to explain everything to you the moment we are inside my private quarters."

She tensed. Her spidey sense was tingling something terrible.

"I come from a billionaire family. I've been around wealth and fame before, Jasiri. Don't worry, I know how to act right in bougie circles. I won't embarrass you."

His face was drawn straight as he looked across the table at her.

"You've been in wealthy circles before, Reigna. But you've never been in royal circles."

She gripped her armrest tighter as she tried to process what he'd said.

"I'm sorry, what did you just say?"

He leaned forward, making sure her gaze was fastened on his before he spoke again.

"Reigna," he spoke her name with quiet strength that let her know he was in control of this conversation. "I am Jasiri Issa Nguvu of the royal house of Adebesi, son of King Omari Jasiri Sahel of the royal house of Adebesi, crown prince and heir apparent to the throne of Nyeusi."

Her jaw dropped as her eyes searched for any hint that he was joking. Unfortunately, the straight set of his jaw and his level gaze didn't say *Girl, you know I'm just playing with you*. Nope, that was a *No lies detected* face staring back at her if she ever saw one.

"You're...you're a...prince?"

"Not *a* prince, *the* prince. As the heir to the throne, I stand above all other princes in the royal line."

She peeled her hand away from the armrest and pointed to herself. "And that makes me...?"

He continued smoothly as if they were having a normal everyday conversation and not one that was literally life-changing. "As my wife, you are now Princess Reigna of the royal house of Adebesi, consort to the heir and future queen of Nyeusi."

Her mind was racing to match the pounding tattoo of her heart. This man, once her lover, now her fake husband, had dropped an unbelievable bomb on her as their plane descended from the sky. And when the wheels hit the tarmac, shaking them in the cabin, four words came out of her mouth.

"Damn. Your. Lying. Ass."

Jasiri watched Reigna as she remained seated in her chair, the picture of calm. He was surprised at just how still and reserved she was. Granted, *Damn. Your. Lying. Ass.* could've been seen as a tad bit aggressive in his circles. But he'd seen Reigna pissed off before, and her response to his admission was pretty tame, considering how he'd thought she'd respond.

Reigna was not a physically violent person. But if you crossed her, she'd cut you into tiny pieces with her tongue, leaving you wondering how someone so beautiful was so lethal that she could make grown men cry.

"You waited until you married me and brought me to your country to tell me you're freakin' royalty? What the absolute hell, Jasiri?"

She unlatched her seat belt with more force than was necessary and stood in the aisle looking down at him. He made the mistake of looking up and meeting the fire flickering in her gaze.

Reigna on any given day was a beautiful woman who could take a man's breath away. Her full curves made him long for the nights he'd had that plush body of hers pressed against him. But the fire in her eyes was indicative of the passion that flamed hot and steady between the two of them. How many times had they argued over something inconsequential that had made desire burn through both like a short fuse to dynamite? Too many to count or too scorching hot to forget.

Watching that familiar flame flash in her eyes made his body tighten in ways and places that he didn't need to entertain at this moment.

She was here to help him save his father and his country. His traitorous body didn't factor into the equation at all.

An ache thrummed through him as if his flesh was saying *Okay, buddy. If you say so.*

Stay focused, Jasiri.

"You are a right SOB, and I knew I shouldn't have trusted your shady ass."

"Reigna," he called, stopping the angry pacing she'd started in the narrow aisle. "We both know if I'd told you before we left America, you would've never agreed to come with me."

"You're damn right," she replied through gritted teeth.

He stood up, blocking her path, making her stand still before him. "My father's health is at stake, and an entire nation rests in the balance. My ascension is about more than me and you. I had to do whatever was necessary to make sure you accepted this deal."

She titled her head, her eyes wide in disbelief as she just stared at him.

"You say that like it excuses this humongous lie. You've been lying to me since you've known me. Your father hasn't been sick all this time, Jasiri. You've been lying to me since day one."

There it was. The real reason for her anger. Oh, he was not the least bit disillusioned in thinking she was mad about finding out his true identity in this moment. This was about their past and all they'd been to each other.

There, in the depths of her angry eyes he could see the sliver of hurt all that fury covered up. He could see it. It called to the soft spot he had for her that he'd buried beneath all the anger and pain of her rejection. It begged to be set free to comfort her.

He closed his eyes, pinching his brow as he actively worked to get a grip on himself. Reigna was not his priority. His father and his country were. That was all he could focus on. All he would allow himself to focus on.

"There are more important things in the world than your feelings of betrayal, Reigna. As the future, albeit temporary, queen of this nation, you'd better learn that the crown comes before everything and everyone."

A tap at the door followed by Sherard stepping into the room stopped all conversation.

"Your Highness." Sherard's greeting made cold coil in Jasiri's chest. It was a reminder that there was no such thing as privacy when you were a royal, something else he was going to have to explain to Reigna. Outbursts where you could be overheard by staff was a hard and fast no.

Sherard and everyone else in Jasiri's service had been forbidden from using any of his royal titles or styles of address when in Reigna's presence. *Sir* had been the only honorific he'd allowed. Sherard's reference to His Royal Highness meant he'd heard every word of the conversation he and Reigna had just had.

"The king requests an audience with you and the princess," Sherard continued. "We should leave at once if you don't want to keep His Majesty waiting."

"We wouldn't dream of it," Jasiri ground out, knowing his longtime adjutant could read the annoyance in his voice. He turned to Reigna, watching the simmer of concealed anger thrum through her tightly held stance that told him she was using every bit of strength she had to bite her tongue in the moment.

Jasiri extended a hand to her, letting it hang in the air as they engaged in a silent battle with nothing but their gazes before she finally took his offered hand.

"Come, Princess. Our king awaits."

CHAPTER SIX

REIGNA LEANED HER head back against the headrest of the seat. Jasiri sat next to her in the limo, and as always, his faithful adjutant sat to their side reading off an itinerary to Jasiri.

Reigna was mad.

She was beyond mad.

She was stewing in a boiling pot of pisstivity that she wanted to pour over one Crown Prince Jasiri. But she figured threatening death to the almost sovereign of a nation was probably bad form, so she sat back with her eyes closed trying to remember the words to "Children Go Where I Send Thee."

It was an African American spiritual whose upbeat cadence and group participation meant fun times for noisy kids. Ace used to get her and her cousins to sing it when they were getting too rowdy around the house. It also required you paid attention to keep all the lyrics in the correct order, so it kept their sugar-fueled brains focused for a short time.

Of all her cousins, she was a pro at this. Could sing all the lyrics in the correct order from one to twelve. But she was so damn mad with Jasiri's I'm-secret-royalty BS and how he'd lied to get her here that she couldn't remember who was born in Bethlehem: Paul, Silas, or the little bitty baby.

"Your Highness," she heard Sherard's voice break through her mental notation of mixed-up Negro Spiritual lyrics in her head. "Is the princess, okay?"

She didn't respond even though a sour *What do you think?* was springboarding off the tip of her tongue.

"It's a lot to take in, Sherard. But she'll be fine."

She'll be fine as soon as she gets you behind closed doors and can wring your royal neck.

The car stopped, and she heard the door open and Sherard shuffle outside of the car before the door closed again.

"Are you going to stay in here and sulk?"

"Sulking is the least destructive thing I could do right now. You might want to leave me to it. Wouldn't want your new wife to cause a royal scandal."

She kept her eyes closed, but she could hear the small chuckle Jasiri let slide into the air. A memory of the full robust laughter he'd gifted her with when they were curled up inside her apartment or in one of the many hotel rooms around the world they'd shared made her rigid muscles want to relax and melt into the supple car cushions.

"Reigna, I've already told you what's at stake here. I need you to play the role of a woman in love with her prince. We have to sell this if I'm to get the backing of my father's ministry council."

"How long are you gonna use that fate-of-the-country spiel as an excuse for being an asshole?"

He chuckled again before letting his thick thigh gently touch hers.

"Reigna, I think we both know I was an asshole long before this accession thing became an issue."

He was not wrong.

Jasiri walked into a room knowing who he was. He knew it now as he sat next to her sucking up all the air with his polished sexiness that made you admire and hate him all at the same time. He'd known it then when he'd burrowed himself under her skin in less time than it took to drink a hot cup of a Brooklyn bodega's coffee.

Reigna's mind traveled back to the first time she'd laid eyes on him. He was sitting in Ace's office at Devereaux Inc., laughing with her great-uncle about something too innocuous to remember now. But what she recalled with perfect clarity was the moment he'd stood and greeted her. He was tall, broadly built, with rich dark skin that made her fingers twitch as she fought the urge to reach out and stroke it.

Jasiri had taken one look at her, given her his assured, cocky smile, and they'd both known he had her soul and he'd have her body shortly thereafter.

He'd asked her to walk him to the exit when he was finished meeting with Ace, and before he'd stepped onto the street he'd said, *"You and I are going to enjoy our time together."*

"Our time together?" She'd looked back toward the way they'd come. *"As far as I know, our time together began and ended in the five minutes it took to walk from Ace's office to the front door of this building."*

He'd pushed his hands in his pockets, hitching the corner of his mouth into a wry smile.

"Fierce and unafraid to speak your mind. I like it."

She'd shrugged, placing her hands on her hips to give him her I-am-not-to-be-played-with glare.

"Not really concerned with whether you like my attitude or not. I don't know you, and after five minutes in your presence, I don't really see a reason to get to know you."

He'd stroked his chin and glanced up into the sky, as if he'd needed to draw his answers from it. But they both knew it was a ruse. Everything about Jasiri, even then, had spoken of the certainty he had in himself.

"Here's the only reason you need."

He had stepped closer to her, taking her hand into his and holding it as if she was delicate and fragile, something to be treasured.

"A self-possessed woman like you needs a man with a purpose. A man who understands his place and power in the world. Anyone else you'll walk like a dog on a leash, and that kind of subservience will never satisfy someone like you who's always seeking to conquer new things, new people, and the world."

His arrogance had rolled off him in waves. That should've been the clue she'd needed to run far, far away. But instead of running, her natural competitiveness and her uncontrollable need to check anyone who crossed her had got the better of her, and even though his asshole-ish ways shone through, she'd found herself in his company and in his bed only a handful of days later.

The worst of it was the pretty jackass knew the power he wielded, and he made no bones about using it to his advantage. That's exactly what was happening now.

She knew exactly what he was doing. It was obvious. He was trying to get on her good side to get her to do what he wanted. He wasn't even trying to hide how obvious he was being. Except somehow, she could feel the armor of her anger chink just a little, and her laughter tried to squeeze through the weakness in the wall she was trying to build between them.

"Yes," she finally agreed, opening one eyelid to peer up at him. "You are an asshole."

"See?" He shifted in his seat, turning his big body so he fully faced her and that bright and dazzling smile of his beamed down on her like a celestial glow. "We're getting along so much better already."

Nope. She was not letting him charm his way out of this. Not with how he'd played her.

"I don't like being jerked around, Jasiri. Manipulating me into agreeing to marry you when you knew what was waiting for me here was a foul move. I don't know anything about being a royal, let alone the spouse of a monarch. If us pulling this off is as important as you say, how could you think this was a good idea?"

He was quiet long enough that she opened her other eye to get the full view of him. He was still there, still wearing the dark, tailored suit that he'd worn that morning at their wedding. The arresting way it hugged his muscles made him a captivating figure then. Seated here in the dark cabin of a limousine, he was no less commanding, no less…desirable.

"Reigna, you may not be royal by blood, but you're the most regal woman I know. My mother will teach you how to be a queen. Nevertheless, the style and grace you possess can't be taught. It's something you're born with. I've always known that about you."

She swallowed. Her throat dry and tight, making the forming of simple words impossible as she stared back at this man whose body and personality took up so much space next to her that she was beginning to feel claustrophobic.

This was the *real* Jasiri, crown prince of a nation.

How had she missed it?

Looking at him now, it made so much sense. His natural assurance, the way he always knew he was in control of a room and his surroundings, she'd thought it was just his success as a diplomat that made him so confident. Now, she realized it wasn't everyday confidence. No, he was majestic. He'd been raised since birth to wield his power. Now it was innate, just as natural to him as breathing.

Get a grip, woman. He's the enemy now, remember?

"You really think your mother can teach me to be a queen?"

She expected his smile to broaden, for him to toss some offhanded joke about her lack of preparedness for this wild journey he was about to take her on. His eyes pinned her against the cushions and kept her total focus on him.

"She taught my father to be a king," he answered. His voice was filled with reverence for both his parents, and it warmed her to think of what kind of parents they must've been to engender this type of loyalty and adoration from their son. In just the way he spoke of them, she knew they'd had to be in another league of parenting than her own. "From the way I've watched you run Gemini Queens, you're ten times the leader he was when he first sat on the throne. I think she'll have a much better time with you as her student."

The silence that filled the car was thick and heavy with anticipation as he waited to see if she'd bolt, and she waited to see if he was going to push her past her breaking point. This was part of who they were, who they always had been when they were together. This edging thing where they pushed until the other grew beyond their own expectations, their own capabilities had been both bliss and heartache. Now, here they were again, doing the same.

Before, he'd pushed her until she felt backed into a corner like a wild animal and her only recourse was to come out swinging. She pulled her gaze away from him and looked out at the sprawling castle that sat atop a hill providing the perfect view of the rest of the nation. She closed her eyes, taking a slow deep breath. What would happen now if they pushed each other beyond their breaking point again? There was so much more at stake today than their broken hearts. If they couldn't figure this out, a man's health and a nation's sovereignty hung in the balance.

"Is your faith in your mother's king-making abilities just the overblown adoration of a son, or do you really think she can get me up to speed so we can fool whoever we need to fool?"

His eyes sparked with the same mirth she'd seen when they'd traded barb for barb in one of their teasing sessions of old.

"Oh, I adore my mother. As the former general of the King's Guard, I have a healthy dose of fear where she's concerned too. I've seen that woman cut a hardened military man down with the slant of her eye. Respect her power and be open to listening, and I have no doubt she'll make you the greatest queen Nyeusi has ever seen."

His hard and sharp gaze narrowed on her. It should've made her uncomfortable the way he was looking at her. He wasn't just seeing her, he was seeing through to her, to the possibility of her greatness. And damn if that wasn't just about the sexiest thing she'd ever seen in a man's eye, his absolute belief that she could be and do anything she set her mind to.

It was intoxicating the amount of belief he had in her. It was also terrifying. His firm and unwavering confidence that she could accomplish anything had been one of the most alluring things about Jasiri. It had assured her falling for him more than his charm and good looks had. That thought made a quiver of concern spread through her.

Never again, Reigna. Don't let him lure you down a path you know can only lead to heartache. You know what love gone bad looks like between your parents and between you and Jasiri.

"Ultimately," he continued, drawing her out of her thoughts. "There's one other reason she'll do her best to make sure you can handle your role."

She narrowed her gaze, giving him the unspoken *What's that?* he was waiting for to continue.

"From a mother's perspective, you're the woman who adores her only son. For that, Aziza, daughter of Nuru, would trade her weight in gold to make sure you had all that you needed to fulfill your duties as consort to the new king."

She understood what he was saying. His parents or, at the very least, his mother didn't know this marriage was fake. She also read the underlying subtext that she could never enlighten them about the truth of their nuptials either.

"Trust me, Reigna." His easy smile returned, breaking up the tension in the small space and making it easier for her to relax for a bit. "You are far beyond any expectation that my mother could have for a daughter-in-law. You are your own woman separate from me, and from everything I know about you, you won't give a damn about life at court. To my mother, a hard-nosed military person, that personality quirk will go a long way in gaining her favor."

Reigna quelled the doubt gathering behind her closed lips. If Jasiri's mother was as astute and perceptive as he said, the woman would no doubt pick up on Reigna's distrust of Aziza's son. Because no matter how nice Jasiri appeared in this moment, he was still the man who had walked away from her without a word, never giving her a chance to explain why she'd turned down his proposal. He was also the man who had said and done anything he had to in order to get Reigna exactly where she was. Reigna wasn't sure if she was a good enough actress to make it seem like none of those things mattered.

They mattered a lot.

Grasping at the idea, she grabbed her purse sitting beside her to signal she was ready to step into her new role, no matter how ill-prepared she felt for it. It wouldn't be the first time she owned a role that hadn't been created for her. Gemini Queens Cosmetics thrived because of her leadership and the ingenuity of her brilliant sister. Like Jasiri had said, this was just a different arena.

"You can do this, Reigna," he promised as he tapped on the door alerting the driver standing at the ready to open it.

"I'll hold you to that, Your Highness."

CHAPTER SEVEN

"GOOD GOD ALMIGHTY."

Reigna tried very hard not to act like she'd never been anywhere or seen anything, but the truth was, nothing she'd encountered in her billionaire world measured up to the grandness of Adebesi Palace.

The outside was made of white sandstone that easily blended in with the cool and vibrant tones of an island. Purple domes accented with gold topped the various towers that sprang up like the points of a crown.

She stepped inside what looked like a four-story building fashioned with the largest of the towers on top to see nothing but granite and wood covering the walls, surfaces, and flooring. All the home training that had been grilled into her about how to act in sophisticated places left her, and she had the urge to run her hand over the interior's surfaces while saying *Ooh, this is ni-i-i-ce* in her Tiffany Haddish voice.

"This is your house? You grew up here?"

She glanced at him, unsure what she was expecting to see in his eyes. He stopped to circle just as she did before meeting her gaze.

"This was our main home. We have several smaller ones throughout the island. But this is the one where most state business is conducted. All our governmental buildings are nearby so that the crown can reach all branches of his government quickly, and they him."

She fastened her eyes on the large central stairway with ornate carvings on the wooden banisters that seemed to be trimmed in gold.

"Did you appreciate how amazing this place is as a kid? Or did you slide your disrespectful behind down those gold-trimmed banisters?"

His face lit up as if he was remembering the very thing she'd accused him of.

"I'm afraid I wasn't as appreciative of nice things back then as I am now. As a kid, those banisters were a source of never-ending fun. Today, I recognize them for the gifts from our people that they are. We reside here and can live this way only because we serve the people."

"A lesson that took way too long to take root, if you ask me."

From a side doorway, Reigna saw the woman she recognized through several FaceTime calls Jasiri had included her on to meet his parents. Mrs. Adebesi, as she'd known her then, and Queen Aziza, as she knew her to be now, seemed to float across the room on grace and Black girl magic, and everything in Reigna just wanted to naturally bow to the regal beauty greeting them with a smile.

"My Queen," Jasiri said as he met her in the middle of the foyer, taking her offered hands and kissing the tops of them. "It's so good to see you again."

She shook her head and then wagged her finger at him as if chastising him.

"I am Mama," she said matter-of-factly and then glanced over quickly to Reigna. "As of today, she is your queen. Understood?"

This woman wasn't even talking to her, and Reigna was

ready to nod right along with Jasiri, agreeing to everything his mother had just said.

She stepped away from her son and headed toward Reigna, and suddenly Reigna felt awkward and uncomfortable. Was she supposed to bow, curtsy, kneel? She had no idea.

This regal woman, who looked to be about the same just over five feet height that Reigna possessed, with her deep curves draped in a form-fitting purple peplum skirt suit and a matching Gele head wrap, that told anyone who laid eyes on her that she ran things, captivated Reigna, freezing her where she stood.

"I'm not sure how to properly greet you. I've never met a queen before," Reigna admitted, not wanting Queen Aziza to think ill of her simply because she was ignorant of their ways.

Aziza's warm brown skin glowed as her mouth spread into a wide grin. "A simple *Hello, Mama* and a hug will suffice."

Not waiting for Reigna to respond, the woman grabbed her up in a hearty hug, one where you had to sway back and forth to keep from toppling over. It was warm and inviting, and even though she'd only known the queen for two minutes, Reigna's body melted into hers like she was starved for matronly affection.

Queen Aziza pulled back sooner than Reigna would've liked. That warmth had felt glorious as it spread from the core of her chest out to her limbs.

"Now, let me take a look at you. You are absolutely gorgeous, daughter."

Reigna blinked at the word, wondering if she'd misheard the woman.

"You are mine, as much as that bullheaded son of mine is."

Reigna glanced over to see Jasiri give his mother a playful eye roll. The way she smiled in response it was obvious she knew her son meant no disrespect.

"Know from this moment on, my darling, it is as if you were born to me too. There are no such things as in-laws here on Nyeusi. Considering how our nation was formed, kinship played a huge role in our enslaved ancestors escaping and building a new world upon this land. Family, whether born or chosen, functioned the same for them and now for us. That means I am your mother now, Reigna, and the king is now your father. That is the Nyeusi way."

Reigna could feel heat suffuse her brown skin, and she had to stop herself from swiping at her eyes or she knew the tears would come.

Never in all her thirty-four years had any woman, even her mother and grandmothers, ever made her feel this loved and cared for the way a child seeks to be nurtured by a mother figure.

Reigna's mother had seen her twin daughters as nothing but a nuisance. She'd snap at them whenever they made too much noise, whenever they'd asked her to play with them. Hell, them breathing too loudly was enough to garner her wrath. Reigna had always ached to leave school and have her mother scoop her up into a big hug like she'd seen her classmates' mothers do. All she'd gotten was an employed driver holding a door open for her and silence when she'd walked into their family home.

Ignoring the ache her mother's absence had caused had become a usual part of Reigna's existence. Ignoring the neglect had meant rarely taking the time to think about how much she lacked for as a girl. Unfortunately, after experiencing just one hug from Aziza, Reigna was painfully aware of how much she'd been denied as a child.

Thank goodness Ace had been everything to his twin great-nieces. Due to his love, it had never occurred to her, and Reigna was pretty sure she could speak for Regina on this point too, that not having a mother figure had meant they'd missed out on something.

But standing in the warmth of this great and powerful woman, Reigna could suddenly feel the emptiness that this woman was actively filling. This role that Reigna was going to actively let her fill even though she knew it was only going to be temporary.

Again, there was no rule saying this entire experience had to be miserable for her and Jasiri and, by extension, his parents. They each could take what they needed. If Aziza wanted a daughter, Reigna would happily accept her as a mother, because in this moment where she was out of her depth, Reigna realized she needed and wanted one more than anything.

"Thank you, Mama" was all she could manage without bursting into a blubbering bag of water. It was also all she could manage to get past the hardening ball of guilt lodging itself firmly in her throat.

Reigna was wrong for this. She knew that as well as she knew her name, all while intentionally ignoring that knowledge. What did it say about her that after experiencing Aziza's genuine affection, Reigna didn't want to be right?

Aziza must have divined Reigna was about to break against her emotional wall because she straightened her shoulders and said, "Now that we've gotten that straight," she took Reigna's hand into her own, "let's go meet the king."

Jasiri walked behind the queen and Reigna, a tight knot balled up in the middle of his chest as he recounted the brief exchange between his mother and his wife. Never having had any kind of real relationship with her own mother, he could see the relief that bled through Reigna's body when his mother had taken her into her arms.

He knew how serious his mother was about their family. He should've never allowed her to get so close to Reigna so quickly, especially since he knew their marriage was on borrowed time. But knowing how Reigna's toxic relationship with her parents had warped her sense of connection, he couldn't take the warmth his mother provided away from his bride.

He shouldn't care. This would only last for two years. But he wanted it for her. Since his mother had given him the excuse to go along with it because it was what the soon-to-be queen mother wanted, he could let it happen and ignore the guilt his dishonestly spun inside him. He could also ignore the extra thump in his chest when he saw his mother fawning over his wife.

This is what they would've had two years ago if Reigna hadn't rejected him. The only difference was that then he could've had the total package. A mother who adored him and the woman he loved. Now he'd just have to settle for his mother adoring Reigna. That would just have to be good enough because that was all there could ever be.

He would never allow a woman, especially Reigna, the power to hurt him, to control his heart, and therefore him ever again. Not even for the happiness of his beloved mother.

His mother opened the double doors to the king's office, and there he found his father sitting behind his desk, looking not as strong as Jasiri would like him to be, but he was in command of himself, the frailty of his hospital bed left behind.

The king stood, walking in front of the desk, and Jasiri knelt on one knee, taking his father's right hand into his and kissing the royal ring of a golden lion's head with purple sapphire eyes to signify his leadership and his royal status.

His mother wore a matching one with a lioness's head, and the same royal purple eyes that embodied her position as the consort to the Great Lion of Nyeusi.

He brought his forehead closer to his father's ring, letting the cool metal touch his skin.

Jasiri had always known this ring would be his one day as the heir apparent. But never had he imagined it would come so soon. He pushed down the sadness thoughts of his father's health brought to his heart and instead focused on the blessing in this moment. Thrones usually passed from father to son in death. Yet his father was still here, reminding Jasiri the upheaval to his life was a small sacrifice to pay to see his father alive and healthy again.

"My King," he uttered as he stood. "I am glad to see you looking better. But don't you think you should stay away from this desk?"

"Do you see this, Aziza? He gets married and thinks he's king already. Where is my new daughter you've brought me? Let me focus on her instead of your fussing."

Jasiri stepped aside so his father could see Reigna standing next to his mother. She looked less uncomfortable than she had upon meeting his mother, and Jasiri knew he was right in asking his mother to take on Reigna's royal training. Any staff member could've taken that on, but his mother would teach Reigna while building her confidence in navigating this new world Jasiri had brought her into.

She needed the confidence of a queen. Otherwise, this would never work. The council would never approve his

accession, and if he took the throne without their blessing, it would leave room for his uncle to try to lay claim
to the throne.

That could never stand.

"Come, daughter." The king waved his hand, bidding
Reigna to step toward him. When she stood before him, he
clasped her hands into his. "You are even more beautiful
in person than you were on the few video calls we shared."

The king returned his attention to Jasiri. "I knew then
from those short chats that you'd chosen well in a partner. I'm glad to see that you fixed whatever was wrong
between the two of you, Jasiri. The wisest decision a king
can make is who he chooses to be at his side."

Jasiri watched as his father returned his gaze back to
Reigna, squeezing her hands in his. "Forgive us for not
revealing to you who Jasiri was. We have always agreed
to support him in however he chose to show up into the
world. It made us proud that he wanted you to know him
as a man and not a prince. It meant that he really wanted
you to love him. My only regret was that keeping that
knowledge from you resulted in you walking away from
what the two of you shared."

He saw the flash of questions in Reigna's eyes, and he
simply nodded. Yes, he'd told his parents that she felt be-
trayed by him keeping his royal secret because it was the
only thing that let both him and Reigna off the hook with
respect to blame. She'd angered him to the point that he
was hardly able to comport himself and be the charming
prince his birthright had demanded he be. But he'd never,
never wanted his parents to think ill of her.

She spoke to the king but kept her eyes on Jasiri. "I'm
sorry I reacted so poorly. I only hope I can show you I'm

made of stronger stuff than my response may have led you to believe."

Was she saying those words for his parents' benefit or his?

Jasiri closed his eyes, trying to keep himself from reading more into this than there was. The truth was, it didn't matter if she was sincere. She'd shown him who she really was when she'd rejected him. She hadn't wanted him then, and he'd never give her a second chance to have him now.

CHAPTER EIGHT

AFTER MEETING WITH his parents, the two of them walked to what Jasiri explained were his apartments, or his wing of the palace.

They were standing in the middle of what looked like a living room but on an elevated scale, with warm shades of brown, burgundy, and beige creating an inviting feel that almost made you forget the vaulted ceilings or the priceless artwork with African heritage sprinkled throughout.

A long quiet stretched between them, and Reigna wasn't quite sure how to deal with it. Something had happened in that brief exchange between them in his father's office, and she didn't know how to handle it.

The smart thing would've been to ignore it and pretend it didn't happen. But Reigna didn't build the business she had by ignoring things. She envisioned something she wanted, and she went for it. Yet that tactic didn't seem quite right when it came to Jasiri. Partly because she was nowhere near ready to admit that she wanted anything from him but his half of Ace's house.

This was an emotionally taxing day. She'd been overwhelmed by so many different feelings that she couldn't swear in a court of law exactly what she wanted. At least that's what her brain was saying. She figured it was a safer option to follow it instead of her heart. Especially when being in the presence of Jasiri's family was doing strange things to it.

"This is our quarters. Our bedroom is through that door to the back right, the kitchen and dining areas are through the front left, and the balcony is through the back left."

He pointed back toward the front door that they'd entered.

"The more formal rooms for gathering, cooking, state affairs, and the library are all on the first floor. The private gardens are in the back, along with a personal gym and a swimming pool. Just ask me or any of the staff to show you how to get to whatever until you learn your way around the palace."

She blinked rapidly at him. She'd heard all he'd said, but her brain kept circling back to one thing.

"I'm sorry," she said and held up a finger. "Did you say *our bedroom*, as in we'll be sharing one?"

"Of course I did."

He loosened the knot of his tie, then removed his jacket before beckoning her to follow him. She'd hoped to find a large room with two beds that would make this *our bedroom* thing make sense. But nope, that's not at all what she found.

A four-poster elevated king-size bed with linen drapes from the overhead canopy tied to each post.

"There have got to be other bedrooms in this palace for me to sleep in."

"Of course there are," he replied. His matter-of-factness grated on her nerves just a little bit.

"Jasiri, this is a fake marriage. What happened to 'I've never had a woman in my bed who didn't want to be there'?"

"That's true. That will always be true," he countered.

He sat down on the foot bench in front of the bed, laying his jacket and tie on one side of him while he patted the empty space on the other.

She complied, figuring blowing up probably wouldn't resolve this issue in any way that was conducive to them keeping this fragile peace they seemed to be attempting since she'd met his parents.

"Reigna, there is no such thing as privacy when you're a member of the royal family. If anyone discovers the true nature of our union, all will be lost. If you and I sleep in separate rooms, the staff will talk. We can't have that getting out."

She ran her fingers through her long braids, trying to make sense of what Jasiri was saying to her.

"I thought all you royal types slept in separate beds all the time, like it was some sort of rule."

He shook his head. "Americans really need to stop using *The Crown* for their only understanding of royal life."

She chuckled because that was exactly where she'd gotten that information from.

"The Adebesis are not any other royal family. It may be customary in some royal homes for couples to sleep in separate rooms, but that's not how it works on Nyeusi. The monarch and his consort are a team, they always present a united front, and they work as one in all things. You must sleep here with me."

Her deep breath seemed to echo off the high ceiling and the walls of the large room.

"Jasiri, you're a cuddler. This isn't going to work."

"No," he corrected, "I was a cuddler with you. But if you want me to keep my hands to myself, I promise that won't be a problem."

She stood up, pacing a bit to get her thoughts together.

Did she think it was a great idea tempting fate by them sleeping in the same bed? No. But they were adults, and she was certain they could make this work.

"You said the monarch and his consort always present a united front. Is that true?"

He simply nodded in response.

"If we're going to do the same, we have to work on you being honest with me, Jasiri."

"Reigna," he said and sighed, "I've already told you why I kept you in the dark."

She held up a hand to stop him. "We're past all that, Jasiri. While I still don't agree with how you kept me in the dark throughout or relationship and you negotiating with me in bad faith, I understand why you did what you did. What I want to know is that from now on, you're going to keep me in the loop from start to finish."

The pinched furrow of his brow told her he was seriously contemplating her words. Good. If this was going to work, he had to consider her.

"Jasiri, I won't be ambushed like this ever again. If you want me to be your partner, present this united front you keep talking about, then I expect to be treated as your partner. And as such, I have a couple of demands I'm going to add to our agreement."

He quirked a brow. "But our agreement has already been made."

"Nope," she replied with an over exaggerated shake of her head. "You're not going to sit here and pretend like contracts aren't addended or outright renegotiated all the time, especially when one party negotiates in bad faith."

She had him, and the reluctant way he narrowed his gaze was confirmation of that.

"Fine. What are your new terms?"

"I want to be the last one in the room with you when you make your decisions. You can't expect me to play my role if I'm kept in the dark. You want me to stay here? To help you stabilize your nation? Then, you do me the courtesy of keeping me aware of everything that's going on. Otherwise," she said and pointed to the window, "I'll be on the first thing smoking out of here and leave you to your own devices."

She meant every word she'd said. Yes, she'd lose Ace's house, but in the moment, somehow, she knew this was a stance she had to take. Reigna didn't do fake. She was either all in or she couldn't be bothered in the first place. Everything she'd witnessed since she'd landed on this island told her this venture with Jasiri would be no different from the ones she conducted in the boardroom. They were either going to work together or not at all.

She watched his dark brown eyes spark with something like interest. Amusement? Pride? Or maybe some combination of all three. Jasiri had always played his cards close to the vest, and she figured the incongruous look on his face was probably his usual when it came to contract negations.

"You really want to be my queen in the truest sense?"

She sighed deeply, pausing a moment before she replied. "I don't think there's any way around it if the scrutiny you've said we'll be under is accurate."

He stood, extending his hand as he said, "I hope you understand what you're getting yourself into. I trust you to know your own mind, however. If you want to be my business partner in this venture, then that's exactly what you'll be."

When she accepted his hand and gave it a hardy shake, she attempted to take it back and he held on to it tighter before looking deeply into her eyes saying, "Long live Queen Reigna of the House of Adebesi. Long live the queen."

Jasiri stood in the gardens replaying the conversation he'd had with Reigna about being partners. This was the best-case scenario he could've hoped for. Reigna bringing her considerable leadership skills to help him settle into his role as king. Then, why did he feel trouble looming just beyond the horizon as he considered what working this closely to Reigna could really mean?

He wanted off this mental roller-coaster, where he couldn't figure out whether to draw near or run for the nearest exit where Reigna was concerned. No matter how much he wanted to accept her generous offer of partnership, in his head, *What happens when she leaves?* played over on a never-ending loop that he couldn't see how to break free from.

Two years. She'd be leaving in two years. That was their agreement. Getting attached would only bring trouble to his feet that neither he nor his people needed. A distracted king was a bad king, and after all he'd sacrificed to ascend to the office, he wasn't going to do his people the disservice of letting himself lose focus on what was important.

Running from the distraction of her was how he'd ended up standing right where he was in the garden. He'd managed to keep things compartmentalized until he'd walked into their bedroom to grab the laptop he'd left on the nightstand when he'd found her asleep, curled up on one side over the duvet in the large bed looking like she belonged there all along.

This was what he'd wanted when he proposed to her. He'd wanted stolen moments like this where he could forget his title and lose himself in the woman he loved.

How did that work out for you?

His cruel memory letting him grasp his hope in one moment while rubbing the truth of his failed past with this woman in his face in the next was nasty work. It was unnecessarily cruel, while warning him away from danger at the same time to make sure he learned his lesson.

"This is not about what you shared, Jasiri." He whispered those words so low he barely heard them himself. "It's about your father and Nyeusi. Nothing more. Nothing less."

He needed to put distance between himself and Reigna and the conflicting thoughts he was having about her. Jasiri left his apartments, walking toward the steps that would lead to the administrative wing of the palace when he heard a loud voice coming from his father's office.

He quickly headed in the direction of the noise, tensing when he saw his father's guards standing at the door poised, ready to move in at the hint of their king's bidding.

"Your Highness," they greeted Jasiri but kept their entire focus on the door.

"What's happening in there?"

"Prince Pili demanded to speak with the king. We tried to keep him away, but the king insisted he'd speak with him."

Understanding dawned. Only one thing could make Pili this angry, and Jasiri was certain it had nothing to do with the king's health.

"Contact the guards in my wing, and have someone bring the princess here to me. When she arrives, let her walk directly in."

If Reigna wanted to be his partner, showtime was about to start now.

He moved beyond the guards and stepped into his father's office seeing his parents sitting on a high-backed sofa together while his uncle paced back and forth.

"I cannot believe you would allow the prince to do something so dishonest. Anyone with eyes can see he only married this American to be able to ascend to the throne. As beloved as your son is, Omari, he is not ready to rule our great nation."

"I'm not?" Jasiri asked, his words stopping Pili's motion dead in his tracks. "Baba, I guess all those civics and comportment classes I've endured over the years have been a waste."

"Nephew," Pili growled, "show some respect for your elders. This is not a joking matter."

Oh, did this man annoy the hell out of Jasiri. He always had. He stood more than a head shorter than Jasiri's six feet two inches. Where Jasiri and his father walked with confidence and treated their countrymen with care, Pili walked through life thinking his royal blood made him special and everyone should bow to him. Unlucky for him, Jasiri had never bought into Pili's self-indulgent script. Even worse, Jasiri's father had taught him that a man was only as good as he treated the least of those around them. By that measure, Pili was the worst example of a man and a king that there could be.

"The only joke in this room is you coming here pretending to care about anything other than your place in the line of succession."

Pili snatched his gaze away from Jasiri and took an angry step toward the king. Jasiri watched closely as his mother crossed her leg and rested one of her hands beneath the crossed leg.

He knew for a fact that as the former general of the

King's Guard, she was never without a weapon or a means to defend herself or those she loved.

As if on cue, his mother said, "Make that the last step you take toward your king, Pili. I wouldn't want to see you hurt." Pili instantly stepped back, to Jasiri's relief. He wasn't worried in the slightest for his mother's or father's safety. Hell, he wasn't even worried for his own. It was mandatory that senior members of the royal family all mastered self-defensive arts. History had taught them all too well what happened when royals thought they were safe.

Jasiri's only concern about this moment escalating was the blasted paperwork he'd have to fill out as a witness to treason against the crown.

He pinched the bridge of his nose to bring his mind back to focus. He would be king soon. Annoyance or threat, he would have to deal with Pili sooner or later. No need in delaying the future.

"Prince Pili," Jasiri called his name with the authority of a king. He wanted this man to know he wasn't speaking to his nephew, he was speaking to the imminent ruler of Nyeusi. "Your concern has been noted."

"Are you dismissing me?" Pili's face contorted into a twisted frown, as if the idea that Jasiri was exerting authority over him physically pained the man.

"Yes, I am. You've voiced your opinion regarding my ascension. What more is there to say?"

Jasiri was about to walk away until Pili said, "You married an outsider." His words were like sharp rocks against delicate skin. The idea of anyone putting Reigna in a box of any kind made his blood boil.

"You would be wise to mind your words, Prince Pili."

"You heard what I said, Jasiri. You married an outsider.

You didn't even have the decency to choose a spouse born of Nyeusian blood. She's one of the Lost Tribe, for God's sake. What were you thinking?"

Jasiri's body tensed, and he had to fight to remember that he was beyond reducing himself to a simple brawl because he wanted to snatch his uncle's disrespectful lips from his face. Before he could restrain his anger enough to be certain his reply would be verbal and not a clenched fist to the jaw, the familiar sound of Reigna's voice filled the room.

"The Lost Tribe?" she questioned with raised brows as she entered. "What exactly does that mean, and how did I end up joining it?"

All eyes focused on Reigna's form. She was dressed in what could only be called as a power suit. The red material pulled over her curves just the right way while the vibrant color and high bun she'd twisted her braids into on the top of her head let everyone know this woman hadn't come to play. If there was any doubt in that, the self-assured way she carried herself in those impossibly high stiletto heels said it all. She never put a step out of place and if you wanted to tussle with her, you'd better come prepared.

CHAPTER NINE

REIGNA DIDN'T NEED to know the specifics to understand what was going on here. The guards had said Prince Pili, the brother of the king, was making a fuss about Jasiri's ascension. From the bit she'd walked in on, he was specifically upset about who Reigna was. Or, more important, what she wasn't: Nyeusian. As a Black woman running a *Fortune 500* company, being unwelcome at the table wasn't foreign to her. As this Prince Pili would soon learn, it didn't scare her either. It just made her more determined to succeed.

Ace had once told her, "If they refuse to make room for you at the table, kick the door open and sit down like you belong there, because you do. Then you stare every one of those cowards in the eye and dare any one of them to try to make you get up."

That was her motto. She owned everything she touched, and this royal thing would be no different as far as she was concerned.

As if she'd done it a thousand times before, she walked into the room and mimicked what she'd seen Jasiri do when greeting his parents. She knelt in front of the monarch and his consort, taking both their right hands in each of hers. She kissed the head of his father's lion ring and said, "My King," then repeated the process for Jasiri's mother and said, "My Queen."

She stood, keeping their hands in hers. "Baba, Mama, please forgive my delay. I guess I was more tired from our travel than I realized. As soon as my head touched the pillow, I dozed off."

Both the king's and queen's smiles silently told her *Give him a show, daughter.*

She felt a familiar weight on her hip and instantly knew Jasiri was touching her. They might have been apart for two years, but when a person touches you with such strength, awareness, and entitlement, you remember it like you remember your own name.

His lips settled on her temple and instinctively she melted into him, placing her hand on his large bicep for purchase. She was playing a role for the benefit of his uncle, keeling over in her stilettos just wouldn't do.

"Did you rest well, my love?"

His voice was so sincere she could almost forget that this was just for show. It felt natural to her ears to hear him use such an endearment to address her, and her body's natural reaction was to calm in the presence of his security.

She closed her eyes briefly, one to revel in the balm of his voice and the comfort of his touch, but also to remind herself that this wasn't real. She had to remember that. Forgetting would cost her a lot more than Ace's house.

"I did rest well. I'm sorry if I delayed any plans you'd set forth." She looked over to where Pili stood with a mix of anger and confusion, as if he couldn't figure out if the scene he was witnessing was real or not.

Good. Confusing your enemy was a good strategy for victory.

"This is my uncle, Prince Pili. His visit was unexpected." Jasiri tightened his hold on Reigna's waist. It could just be part of the ruse they were putting on. Somehow, it didn't feel that way. She was pretty certain it was a protective measure.

In all her years in the corporate world, she'd learned to follow her instincts. So if Jasiri's was telling him to keep her close in the presence of this man, she wouldn't fight him.

"Princess." Pili cleared his throat. "Forgive me. I meant no disrespect."

She raised an eyebrow. The way Pili's eyes darted from side to side said he'd realized he'd said the quiet part out loud.

"Sure you did, Pili." His features held still. That was the true markings of a politician or a PR person. But he couldn't hide the slight widening of his irises that expressed his shock. "I might not know what the Lost Tribe is, but it's obvious it wasn't meant as an endearment. What I do understand is that you'd prefer Jasiri had married someone who was born on Nyeusi and raised in its culture."

She stepped out of Jasiri's grasp because everyone in that room knew that Pili was now on the ropes. He'd relinquished any standing the moment his elitism had gotten the better of him.

"The problem is that's not who Jasiri chose. I'm not just some random person off the street. I'm someone who your nephew took the time to learn about and love."

She turned slightly to glimpse Jasiri. His face was inscrutable, and she couldn't readily read what was going through his head. Whatever it was, he extended his hand to hers and when she took it, he laced his fingers through hers, anchoring her in the moment and in her place by his side.

"If given the same opportunity," she continued. "I would like to learn about and love Nyeusi's culture and her people as well."

She bowed her head slowly toward the king and queen, hoping she conveyed the sincerity she had in her heart. This marriage and her role may be temporary, but she would do all she could to support this family and this nation for the duration of her time here.

"If that's your only concern about my marriage and Jasiri's ascension, I can promise you that you have nothing to worry about. As his consort, I will always put this nation first, no matter where I originate from or where my bloodline traces back to."

"Princess," Pili tried to interrupt but she ignored him and continued on. It wasn't in her nature to give elitist bullies a moment of grace.

"Pili, as I said, if your concerns about my marriage and Jasiri's ascension rest in fear regarding the preservation of this country's culture and history, you have nothing to worry about. But if your concern rests in the fact that you don't want Jasiri on the throne because you want it for yourself, then you'll come to understand what everyone who underestimates me does. To do so pretty much solidifies your own peril."

Pili flinched as if she'd struck him, and Reigna smiled. She'd thrown down the gauntlet and let Jasiri's enemy know she wasn't to be played with. It was up to him now to decide if he'd heed her warning or not.

She turned to the king and queen and gave a quick bow of her head. "Baba, Mama, if you require nothing further of our presence, the prince and I aren't yet settled into our apartments. Please excuse us."

"Of course." The queen stood, grabbing Reigna into

another tight hug. "We know you two must be tired after your journey. Take the night and the day to get settled and meet us for dinner tomorrow in our private quarters at six sharp. We await your arrival."

"Thank you, Mama."

She looked down at her and Jasiri's entwined fingers, realizing he hadn't yet released her. She made no move to disengage them. She liked the feel, the power of them joined together.

"My prince," she said as she purposely softened her features and offered him a welcoming smile. "Shall we?"

He nodded, then gave brief nods to his parents. He led her to the door, stopping to open it. He turned his gaze to his parents once again.

"Baba, Mama, don't overexert yourselves." He narrowed his eyes and gave Pili a hard glare. "Uncle, do not overstay your very limited welcome."

Just like that, Jasiri ended the discussion, and they walked out of the room. Two things had happened in that encounter. One, she'd made it clear that she was Jasiri's partner, and she wasn't afraid of his uncle. Although her family was wealthy, Reigna had grown up in Brooklyn, and she wasn't unaccustomed to metaphorically scrapping when she needed to. Two, Jasiri had made it clear, he was the next and true ruler of this nation, and if Pili wanted to challenge that, he'd have the fight of his life on his hands.

When they were back in their apartments, Jasiri turned to her and said, "I'd forgotten how fierce you were in a power suit."

She slid her hands down the front of her suit and then the sides of her updo hairstyle.

"I don't play when I'm in my battle armor."

"A note well taken." He took a deep breath before he

turned serious eyes to her. "You really meant it when you said you wanted to be my partner in all this, didn't you?"

She tilted her head as she gazed up at him. This wasn't small talk. Jasiri truly wanted to know her answer to his question.

"As I said before, I'm still pissed with the antics you pulled to get me to agree to this, Jasiri. But after meeting your uncle and suffering his bullshit elitism, I'm in ten toes down. There's no version of this where I sit back and do nothing while he tries to steal your throne. If he wants a fight…"

She squared up like she was facing an opponent in a boxing ring.

"Then ring the bell, dammit, and let's go."

CHAPTER TEN

JASIRI STOOD ON the balcony looking out over the ocean view. He'd specifically chosen this part of the palace as his own because of the calming effect the push and pull of the ocean to and from the coast always made him feel whole. It was like the waves were reaching for him, returning each time to come back to him.

Once he'd returned home after Reigna rejected him, part of him had held on to the dream that someday she'd come reaching for him too, the same way the great waters that fed life to his land did.

"Jasiri?"

As if he'd conjured her with his mind, Reigna stood in the sitting room, just beyond the doors to the balcony.

"I didn't mean to disturb you. I thought it might be nice to get some air on the balcony." She pointed her thumb over her shoulder before continuing. "If you want to be alone, I can certainly find somewhere else to be in this ridiculously large space."

"It is rather ridiculous, isn't it?" Having grown up in this space, he spoke those words with honesty.

Her eyes widened as she held out the palm side of her hand.

"I didn't mean to offend you. This place is the most gorgeous thing I've ever seen. I just never imagined anyone living in something that looks like it was magic, hand-painted by God. Considering I grew up in luxury, that's saying something."

"No offense taken." He gestured for her to stand beside him, and he was glad to see she'd come willingly. "Everything is relative. It wasn't until I'd become the Nyeusian ambassador that I realized just how extravagant my life was. It humbled me. Kept me grateful for who I am and grounded about the duties I was born to fulfill."

She studied him for a moment, and he wondered what she was trying to see. She'd already known Jasiri the man. He'd never had the opportunity to show her Jasiri the dutiful prince, though.

That regret, like so many others he buried in his gut trying to forget and disassociate himself from, sat heavy at his core. It weighed him down, kept him tied to it no matter how desperately he wanted to be free.

"Have you eaten, yet? I didn't have the heart to wake you after you went down again once we dealt with Pili in my father's office."

It was an obvious ploy to throw her off his scent. Her pointed gaze and the wry twist of her mouth told him she wasn't fooled by his antics either.

"I found the kitchen and made myself a quick sandwich when I woke up. I guess between the travel, stepping inside a real-life palace, and meeting a king and queen—not to mention the opening scrimmage with your uncle—I couldn't seem to keep my eyes open once I sat down."

She looked out into the ocean, seemingly captivated by the same ebb and flow that had him rooted to this spot himself.

"Speaking of Pili, he's not going to make your ascension easy, is he?"

"Not one bit," he replied making them both chuckle at the inevitable fight they knew awaited them.

"I'm not afraid of him."

Although she continued to gaze at the water, her words gripped him, making him look directly at her profile. She was breathtaking, no matter the angle. Watching the light breeze shift her braids, his fingers itched to touch the end of one. He wanted to twist it back and forth between his fingertips over and over again until his stress bled out of him.

"I know you're not afraid of him, Reigna. That's why I brought you here. I knew you were the one person I could trust to have my back when it came to Pili."

Her brows furrowed and she pursed her lips, silently asking why.

"Two reasons. One, you're the most loyal person I know. Just look at the lengths you went to just to snatch Ace's home from my clutches."

She opened her mouth to speak and then closed it abruptly because they both knew his recollection of the facts was true.

"Two, you don't like bullies. I've seen you cut some of the richest and most powerful people down to size in defense of someone who couldn't defend themselves. I knew you'd never willingly stand by and let Pili corrupt the throne."

Her hands were on her hips, and he could see her searching for an argument where there was none. She glanced up at him, taking a deep breath and then releasing it into the quiet of the night.

"I guess you got me there. I really can't stand that man, and I only spent five minutes in his presence."

"Pili tends to have that effect on people." He moved

closer, laying one hand on the stone railing and using his finger to pull her gaze up to his. "Never underestimate him, though. He's sneaky, ruthless, and relentless. Always keep your guard up when it comes to him. I don't want to see anything happen to you, Reigna."

He hoped she could understand what he was really saying. He certainly didn't have the words to express it verbally. The idea of her coming to harm because of Pili burned through him like hot metal on skin. It would mark his soul in a way he wasn't sure he could ever recover from.

"I see it now."

"See what?" His voice was gruff but not as stern as he'd wanted it to be. It seemed whenever he was in this woman's presence he could never get his body to do as he'd directed.

"All the arrogance and obsession with control, I thought it was just your overinflated ego. It was more than that, though? Wasn't it?"

She leaned closer to him, placing her hand atop his on the stone railing of the balcony.

This is not good.

He should've heeded that thought and left right then before her wide, soulful eyes looked up at him. The glint of the moonlight bounced off the ocean and into her pupils, making the brown pools turn to glass. Glass that reflected into the depths of his soul giving a clear view of everything he was trying to hide from her.

"Yes."

The word slipped from his lips like a petal on the breeze, easy, without the ability to steer or control where he'd land. He gripped the stone beneath his hand in an effort not to grip hers. If he returned her touch, it would be his undoing, and then where would he be?

Right back at her feet, rejected at her whim.

"If meeting my uncle today didn't teach you anything else, it should relay how heavy the burden of succession is. My life has been written for me since before I was born."

He tried to stop there, but her pleading gaze silently asked him to continue, and he couldn't help but oblige.

"My name, my occupation, my education, my place in the world, it was all locked in place from the moment my parents learned of my conception. It can easily take control of you if you don't have the skills or the desire to control it."

"Don't you ever get tired of always being in control, hypervigilant, Jasiri? Don't you want to let go sometimes?"

Her hand began to glide up his hand and beyond his wrist. He stood rod straight, apprehensive about where her touch would lead to but still so desperate for it, he refused to push her away. She let her hand move up his arm and over his chest, resting it above the strong thud of his heart before her eyes met his.

"If only for one night," she continued as she stepped into the circle of his arms and pulled them around her. "Don't you just want to let go?"

"Every goddamn second of every day."

His voice was gravel against rough sand, scraping up the tender flesh of his throat as he ground those words out. The closest he'd ever come to it was the moments he'd spent in her arms. Her touch had done more than just excite him: it had healed something broken in him that he'd never been able to name. With her looking at him, no, through him, he could see from her perspective what had been missing before and after her. It was his ability to just be himself.

With Reigna, he didn't have to carry a title or responsibilities. The crown wasn't looming over him like a recurrent bad dream that was just waiting for him to fall deep enough asleep until it hijacked his dreams. As long as he was with her, his title felt like a job he left at the end of the business day. When he crossed Reigna's threshold, he was a real man, not a title. Not a cog in a nearly three-hundred-year-old machine.

"Jasiri?"

She put her hand in his and slowly walked them to the bathroom. She left him standing in the middle of the large room to turn on the shower heads. Like so many other places in the palace, it was too large and ostentatious to be called by its functional name. Yes, this was technically a bathroom. The multihead shower with the large marble bench long enough that Jasiri at over six feet could lie comfortably on it took up one wall on its own. Its glass enclosure so clear you could hardly tell it was there. This was a spa.

Even if you could ignore the shower, the gold-encrusted basins and the wall and flooring tiles made of onyx and marble made it clear that this room, like every other in the palace, was an experience.

Reigna made quick work of undressing them both. Once she covered her head with a shower turban, she waited until he donned his too, then without preamble she pulled them inside and under the spray.

The moment the water touched his skin all the noise in his head stopped and all he could see was her. Her full, luscious body slick with water, begging for his touch. He'd been taught to control his urges lest they control him. As a king, you could never allow anything or anyone that kind of power over you. Her full lips with the perfect bow opened slightly and said the two words he'd never been able to resist coming from her.

"Jasiri, please."

He heard the brittle snap of his control echo off the glass enclosure and any hopes he had of resisting Reigna were gone. He pulled her to him, consuming her mouth in a greedy kiss as he pressed her back into the cool wall. She'd wanted him to let go, and dear God, he'd give her everything she'd asked for.

"On the bench now, Princess."

Reigna had meant to comfort the man, help him lay down his heavy burdens for just a few moments. How that had landed with her in the supine position on this giant marble bench while Jasiri stalked over her like she was his prey, she didn't know, and she didn't care. The same fire that blazed in his eyes before he wrung both their bodies dry of pleasure flashed in front of her now. This wasn't a warning. It was a promise, and Reigna was here for every pledged moment of it.

Jasiri's hands were all over her, stroking her expectant skin. His mouth found her nipple, licking and grazing it with his teeth until it was taut and stiff. He worried it until she was squirming with need beneath him.

Jasiri's touch had always been the truest thing she'd known in her life. His touch instantly meant she'd splinter into pleasure, and there had never been a moment when that wasn't true with him.

He loomed above her with his one hand planted just above her head on the marble bench and one of his knees rested against the outer shell of her hip. She felt his other hand slip between her wet folds, caressing her nub until it hummed with a delicious ache. She lifted her hips, chasing his touch, and he rewarded her by applying a light pat against it that made her shudder with her desire for him. Before she could recover, his fingers were inside her, plunging, searching, and scissoring until they found that hidden spot within her core that made her body tighten and her breath catch.

Their eyes met in the haze of the water, steam, and need, and when she lifted her hips again, this time he didn't make her wait. He knelt before her, pressing her thighs apart, licking her slit until she was open and exposed to him just the way he'd always like her.

To be devoured by Jasiri was to be worshipped. He lapped at her core like she was made of the sweetest nectar he'd ever had, and with the expert use of his mouth, tongue, and fingers, he was going to consume every last drop she possessed.

The orgasm was so quick and fierce that her body seized in one long spasm as she succumbed to its power. Jasiri gave no quarter; he kept at her until another climax was crashing down on her again, rendering her at his mercy.

He shifted, reaching under the bench, and when she could see his hand again, there was a condom between his fingers.

"I won't make any assumptions because we're technically married."

She understood what he was saying. This wasn't about sexual health. To marry a royal meant you were given a battery of tests to make sure both parties were in optimal health. At the time, she'd assumed those tests were a requirement to get a Nyeusian marriage license. After learning who Jasiri really was, she knew and understood the real reason for such thorough documentation of her health. This was Jasiri's way of acknowledging her agency and caring enough about her needs, that he would protect her for as long as she wanted.

He handed her the condom and then whispered, "Get me ready, baby."

Needing no further encouragement than the smooth sound of his deep voice, she snatched it from his hand, opening it as quickly as she could and sliding it down his length in eager anticipation of having him inside her.

This had started as a way to help him let go and somehow, he'd turned the tables on her and all she could think about was him burying himself inside her to satisfy the ache that throbbed so deeply inside, she wondered if it could ever be reached.

He pulled her up from the bench and turned her until she was facing the glass with his chest plastered against her back.

"You said you wanted me to let go, right?"

He slipped inside of her in one rough stroke, filling her to the hilt. The burn of the stretch nearly took her breath away. He slipped his hand between her folds, caressing her clit until her body began to relax in pleasure, and once it did, he snapped his hips forward, his length grazing her sensitive flesh driving her over the edge again.

He was relentless, never letting up, never letting her go until her body was no longer hers to control. It obeyed every filthy command he gave, and each time she did, he rewarded her with raw pleasure that made her weep in satisfaction as her sheath spasmed around him again as the wave of her climax pulled her beneath the current.

"God, Reigna, you still fit me so well."

His breathing was erratic, and his movements faltered as he slammed into her over and over again until she splintered apart one last time and he fell over into his own climax too.

When he turned her to face him, panting, his muscles still twitching from overexertion he looked at her with wild, lust-filled eyes before he placed his hand at the base of her throat.

"Damn, woman!"

She shook her head, trying to fight her way through the lust-induced fog of her brain to focus on him.

"You would destroy me if I'd let you."

She licked her bottom lip, holding his gaze and returning all the fire she saw in them.

"I'd do any and everything you'd ask me to."

Jasiri's chest heaved, his pupils becoming pinpoints as he stepped away from her. Despite the steam from the hot spray surrounding them, the air inside the shower was almost frigid, causing her to wrap her arms around herself as she watched the passionate man she'd just shared amazing sex with fade into this detached representative that she didn't recognize. He closed his eyes and took a breath, somehow completing his transformation. When he opened them again, Jasiri of a few moments ago was completely gone.

He reached for the shower door handle and said, "That's exactly why this should never have happened. It's exactly why it will never happen again."

CHAPTER ELEVEN

"YOU WERE QUIET tonight at dinner with my parents. Is everything okay?"

Reigna turned to the sound of Jasiri's voice, puzzled by the concern she heard there.

They were standing at the back of the palace, on the veranda to be exact, a few steps away from the garden path they'd taken to walk toward his parents' private rooms in the palace.

"Is that actually concern I hear in your voice, Jasiri?"

"Reigna, don't start."

She shook her head, then narrowed her gaze into such tiny slits she could barely see all of him in full view.

"Oh, I'm not only about to start, I'm about to finish too." She stepped closer to him. "I'm sorry, but after I sleep with a man and he instantly tells me he regrets it the moment it's over, I tend to feel a little less chatty than usual. Excuse the hell out of me."

He let a soft sigh slip past his lips and pointed to a cement bench at the foot of the veranda. Still annoyed with him, she paused as she contemplated whether to grant his request.

"Please, Reigna, just hear me out."

She nodded and sat next to him, waiting to hear what he could possibly have to say to her after last night.

"I didn't say I regretted what happened between us."
She opened her mouth to refute him, but he held up his
hand silencing her. "I said it shouldn't have happened."

"I fail to see the distinction."

"Reigna," he began slowly, as if he was searching for
the right words to say. It was rare for Jasiri to struggle with
expressing his thoughts, and seeing him do so made her
settle, giving him the chance to continue.

"I don't regret what happened between us in that shower,
Reigna. I just know that it has the potential to complicate
things in a way I can't afford right now."

He kept his gaze forward, never once allowing himself
to lock eyes with her. It was as if he needed the separation between them for some reason she couldn't fully understand yet.

"While I may still harbor resentment for the way you
publicly humiliated me when you rejected my proposal,
I do not wish to mislead you, Reigna. Nothing should've
happened between us without me clarifying that nothing
beyond the physical could ever happen between us. It's not
what I want, and it's certainly not what I need right now."

When he finally looked at her, the seriousness in his
gaze and the sharp angles of his face expressed how sincere he was in this moment. He truly believed what he was
saying. The only proper response Reigna could come up
with was to laugh right in his face.

Right there in front of him, she dissolved into giggles
that she couldn't stop. Leaving him to sit there watching
her in disbelief as his brows rose.

"I fail to see what's so funny about this situation,
Reigna."

"Of course you wouldn't get it, Your Highness."

She intentionally addressed him with a bit of sneer in

her voice, and she knew it had landed exactly as she'd intended when the muscle in his jaw ticked.

"Jasiri," she began as her laughter died down, "you have a very essential role here on this island. Please don't confuse your importance here to your importance to everything else in the world."

She stood and stepped in front of his sitting form to make sure he understood everything she was saying.

"We had good sex. That in no way indicates that I'm looking for anything more than another orgasm from you. I don't want a do-over as far as our relationship is concerned. Or are you so stuck on yourself that it never occurred to you that after being dropped into a situation I'm wholly unprepared for that it might do me some good to let go with someone familiar for a few moments?"

She couldn't tell if it was her tone or what she'd said to him that had his pupils shrunken down into pinpoints and she didn't care. The absolute nerve of him to think good sex with him would make her lose all common sense. The fact that it had in the past wasn't the point. She was different now. They were different now, and she had no intention of letting this man anywhere near her heart again.

"Unless I tell you otherwise, please assume that its strictly physical between us. That is, if I ever decide I want someone so arrogant inside me again."

She stepped calmly away from him, making sure he understood how unbothered she was.

If you're so unbothered, why did his regret upset you so much?

She ignored the nagging voice in her head and walked into the garden where there were tall pillars of greenery suffused with flowers of varying shades of purple with hints of gold. She was beginning to notice that purple was a theme. First his and his parents' royal rings and now the gardens. To keep up the charade that she was unaffected by this entire conversation, she decided to focus on the color scheme instead of the unexplainable disappointment his words had stirred in her.

"Is purple and gold your national color scheme or something?"

He stopped, raising a brow to let her know he knew exactly what she was doing. She didn't care. She would never admit that his not wanting her had wounded her in some way.

"Purple is considered the color of royalty. But yes, purple trimmed in majestic gold is our national color, our brand if you will. Everything from our flag to our coat of arms is fashioned in those colors. When the monarch dies, we mix it with a rich ebony to symbolize the loss."

She walked over to a pillar, fingers delicately tracing a purple petal. Its softness and its vibrant hue were calming. Unfortunately, her nerves were so loud in her head, she wasn't sure the island possessed enough purple or flowers to get her to chill the hell out.

She anticipated his heat before she heard him step closer. No matter the physical distance, Jasiri's heat always seemed to channel to her whenever they were orbiting each other. It was both reassuring and unnerving and she wasn't sure she'd ever get used to it or if she ever wanted it to stop.

"Well played, Your Highness." His words rattled her, but she stood firm, refusing to allow him that knowledge.

"You've taken me from concern over your feelings to wanting to prove to you why our bodies coming together can never be just physical for either of us."

She kept her back to him, too afraid that whatever she

saw in the depths of his eyes at this moment would be too much to handle in her unsettled state. She wanted him to prove just that. But admitting that would be the first missed step in her downfall.

She finally found the courage to turn around and look up to him. The moon framed his solid form in a celestial glow. His features were relaxed, something she couldn't quite understand considering the twisted ball of tension her body was at the moment.

Then the corner of his mouth hitched into a knowing grin, and heat quickly burned inside of her.

He closed the space between them, slowly resting his large palm against her face, letting his thumb gently caress the skin on her cheek.

"You, Reigna Devereaux, are turning into the very queen I'd hoped you'd be when I proposed to you two years ago. Your determination to forge your own fate while caring to make a difference made me secure in my decision to ask you to be my wife. I knew that with you as its queen, Nyeusi would only prosper."

He'd never told her why he'd proposed to her. She knew it was because he loved her. Love and connection had never been an issue for them. A complicated man like Jasiri, however, would never make such an important decision based solely on how he felt about her.

Hearing him say this now, it unraveled that knot in her chest that her worry had tied.

"Why are you telling me this now, Jasiri? We're long past this. You just told me things couldn't get personal between us."

"Yes, but somehow things always manage to be personal between us even when I don't want them to be." He whispered those words to her as his fingers lowered to her neck before he burrowed them in her braids. "I thought we were past this too."

Her parted scalp tingled with the awareness of him. Her senses ignited at his touch, filling her with the remembrance of what it was like to give herself over completely to this man's ministrations.

"But seeing you throw yourself into this drama and watching you show more care for my country and its people than my uncle, who has lived here all his life, it's doing something to me, Reigna. Something I don't want, and yet it's something I can't seem to control or ignore. It's damn inconvenient if you ask me."

Her tongue swiped against the dry flesh of her bottom lip, trying hard to remember how to speak as she did.

She pressed her hands to his chest, leaning into his warmth, to his demanding presence that seemed to surround her.

"What do you intend to do about it? According to you, last night was supposed to be a one and done. I'd think touching me this way would be strictly forbidden."

His eyes flickered with amber flames of desire as he stared back at her. Without fear or hesitation, his hard gaze bore down on her, and he said, "Didn't you hear I'm about to become king? That means I can veto or reverse any previously made edicts whenever I want, without explanation."

CHAPTER TWELVE

JASIRI'S MOUTH SLAMMED down against Reigna's and immediately silenced every reasonable thought that told him he was flagrantly traipsing on dangerous ground.

Dangerous and torturous, to be precise.

He'd intended for the first press of their lips to be gentle, reassuring. But he was a fool. Things had never been gentle between him and Reigna.

His mouth on hers was like a clap of thunder in the sky, its rumble hard enough to shake their mooring, forcing them closer together for purchase.

She met him with equal fervor. Her arms wrapping around his waist in the familiar way they used to anytime their bodies found each other near. It anchored him, made him feel like he was strong enough to take on the world as long as she held him close like this.

He threaded his fingers through what seemed like a million tiny box braids, each one pulling him back into the memory of what it felt like to have them slide across his chest, his stomach, his thighs.

Jasiri's fingers tightened as his mind gave him a quick glimpse of the moments where she'd owned his body, his mind, and his manhood hadn't suffered the least bit because Reigna touching him always meant pleasure so pure and overwhelming, all he could do was experience it.

When his fingers scraped her scalp, she moaned, her voice thick with need. He took advantage of her parted lips to lick inside her mouth, tasting the remnants of the sweet confection they'd had for dessert. She held him tighter, and his heart pounded behind the cage of his ribs.

He could feel himself thickening in his slacks, and it appeared so could she, because she tilted her hips up, touching the ridge of him, taking him from semierect to full-on hard with just one motion.

He tore his lips away from hers leaving them both gasping for air as they stared at each other. Her pupils were wide from arousal. As his own need pulsed in his aching flesh, he was certain if he looked in a mirror, his would be near blown.

"You're playing with fire, Reigna."

His voice was raspy, like sand against gravel. If he could focus on anything but Reigna and the way her heavy breasts pushed against the fabric of her button-up shirt, he'd clear his throat and use all those comportment lessons that taught him how to modulate his voice and tone depending on the situation. Being near Reigna messed with his head and therefore with his ability to exert control over himself and the situation at hand.

"Heat was always my thing, Jay. Or have you forgotten?"

His hand rested at the base of her throat as his thumb pressed against the excited pulse that thumped at the base of her neck. The mention of her nickname for him was always like a switch she flipped at her leisure to make him forget everything he'd been taught about how a proper royal should behave. It stripped Jasiri down to his elements where he was just a man, her man.

"I've forgotten nothing."

Before either of them could think about what they were

doing, he had her pressed against a nearby pillar. The minute her back was against the structure and it stopped their motion, all bets, all rules, and every bit of common sense either of them possessed was gone.

Reigna's fingers were rough against the silk of his shirt, and if she kept raking at the material, he was certain she would shred it. She must have come to the same conclusion, because she pulled at the soft material until it was free of his waist and her hands clamored underneath until her nails reached his skin.

Talk about fire.

His skin lit up from her touch as if a torch has been placed against it, searing him with her brand. Jasiri had never wanted a tattoo, but the idea of being branded by Reigna made him ache with need.

He let his hands wander away from the safety of her neck and face. Not that they'd prevented them from crossing the line they were racing closer and closer to. He'd fooled himself into believing if his hands remained above the rest of her body, he'd protect them both from letting their passions get the better of them.

No such luck.

The need he had for her burst free of the iron cage he'd kept it behind for the last two years. As soon as the lock gave way, it rushed forward, overtaking him, leaving him unable to do anything but feel.

They moaned in unison when his palm surrounded and caressed her heavy, cloth-covered breasts.

Reigna was so sensitive there, and if they were in the confines of his bedroom where he could be sure he would be the only one to hear her moans, he'd rip her shirt open and close his lips around one taut peak and then the other.

Instead, he kept his hands moving. He was tempted to

swipe the blazer she wore from her shoulders, eager to have every part of her bared to him. But they were outside, and even though he knew they were in a part of the garden that held a small blind spot from security, that blazer would provide them with some cover.

His hands reached the button of her jeans, and the realization sobered him just slightly. He was caught up in his need for Reigna. He needed to check in with her to make sure they both wanted this.

His eyes locked with hers as his fingers hesitated over the metal button. He saw heat and need there that would match his own, begging for him to give them both what they wanted. When he stilled his hands, she nodded, granting him permission to continue. Wasting no time, he flicked his fingers, separating the placket that gave him entry to what he wanted.

Jasiri had always been a thorough lover. That was doubly true with Reigna because he could never get his fill of her. This had to be quick, though. There was the threat of discovery that heightened his need to bring her to climax quickly. There was also his fear that his practical mind would finally reign in his lizard brain, and he'd have to think about what would happen beyond the moment she broke apart for him.

Before he could let his thoughts interfere with his movements, his slid his fingers beneath the lace of her panties until he met her wetness at her slit.

He groaned, his length twitching as blood rushed even faster through his veins making him ache with the need for release.

"Dammit, Reigna. I've barely touched you and you're already dripping for me."

He dipped his fingers between her folds, twisting them in a circular motion, drawing a beautiful moan from her lips. He smiled down at her, loving the glassiness in her eyes as she met his gaze.

He leaned down to her ear, stilling his hand as he spoke.

"We can't be seen here, but the cameras can pick up sound. I don't want anyone else knowing what you sound like when you're coming for me."

He let his fingertips graze her nub and she tremored.

"Be a good girl and keep quiet. I promise I'll make it so good for you if you do."

She tugged her bottom lip between her teeth and that was all the confirmation that he needed that she would comply. To add to the running list of everything that was sexy about Reigna, the fact that she was so eager to please him in bed was like a match to gasoline taking his desire from a simmering boil to an outright explosion in minutes.

She was a strong woman who knew her own mind and ran her life and her business with the confidence of someone who knew what she wanted and made no apologies about it. The fact that she trusted him enough to let go when she was with him, to let him take the reins, giving her a reprieve from carrying the world on her shoulders, made his chest swell with pride. Last night, she'd been that for Jasiri, allowing him to lose himself in her and lay down his worries for just a few precious moments. Tonight, he would be that for her, removing this burden of pretense from her. Like him, she would have to face the fact that there would never be a time where they didn't want each other. Tonight, he would ease her need to fight that realization. Perhaps, if they both admitted it, they'd find the combined strength to overcome it.

Jasiri's hand began moving again and Reigna had to shut her eyes as she damn near bit a hole in her lip trying not to make a sound. The feeling of his thick fingers sliding against her slick flesh had her hips bucking and chasing the pleasure he was giving her.

When he slipped one finger inside of her, she dropped her head to his chest, needing to be closer to him, needing the lull of the thumping of his heart to soothe her, but also needing his strength to keep her from dissolving into a liquid mess at his feet.

Soon, he'd added another finger, stretching and filling her walls just like she liked, just like she needed. His thumb circled around her nub, and she could feel herself getting closer to her peak. She tried to back away. She didn't want it to be so quick she could hardly remember it.

She no longer held any illusions. She wanted Jasiri so damn bad every inch of her ached for his touch. His previous retreat from her stoked her need to savor every stroke, every touch that this moment had to offer. If he refused to touch her again, she'd only have last night and this impromptu moment in the garden to hold on to.

Jasiri was having none of her hesitation, though.

"No retreating," he crooned in her ear. "I want it. Be my good girl and give it to me."

Why this man calling her his *good girl* twisted her up inside into a raging ball of pleasure, she did not know. She truly didn't care. All she knew was that her nerve endings sizzled with need and raced toward a delicious end every time those words graced his lips.

She bucked her hips again, and he rewarded her with another finger, three now. They rubbed furiously against that hidden spot that held the trigger to her release. A few more strokes, and she was rooting against his chest, biting down through the fabric, and not caring if she left a mark on the material or him.

It was his own fault if she did. No man had the right to be this goddamn sexy. He had no right being able to bring her to such heights with his hand and his voice. It was criminal, sinister, and she was here for every damn minute of it.

Before she could breathe her next breath, her body seized with release, and air ceased to move in and out of her lungs.

She buried her nails into his arms, grateful that they were covered with fabric that would keep her from breaking his skin there…probably.

She broke apart for him, writhing against his body, riding his hand desperately like she would him if they were horizontal. As good as this was, she knew it would never be enough. This stolen moment in the royal gardens had reaffirmed what last night had revealed. This thing between them was living and thriving, and it refused to be shoved into the dark depths of her emotional closet where she could pretend she didn't remember it or want it anymore.

Reigna had been telling herself a bold-faced lie that she couldn't deny any longer.

As her release crested and shattered her, her sheath pulsing in rhythmic waves as her climax controlled every muscle she possessed, she decided if she couldn't ignore it, she wasn't going to allow Jasiri to ignore it either.

"There's my good girl," he whispered, prolonging her climax and his control over her.

When her release finally ebbed, he pulled his fingers from her, sliding them inside his mouth and licking them clean. Before she could get lost in how the sight of him licking her release from his flesh made her sex clench, he pressed his lips to hers, letting her taste her on him, and it was the headiest flavor of spice and sweetness, making her ache for more of him, more of them.

She slipped her hands down his sides and to his front. Not caring about her lack of finesse, she shoved her hand into his pants, needing to feel her hand wrapped around his girth.

"There's my eager girl, ready to take what she wants."

Need trembled through him as she stroked him through his clothing. She needed him to experience more so she could experience more.

Getting Jasiri off wasn't just about him reaching release. It was about knowing she could turn such a controlled, refined man into a rutting beast if she touched him the right way or swiveled her hips in the right direction. That kind of power was addictive, and after he'd laid waste to her in a matter of a few moments, she needed to return the favor in spades.

She opened his zipper; her fingertips just having made the edge of his underwear when a knock from a distance shattered the spell they were hiding in.

"Your Highness, please forgive the intrusion."

Panic welling up in her as realization took root. She was standing in a garden, at a palace no less, allowing herself to be debauched and just as eager to do some debauching of her own, where anyone could've walked in on them in the act.

She pulled back her hand as if fire had scorched it. She tried to pull away from Jasiri, forgetting there was a pillar behind her. But even if there weren't, Jasiri's strong hands on her shoulders would've kept her right where he wanted her, plastered against him.

"What is it?" Jasiri replied. His tone not hiding his annoyance.

"The guards will be making their mandatory rounds soon."

The disembodied voice said nothing else. It didn't need to. This was the royal security giving them their privacy even when the nature of their way of life provided little of it.

"Thank you" was all Jasiri said and the same loud footsteps that had drawn their attention in the first place receded.

"It seems it's time for us to leave."

He adjusted her clothing and then buttoned her jeans, then did the same for himself.

He stepped away from her, and the space between them, even though small, felt like they'd been ripped so far apart a chasm could exist between them.

With his shoulders squared, he pulled himself to his full height. When she looked into his gaze, the fire that had burned between them only moments ago was being replaced by cold reason. Whatever fantasies she had about them continuing where they left off before they were interrupted was over. Prince Jasiri, the man she was in a business partnership with, had now returned.

She straightened her own shoulders in response. Prince Jasiri may have returned, but Reigna Devereaux was here now, and she'd be damned if she was the only one who was going to deal with this thing between them that wouldn't die.

He held out his hand to her and said, "Shall we go?"

She gave him a confident smile before placing her hand in his. "We shall."

CHAPTER THIRTEEN

JASIRI ISSA NGUVU, Prince of the House of Adebesi, was a coward.

There was no more apt a word to describe how he, the man who was about to stand before his father's ministry council and ask their blessing of his ascension to the throne, had spent the last two weeks avoiding his wife.

Oh, he'd seen Reigna plenty, at their meals, during official briefings, during some of the lessons his mother arranged to help Reigna acclimate to her role as current princess and future queen of Nyeusi. He'd even spent time with her privately giving her tours of his homeland or simply watching movies in their apartments.

He'd mostly allowed Reigna to choose what they watched which meant they'd mostly viewed her favorite genre, Blacksploitation and Neo-Blacksploitation movies. Everything from *Foxy Brown* to *They Cloned Tyrone* kept them in each other's presence without the need to engage each other beyond commentary on the films.

It was the only way he could be in her presence without... He couldn't even bring himself to think it. To think it would have his body responding to the new memories of what Reigna tasted and felt like when she was in his arms.

His skin warmed, and he took a deep breath trying to cool himself down.

He'd thought he was rid of this hold Reigna possessed over his mind and body. The moment she'd turned his proposal down, steel walls caged his heart, and the only thing he could feel when he thought of her was anger.

Somewhere between seeing her battle a panic attack at Ace's funeral and watching her own his uncle upon first meeting, she'd burrowed underneath his skin, so much so, he'd been secretly sleeping on the oversize and, fortunately for his body, ridiculously comfortable chaise lounge.

He made sure he stayed up after Reigna fell asleep and woke up before she rose to make certain not even she knew he wasn't sleeping next to her.

It was a chickenshit way to handle his growing need for the woman who was distracting him with her mere presence. It was the only safe way to be near her and not give in to baser needs at Reigna's expense.

His insides twisted at the thought of how poorly he'd treated her in the gardens. She was here helping him. Although he'd essentially blackmailed her to be here, she'd stayed and agreed to fight for his nation.

The moments in the shower and in the gardens were pure bliss. Touching her, her touching him, her body yielding to his commands, no title could augment his sense of self-worth the way Reigna's needy moans did. He may not technically be king yet, but Reigna's body pressed against his certainly made him feel like he was.

"Son, you seem to be deep in thought this morning."

Jasiri looked up from where he sat in the corner of the large sitting room to find his father looming large in the doorway in his royal guard uniform. The jacket and pants were a deep purple, so deep they almost looked black in dim light.

His jacket was adorned with all the monarch's insignias, making an imposing yet dashing presentation. Jasiri's formal dress nearly matched his father's perfectly, except for the crown. His gold crown adorned with large purple sapphires rested perfectly on his brow as did his sword rested against his hip. As prince, Jasiri's crown and sword were smaller incarnations of his father, because no one was larger or more important than the king.

His father's eyes caught sight of Jasiri's sword resting on the marble of a nearby tabletop. With their departure imminent, it should've been attached, and Jasiri should've been standing at the ready.

"Consumed with thoughts of your new bride?"

Jasiri's heart beat a bit faster at his father's question. How could he possibly—

"I was a newlywed prince once myself."

His father's broad smile and the distant twinkle in his eye indicated he had momentarily taken a jaunt back to the time when he and the queen were first married.

"When you have a good woman beside you, it can be hard to think of anything else."

His father certainly wasn't wrong about that.

"How long did it take you to get over your fascination with your new wife?"

His father's brow drew into a V and amusement showed in his eyes. "I never did, and I have no intention to. How do you think we've been happily married for more than forty years?"

"Then, how—?"

His father placed a firm yet loving hand on his shoulder. It was how he'd always calmed Jasiri when his fixation on something immobilized him. It worked then pulling him out of whatever problem had him tied in knots, and it worked now when his mind was overwrought with thoughts of the bride who remained untouched in his bed.

"Your mother's presence became my reward, my reason for doing any of this. If I completed my work, I was doing it for her and gifting myself time with her as a result. Make Reigna your reason, son, and there is nothing you can't accomplish in her name."

His father's remedy made perfect sense and at the same time erased any hope Jasiri could find a way to break Reigna's hold over him. She couldn't be his reward, his reason for a job well done. Not when he'd been so careless with her in those gardens.

"Father, I thought the reason any of us ascend to the throne is for the people, for our home."

"Who do you think is my home, son? Is it the title and power I wield? Is it the riches we enjoy? Is it the insufferable administrative things that comes with the title?"

The king shook his head in answer to his own questions.

"No," the king replied. "My home is and has always been your mother and, once you came along, you."

His father's words created an ache in Jasiri, a longing for what his parents had. Unfortunately, entering this bargain with Reigna, he'd forfeited the possibility of that. His reunion with Reigna wasn't one of the heart; no matter how much his body ached for physical closeness to her, her heart would never be his again.

After everything he'd done to bring her here, he wasn't even worthy of any of the kindnesses she'd shown him since arriving. There was no version of this where he was actually worthy of her heart.

"A miserable king cannot justly govern his people." His father's words broke through his rumination. "If you want to succeed in your new role as king, you will have to find an anchor, a support system that will hold you up when you're weak and ground you when the arrogance your position encourages makes your head too big for your shoulders."

"Reigna is more than a prop to hold me up, Father."

"Son, you misunderstand me. Your mother isn't my prop. She's my better. Loving her means I'll do anything to be worthy of the love she so selflessly gives to me."

What an orator this man was. He was able to make anyone believe in him. That was part of what made him such a great king. Jasiri wasn't so sure he'd inherited that ability. After all, he'd chosen to blackmail Reigna into agreeing to be his bride. Sure, he'd put forth a cursory request first. Yet, he already had his plan shaped around using Ace's bequeathal as a means of bringing her to heel.

"Anyone with eyes can see that woman is your better. You just need to admit it to yourself and stop wasting time pretending you're her equal."

"Trust me." Jasiri stood, walking toward the fireplace. "I more than anyone am aware that Reigna is my better in every way that counts."

He looked up at the large painting of his mother and father on their coronation day that ran from the vaulted ceiling to just above the mantle. Its frame was fashioned from Nyeusian iron, representing the strength of their union and their commitment to the people of Nyeusi.

He scanned the painting that was older than him, relishing the regal aura captured by the artist. This was what his nation needed, reassurance that its leaders were in sync and united. Something he knew he couldn't truthfully offer them, no matter the temporary facade he and Reigna would portray for two years.

"Whatever you need to do to get your head on straight, you must, Jasiri."

Jasiri's shoulders straightened and his form tightened, falling into his royal stance with his hands clasped behind him. When Jasiri's father was speaking to him as a father, he rarely used his first name without possessive pronouns attached to it. He'd heard *my Jasiri* and *our Jasiri* so much as a child, he'd almost believed those were his proper names.

But *Jasiri* alone was tantamount to his father calling him by one of his royal titles. It was his way of easily transitioning from the personal to the regnal.

"Father," Jasiri said making sure his voice was confident and hopefully reassuring, "I will not fail you. On this day I will show the council I am the king they and this country needs."

His father's assessing gaze looked to find any signs of weakness in Jasiri's declaration. He wouldn't find any. Jasiri meant every word he'd spoken.

"Good. Then, go get my daughter, and I'll find your mother, and we'll meet back in the foyer."

"No need to go searching for us, darling." The queen's voice pulled their attention to the doorway. "The women of the House of Adebesi are here."

Jasiri spared a glance to his mother. She looked powerful in her gold pantsuit with her royal purple sash adorned with her royal and military insignias pinning the sash in place diagonally from her shoulder to her hip. Her shoulders were covered by a purple velvet mantle. The final detail that completed her ensemble was the majestic lioness crown. It was covered in large oval diamonds with an accenting row of purple sapphires.

As glorious as a picture his mother made, it was the woman standing next to her who took his breath away.

Reigna stood in a form-fitting purple suit with an asymmetrical single-breasted jacket that reached just above the swell of her curvaceous hip on one side, and on the other, a long train with billowing ruffles that swept the floor. Her purple sash adorned with royal insignias befitting the wife of the crown prince complemented the outfit nicely. But it was her diamond tiara against the intricately styled braids that turned Reigna from a beautiful woman who set his senses on fire to Her Royal Highness Princess Reigna of the House of Adebesi.

Reigna stepped inside the room. Each step stole a little of the air in his lungs. By the time she reached him, he'd suffer air-hunger for certain.

"Omari, my love. Why don't we give them a moment?"

Jasiri didn't know whether his father agreed with his mother or not because Reigna filled his vision. They must've gone, though, because Reigna gave a little wave over her shoulder before returning her gaze to him.

"I hope I look okay. All this royal gear," she said as she touched her fingers carefully to the tiara fixed atop her head. There was no need. He knew from his mother that those things were nearly fastened to the scalp with an unbelievable number of hairpins.

"You are by far the most beautiful princess to ever wear that tiara. Everyone who glimpses you will be drawn to you, unable to look away."

"Not everyone." The smile slowly dripped from her lips making him want to forget uniform protocol and take her in his arms and hold her near. "You seem to do a perfect job of keeping your distance from me."

He opened his mouth to speak, but Reigna held up her hand.

"You're sleeping on the couch, Jasiri. No matter how fancy and expensive it is, it's still a couch."

"Reigna."

"Don't lie. I know what it feels like to sleep next to you. Even though we haven't slept together in years, I remember what that felt like."

"I do too." Those words seemed so fragile slipping from his mouth. Waking up with Reigna snuggled next to him, enveloping him with all her lovely heat. "I'm sorry, Reigna."

She shook her head, concern marring her beautiful features.

"I should be the one apologizing, Jasiri. I overstepped in the shower and the gardens. We are not together anymore, and I hadn't meant to make you so uncomfortable that you can't sleep in your own bed."

Understanding dawned and struck him in the middle of his forehead like a mallet.

"You think I'm uncomfortable with what has happened between us?"

"Obviously you are. Instead of picking up where we left off, you've been avoiding me during the day and sneaking out of our bed every night since. I'm just saying you don't have to make this weird. I won't cross that line again."

His anger simmered, trying to reach a full-on boil, and it was all directed at himself. Yet again his actions had caused this woman harm.

His pulse pounded in his ears making it impossible for his thoughts to coalesce into something concrete. He reached his hand out, startling her when it snaked around her neck and drew her to him.

Before sound could cross her lips, his mouth was on hers in a brutal kiss. He knew it was rough, demanding she yield to him, open to him. Her flesh would be swollen when he was done and that was exactly what he wanted, for her to wear his mark.

When his lungs demanded air, he tore his mouth from hers, using the hand at the back of her neck to keep her fixed right where he wanted her.

"Reigna, there is no version of me that doesn't want you. I think after all that's happened between us, it would be silly of me to deny it. I have always wanted you. Even when I was hurt and angry after you rejected me, I still wanted you."

Her brows rose in surprise as if she hadn't considered what he was saying could be a possibility.

"I tried to put distance between us after the first encounter because I didn't want to give in to that need. I've been keeping my distance since the gardens, because I felt I failed to protect you there. I have grown up under a microscope. It's the price I pay for my position in this life. But you aren't used to this. The fact that I was so consumed by my need for you that I believed hiding in a blind spot from the security camera was enough to protect you from the scrutiny being attached to me brings just shows how out of control I was. I am angry with myself, Reigna, never you."

"What if I don't want your protection?"

He watched her intently, his stare searching for any hint of deception or, worse, regret. She took her his hand in hers, and he was forced to look down to where she'd laced their fingers together in a beautiful latticework that he would never tire of seeing.

"If my eagerness in those gardens wasn't enough of an indication, I want you too, Jasiri."

"Our agreement doesn't call for this, Reigna. By indulging in what we want, it could be our undoing."

He closed his eyes, breaking free of her hold and stepping away from her.

"My undoing," he whispered as he touched their foreheads together and then placed a light kiss on hers.

"No matter how badly I want it, I can't risk it."

He took her hand, reaching into his pocket and presenting the final emblem of her position and connection to him.

It was a lioness's ring. The same as his mother but slightly smaller to symbolize her position next to the queen. He glanced to see confusion in her eyes. Confusion he'd put there, no matter how unintentionally.

He slid the ring on her right forefinger, bringing it to his mouth and kissing it before lifting his gaze to hers.

"We are Prince Jasiri and Princess Reigna until my ascension is blessed. This is the only connection we can focus on."

He could see the hurt swelling in her eyes, and his chest ached with the need to fix it, to give her what they both wanted so desperately. Then he remembered what happened the last time he'd allowed his heart to rule him where Reigna was concerned, and it fortified his decision.

Back then, he wallowed in his pain, shirking his responsibilities to the throne, to his parents, and to his countrymen. As the next in line to the throne, he'd always known to be cautious with his life because there was no spare. If something happened to him, his father's branch of the House of Adebesi would cease to exist.

The pain of being rejected by Reigna made him lose control. It made him take risks with his life by engaging in reckless activities like high-speed racing on dark streets and overindulgence of alcohol that sometimes left him unaware of how he'd gotten from one place to another.

It had taken Sherard pushing him into a shower stall

fully clothed and blasting the cold water on him to clear his head enough for the man to give him the stern talking to he'd needed. From that moment on he knew he could never allow anyone to have such a hold on him again. While he believed he was past the hurt and anger those wounds had inflicted, he was left with the fear of how losing control could cause him to spiral again.

Kings couldn't spiral into despair. Not if they intended to be of any use to their kingdom.

"Did I hurt you so badly, Jasiri, that we can never get past my awful mistake?"

He searched her face for any signs of artifice. Was she playing a role, saying what she thought he wanted to hear just to get what she wanted?

No, he couldn't allow himself to go down that particular rabbit hole again. Not when there was so much at risk.

He stepped away from her, needing distance before he answered her.

"Yes."

It was a complete sentence that poured ice-cold water over both their heads. It was shocking but necessary to keep their minds and expectations clear.

Sherard materialized at the door. The royal staff had to know how to be at the ready while blending into the walls, giving the royals a sense of freedom from the scrutiny of the crown.

"Your Highnesses, pardon my interruption, but we must leave if we're to make it to the council on time."

Jasiri gave him a slight nod, and Sherard disappeared as quietly as he came.

"Shall we, Princess?"

Her face was inscrutable, and he desperately wanted to

know what was going on behind those deep, soulful brown eyes that haunted him in sleeping and waking hours.

She lifted her chin and straightened her shoulders, clear signs that she was preparing for a battle. It should've alarmed him, made him lift up his own defenses.

Instead, it made need rise and his uniform pants tighten conspicuously.

"Your ascension to the throne may be a foregone conclusion, but you are not the boss of me. We are partners."

She raised her finger and jabbed it into the air with each spoken word.

"In. Every. Sense. Of. The. Word. You do not get to dictate to me. We either come to an agreement, or nothing changes until we do."

Her brown eyes flamed with specks of amber as her anger seeped into the air and into his bones, pushing aside the cold regret that rested within them. Her blaze was so damn inviting, he wanted to draw nearer to it, allow himself to be consumed by it.

"Reigna, you rejected my marriage proposal two years ago. Two weeks ago, you didn't want anything to do with me. Now, after some time in my palace and in my bed, suddenly, you can't let me go?"

He didn't mean a word of the garbage he was slinging at her, but it was his only defense at this point. She had whittled down his restraint to a bare thread, and he was ready to give her anything she asked if she said much more.

"I meant what I said, Jasiri. You don't get to dictate to me. I don't care who you are."

"How dare you speak to me like that." His voice was hard and sharp, and anyone with sense would've shrunken away from it. Not Reigna, though. Everything he knew about her said she'd choose fighting over acquiescence any day. It was why he was a fool for picking this fight. What alternative did he have when just being in her presence was wresting his control from him?

"You do realize I can turn this palace into a prison and make life a living hell for you, don't you, Reigna?"

"And you do realize I'm a goddamn Devereaux and we are bred for battle? We got hands for days and we never lose. And if you fight one of us, you're gonna have to fight all of us. Trust me, you don't want that smoke."

Did she just threaten him with physical violence? He was about to be a damn king in a matter of hours, and she was talking to him like some commoner on the street?

He was so disoriented by her words, the want he was trying to ignore, and the need thrumming through his body that he couldn't really tell. Also, he wasn't as fluent in African American Vernacular English as he should be, especially after spending two years in a relationship with a native speaker, that he could swear to the proper translation either.

The truth was, it didn't matter if she was actually threatening him or if her language was simply figurative. Either way, he was turned the hell on and two seconds from dragging her upstairs to their apartments where he'd strip every inch of that purple silk from her skin.

She folded her arms, lifting her full breasts and the tantalizing line of her décolletage to his gaze. His hands fisted, and his blunt nails bore into his flesh as he tried to keep from reaching for her. Soon, he was either going to draw his own blood or pull her into his arms. The jury was still out on which.

"Let me give you some sound Brooklyn advice, *Prince* Jasiri." The word *prince* pierced his chest like the sharpest Nyeusian blade. It was a precise blow, showing him his demise was eminent.

He couldn't win this battle, and they both knew it.

"Don't start none. Won't be none. Remember that before you try to use your I'm-about-to-be-king voice on me again."

She smoothed her hands lightly against her hair and her jacket before presenting a calm, unbothered affect.

"This thing between us," she said as she moved her finger back and forth between them, "is over when we both have gotten it out of our system. I don't need to be in love with you to screw you. So unless you're so in love with me you can't just keep it physical, we will continue as we are until we both decide this no longer serves us." She stepped close to him, wiping imaginary lint from his shoulders. "But you will not make unilateral decisions about something that involves us personally without mutual agreement."

He stood there stunned silent, unsure of what to say next. He needn't have worried how he should reply to her because she smiled up at him and said, "Now." Her voice was soft, yet firm, establishing once again that, despite his title, she was the one in control here. "Let's go make you king."

CHAPTER FOURTEEN

"ALL HAIL KING JASIRI and Queen Reigna! May the ancestors grant you wisdom, bravery, and longevity."

All the ministers repeated King Emeritus Omari's edict in unison, their words and voices so powerful Reigna might've tilted on her stilettos if Jasiri hadn't held her hand as they stepped off the dais and in front of the center aisle of the chambers.

"Rejoice, Nyeusi. Rejoice!"

The former king's voice bellowed above the crowd as Jasiri walked them through the well-wishers in the chambers. Just before they reached the exit, Reigna glanced up into the balcony seats and saw none other than Pili sitting where everyone else stood, face drawn without a hint of anything except anger.

She'd known she'd find a problem eventually in this room. There it was, looming above her like a daunting promise of her demise. Pili was officially waging war against her.

That was fine by her for two reasons.

She would not run.

She would not lose.

Death on the ocean floor over life in chains on the land
EST August 8th, 1741

Reigna read the words carefully on the looming memorial right outside of the ministerial chambers. The granite held the likeness of five men. From their full lips, high cheekbones, and tightly coiled hair, she could tell they were of African descent. One stood at the top of a rock holding an ax in one hand and a broken shackle in the other. His features were drawn taut, and his mouth was open as if he was yelling something powerful, and the four men behind him held similar poses, expressions, and stances, as if they were making some sort of battle cry.

"What's this memorial for, Jasiri?"

"It's to commemorate the victory of emancipation that occurred when our ancestors reached these shores."

He stood closer to her, resting his hand on the cool granite and bowing his head in reverence before speaking to her.

"Have you heard of the New York Conspiracy of 1741?"

She nodded. "Yeah. When I was ten, Ace spoke about it at the reburial of the enslaved remains found in Manhattan. It was pretty much the Salem Witch Trials of Manhattan, but the enslaved and poor whites were the targets. They were accused of setting fires all over New York, including the governor's house."

The muscles of his face relaxed as if he hadn't expected her to know that. If Ace didn't teach her anything else, he made sure she knew her people's history, even the painful parts.

"The accused were either executed or exiled from New York if they were white or shipped to the Caribbean for harsher enslavement conditions. One such ship was headed for Jamaica when the ancestors changed the wind and battered the ship with a storm. Half of the ship's crew were lost at sea, and when the remaining unshackled some of the enslaved to replace the lost crew, a revolt broke out. By the time the boat was shipwrecked on these uninhabited lands, it was only the enslaved who made it to the shores. The five men are the ones who led the revolt, and once they arrived on the island, the one standing on top of the rock became our first monarch. King Dakarai Adebesi."

"You ancestor led the revolt?"

She tried to hide the wonder in her voice but couldn't. It wasn't every day you learned your husband was related to a real-life folk hero who turned the enslaved into champions and built a nation.

"I told you, Reigna. Protecting our people and our nation is written in my DNA."

He certainly had told her that. Hearing the details of how this nation came to be spotlighted that point in bold bright rays that made him look less like the asshole he'd been to her before they'd left the palace and more like a flesh-and-blood hero.

"Does this origin story have anything to do with what Pili meant when he called me part of the Lost Tribe?"

"It's connected," he replied, "but not in the way Pili intended it." Jasiri placed a gentle hand at the small of her back as he continued to stare at the statue.

"The Lost Tribe refers to Africans who were enslaved and relocated all over the world and their descendants. African Americans would be included in that grouping."

When he looked down at her she could tell he was questioning if she understood what he was trying to say. She did. Pili was trying to say she didn't belong. She looked into Jasiri's eyes and saw an apology there for the way his uncle had previously used the term. She smiled up at him, hoping to dismiss any misplaced guilt he felt in the moment.

"That's actually kind of beautiful." She saw the slight pinch in Jasiri's brows as he was trying to figure out where she was going with this. "African Americans are socially taught to be ashamed of our ancestry, as if it was somehow our fault that our ancestors were stolen, enslaved, and kept in bondage for four hundred years. *The Lost Tribe* means we belonged somewhere. It implies there's a people, a community, a land that misses us and aches for our return."

"That's how the phrase was intended to be interpreted, My Queen." Jasiri's welcoming voice made Reigna turn to face him. "What my uncle forgets is that we here on Nyeusi are members of the Lost Tribe too." He pointed back to the statue before them, pride written into every fiber of his being as he paid homage to his ancestors. "That's why we provide open citizenship to all people in the Black diaspora here in Nyeusi. We want our people to know that there is a people, a community, a land that misses their presence and aches for their return."

Her heart leaped in her chest. This man was supposed to be her business partner. Every time he spoke of his love for his country, it made her want to become a part of it and him. Sure, he'd angered her beyond reason before they'd left for the ministerial chambers. Yet when he talked about his nation and its rich history, she could forget how enraging he could be. Listening to him express his love for his nation felt like he was welcoming her into much more than the office his family held, but into his homeland and his life too.

She wanted that feeling of belonging to be real. As he tightened his arm around her, drawing her in to his side, she decided it would be as real as she needed it to be for as long as she needed it to be. After all, she was the queen. Who would dare tell her different?

Jasiri leaned down and ran his hand just under the inscription and pointed to a gold plate that read

Donated by Jordan Dylan "Ace" Devereaux,
I to the loving people of Nyeusi

"Ace and his love of Black culture and history across the diaspora made him such an incredible champion of Nyeusi. When the original memorial was damaged by a hurricane, he donated a new one to us. That and his countless other philanthropic endeavors on the island made him a favorite of the people. He and my father's friendship truly benefited our people and our nation."

Her heart swelled in thinking that her great-uncle's greatness lived on in places besides Brooklyn. His good works around the world meant his legacy would live on.

She tightened slightly as a realization hit her that in all the upheaval of the last few weeks she hadn't yet considered.

"He knew you were royalty, didn't he?"

The sliver of regret in his eyes was answer enough for her. However, before she could let this knowledge turn into something ugly in her mind, he ran his hand up her shoulder before enclosing her fully in his arms.

"He loved you, Reigna. He truly did. Him keeping this secret for me was never about you. It was about protecting me. My work as an ambassador was about more than me learning diplomacy. It was also about giving me a brief moment in my life where I had some modicum of freedom to be just a man so the crown wouldn't feel like such a noose when I finally had to wear it. It was a moment to allow me to really learn who Jasiri was without all the formal trappings of the crown. Ace knew just how vital that would be to my future and to Nyeusi's future. That is the only reason he kept my secret from you."

She rested her head on his shoulder, loving Ace more in this moment than she ever could convey with words. He'd protected Jasiri and allowed him to become this man that she was falling harder and harder for each day.

Yes, she knew what she'd said to Jasiri about not needing to love him to screw him was a lie. It was all BS she'd spouted just to win in the moment. The truth was, the more she saw him love his country and embrace his place and position in it, the more she loved him. Now, she'd just have to play her cards close until she could get him to admit the same. She had no doubt he loved her. There was no way he could comfort her this way if he didn't.

She stepped out of his embrace and leaned down to run her fingers over it when she saw a shadow darken her periphery. She stood up just in time to see a young boy, probably no more than thirteen, charging at her with wild eyes.

She braced for the inevitable impact but felt Jasiri's strong arms grab her up before pushing himself in front of her. Two guards stopped the boy before he could reach the first step of the monument.

Her heart was pounding so loudly she could barely make out voices. From the way the police and their guards were talking into radios and phones, she knew there had to be chaos all around them.

Shaking her head to try to focus, she opened her eyes, and the noise assaulted her. Instead of the radios and sirens she knew had to be blaring, she heard, "Please, ma'am, I meant no harm. I just wanted to give you this."

She looked down at the rolled-up piece of paper thrown to the bottom of the monument before he was tackled. She tried to step aside Jasiri to get it, but he shoved out an arm.

"Jasiri, he wasn't trying to hurt me. He's a baby. Just let me see what he was trying to give me."

The muscle at his jaw ticked as she placed a hand on his arm. "Please, Jasiri."

He motioned to one of the guards, and they handed the paper to him first. He unrolled it, then let out a harsh breath before giving it to her.

It was a portrait of her in front of a backdrop of Adebesi Palace. She stood tall with a crown on her head and a lion's skin over her shoulder. At the bottom it read *The Great Lioness*.

Since she wasn't wearing the same outfit in the painting as she wore now, she knew this child had made this painting for her...before today.

This time when she pressed at Jasiri's arm, he moved, letting her step in front of him walking toward where the guards still held the boy.

He was upright now but still being caged by the burly guards.

"Please let him go. I don't believe he will harm me."

They did as she asked but still bracketed the boy.

His T-shirt was smudged with grime, and she could see a small scuff on his cheek. She reached inside her purse and pulled her handkerchief out of it, slowly extending her hand to give it to the boy.

His smile quivered as he bowed as best he could with the guards standing so close.

"Thank you, Your Majesty. I meant no harm."

"I know you didn't. These two..." she pointed to the guards on either side of him "...get a little bit antsy when they see someone charging their new queen."

She opened the paper roll and showed it to him. "Why did you paint this for me?"

"Because you love our king, which means you love us. I wanted you to know we love you too."

She looked down at the painting because if she kept her eyes on that sweet boy's face she was going to burst into a bag of water. She saw a name scribbled in the corner.

"Kofe?" She chanced a glance at him. "Is that how you say your name?"

He nodded eagerly, his little chest growing ten times its size with pride.

"Thank you so much for such a kind welcome, Kofe. I will treasure this always. May I hug you?"

His shirt was yet smudged, and dirt was still on his face, but she didn't give a damn whether her designer clothing looked like an off-the-rack special after this, she was hugging this boy with such a beautiful soul who had risked so much just to honor her.

She pulled him into her bosom, holding him as hard as she could without hurting him before she pressed a kiss atop his head.

"Thank you so much for this gift, Kofe. I will treasure it and you always."

She stepped back and cupped his cheek before saying, "Next time, just be sure to get permission to talk to me first. I don't want to see you get hurt just to talk to me. You understand me?"

"Yes, ma'am."

"Good." She gave his face a soft pat before turning to Jasiri and following him and their guards back to the car.

The limousine was silent the entire ride back to the palace. Jasiri's entire being was still tightened as if the perceived threat was still in play. The only thing keeping him anchored to the back seat was Reigna's hand clasped in his.

Touching her grounded him, kept his mind from jumping to the million and one horrible scenarios that could've
unfolded if that child had meant anything other than adoration for his new queen.

Jasiri shuddered at what could've happened to that child
if Reigna hadn't recognized he wasn't trying to harm her.
All he had seen was someone pushing through to get to
her, and his instincts had told him to protect her with his
very life if need be. He'd posit that later because trying to
make sense of it now would only serve to frustrate him
more, and he didn't need to deal with anything else that
would distort his insides the way the incident had him
twisted up in knots right now.

The car had barely come to a full stop when he'd pushed
the door open and stepped out of it. The staff nearly tripped
over themselves trying to open the door for him, but he
was too quick and too focused on the only thing that mattered: Reigna.

He was around the car and opening her door, extending his hand to help her, but to also connect with her, to
remind him she was alive and so was he.

They made it back to their apartments quickly, allowing
the staff to remove their crowns and regalia and quickly
take them away to the vault.

Once they were alone, Reigna removed her jacket and
shoes, and by the time she plucked the last pin from her
hair, Jasiri was in standing in front of her, looming.

"Jasiri, are you—?"

He didn't give her a chance to finish her sentence. His
mouth was locked on hers, and he'd pulled her into his
arms so quickly, she'd nearly stumbled against his chest.

If he was half the man his mother raised him to be he'd
gentle this kiss, step back, and give her space, talk to her

about how fear and regret had wound him up when he thought she was in danger. But that would require him to stop what he was doing, and touching her, her touching him, it was the only thing that kept him from sinking into despair.

His hands pulled her closer to him, as if he was trying to take her inside of himself. She purred for him, and it was like a volcanic explosion. His hands on her ass, Jasiri picked her up until her legs were around his hips. They made it as far as the dresser in their bedroom before their hands were all over each other again.

He leaned back just enough to grab the silk camisole covering her breasts and tear it in two, as if the delicate fabric somehow offended him. The strapless bra holding those ripe mounds of flesh would've been next if she hadn't held out her hand.

"This is a La Perla exclusive. You can't buy this anymore, and I will not let you destroy it no matter how much your growly caveman bullshit is turning me on."

He tilted his head, feeling the corner of his mouth hitching up into a grin. She wasn't joking in the least little bit, and it was both amusing and intoxicating all at the same time.

"I want it off. Now."

She slipped from the dresser to remove the bra, and he stepped away to get what they needed in the nearby night table. When he looked up again, Reigna was standing beside him, her body free of clothing as she slowly crawled into the bed, her back arched like the fierce lioness he knew she was.

She lay down on her back planting one foot on the plush bedding before she slipped her fingers between her folds, stroking herself slowly and deliberately. The delicate skin of her sex glistened with her arousal, and if he hadn't been rock-hard already, the sight of her pleasuring herself would've taken him from soft to ready to cut diamonds within seconds.

"Are you waiting for an invitation?"

He disrobed quickly, holding himself over her as she continued to bring herself closer and closer to release.

"If you come before I have the chance to fill you, I promise you'll regret it."

She pulled her bottom lip between her teeth, as a glint of mischief sparked in her gaze. "I guess you'd better hurry up, then, because I'm nearly there."

He sheathed himself, taking both her hands in one meaty palm and locking them in place above her head as he used his hips to make her open to him. He ran the covered tip of his domed cap over her sensitized flesh, his entire body loving the sweet ache that flared inside him. She was so wet, her arousal coating him, making the glide that much smoother, taking him from painfully hard to steel and making his balls heavy with his release.

Her moans were becoming louder with each swivel of his hips as he caressed her swollen flesh. She was almost on the edge, and he wouldn't miss the unadulterated joy of having her hot and dripping, nearly squeezing the life out of him as she bore down on him throughout her release.

He slipped quickly inside, riding her hard, nearly drowning in the pleasure of her body molded around his as if she were made explicitly for him. The first spasm of her release made him snap his hips harder, angling himself from muscle memory over that spot that made her explode. Just like he remembered, her body convulsed beneath him as she called his name over and over as if it was a lifeline to her salvation.

He'd needed this. To see her alive, vibrant, and beautiful, taking his strokes so good he had to fight not spill from the second he'd entered her. He placed his hand at the base of her throat, letting his thumb rest softly against her racing pulse, confirming that she was here, with him, and in danger of nothing except the pleasure pouring over her.

When her release subsided and her eyes focused on him again, she saw something. She gripped the hand around her throat, relocating it to rest flat against her left breast, and she kept it there as he plowed into her.

"I'm here, Jasiri. I'm okay."

The knowledge that she understood what was driving him, this uncontrollable need he had to bond with her, to reassure himself that his worst fear hadn't happened today, it melted something in him. He couldn't afford to be vulnerable in front of Reigna, not when he knew the pain of her turning his world upside down. But in this moment, he couldn't hold back his need to be not just near her but in her and around her.

He fell forward, catching himself on his elbow as he buried his face in her neck. Here, she couldn't see how afraid he'd been for her and himself. Here, she couldn't see the relief her safety brought him. Most of all, here, she couldn't see how much she'd wrapped herself around his damn heart. Reigna could never know she had that kind of power over him.

She wrapped her arms around him, rubbing his back and whispering soothing things in his ear until his body was one big knot of tension that snapped so tightly that when his climax rushed through him, he'd nearly blacked out from the unending pleasure. Her body spasmed around him, milking him, drawing his orgasm out longer until his skin was so sensitized he shook.

He'd told her this should never happen between them again the last time he'd found himself buried in her body. As his muscles slowly relaxed and his breathing became somewhat normal, he realized how wrong he was. He needed her. He needed them. He couldn't go on pretending otherwise.

CHAPTER FIFTEEN

"DID YOU MEAN IT?"

Reigna stretched, a smile tickling the corners of her lips when she felt the hard planes of Jasiri's naked body pressed against hers.

His arm hung possessively over her hip, pulling her into the cradle of his lap until he was so close she could feel the strong beat of his heart.

"Sir, you just sexed me stupid. I'm gonna need more information if you expect me to hold a coherent conversation with you."

The rumble of his laughter in his chest made her snuggle closer to him, his warmth so inviting she doubted she could pull herself away even if she wanted to.

"When you said you didn't need to be emotionally attached to me to have sex with me."

The languid relaxation that had her bones malleable just a second ago began to stiffen. As if he'd sensed her need to flee, he pressed a gentle kiss on her bare shoulder and gave her a squeeze around her waist.

"I need to know, Reigna."

She turned in his arms and met his gaze. There was a vulnerability there she'd never witnessed before. This man was a whole king. People had literally fallen at his feet and heaped praises on him as a matter of course like someone serving her coffee in her favorite brunching place. But here he was, needing reassurance from a wound she realized had been festering for the last two years.

"No," she replied with a smile. "That was just bravado. I had to save face after you basically told me you didn't want anything to do with me."

He held up a finger. "That's not exactly what I said."

She shrugged. "Doesn't matter. That's what I heard, what it felt like." She leveled her gaze at him before speaking again. "What about you, Jasiri? Is this just physical for you?"

He huffed in feigned frustration. "My life would be so much easier if it was."

She slipped her thigh over his as she placed a small kiss on his chest, and his body instantly reacted, his skin pebbling up at the site of her touch.

"That's not an answer, Mr. King."

"I think you mean *Your Majesty*."

She raked her fingers down his chest pulling a needy moan from him.

"That's not an answer to my question, Jasiri. Is this just physical? Is that how you'd like us to proceed?"

She raised her eyes to his, needing to see his response as well as hear it. She couldn't be in this alone. Not after everything they'd been through.

"No matter how I've fought it, you are part of me. I don't want to fight this thing between us anymore, Reigna. I want us to be real again."

Her heartbeat was just this side of too fast as she listened to him. He didn't just want her, he wanted them. She'd known that. But hearing him say it, it soothed the unease she'd been carrying since she'd recognized she was losing her heart to him again.

"It's just…we said this arrangement was temporary. It would be unfair of me to try to change the rules now."

"I seem to remember a certain king-to-be telling me he could change his mind at any time without explanation. Is that still true, Your Majesty?"

She moved her body against his, making him shudder. His responsiveness to her touch had always heightened her physical need for him. Now that he'd admitted she wasn't the only one losing in their misguided battle of wills, she needed him to dive into this headfirst just like she was.

"Is that still true, Your Majesty?" she repeated.

"Only if you agree to forget about our contract and stay."

A tiny sliver of panic inched up her spine as her inner commitment-phobe tried to raise a red flag. She closed her eyes, refusing to permit it to surface. Fate was giving her a second chance, and she wasn't going to let her irrational fear keep her from getting everything she wanted.

Hell, she was already married to the man. That had to count toward getting over her commitment issues, right?

She locked gazes with him, making sure he saw nothing but her sincerity in her eyes. "As far as I'm concerned, that contract has been chewed up in the shredder. I'm here for as long as you want me, Jasiri."

She laced her fingers through his and gave them an encouraging squeeze. She let her hand slide down his chest until her fingers were tracing over the hard ridge of his abs. She kept going, her fingers threading through the thicket of curls at his groin.

Her fingers descended until they met his half-hard length. She cupped him, and he spread his legs wider, giving her an open invitation to continue her exploration.

A growl simmered at the back of his throat, making the sensitive flesh between her legs tingle.

She gave him a single stroke, and his flesh lengthened. It was thick, long, and heavy in her hand, its weight making her mouth water.

She didn't wait for him, buried her nose in the cleft where his thigh met his groin, taking an intoxicating sniff of his spicy scent. She stroked him once more, and then licked him from his base to his tip, before swirling her tongue around his proud dome.

His hips bucked, searching for the warmth of her mouth, and she didn't disappoint him. She glanced up while she took him as deep as she could, loving the heft of having him on her tongue. And when her eyes met his and she could see him fight for control, she knew she'd won this battle…for now.

Jasiri didn't trust her completely, that was evident in the way he couldn't let go. But she wouldn't relent. She would show him better than she could tell him what she wanted and that he could trust her with his heart again. Until then, she would break down his walls one lick, one kiss, one caress at a time.

"This is heaven."

After three weeks of him and Reigna working themselves to the bone to make the transition of power as smooth as possible, Jasiri had decided a weekend away with his new bride on the royal private islet was just what the two of them needed. The brilliant sun, gleaming white sand, and doing nothing but lounging, eating, talking, and making love would cure the weariness their new roles caused.

Jasiri watched as Reigna plopped down on a thick beach towel spread out upon the plush chaise of the cabana. Her deep brown skin glistened with rivulets of water that cascaded down every inch of her. Between the sheen of water on her dewy skin and her pinup-girl-style two-piece swimsuit, Jasiri's body responded the same way it always did when he was this close to her: with want.

"I take it you're enjoying Bandari Ya Kisiwa." She cracked one eye open as she regarded him.

"Bandari, who now?"

He found so much amusement in her forthrightness. Unlike many he'd met from such a privileged background as hers, there was no pretense where Reigna was concerned. She wasn't brash. She didn't speak carelessly or without thought. Her business would never have become as successful as it had if she hadn't learned how to prevent people from knowing exactly what she was thinking.

But there was no cowering behind artifice for her. She spoke plainly so that her audience knew she'd meant exactly what she'd said.

"Bandari Ya Kisiwa. It translates roughly to Haven Isle in Swahili."

She pulled herself up on her elbows, giving him her full attention and a full view of her plump bosom, and for a moment he was more than a little distracted. When he heard her calling his name, he returned his gaze to her face.

"Jasiri, you speak Swahili?"

"Among several other languages. You kind of have to be a polyglot if you're going to be a dignitary. Swahili, Yoruba, and English are our national languages, so I was taught all three from birth."

She tilted her head, and he could see the questions forming in her head. Since she'd arrived, anytime she'd wanted to know more about his country's or his people's history, she always reproduced this gesture.

"I thought Swahili was an Eastern African language. If most people stolen during the Transatlantic Slave Trade were from the west coast of Africa, how did Swahili become one of your people's national languages?"

"The people who founded this nation were a mix of enslaved people who'd been born in the American colonies, recent Yoruban abductees from Nigeria, and new abductees who were taken from what is now known as the Democratic Republic of the Congo where Swahili is still spoken. That's how all three languages became our national languages."

Something bright shone on her face, and he wasn't exactly sure what it was. It was sort of wistful yet reverent, and he wanted to know more about it.

"African American culture is rich and deep. Its connection to the ancestral lands we came from are still strongly visible. But our culture isn't treated as if it's part of the American cultural identity. It's a subculture, something niche, and often positioned as oppositional to American culture. Sitting here listening to you talk about your historical legacy and knowing it's celebrated by your people and your government, it's...inspiring."

He'd heard it said that the way to a man's heart was through his stomach. For Jasiri, his national and ancestral pride was a gateway to his.

Her awe of his history, his people, his land, it was like a magic rope threading itself around his heart, and Reigna knew how to tug on it just so it was near bursting in his chest.

He pulled her into his arms, something he was doing more and more since that night three weeks ago where fear for her safety had driven him to forget about the detachment he tried to encourage between them. Sitting here with her now, he was so glad his foolish plan hadn't worked because being near her, with her, did something to his soul that he couldn't willingly relinquish if he tried.

"Every time I hear you speak about Nyeusi, its history, and its people, the more I know my wisest decision as king was choosing you for its queen."

She wrapped her arms around his waist, tugging herself closer to him and covering his leg with hers. He tightened his hold on her, a pleasurable sigh escaping his lips as his soul reveled in the peace being in her arms brought.

They remained silent until a loud grumble rent the calming sounds of the water's movement back and forth across the shore.

They chuckled in unison, Reigna taking her hand and placing it across the soft expanse of her belly.

"I guess I worked up an appetite swimming."

"If my queen wishes to feast, then she shall feast."

He grabbed his phone from the nearby table and sent off a quick text.

In a matter of moments, several staff members stepped into the grand cabana made of sandstone and cedar, placing platters of food on a long table.

Once the staff was gone, Jasiri took her hand and guided her to the table where she could choose her fill.

She pointed to a white pastry box sitting in the center. "Are those from…?"

As a surprise, he'd had an order of pastries hand-delivered from Buttercooky Bakery, her favorite bakery in Floral Park, New York. It was an extravagant thing to do that he normally wouldn't indulge in. Seeing her full lips pull into an excited wide grin, he decided he'd have fresh pastries from this place every day and twice on Sunday if she gifted him with such a beautiful smile.

"Yes," he replied. "I know you love their raspberry-filled croissants, so I had two dozen flown to the island."

"You really are like a prince from the fairy tales."

He shook his head while grabbing a plate and utensils and then presented her with the golden-brown croissant with thick red ribbons of stripes of raspberry swirling around it.

"No, I'm a real-life king, milady. Way better than those fairy tales."

He handed her the plate and she sniffed, the aroma making her smile grow wider.

"These smell delicious." She took another sniff before looking up at Jasiri.

"Is everything okay?" He waited for her to respond. He'd wanted this surprise to be perfect for her; if something wasn't right, he needed to know.

"Nothing's wrong," she said and sniffed it again. "Just different. I think they may have started using some kind of almond extract or flavoring because there's this almond scent mixing in with raspberry and butter that I don't recall."

Panic rose up in Jasiri, forcing him to smack the plate out of her hand as he yelled, "Don't eat that!"

He pulled her away from the table as he pressed the screen on his smart watch, activating a blaring alarm that made them both cover their ears.

His adjutant and several guards poured from the beach house and crowded around the cabana in a protective, military stance.

"What's happening, My King?" Jasiri could hardly make out Sherard's words over the loud beating of his heart blending into the shrieking alarm.

"Someone just tried to poison the queen."

CHAPTER SIXTEEN

REIGNA WAS DONE.

She was so done as soon as she opened the door to their apartments and found four guards positioned at the door and in the corridor. She was sure there were more she couldn't see making themselves blend into the walls to go unnoticed.

She slammed the door and screamed out her frustration, only to have one of the guards stick his head in the door to make certain she was okay.

"I'm fine!" she barked, never feeling more violated than knowing she was living under a microscope since the attempt on her life. The guard gave her a remorseful look, trying to impart how bad he felt for her. No matter how bad he felt, she knew he'd never let her out of his sight on pain of death.

She'd been in Nyeusi for eight weeks. The last three of which she'd spent locked inside the palace like some fairy-tale princess in a tower, and it was driving her mad.

They'd discovered the kitchen staff had been infiltrated by a Pili supporter. He'd claimed to have no official connection to Jasiri's uncle, but no one believed that. Unfortunately, they couldn't find proof to substantiate their beliefs. This deluded young man would stand trial for attempted regicide, and Pili would be as free to come and go as the waves rushing and then pulling away from the shore.

Reigna sat down on a high-backed chair by the balcony, lifting the receiver and punching in a number she knew better than her own.

"If it isn't Queen Reigna I of Nyesui blessing her lowly sister with a phone call."

Reigna forgot how annoying her sister could be, even from a distance.

"Don't start, Regina."

Her words were terser than she'd planned, and she could feel Regina's energy change through the line as soon as she said, "What's wrong, Reigna?"

She paused a minute. Ringing the alarm in the Devereaux family was like having all the emergency responders from everywhere converging in one place.

"I'm just missing my sister, and it's making me grumpier than usual."

"You sure Jasiri hasn't done something?" Her sister's voice had a healthy dose of suspicion that couldn't be denied. "You know I don't play about my sister. If I have to come remind His Highness of that, I will."

Instantly, Reigna's mood lightened not because her sister was essentially offering to wage war for her, but because she knew her sister well enough that she'd have Jasiri crying for his mother if Reigna really believed he'd done something to make Reigna unhappy.

"Technically, it's *His Majesty*, and Jasiri is fine," she said, fudging that truth. He was physically okay, but he was a walking ball of rage that couldn't be reasoned with right now. A fact Reigna would not share with her sister.

"He's just busy with running the government. I get to

help a great deal, but then there are times when even the queen can't take part in the secret meetings."

That bit had added to her frustration at present. Before the attempt on her life, Jasiri had always allowed her to take part in his governance of the country. Now it was as if he'd shut her out of everything to keep her wrapped up in a tiny closet, if that closet was a sprawling palace.

She knew this was just because Jasiri was scared. His concern aside, he was honestly ticking her off.

"I just miss you." Reigna tried her best to keep her frustration out of her voice. She and Jasiri hadn't really discussed this yet. In that moment, as much as she was annoyed with him, she still wanted to protect him too. "Why don't you come visit? I know you're coming in another month for the coronation and wedding. I just would love to have you with me now, if you can get away."

That wasn't a lie in and of itself. She did miss her sister. They had been inseparable for most of their lives. But there was another reason for this visit Reigna didn't quite want to acknowledge. Jasiri's insistence on isolating her was triggering all those old fears imprinted on her by her parents' toxic marriage. She recognized there was a part of her that was ready to run when things got hard. She hoped having her sister here might soothe her jumpy nerves that were making her itchy for escape.

"If it means that much to you," Regina began, "I can come out in a few days."

Regina coming to visit her meant everything to Reigna. It meant she wouldn't feel so isolated and alone while Jasiri was on his master-of-the-land rampage. It meant she might just live up to her vows and stick around through better and worse.

"I have that gala you asked me to attend in your place,"

Regina continued. "I still don't get why I must pretend to be you at this thing."

"Because I can't get away. If I go, there's just going to be too much to plan security wise for Jasiri and me to be there. Has word of our marriage or accession reached the States yet?"

"Surprisingly, no," Regina replied. "I honestly was expecting it to be all over the world by now. Your husband must have some major PR sway."

Reigna chuckled at that. She was certain Jasiri did have sway with the media to keep their union and his ascension out of the global news.

"You know the British royals are the only royals the world cares about. Luckily that means you can attend this gala in my place and get those folks with deep pockets to sponsor the Alva Grace Trust."

Ace had started it after his wife, Alva, passed away. It granted scholarships for young women entrepreneurs in Brooklyn.

Rich people were stingy with their money. They liked to feel catered to when they were giving it away. That meant if the chairman of the fund didn't show up to schmooze with them, they'd be less likely to dig as deep as Reigna needed them to in order to keep the fund growing.

"Fine," Regina groaned as she acquiesced. "I'll go to this stupid thing and smile like you for an hour and then I'm out. You better have one of the crown jewels prepped as my reward."

"I'll do you one better," Reigna replied. "I'll let you into my closet where they've stocked it with the most gorgeous, and ridiculously expensive clothing you've ever seen. Do this right, and I'll let you take something. If you exceed our fundraising expectations, I'll even let you into the purse and shoe closets too."

Knowing how her sister loved shoes and purses, Reigna was pretty certain Regina had been shocked speechless on the other end of the phone.

"Fine." Regina's harrumph made Reigna's shoulders shake with amusement. "I'll be there. But you'd better make sure you have your butt back here for the private memorial we're having at Devereaux Inc. in Ace's honor. I'm not going to be answering fifty-'leven-hundred questions about where you at and why you didn't let nobody know you got married."

Reigna laughed at her sister's use of the mythical and exaggerated number used in Black culture to express when something had been done, said, or asked with exhaustive frequency. She wasn't sure which one of her ancestors came up with that particular idiom. But it would live in infamy in the minds and vocabulary of Black people now until forever.

"God, our family is nosy," Reigna lamented having momentarily forgotten about that fact. There was too much going on when she'd agreed to Jasiri's business proposal to even think about all the questions her cousins and the like would have.

"Exactly," Regina agreed. "You will not leave me here to deal with that alone, Your Majesty."

"You know, Regina, that phrase is usually said with the utmost respect for me."

"Heifer, please," her sister laughed obnoxiously in her ear. "I shared an amniotic sac with you. The chances of me ever caring about your fragile feelings are nil."

"I hate you," Reigna replied.

"You adore me. That's why your ass is begging me to come stay with you in your palace."

"When you're right, you're right."

Reigna wouldn't even try to deny it. She did adore her sister, and if admitting that would get Regina here sooner so Reigna could deal with the current level of angst Jasiri had her living under, she'd say it a thousand times more.

"Sire."

The sound of Sherard's voice forced Jasiri to look up from his computer. He glanced at the time and saw it was nearing midnight, making this the earliest night he'd stopped working in the last three weeks.

"What is it, Sherard? I'm about to retire."

He ran an exhausted hand down his face, pinching the bridge of his nose briefly to relieve some of the pressure this never-ending stress headache was causing.

"I tried to bring this to your attention earlier this evening, but you said you didn't want to be disturbed when in discussion with General Askari."

Jasiri straightened. Whatever Sherard was about to say, he instantly knew he wouldn't like it. He also knew he'd have no one to blame for his anger but himself because Sherard was reminding him of his own edicts.

"What is it, Sherard?"

"The queen called her sister today. She made arrangements for Ms. Devereaux to visit in a few days. Neither disclosed how long the visit would be."

Jasiri stood and walked to the floor-to-ceiling window that looked out over the gardens. It was a place that was supposed to offer calm, peace. He felt none of those things at the moment.

"Sire, did you wish me to prepare the palace for her twin's arrival?"

Jasiri's stomach dropped as if an unforgiving brick was lodged in it. Reigna was already unhappy with him. Their cold bed and their even colder exchanges since the incident were all the proof he needed his wife was definitely not pleased with his security mandates. Making the wrong choice could be the breaking point for them and the union they were building.

He knew Regina would give her life for Reigna. He also knew how devastated Reigna would be if Pili harmed her sister in an attempt to get to her. He didn't need another person to have the royal guard focusing on. All his efforts had to be centered on protecting Reigna, even if she ended up hating him for it.

"Contact Ms. Devereaux first thing in the morning and cancel her trip. Between plans for the coronation and the wedding, providing Pili with more targets would not be wise."

"Should I tell the queen?"

Jasiri looked out into the dark night, unable to help but see the blackness as a forewarning for what was to come.

The attack on Reigna had made one thing clear for Jasiri. The thought of living without her caused him unbearable pain that seeped down deep through his bones, into his cells, and right into his soul.

He loved her.

Not just as a companion who was helping him run his country, either. He was in love with her.

The paralyzing fear he felt when he realized her pastry might be laced with cyanide was his first clue. The moment that suspicion had been confirmed and he recognized how close he'd come to losing her forever, desperation took root in him, coloring every thought he had.

"No," Jasiri answered. "I will tell her in the morning. Please make the cancellation your priority at the start of the day."

Sherard left just as quietly as he'd come, leaving Jasiri to wrestle with his demons. He had no doubt he was going to incur Reigna's wrath over this. In comparison to what placating her anger might cost him, he couldn't be concerned with it.

Her anger he could handle. Her not being in the world would effectively end him.

Jasiri slid into bed, reaching for Reigna's warmth the moment his weight was completely pressed against the mattress. He'd been working around the clock for the last three weeks and his time with her had been limited to the few hours he slept next to her.

He wrapped his body around hers, needing to know she was safe in his arms where she belonged.

She stirred in her sleep, her full bottom pressing against the swell of him.

"Jasiri?" His name was a sleepy whisper on her lips, and it was his undoing.

He'd planned to pull her into his arms the way he did every night, to make sure she was safe, warm, and protected. Hearing her call his name like that, as if it meant everything to her, soothed him, made him feel whole.

If the anger and fear his uncle had wrought had torn away half his soul, Reigna's anger had gutted him hollow.

Not with harsh words or a loud voice: no, she'd chosen an even deadlier weapon. Her silence.

She'd refused to talk to him beyond what was necessary

or be with him during the day. The result was him barking at everyone around him like he was some sort of tyrant. Holding her was the only way he found a moment's peace.

He'd taken to sneaking in their bed, needing to gather her to him, just to quiet the fear and anger that seemed to be his constant companions.

"I need you."

He felt her stiffen, and he worried that she'd leave him there to suffer just like he deserved for putting her in danger and for not finding a way to stop Pili yet.

"Just let me hold you."

She turned in his arms without a word, pressing one hand gently against his pec and slipping the other around his waist.

He'd wanted to hold her to make sure she was safe, but as her body intertwined with his, he realized it was him that felt safe and protected.

She pressed her hand against his shoulder and kept pushing until he was flat on his back, and she was straddled atop him.

"I wasn't trying to—"

"That's your whole problem Jasiri. You're focused on the wrong thing. Instead of stalking around this palace yelling at everyone," she pulled the silk nightgown from her body exposing all of her to him, "you could be here with me focused on all of this."

She leaned forward, letting his cloth-covered sex settle between her naked folds, and he gripped her hips forcing her to sit still.

Her lips quirked into a lopsided grin. The little minx was enjoying torturing him. She ground down on him forcing a needy groan from him that was strong enough to shake the walls.

"I'm either going to come like this," she said as she swiveled her hips again while she cupped her heavy breasts and tweaked her erect nipples, "or you're going to take off those silk pajama bottoms you love so damn much and give me what we both want."

She lifted and he removed them. As soon as they were gone, she lowered herself to him, and when her wet heat engulfed him, pleasure seeped through his skin, firing every nerve he possessed.

Her naked heat sliding down his flesh drained his lungs of air and made them burn with the need to breathe. Her movements were slow and deliberate, almost surgical in how they elicited pleasure from him. If she kept this up, she'd kill him, and he'd have the shortest reign in history.

Jasiri decided right there that if she was going to kill him, if he was going to be undone by their joining, he'd be damn sure to take her with him too.

He wrapped his arm around her waist, pulling her down to the bed and flipping them, notching himself between her thick thighs. He slid inside of her in one stroke, filling her to the hilt.

Her back bowed, and he used the canting of her hips to deepen his stroke. Her body clamped down on him, and he nearly collapsed. He dropped forward, locking his elbow above her shoulder, hooking her thigh over his arm so he could plunge in and out of her.

He found that tempting spot where shoulder met neck, biting down on it gently to heighten her pleasure.

She moaned, her hands grasping his ass, pulling him deeper as her core quivered around him, as she neared her peak.

His gaze locked onto her face. Reigna in the throes of passion was a beautiful sight. Her face contorted with need as she climbed higher, trying to grasp the prize that Jasiri kept just out of reach for her.

It was only when she said "Please, Jasiri" that he slid his hand between them, circling her swollen nub as he stroked so deeply inside her, he thought they'd become one.

His balls were heavy and aching, and he could feel the electric spark of his release tightened at the base of his spine. When she broke apart, strangling him with her sheath tightening around him like a damn vice, Jasiri's climax pushed through him breaking the hold his anger had on him and filling the empty space Reigna's absence had left him with.

When he spilled the last drop of himself inside of her, he slumped against her, taking her mouth into a deep kiss. The kiss was meant to connect, but it was meant to conceal too. It kept him from having to speak or to give her the chance to look at him and see how raw he was inside.

Reigna had ruined him, and he'd let her. And as they cleaned up and she burrowed into his chest falling into a satisfied sleep, he realized he'd let her ruin him again, as many times as she wanted to. Just as he was about to slide into a blissful sleep realization hit him and he stiffened.

"Reigna, we didn't use a condom."

"I know," she replied on a yawn. "I was there."

"Reigna—"

She held her hand up, stopping whatever he was going to say next.

"We got carried away, Jasiri. Neither of us planned it. I'm okay with any consequences that may arise from it. Are you?"

Their pre-marital health screening established their was no medical reason for their continued use of condoms. But they'd never discussed starting a family.

Suddenly the image of Reigna swollen with his child filled him with warmth and pride, burning itself into his soul.

"Reigna, are you saying you're okay with a possible resulting pregnancy?"

"Yes I am."

Her words rang clear in his head and he couldn't help the smile curving his lips. He went to tighten his embrace around her, but she pointed a finger at him instead.

"I'm mad as hell at the way you've been keeping me locked away in this palace, Jasiri. That said, I'm still not going anywhere. Not for anything or any reason. I'm here for the duration. I'm with you for as long as you want me."

Fear gripped him. There was no question he wanted Reigna through this life and the next. Nonetheless he knew once she found out what he'd done, there was a possibility he'd pushed her beyond her breaking point, and he would lose her, and now possibly his child, for good.

CHAPTER SEVENTEEN

"Everyone out. Now."

Jasiri's office was filled with his administrative staff, all of whom worked for him and honored him as their king. Not one of them looked to Jasiri, who sat in the middle of the room behind his massive desk, for confirmation. They all stopped what they were doing and began making their way out of the room.

Maybe it was Reigna's stiff stance or maybe it was the steel in her voice. Whatever it was, she must've had *I am not to be played with* tattooed on her forehead because those folks scattered like they were running from explosive hot lava raining down on their heads.

When the door clicked closed behind her, she stepped toward him with her finger pointed at him.

"You sneaky—"

He raised his hands palm side up, cutting her off as if she were one of his servants. She'd thought she'd been mad after the call she just received from her sister. With just that simple gesture he'd taken her from angry to enraged, decimating any chance they had at having a reasonable conversation.

"Reigna, I—"

"I don't want to hear it, Jasiri. Canceling my sister's visit without consulting me? You've gone too far."

She stood looming over him, her fury vibrating through her resulting in seismic quakes through her body.

"You've kept me locked up in this damn palace for three weeks as if I'm the one who did something wrong. I hate it, but I knew you were doing it because you were scared, because the thought of losing me scared you stupid."

His widened eyes almost made her laugh. Apparently, he'd really thought he was hiding that well.

"If you know that, you should understand why I canceled your sister's visit."

"Jasiri, I am your wife. We agreed that I would also be your partner in this royal endeavor. Instead, you've sidelined me as if I'm some helpless, fragile damsel who can't fight for herself."

"Reigna, I—"

"I said shut it!" she bellowed, not caring if anyone on the other side of that door could hear. "You are the king of this nation, Jasiri. But you are not God. You do not get to make decisions for me without consulting me or getting my permission."

Fire flashed in his brown eyes, and she saw the moment his restraint snapped. He stood so quickly his chair crashed to the carpeted floor with a loud thump. Jasiri ignored it, focusing only on her as he stalked around the desk and stood before her.

"Pili tried to kill you, Reigna! He tried to kill you, and I can't find a goddamn thing to tie him to his attempt, which means he's free to try again."

His locs hung free, swinging and moving with the same angry staccato that his words took on.

"I will not let him take you from me."

He spoke through clenched teeth. His features were twisted with fear and rage. She'd seen Jasiri undone when they'd made love. But she'd never seen him so out of control with anger that she could hardly recognize the man in front of her.

"If I have to lock you in the goddamn dungeon and throw away the key, I'll do it with not a single ounce of guilt because as pissed as you may be with me, you'll still be alive."

He shoved his fingers through his hair, tugging them angrily through the neatly twisted strands. It looked painful, but in that moment, she thought he might somehow welcome the pain.

"Don't you understand, Reigna? I love you."

He slapped his hand against his chest as he spoke each word again.

"I. Love. You. And the idea of letting him take you away from me sets fire to my soul. If he takes you, what will be left of me? If he takes you, then everything I have sacrificed to protect my nation, my people, my family, it will all be for naught. Because if he takes you, there will be nothing left of me that will be fit to live, let alone rule."

Heat burned through to her skin as tears pooled in her eyes. This beautiful and strong man had been so broken by his fear he was closing the rest of the world out to keep the thing, the person he was fixated on, with him.

"Oh, Jasiri. Don't you see? If Pili had really meant to kill me, I would be dead. What he wanted was to get in your head and he's done that. This is not love, Jasiri. This is obsession, and I cannot condone it. I won't live like this, not after watching how my parents spent years manipulating each other for their own gain. I won't let you turn us into them, Jasiri. That would be the thing that actually kills me."

He leveled his gaze at her, shaking his head as he stood

before her. "You're not taking this seriously, Reigna. I'm trying to do what's best for you."

She placed her hand against her chest to still the tremors shaking her digits. "That's what my father told my mother when he insisted they get married once he and his family discovered she was pregnant. It's also what he said to her when he demanded she give up her dreams of earning a college degree because he was a Devereaux and his wife didn't need to work when he was more than capable of providing for her. It's also what he told her when he isolated her from all her friends and family who were trying to warn her that my father's controlling behavior wasn't healthy. I won't let you do that to us or me, Jasiri. No matter how good your intentions are."

"We are under threat, Reigna—"

"My sister is not a threat, and you know that. But your fear is controlling you, poisoning your way of thinking and making you see threats where there are none. They're making you try to strip me of my freedom just to keep me by your side."

She stepped closer to him, placing careful hands on his face and pressing her lips gently against his.

"I love you, Jasiri. I never stopped loving you. But I cannot watch you destroy yourself by playing into Pili's long game. I won't live as a prisoner, and I won't watch you turn our love to bitter hate because you can't let go."

She stepped away from him. Closing her eyes until she could find the strength to meet his gaze.

"I'm going back to Brooklyn today."

"Reigna, we had a deal."

His words were soaked in anger, but she knew that was a disguise for the hurt she could see gathering in his eyes, in the way his shoulders slipped just a little.

"I will honor that deal. I will show up for any royal appearances you need me to. I'll return for the wedding and the coronation. But I cannot live here with you, like this. When you are ready to hear reason and see that I am an asset to you, a weapon to be wielded instead of a source of weakness, then I will return to this island so fast it will make your head spin. Until then, I can't stay here with you and watch you turn us into my parents."

She walked toward the door and stopped abruptly when he said, "You know I can stop you if I choose. All it would take is a word."

Her tears began to flow, there was too much pain gripping her heart for her to hold them back now.

"I know you can. But you should also know that I spoke to my sister on my private cell phone, the one I came here with. If she doesn't receive a call from me with my flight information in the next fifteen minutes, she'll use every resource the Devereauxs have to start a media shitstorm."

She placed her hand on the doorknob before her as she continued. "You told me once that the most vulnerable time in any government is during the transition of power. Do you really want to test whether the monarchy can weather the global media scrutiny of you keeping an American citizen here against her will?"

When she didn't hear him stomping after her or calling for his guards, she released a breath. Before she could twist the knob and open the door, she heard a sad small whisper rent the air.

"Before you go…" His voice was shaky and frail, and if she hadn't known that they were the only two people in this room she wouldn't have recognized it. "Please tell me what's so terrible about me that your first response to trouble is always to leave me."

His words hit her like stone against brittle bones, making her want to drop down into the fetal position to try to protect herself from the emotional blow.

She turned around, and her knees nearly buckled when she saw the shimmer of unshed tears filling his eyes. "I said *no* not because I didn't want to be your wife but because I didn't know how to be anyone's wife."

He flinched, as if her words struck him across his jaw like a skilled fist trained in the art of hand-to-hand combat.

"We hadn't talked about marriage. I had no idea you were even thinking along those lines. I needed time to prepare, Jasiri. Time to understand that I wasn't my mother and you weren't my father. Instead, you sprung a very public and unexpected proposal on someone you knew from jump was commitment-phobic and when the expected happened, you walked away from me without a word."

She glanced up at the ceiling briefly to gather strength to continue.

"You left. You cut me off, blocked my number with no means of contacting you. And when I went to the consulate to try to speak with you, I was told I was no longer allowed on the premises. You decided we were over, Jasiri, and I wasn't given a say in it. I will not let you do the same thing to us again out of some misguided attempt to protect partly me, but mostly to protect yourself."

His jaw tightened, and she could tell he hadn't ever considered how their breakup had affected her. She'd been too afraid to say these words then, a mistake she wouldn't repeat now.

"I won't cut you off the way you did me. I will always keep the lines of communication open between us because what we have is worth fighting for. But right now, you're not ready to fight. You're running scared, Jasiri, and that fear is pushing me away."

She wiped her fingers across her face to stanch the river of tears sliding down her cheeks, hoping to say this one last thing before she completely devolved into sheer emotion and no reason.

"The first time I left you was because I was afraid of me, Jasiri. Now I'm leaving you because I'm afraid for you."

And with that, she turned around and opened the door, stepping into the empty hall, walking away from the man she loved quite possibly forever.

CHAPTER EIGHTEEN

REIGNA SAT AT her desk, making the final arrangements for the rechristening of the library in the Devereaux Inc. building. Her cousins and sister had handled most of it, but there was a new development that only the queen of Nyeusi could carry out.

"Do you think Jasiri is going to handle this well?"

Reigna looked up at her sister's question and saw Regina and their five cousins filing into her office.

Regina, Jeremiah, Trey, Lyric, Amara, and Stephan all stood in the middle of the room like a protective barrier from the wind, waiting to cover her when her world was crumbling around her.

"If he knew what my plan was," Reigna began, "I don't think he'd be handling it well at all."

Reigna had known the moment Jasiri had crossed that final line that if she was going to save their marriage, she'd have to find a way to deal with Pili and end the head games he was playing with her husband. To make that happen, though, she needed her family, and she needed to change the arena in order to capitalize on home-court advantage.

Jeremiah spoke up. "Everything is settled on my end, Reigna. My connect has everything set up. They'll be by the morning of the event to get everything arranged and go over the detailed plan with you. We're gonna finish this once and for all."

His wife Trey placed her arms around his waist and smiled at Reigna. "Jeremiah's right. We're gonna teach this fool that if you come for one Devereaux, you come for us all."

They all nodded in agreement, including Reigna. This family didn't play about theirs, and Prince Pili of Nyeusi was about to find that out the hard way.

Her family exited her office, and she knew it was time to set the most important part of her plan in place. She took in a breath and dialed, expecting to get a notice that her number was blocked. Instead, Jasiri picked up on the first ring.

"Reigna?" His voice was rushed, tinged with a bit of relief. When she didn't answer immediately, he spoke again. "Please tell me you're safe. Are my guards near?"

"I am safe, and your guards are just outside my office door. I have complied with all their demands. I wouldn't risk my life unnecessarily. Not when I want to come home, Jasiri. I don't want to be without you any longer than I have to."

"Then, don't, baby. Come back to me."

The sound of his voice melted through the cold numbness she'd carried around in the two weeks she'd been gone.

"I want to. But I need to know you trust me to make decisions for myself. I need to know you trust me to fight at your side. I need to know you trust me to fight for you when you can't or won't fight for yourself."

"Reigna, what you're asking—"

"Jasiri, I know part of this is my fault because I ran without an explanation, and I hurt you as a result. I'm trying to tell you now that this is different. I'm not running because I'm scared, I'm fighting for us and for Nyeusi. The question is, will you trust me enough to fight with me?"

Reigna made her way through the crowd, stopping to chat with friends and colleagues of Ace as they praised the work she and her cousins had done to create such a touching memorial to her uncle. It was then that Reigna caught sight of Jeremiah, and he gave her a quick nod letting her know it was go time.

"Sweet Lord in heaven, please let this work. Not only is the future of a whole nation on the line, but so is my heart."

Her prayer said, she gathered the flowing skirt of her evening gown heading toward the executive elevator. With her royal guards falling in step behind her, she found herself and them emerging from the elevator and onto the executive floor in no time.

She stepped inside of the dark room, forgoing the wall light for the dim lamp she used when she was working late or needing to think in silence and semidarkness.

She sat behind her desk, looking out into the window that made up the back wall. From here she could see the serenity of the lights of the Brooklyn Bridge stilling her nerves. That bridge was Brooklyn's strength and resilience personified, and if she needed any more encouragement, she could hear the rap goddess Lil' Kim telling her Brooklyn didn't run from ish to soothe any uncertainty she had about executing her plan.

The glint of metal reflecting in the window glass shut down any remaining doubts she had. She was Queen Reigna I of Nyeusi as well as Reigna Devereaux of the Brooklyn Devereauxs. Just in case there was any misunderstanding, she was ready to set shit off.

"Prince Pili," her lip curled a knowing grin as she slowly spun around in her chair to face her husband's uncle. "Right on time as scheduled."

"As scheduled?" he huffed with a dismissive tone, as if he was shooing her away with a condescending *silly girl.* "There's no way you knew I'd be here tonight."

Reigna raised her brow, keeping the rest of her body still in the chair.

Pili walked toward her slowly, taking the seat in front of her desk as if she'd invited him to sit down. Entitlement just oozed from this man, and Reigna couldn't wait to be done with him.

"What can I do for you, Pili?"

"Oh, My Queen, I am the one who is here to do something for you."

She leaned back into her chair, crossing her leg and granting him permission to speak with a wave of her hand.

"It's been brought to my attention that the king isn't doing well since that unfortunate attempt on your life."

Reigna shook her head, already over this man's feigned concern. "An attempt we both know you're behind, so why don't we stop with the pretense and get directly to the point of your visit, shall we?"

He chuckled as if she were amusing him, and she smiled in return. This man was underestimating her, and he had no idea what a foolish move that was.

"Well, then, if that's how you want it, I'll be perfectly honest. Yes, I was responsible for the so-called attempt on your life. But since I abhor murder, you should know that I had no intention of bringing harm to you. I just knew that thinking you were in danger would send my besotted nephew into a tailspin."

She steepled her hands together as she looked at him.

"I don't understand how you thought provoking Jasiri this way would benefit your cause."

"You wouldn't," he sneered. "You haven't been at court long enough to know that a king more concerned with his wife than his kingdom isn't fit to rule. By whipping Jasiri up into a frantic tizzy, I have all the proof I need that the king is not fit for the crown. I didn't need to kill you to accomplish that. I simply needed to make it look like I was."

She breathed slowly through her nares to control the anger swelling in her chest. She was almost there; she couldn't let him win now.

"The only problem is you had someone plant real cyanide in my pastries. If I'd taken a bite of one, I'd certainly have died."

He smiled as if any of this was the slightest bit funny, shrugging nonchalantly as if this were all some sick, twisted game.

"But you didn't, so it all worked out in the end, right?"

She closed her eyes, smiling before she looked at him again.

"Pili, you are absolutely right. It did work out in the end."

"I'm glad you see things my way," Pili responded. "Now, if you want me to stop my mental warfare on the king, have him abdicate, or I promise you I will ruin him before the eyes of the Nyeusian people."

Reigna leaned forward, chuckling as she did so. "You really do think you've got me right where you want me, huh?" When he opened his mouth to speak, she held up a hand to stop him. "It was a rhetorical question. This attack on Jasiri was cute, and it might have actually worked if he were married to any other woman but me."

Pili's smile slowly dripped off his face as he watched

her, as if he finally realized he might not be as in control of things as he thought.

"Pili, while you were playing checkers, I was playing chess. You see, in Brooklyn, you've always got to know somebody, because knowing somebody is how we get things done. So when I called my cousin Jeremiah to tell him about my plan to get you out of my hair once and for all, he was all too happy to call one of his friends from way back in the day who just happened to be an NYPD captain. Captain Heart Searlington, would you like to introduce yourself to Prince Pili?"

From the shadows of the office, a tall Black woman with her dark hair pulled into a tight bun stepped into the dim light. She wore a bulletproof vest emblazoned with *NYPD* as she slowly stepped toward Pili's chair.

"Prince Pili, is it?" Her question was rhetorical, but to a megalomaniac like Pili, failing to acknowledge him was a cutting blow. "It seems you've been a bit chatty. You actually admitted to attempted murder in a room where anyone could be listening." She pulled a radio from her waist and spoke into it. "Did we get that, boys?"

"Copy that, Captain," crackled through the airwaves leaving Pili gripping his armrests as his jaw dropped in shock.

"You were recording me?"

Pili had found his tongue, apparently, and his backbone too, because his shock turned visible as he sat ramrod straight in his seat.

"Well, you villainous types like to hear yourselves talk a lot, so I figured it shouldn't be that difficult to get you to admit your crimes on tape."

His brown skin flushed with anger, as his eyes turned nearly black with rage. If it weren't for the fact that a police officer was in the room with them, she had no doubt Pili would've chosen violence in that moment.

Catching himself, he recovered quickly and fell into his royal facade easily.

"It doesn't matter what you've recorded. I have diplomatic immunity. I could've assassinated the king in front of this officer, and there wouldn't be a thing she could do to me."

"That's easily fixed." Reigna smiled as she spoke to him. "I'm revoking your diplomatic immunity right now."

Pili laughed loud enough to shake the walls. "You've been queen for all of, what, five minutes? I think you need to take some more civics lessons to figure out how diplomatic status works in Nyeusi. Only the monarch can grant or remove diplomatic status." His lips pulled into a loathsome grin. "Being the whore he beds doesn't give you any power over my status."

"Oh, Uncle."

At the sound of that deep and powerful voice, Pili's confidence slid off his face, turning his skin from a deep brown to an ashy death gray.

Jasiri stepped into the room flanked by his adjutant Sherard on one side and General Askari on the other.

"When my wife…" Jasiri let the word dangle in the air as an open objection to his uncle's attempt to disrespect and degrade Reigna "…arrived in the United States, she did so as my regent. As my regent, she wields the full power of my office in the capacity I have granted her. Today, that would be in state matters where she can decide which of our emissaries will be covered by the might of our nation."

Jasiri pulled a folded piece of paper from his pocket,

opening it and holding it in front of Pili's gaze. "Two hours ago, she signed the paperwork revoking your diplomatic immunity. An hour before that, she had my written permission to do so."

Pili's eyes widened, and his jaw dropped open as realization hit.

Jasiri moved to stand near Reigna's chair, pulling her to her feet and placing a protective hand at her waist as he pulled her into his side.

"You can either return to Nyeusi and be tried and convicted of treason and attempted regicide, where the penalty is death." Jasiri gave a brief nod to Captain Searlington before he continued. "Or the captain can arrest you and you can face trial in the American justice system for your admission of the attempted murder of a foreign dignitary. Either way, you will never be free to come near my wife again."

"Nephew." Tiny beads of sweat bubbled on Pili's top lip and forehead. "You can't do this. We are blood. Think of your father." Pili had been reduced to bargaining for his life. He was a dead man walking, and he knew it.

Jasiri pointed at himself before speaking. "I am king of Nyeusi. I decide how to handle all threats against the crown. My father mourned his brother the moment you made an attempt on the queen's life. He knew then there would be no version of this where you would walk free of your crimes. Make your choice, and make it quickly. My general is aching to throw you in the dingiest cell he can find."

Captain Searlington handed a thwarted Pili over to her lieutenant. When she returned her gaze to them, Jasiri reached out and shook her hand.

"Captain Searlington, you have the appreciation of all

Nyeusi for protecting our queen. Should there be anything I can do to repay the favor, you have but to ask."

"I appreciate your offer," she said, sharing a reassuring glance with Reigna before she returned her gaze to Jasiri. "My husband has had a twisted family member put him in harm's way too. I know the worry you must've felt. This was a freebie. You don't owe me anything."

She turned to walk out the door but looked over her shoulder and said, "There's a bunch of Devereauxs that are clamoring to get upstairs. You want me to let them up?"

"No," Reigna responded, "I need to speak with my husband alone."

Captain Searlington left the room followed by Sherard and General Askari.

As soon as the door clicked, Jasiri had Reigna in is arms and his mouth pressed against hers. He devoured her. Not just in a sexual way, he was drinking from her, drawing life from her into himself.

He finally tore his mouth from hers, leaving them both fighting to drag air into their lungs.

"You took years off my life," he choked out. "Don't ever do that again, Reigna."

She smoothed her hands out over his cheek, so grateful to be in his arms again.

"You trusted me to fix this, Jasiri."

The sentence came out half statement, half question. Like she'd witnessed a miracle unfold before her own eyes.

"I had no choice, Reigna. I needed you back. This was so different than our breakup two years ago. Then, all I had were crafted fantasies about what it would be like to have you by my side as queen. Now," he said and cupped her face, sliding his thumb along the gentle line of her jaw, "now I know what that feels like, what the reality is, and my fantasies can't compare. I was so out of line, Reigna."

He closed his eyes, shaking his head while he admonished himself. "I would definitely understand if you wanted nothing to do with me."

He took her hand and bent his knee as he looked up at her with contrition glimmering in his gaze.

"Kings don't kneel before anyone but God, Reigna. But this king would take the knee as many times as you deemed fit if it meant you'd give him another chance to prove he will be better."

She tugged at his arm, bidding him to stand before her.

"This queen does not seek to put her king on his knees. All she has ever wanted was to stand by him, to fight with him, and to fight for him. When you are weak, it's my job to fortify you. As long as you remember that, I'm packed and ready to go home right now."

The smile on Jasiri's face warmed her heart airing out the dank places that pain and mistrust had left to rot.

"If you won't accept my supplication, I hope this will express how much you mean to me and how committed I am to having you by my side."

He reached into his inside jacket pocket and pulled out folded documents. He gave them to her, and she wasted no time scanning through them.

"You've turned complete ownership of Ace's house over to me?" The words tumbled from her mouth quickly as she continued to read. Then her gaze slid across the last line of the transference, and a tear slid down her cheek and onto the page, blotting the corner it had fallen on. "This says you signed these on our wedding day?"

He let a gentle finger slide across her cheek to collect her tears as he smiled down at her. "When I told you who

I was, I expected you to end our deal and demand I take you home. You completely surprised me when instead you demanded to be my partner, to stand by me and share the load. I knew then that you deserved better than me holding something significant to you over your head. I had my lawyers draw up the papers that very day. I signed them digitally and had the forms notarized and filed in America. This house was always supposed to be yours. I was simply correcting my great wrong."

His palm cupped her cheek, and she burrowed into it, letting his warmth fill her. This man had loved her and protected her even when they both refused to acknowledge their love in that moment.

"Take me home, Jasiri."

He nodded and then clapped his hands, and the door to her office opened with Sherard standing at the ready.

"Sherard," Jasiri said without taking his eyes of Reigna, "the queen and I are ready to return home. Make it so."

"By your command, My King."

EPILOGUE

"WHAT DOES MY queen yearn for if her mind is so far away from me?"

Jasiri's arms closed around her, bringing a smile to her face as she leaned back, resting her head against his chest. They stood in the palace gardens at their favorite column that hid them from the rest of the world.

"I was just thinking that when we met again, I was going through the worst pain of my life. Ace was gone, and then I found out he'd given away the one thing he'd promised me."

He didn't speak. Jasiri knew her well enough that he understood she didn't need to be rescued, just heard and considered. Of all the things she loved about her husband, it was that he'd taken the time to learn who she was now.

"Ace's house."

He hugged her to him, and again she let his strength seep into her.

"It was never about the house. It was about holding on to the only person who'd loved and protected me the way I'd needed. I was so damn angry with that old man for doing me dirty and giving you half that house. I realize now, he'd known exactly what he was doing. He knew I would fight like hell to get what I thought was mine."

Jasiri chuckled. "Ace was always ten steps ahead of all

of us. If I didn't know any better, I'd say he planned our reconciliation down to the royal wedding."

"Knowing my great-uncle, I wouldn't put it past him."

She turned in his arms, placing a gentle peck on his lips. "Because of Ace's meddling, the worst pain in my life turned into my greatest joy, Jasiri."

She was so grateful to Ace for all his wisdom, grateful for all she'd gained because of it, but most of all, she was grateful for the love she shared with Jasiri.

The celebration in the palace blared, drawing their attention. She hooked a thumb over her shoulder toward the palace. "We should probably get back to the party before they send the King's Guard looking for us."

"It's the second reception today." Jasiri tightened his arms around her. "They can do without us for a little while."

"True, but this reception is the private one for our family and friends. I actually want to attend this one."

He stepped away from her, bowing dramatically. "Whatever my queen wants, I shall provide."

He gave her his elbow, and they walked until they were positioned in front of the doors to the grand hall.

The doors opened, and music surrounded them as they danced their way to the center of the floor to the sensual tune of Gyptian's "Hold Yuh."

She'd spent all day following the proper protocols for the royal wedding, immediately followed by the coronation, and then the reception for all the heads of state. But this one, this was what she and her fellow Brooklynites would call a full-on bashment party.

Yeah, it was on the bougie side because it was being held in a palace. The important things like a fire DJ and all their family surrounding them, cheering for them as they lost themselves in the rhythm and lyrics were still present, though.

This moment was the real start of their lives together. The one she would remember every moment of her life. And when the song blended into another, and her husband smiled down at her, she knew this was the perfect time to give him his wedding gift.

His hand was lovingly resting low on her waist. She threaded her fingers through his and slid his hand forward, flattening his protectively over the bottom of her stomach.

Jasiri caught the motion immediately, his gaze locking with hers as his eyes asked the silent question.

A smile and a tiny nod was all it took before he grabbed her up in his arms and swung her around.

She placed her mouth near his ear so he could hear her over the music. "Put me down, you maniac, before my morning sickness starts again. Your heir doesn't like sudden motions."

He placed her gently on her feet before pulling her to him and kissing her breathless right there on the dance floor. The music was blasting, and the lights were flashing, but the only thing Reigna could see was the man she loved so overwhelmed with joy at the news of her pregnancy that her heart was fit to burst.

"I love you, Jasiri."

A happy tear slid down his face as he placed a finger under her chin and lifted.

"And I love you more, My Queen. Just as it should always be."

* * * * *

ITALIAN'S CINDERELLA TEMPTATION

CAROL MARINELLI

MILLS & BOON

PROLOGUE

THE TROUBLE WITH BROTHERS?

They know.

Before heading into the meeting, Sevandro Casadio slid open the private drawer of his desk to collect his wallet and caught sight of a wedding band.

It still startled him—as if a foreign object had been placed in his drawer...something that didn't belong to him. Here in Dubai, aged twenty-three, it still didn't feel real that back home in Lucca he had a wife.

He'd never worn the ring—on his wedding day his hand, thanks to a fight with his brother, had been too swollen. But Sheikh Mahir had made a comment, pointing out that the wedding had been three months ago and surely his hand was better now.

Sev had got the implication. Sheikh Mahir was very much a family man, and his relief had been evident when, a few short weeks after commencing work in Dubai, Sev had told him that he was marrying a girl from home.

'That is excellent.' He had smiled at Sev, the young gun who was determined to make waves in the hotel industry. 'A stable home life is good for business.'

Sev had attended the same prestigious Milan school as the Sheikh's son, Adal. They hadn't particularly been friends—Sev was guarded and did not make friends easily. Still, one year he'd invited Adal to the summer festival in Lucca. In turn, Sev had been invited to spend time in Dubai.

More recently he'd approached Sheikh Mahir, telling him about a hotel in Tuscany that was about to go under and explaining his well-thought-out plan, but Mahir had been uninterested.

'I have enough going on here...'

'I recall you saying you were looking for investment opportunities in Italy.'

'That was when Adal was considering living there. I wanted a project for him.'

'This could be one,' Sev had persisted, knowing very well Adal wouldn't lift a finger, but sensing an in for himself. 'Adal and I get on.'

Barely... But he would take the idle Adal off his father's hands for the duration if that was what it took.

Sev wanted capital and, as he'd told Sheikh Mahir, 'The owners need a quick sale—it's too good to pass up.'

'If it's such a good opportunity, why did your grandfather say no?'

'I haven't discussed it with him,' Sev had admitted. 'I'd prefer to keep family and business separate.'

'An impossible ask.' Sheikh Mahir had sighed heavily. 'Everything we do is for family.' He'd paused then, and taken a long, pondering look at Sev. 'What if I told you I had a project here? Well, it's more Adal's venture...'

It had taken him a moment to register that Mahir was offering him opportunities in both Italy and in Dubai, and Sevandro had embraced both. He'd flown back to Lucca to celebrate...perhaps celebrated a little too recklessly one night...

Sheikh Mahir had been correct.

The moment Sev had found out he was to be a father his

priorities had changed. While work had always taken prece-
dence there had always been plenty of time to indulge in his
playboy ways. No more. He would work not just to fulfil his
own ambitions but for Rosa, and the baby they had made, in
a heady, brief encounter.

Everything he did now was for family.

There had been a brief honeymoon, then back to work
in Dubai. Rosa did not understand why he didn't remain in
Lucca—after all the Casadio Winery was as good his.

She didn't understand that he might want to make his
own way.

And he didn't understand the delay in announcing her
pregnancy.

'People will talk,' Rosa said. 'Let's wait a few more weeks.'

But then she'd called him in Dubai and told him she was
bleeding. He'd flown home immediately—but to the news
that their baby was gone…

He'd grieved alone.

Rosa refused to discuss things. Her parents, with whom
she was staying, stonewalled him too, calling him insensitive.

'It was my baby too,' he'd pointed out, and then called over
their shoulders so that Rosa could hear, 'We have an appointment with Dr Romero.'

He'd made several on his many trips home since the loss,
but there had always been a reason she couldn't attend.

His family, unaware of the baby's existence, hadn't noticed that Sev, always solemn and serious, was even more so
on these trips. His brother Dante might have picked up on it,
might have heard he was staying at a hotel, but they were no
longer speaking—and anyway, Dante was back in Milan…

In Dubai the frenetic pace continued, with deadlines to be
met and meetings to attend, but for now, with his marriage
well into injury time, they could wait.

He didn't just want answers—he needed them.

Certainly he wasn't going to put on a wedding band just to appease Sheikh Mahir. Placing it back in the drawer, he looked out at the glittering view of the Persian Gulf.

He took up his phone and was about to call Dr Romero's office to make an appointment to speak with the family doctor and find out what the hell had gone on, when Dante's name flashed across the screen.

At first he thought his brother must be calling to apologise for what he had said about Rosa. Dante's words had been the reason for the groom's swollen hand on his wedding day, and the best man's cut and blackened eyes. Unsure what to say to his brother, he let the call go.

But had Dante been right in his assessment of Rosa? Had there been a baby at all?

Dante called again and this time Sev he answered.

'Sev.'

The moment he heard the strain in his brother's voice, and then a sharp intake of breath, Sev knew this was about more than their fight.

Brothers know.

'I have bad news…' Dante started.

But his words were followed by the ache of a long pause and Sev's back stiffened, his jaw clenched as he braced himself for whatever was to come.

'The helicopter…' Dante said, referring to the family helicopter that buzzed over the hills regularly. 'It went down just after take-off. The rescuers are on their way.'

'Who?' Sev tried to ask, only no sound came out. 'Who?' he said, this time abruptly, knowing it would likely be their parents, for they used it frequently.

Sadly, he was right. 'They were on their way to Milan to see me.' Dante's voice was strained as he said what he must. 'Sev, Rosa was also on board.'

His reaction was silence, and yet there was a huge roar in his head—so much so that he swung on his chair and looked out of the window, almost expecting to see a fighter jet had gone up. But no, the sky was Dubai-blue and the ocean was glittering and azure as it had been a mere moment ago...

There were no survivors.

Both brothers were pallbearers.

Together, but apart.

Sev helped carry their father's coffin into Lucca's magnificent cathedral. Dante walked behind, helping to carry their mother.

They took their places in the front pew, either side of their grandfather, holding up the devastated Gio. At the cemetery they greeted the mourners, then stood side by side as their parents were buried together.

The wake was held at their property, a huge palazzo on sprawling grounds, set on Lucca's ancient medieval walls. It was an elegant affair, with people speaking in low funeral voices—

'Che tristeza!'

'How sad!'

'Such a vibrant couple...'

'They were so happy...'

'It's so hard to believe just three months ago they were celebrating Sevandro and Rosa's wedding...'

Their voices would trail off for a moment. Then...

'How is he doing?'

No one knew.

Least of all Sev.

Sev had never been one to reveal his feelings, and wasn't about to start on this day.

He could hear the comments, though.

'Have you seen Dante's scar?'

'Hopefully this will reunite the brothers—they need each other now.'

'Twenty-three is far too young to be a widower...'

As the last mourners left, Sev checked in on Gio, who lay pale and fragile on a vast bed, still in his funeral suit.

'I never thought I'd say this,' Gio sobbed as Sevandro undressed him, 'I am glad your *nonna* is dead.' He'd mourned her for as long as Sev could remember. 'This would have been too much for her.'

'Try and rest, Gio,' Sev told him, dimming the sidelight. 'Dante's fetching your tablets and then you need to sleep.'

'Yes...' Gio lay back, closing his eyes on the day he'd buried his son and his daughter-in-law, but then he must have realised there was more grief to come, for he suddenly rallied, reaching for Sev's arm and grabbing the sleeve of his black suit. 'We'll be there for you tomorrow.'

'I know that,' Sev said, looking at the thin pale fingers clutching his arm, not turning his head as Dante came in with Gio's medicine.

'Dante?' Gio said, even deep in mourning attempting to heal the brothers' rift. 'I think you should help carry Rosa's coffin tomorrow—'

'No need,' Sev interrupted. 'It's all taken care of.'

He stood and left Dante to say goodnight to their grandfather and walked down the long corridor, taking the stairs up to the floor that had once been his and Dante's. Stepping into his old bedroom, he flicked open his case and started to pack, only briefly glancing up as Dante came to the door. The scar that ran through his eyebrow was an angry pink. Garish and vivid. But then so too were the memories of their fight on the eve of his and Rosa's wedding.

'You're packing?'

Sevandro said nothing.

'Are you going to stay with Rosa's parents?'

Sevandro made a slight hissing noise, one that said, *When hell freezes over*—or at least it did to the brother who had once known him so well.

'So where?'

Sev gritted his teeth and snapped the case closed.

'Don't stay at a hotel tonight…'

Sev had been staying at hotels a lot since his marriage, but he wasn't about to discuss that with Dante now and, picking up his case, he left.

'Sevandro.' His brother bounded down the stairs behind him, then beat him to the vast doors. 'Please…' He attempted to halt him. 'What I said on the eve of your wedding—'

'Not now,' Sev cut in. No, he didn't want to hear it on the eve of Rosa's funeral. 'Just—'

He could not complete his sentence. Since the news had hit—since the roar like a fighter jet had faded—he'd been numb. Completely numb and unable to place a label on a single feeling. He didn't know if it was grief, or anger, or even guilt because he'd never loved his wife. It was as if a fog had descended and wrapped around him, seeping into his veins, sedating all emotion. And that was how he'd got on the plane home. That was how he'd dealt with his family, as well as Rosa's, and yet now the fog seemed to lift for a moment, a brief surge of something hitting him—and it was something he could finally label.

Protectiveness.

A surge of protection towards Rosa.

Tomorrow he would lay his young wife to rest in the ground. However bad the private hell of their marriage had been, tomorrow he would do the right thing by her. He looked at his brother and thought of all Dante had once said about Rosa and knew there would be no reconciliation tonight.

'We'll keep things polite for the sake of Gio, but don't even think about carrying her coffin tomorrow,' Sev warned him. 'Or I'll put a matching scar over the other eye.'

Rosa's service was held in the church they had been married in. Out of town, it was nestled in the foothills of Lucca, close to both families' wineries. Sev, along with Rosa's father and her cousins, carried the coffin. Watching her being lowered into the ground all he could hear was their final row, when once again she'd refused to see a doctor or answer any of the many questions he had.

'Please don't leave me, Sevandro,' she'd sobbed. *'What will people think?'*

Her wake was held at the smaller De Santis Winery, and Sev felt a hypocrite as he accepted the handshakes and condolences. Rosa's parents, who had known he was on the edge of ending the marriage, seemed to have forgotten all about that—they sobbed and spoke of the happy couple and how in love they had been.

It was hardly the place to correct them.

Stepping outside, he walked away from the rather dilapidated cellar door, where the mourners were gathered, and found a secluded spot. But there was no solace there. The wreckage of the helicopter was still in the hills ahead of him.

Dante came and joined him, leaning on a fence. 'How are you holding up?'

Sev didn't answer, because he didn't know himself.

'It's pretty grim in there.'

'Well, what did you expect?' Sev responded, not turning his head, just staring at the wreckage. But then he had a question for his brother. 'Why were they going to Milan?'

'Rosa was attending Fashion Week.'

'I know that.' He'd found out that Rosa had asked his mother to secure her an invitation—clearly, she had recovered quickly from their final row. 'But our parents weren't attending—they were going to have lunch with you. Why?'

'To talk about us,' Dante admitted. 'You and I. They wanted to know why we'd fallen out.' He could feel his brother's eyes on him. 'Sev, I should never have said what I did that night. I don't know if studying law has made me cynical, but at the time I really thought Rosa might be just *saying* she was pregnant.'

Rosa had been saying exactly that.

'Sev,' Dante continued with urgency. 'I was worried she might be trying to trap you into marriage. Clearly, I was wrong.'

Sev did think of correcting Dante—telling him that very possibly he'd been right. Dr Romero had been there at the funeral, and Sev had even thought of making another appointment to see him, getting the answers to the questions he'd been coming around to asking before the news of the accident had come in.

For what purpose, though?

While he might have married Rosa out of duty, it didn't end just because she'd died... There was the scent of soil in his nostrils, the memory of her last words—how she'd cared what others might think.

So he did not reveal to his brother the hell his marriage had been. Instead he pushed up from the wall he had been leaning on to head back to the wake and accept the handshakes and condolences and honour other people's memory of Rosa.

'Leave it,' he said to his brother.

'Sev...'

'Let her rest.'

It was all he could do for Rosa now.

CHAPTER ONE

Almost ten years later...

'THIS WAY...'

From beneath the hood of her coat, Juliet Adams resisted rolling her eyes as Louanna walked ahead of the small group—she was clearly in good spirits.

It was damp and misty, and Juliet was worried.

There were grey clouds over the Tuscan hills and they seemed headed their way.

Beneath the hood her long red hair was worn down, but clipped back from her face, there were pearls in her ears and the black halter neck dress she wore was more suited to a cocktail party than the middle of the day...

It wasn't her hair or her attire that concerned Juliet, though. It was the instruments they carried. 'Louanna we can't play outside.'

'But it's Valentine's Day in Lucca,' Louanna insisted, carrying her cello case with practised ease. 'Lots of love and music to be made.'

There were four of them. Juliet was English, the others Italian, and they all attended the music school here in Lucca and had formed a string quartet—though offers for work weren't exactly pouring in. Lucca was full to the brim with talented and emerging musicians, and their little ensemble was struggling to get bookings.

Juliet was in her final year and hoping to turn professional soon—though she had exams to focus on and, given her work commitments at the ice-cream store and a local bar, she was behind on practice.

Behind on everything...

Louanna, the cellist and their self-proclaimed manager, had decided to capitalise on this romantic day and persuaded them to perform for free on Lucca's famous ancient walls.

'It's threatening rain.' Ricco glanced up at the ominous sky. 'Look, we can't play. Why don't we head to the square... set up somewhere sheltered?' He nudged Juliet. 'For Valentine's Day they're holding speed-dating there. You could give it a go.'

'Sorry?'

'Speed-dating—it's great fun.'

'In the square?' she checked. 'You mean, in front of everyone?'

'Maybe try it. That is how Gabriele and I met...'

Juliet could honestly not imagine anything more horrific— she was shy at the best of times, but to have an audience watching you blush and bluster your way through first introductions...!

'It's perfect,' Ricco insisted.

He was always trying to matchmake, and lately Juliet seemed to be his project. She found she could talk a little with him—perhaps because he only liked men.

'You say you don't have time to meet anyone...' he went on. 'There will be ten, maybe twelve guys on each table. It's short—a timed session. If you don't get on with someone it will drag, but if you click...'

'Oh, please.' Juliet had never *clicked* with anyone. 'What would I say?'

'They'll know you're English, they'll see you're gorgeous.

Say you're studying music and hope to be a professional musician,' he turned. 'What else?'

'There isn't much else.' It was the truth—she lived and breathed music and worked to support it. 'I could say I'm hoping to get my residency here...'

'Too much, too soon,' Ricco said. 'Keep it light.' He thought for a moment. 'Okay, what's your ideal first date?'

'A nice restaurant?'

'You're as broke as me.'

'A picnic, then. Flowers? I don't know...'

'Just be yourself. But don't go on about your exes...'

'I'm not doing it,' Juliet said, rather than tell him that there weren't any exes.

Well, hardly.

She'd never got past the getting-to-know-you part—or rather, when her date got to know that she'd never seriously dated, let alone slept with anyone, any fledgling romance came to an abrupt end.

As if being twenty-five and a virgin, and seriously single, meant she must have issues...

'Give it a go,' Ricco pushed, but she shook her head.

'I'll think about it once my exams are out of the way...'

'What is there to think about?

She was saved from answering by a welcome drizzle of rain, and Dario spoke up. 'I'm not playing outside in this.'

'Okay.' Louanna turned around and put up a hand to halt both their protests and their steps. 'We're not playing on the walls—we have a booking...' She pointed to a bench. 'Perhaps take a seat?'

Louanna was a little bossy—albeit effectively so, because they all did as they were told as Louanna stood leaning against the stone wall.

'You've all rehearsed the piece I suggested?' Louanna checked, nodding to Juliet because, given they shared a flat, she would have heard that she had. Ricco and Dario said they'd practised too. 'That's good, because we have a wedding booking.'

'When?' Dario asked.

'Right now!' Louanna said. 'Six hours' paid work and hopefully good tips.'

'Why on earth didn't you say?' Juliet sat up. 'I've been panicking about giving up a shift!'

'I know, but this is a top-secret event. It's Gio Casadio's wedding,' Louanna said, as if that name alone explained everything.

Actually, it did.

'The owner of the Casadio Winery?'

'Yes—amongst many other things.' Louanna nodded. 'Serious wealth. This is the break we've been hoping for.'

'But...' Juliet shook her head at the impossibility of them playing at such an elite function. And it had to be elite—the wine they produced was so well-renowned that even in England she'd heard of it. Not that she'd ever tried it.

Then she swallowed. Actually, she had...

Susie—her and Louanna's flatmate—had brought some home the other week, along with some other fabulous treats, and invited them to help themselves...

Juliet loathed rumours, but she'd have to be living under a rock not to know that Susie and the very out-of-town Dante Casadio had supposedly had a fling when he'd briefly returned.

'This is huge for us,' Louanna said. 'I nearly died when the event planner called. She asked for our demo tapes before committing and insisted I keep it to myself.'

'I'd have told everyone,' Ricco freely admitted. 'Are you for real, Louanna? Gio is getting married? He must be eighty?'

'The bride isn't much younger!' Louanna had saved the best to last. 'It's Mimi!'

Ricco was so excited to hear Mimi's name that he jumped off the bench and covered his mouth, moaning with excitement.

'Mimi?' Juliet gulped. She knew that name—and not just because the woman was helping Susie with her Italian. 'The famous opera singer?'

'That's the one,' Louanna smiled.

Mimi was incredible.

As soon as she'd heard who it was helping her friend learn Italian, Juliet had fallen into an opera-shaped rabbit hole and started listening to her—studying her, really. Mimi, if she so chose, could stand right where they were now, on the walls, and her voice would reach the beautiful Tuscan hilltops in the distance.

'Why us?' Juliet asked, feeling sick with nerves. 'She could have anyone.'

'They wanted no fuss…just a small family meal after the service…but Gio has decided to surprise her. Mimi has no idea that there's to be live music. Pearla's is catering…'

'Pearla's?' Juliet frowned, glancing along the walls towards the very exclusive restaurant where Susie worked. *Oh, goodness…* 'Is the reception being held at the restaurant?'

'No, no.' Louanna said. 'It's all being held at Gio's home— the planner is there setting up now. Pearla's are tearing their hair out at the short notice—Valentine's is their busiest day. But of course they're not going to say no to Gio. And musically everyone was already booked.'

'Are both Sevandro and Dante going to be there?' Dario asked. Then he added for Juliet's benefit. 'They're Gio's grandsons.'

'Yes, as well as Mimi's sister. It's really small, just a party of five, so there's no room for error…' Louanna warned. They all knew that a bigger audience was in many ways easier. 'Today could lead to much bigger things, so we have to get everything right. There're a few details to run through. Juliet, you especially need to hear this—the guys will know most of it already...'

Juliet nodded. Performing at a wedding wasn't just a matter of plonking down and playing, especially in such an intimate setting as someone's home, so she listened carefully.

'It's a second marriage for both,' Louanna explained. 'Gio's first wife died years ago, whereas Mimi was widowed more recently. She moved in with Gio apparently to help him in the house—though I think they told people that to keep things above board. Gio's very old school...that's why they want low key.'

Juliet nodded and smiled, about to pick her violin case up. She assumed they'd discuss the music selections on the way to the venue, as they usually did, but Louanna waved her to sit back down.

'Wait, Juliet, this is important. A few years ago—actually, it must be almost ten—there was a dreadful accident. Over there.' She pointed out to the hills. 'Gio's son, along with his wife, were travelling to Milan in a helicopter...'

'He was Gio's only child,' Ricco added—which told Juliet he must have died. 'No one survived. It came down just after take-off. My mother actually saw it happen.'

'They were a stunning couple,' Louanna elaborated, as she always did. 'Really prominent here, and so glamorous...'

Juliet looked out to the hills, currently all misty and grey, as Louanna spoke on.

'Sevandro's wife, Rosa, also died in the accident. They'd only been married a few months...she was so beautiful, so young, and there were whispers she was pregnant.'

'She wasn't,' Ricco said. 'My mother—'

'Guys,' Juliet cut in. For while it helped to know what

had happened, she didn't need intimate details. She asked instead for more pertinent information. 'So what music's on the forbidden list?'

'Plenty...' Louanna gave a dramatic sigh. 'I've gone through it with the event planner...'

They started to walk as they discussed the musical selections. There was a lot to avoid. Not just from the funerals, but also the younger couple's wedding.

'It's a musical minefield!' Louanna said as they came to a set of huge gates.

She took out her phone to call the organiser and make sure the coast was clear. As they waited Juliet peered in. There were magnificent buildings all over Lucca, and she'd walked past this one often, assuming it was an old palace or a stately home, perhaps a government building. Even now, looking at the fountains and beautiful gardens, it was hard to fathom it was actually someone's home.

'Let's go,' Louanna said as a groundsman let them in. 'We have half an hour to set up and hopefully rehearse that piece.'

'Should we warn Juliet about the brothers?' Ricco queried as they entered the grounds and walked towards the grand residence. But then he told her anyway. 'There was a big fall-out—'

'I don't need to know.' Juliet felt she'd already had enough of a window into their world.

But Louanna carried on regardless. 'They're rarely together, Sevandro's based in Dubai—he's some big shot in the hotel industry—and Dante is in Milan. He's...'

'Fine,' Juliet snapped.

She'd already gleaned from Susie that Dante was a divorce attorney. Oh, please let Susie not have been roped into working at this function...

'They had a big fight the night before Sevandro's wedding,' Louanna rattled on. 'You'll see the scar on Dante's face—'

'I get it!' Juliet said.

She simply loathed unnecessary talk about people—and with good reason. Her parents had broken up thanks to careless gossip. Worse, Juliet was the one who'd caused the breakup, having repeated what she'd overheard at school…

'Sevandro's a cold bastard.' Louanna just loved to talk. 'He doesn't even visit Rosa's grave when he's back. In fact, you might see him in the square,' she added sarcastically. 'He certainly enjoys speed-dating…though I don't think there's much *dating* involved.'

'Stop!' Juliet hated confrontation but, blushing horribly, she turned and faced her. Louanna was simply too much at times. 'We've been invited to play at a family wedding and we are taking their money,' Juliet reminded the group. 'I don't think it's appropriate to be talking so nastily about any of them.'

'I'm just telling you what you need to know.'

'No.' Juliet shook her head. 'I don't need to know that!'

'Juliet's right.' Ricco backed her up. 'Let's go in there and share in their celebration and make the best music we can.'

It was, though, rather daunting…

The event planner led them into a vast entrance hall with an impossibly high ceiling and a curved staircase. It was all so grand and formal that it was even harder to think of it as a home.

'The dining room is being decorated now,' they were told. 'I'll let you know when the wedding group start to head back so you can stop tuning. It's to be a complete surprise.'

'We can store our things here,' Louanna told them, taking out a key and opening up a door beneath the stairs. She turned the lights on. 'I brought the stands over last night.'

It was far too large to be called a cupboard—one wall was lined with hooks and there were long benches. Removing her coat, Juliet guessed it had once been a cloakroom, and could picture grand balls and counts' and countesses' coats and capes being hung there.

It was nice to have a safe place to leave extra instruments, and such—somewhere that drinks wouldn't be spilled or have people tripping over them. And it was a treat to have a suitable place to hang their coats and check their appearance before setting up.

In contrast to the austere entrance hall, the dining room was more welcoming. While very grand, the elegant furnishings were rich with family photos and mementoes. French windows led onto a tiled portico and beyond a less formal garden, giving it a cosier feel. It was currently being dressed for the wedding, with portraits of both Mimi and Gio being positioned on easels.

As they set up Louanna nudged her. 'There's Susie—she's in her waitressing gear. I wonder if Dante knows she'll be here?'

Then she must have recalled Juliet's rare outburst and abruptly stopped.

'You could have at least warned her about the wedding,' Juliet chided. 'This morning before we left.'

'I didn't know she would be waitressing,' Louanna retorted. 'I thought she was working in the kitchen at Pearla's now. Anyway, I promised not to reveal anything.'

'But surely…?'

'No.' Louanna shook her head. 'The management at Pearla's have kept it from their staff till the last minute. You told me off for gossiping but now question why Susie wasn't told. You can't have it both ways, Juliet.'

Louanna made a good point—but what about loyalty and friendship? Susie was as pale as a ghost, Juliet thought as she gave her friend a wave. She'd been worried about her for a little while. If she *had* had a fling with Dante, it would be dreadful to have to work at a function he was attending.

It was rather a rush to set up, but they tuned their instruments and then rehearsed the piece they'd practised separately before the event planner called for them all to stop.

'They're at the main gates…'

'Quiet, everyone!' someone else called, and the main doors to the dining room were closed to shut them in.

Susie came out of a small butler's pantry carrying a silver tray with glasses of champagne. She was dreadfully pale, as she had often been of late, and Juliet found her eyes drifting down to Susie's stomach. She was relieved that it looked completely flat, telling herself she was imagining things. But she was truly worried for her new friend.

The pause was long, and they all sat quietly, taking one last look around the beautiful room, and then, as footsteps approached, they took their positions, ready to play.

There was chatter and laughter outside, and then the doors opened…

'Oh!' Mimi gasped, as she stepped in, looking so stunned that she lost that gorgeous voice for a moment as their music gloriously welcomed the bride.

She was dressed in emerald silk, her silver curls piled high, and she walked around; her hands clasped, red lips smiling.

'Oh, Gio…' she kept saying, clearly overcome as she went over to the portraits.

And even though Juliet's ears were on the music they played, the piece was so familiar that she allowed her gaze to drift to Susie, her tray proffered as a man came in.

It was Dante. Juliet knew that not just because she'd seen him on television, more because he and Susie were trying too hard to ignore each other as he took a champagne flute from her tray.

Then the other grandson walked in.

About to turn back to her fellow musicians, return her full attention to the music, suddenly Juliet heard the chatter, the laughter, even the sound from her own violin, seem to fade. It was as if she was observing from one of the audio booths at music school. The world seemed to hush even as she played on.

That must be Sevandro.

He wore not a scowl, but a stern expression—as if he were walking into a funeral rather than a delightful wedding. His thick black hair was longer than his brother's, he was a little taller, a little broader, and quite simply, to Juliet, a whole lot more...

He took a champagne flute from the tray, and whatever he said made the still-tense Susie briefly smile as he turned away.

His suit was the darkest grey, his tie a few shades lighter, and Juliet was filled with a sudden urgency for more detail. Not the salacious kind Louanna so freely gave away, but different details, like the sound of his voice, or the colour of his eyes, but he was too far away.

Deliberately she checked herself, looked at her music, tuned back into the world. Her slight absence had gone unnoticed, the music was sublime... But then she found her eyes drifting again, on high alert when she saw Sevandro was walking towards her.

Juliet's stomach clenched as it might have if the catch on a jaguar's cage had been unexpectedly released and the beast sauntered out. There was a sudden confliction, an odd acknowledgment of danger, and yet also a fascination that held her trapped for a moment as he walked towards her.

He was coming over, and so heavy was the pull, so dense the feeling low in her stomach, it seemed almost apt that he should acknowledge her. It took a couple of seconds for her to self-correct and register that rather than walking towards her, he was just moving in her general direction.

Of course...

She played on, unseen and unnoticed, watching from a safe distance as he approached the happy couple. Inwardly she scolded her own overreaction, watching his almost-scowl fade into a slim smile as he congratulated his grandfather and his glowing bride.

She looked away, tuning in to the music, and they were about to move into the second piece when Mimi announced, 'I have to sing!'

The musicians paused and, still a touch bewildered by her reaction to the very handsome stranger, still on alert, Juliet flushed with pleasure as the gorgeous diva came over. Mimi was the best form of distraction—and Juliet was utterly starstruck as she introduced herself to the quartet and asked everyone's names.

'"Una Voce Poco Fa",' she said. "A Voice I Once Heard" from *The Barber of Seville*.

Thank goodness Louanna had made sure they'd practised it.

It was truly a privilege to be there and to accompany Mimi. So much so that it allowed Juliet to put aside thoughts of the handsome widower as she played, revelling in Mimi's voice that moved like a swan floating on the water; the words so sensual, so seductive, it was as if Mimi was truly transformed into the flirtatious and spirited Rosina.

There was applause from their small audience afterwards, and a couple of 'Bravos!'—though of course they were for Mimi.

The ensemble played beautifully.

When a performance went well, it felt as if it was just the four of them, appreciating each other, meeting each other. Their instruments complementing rather than competing. Their little squabbles forgotten, the hours of practice paying off as they barely noticed the hours flying by.

Juliet escaped into her music and almost forgot he was there.

Almost.

'We'll take a break,' Louanna suggested after a suitable time had passed.

But as Juliet put down her violin, stood and smoothed her dress, that aching awareness returned. Her head seemed to be fighting with her neck not to turn.

They were led downstairs into the main kitchen.

'Well done,' Cuoco the head chef at Pearla's congratulated them as they came in. 'Now it is my turn to take care of you.'

It was a sumptuous lunch, and they all fell on it. Performing really was hungry work at times, and today it was profitable too.

The event planner caught up with Louanna and handed her the pay envelopes. 'You're here till seven?' she checked, and Louanna nodded. 'Can you stay later if they ask?'

'Of course,' Louanna said.

'Did you bring concert dress?' the organiser asked.

'No,' Juliet said, worried she'd messed things up for the group, who had.

But Louanna wasn't letting this opportunity slip by. 'Can someone go out and get Juliet some make-up and black stockings?' she asked. She turned to Juliet and added, 'I have a bolero you can borrow.'

'Thank you,' Juliet said, looking at the cash figure on her envelope. She'd wear a bobble hat if they asked her to! The pay was so generous it meant that for the next couple of weeks she could breathe, as well catch up on exam practice without working at the bar to make her rent.

Thank goodness, she thought as she put her wages in her bag in the room under the stairs. But of course it was unsustainable; there wouldn't be many exclusive events like this. They really had lucked out.

Stepping out of the large cloakroom, Juliet was almost tempted to duck back in when she saw Sevandro—or rather, Sev, as his family seemed to call him—walking briskly past.

He didn't notice her—or more likely the Casadios were very used to staff—and he strode through the entrance hall, opened up a door and disappeared into a room, closing the door behind him.

Juliet stood for a second, wondering how the mere sight of someone could make her a little breathless. And why was she staring at the door he'd gone through and picturing him behind it?

What sort of force did he have that she wanted to walk over there? To go in...to see how he was?

How he *really* was.

It was no business of hers—nothing to do with her. But it was as if she could feel the tension behind that door and understood his need for a moment or two of escape.

It was the same with her and her own family.

Oh, her family surroundings weren't anywhere near as lavish, but she'd sat at too many family dinners, smiling and pretending everything was okay, or rather wishing it was... Wishing she could take things back and that she'd never repeated what she'd heard...

'Juliet?' Louanna had drifted up from the main kitchen with the others. 'Shall we go back in?'

'Sure.'

'*Scusi...*'

As they moved back to the dining room a male voice called to them and Juliet knew it was his. Deep and rather curt, it halted her, and yet she dared not turn. Instead, she left it to Louanna to take the query, and with Ricco and Dario went back to their instruments. Juliet felt too shy to speak, even in a professional capacity, terrified of blushing or stammering and making a fool of herself.

'We're staying on,' Louanna whispered as she joined them.

Sevandro returned to the dining room too, and took his seat at the large, polished table.

The afternoon session went well, and they took a supper break in the evening, when the family went to freshen up.

Having eaten, they prepared for the evening session— Ricco and Dario heading back quickly, having changed into jackets and bow ties, leaving the women to change.

As Louanna put on a long black dress Juliet pulled on the new pair of black tights and Louanna's bolero, then took out the make-up bag the organiser had sourced, unwrapping the lipstick—a very dark shade of red.

'I don't think my concert dress would have been up to the occasion,' Juliet admitted. 'I think it would look a bit faded for here.'

'That dress is too,' Louanna told her, in her oh-so-assertive way. 'Look at it compared to my bolero. You need to sort out your wardrobe.'

Juliet bit her bottom lip rather than respond. She might not like what Louanna had to say, but unfortunately she knew it was right.

Coiling her long hair into a chignon for a final touch, she added the lipstick. 'How's that?' she asked, expecting another little telling-off.

'Sexy,' Louanna said, and Juliet laughed in surprise.

'Back to it,' she said.

It felt different.

There was no Susie to look out for—the caterers had gone—but there was a new feast spread out on the table, and there was whisky being drunk now, rather than Casadio wine...

Heavy jade drapes had been drawn the full length of the French windows, and the large dining room seemed to have shrunk in the darker, more intimate light. The guests were at the table, the older couple chatting animatedly, while the brothers were more muted, sitting opposite each other, both their chairs pushed back a little. It was as if they were leaning as far back from each other as they could.

The ensemble played quietly, all their favourite pieces. Sometimes a family member would look over and thank them, or suggest something, but really they were background music and enjoying being so.

Goodness, he was handsome, Juliet thought as Sevandro stood and wandered around, looking at the many family photos on display.

'It's a long time since we've done this,' she heard Gio comment.

'I was here in December.' Sev turned his head a touch.

'For a quick visit,' Gio said. 'You left before Dante arrived. We should get together more. I was thinking for the memorial we might…'

Juliet watched Sev's shoulders stiffen, his hand, holding a photo, go still. He was not looking around, but perhaps Mimi saw him tense too.

'Gio,' she intervened gently. 'Let's not discuss that today.'

It was as the night was winding down that the tensions started to rise. Mimi's sister left, and the newlyweds rose to see her out. Juliet didn't close her eyes as she played, but nor did she look at her music. Her eyes were drawn to the two brothers, alone for the first time today.

Neither said a word, but there was a certain arrogance to Sevandro as he poured himself a drink but didn't pour his brother one. Juliet was riveted, and found she could not pull her gaze away. She just stroked the strings with her bow, watching how the brothers stared across the table at each other, neither looking away and neither saying a word, the tension palpable.

Despite her outburst with Louanna, Juliet found she

wanted to know more—wanted to know why the brothers didn't speak.

But there would be no answers tonight. In a slightly insolent gesture Sevandro pushed his half-empty glass across the table and made to stand. It looked as if he was about to go.

'Boys,' Mimi said as she returned. 'Stay.'

They might be boys to Mimi, but as the night progressed the air had become thick with testosterone, and Juliet wasn't sure that Mimi's suggestion to prolong the night was the wisest choice. There seemed to have been a slight loss of control in the carefully curated proceedings—or just a true glimpse of the Casadios when duty was done.

Juliet found that she rather liked it.

Louanna was applying rosin to her strings and Ricco was replacing one of his. She took a sip of iced water, the conversation from the table drifting over to her.

Mimi was lighting a cigarette and Gio was telling her off. 'Watch that beautiful voice,' he told her, even as he lit his own.

'It's my wedding day.' Mimi pouted.

'Dante?' Gio said. 'Are you able to visit the winery while you are here?'

'I can't,' Dante gave a curt shake of his head.

Gio sighed. 'Sevandro? How about you? How long before you head back to Dubai?'

Juliet didn't get to hear the answer as the music resumed, but soon there were more signs that Sevandro was leaving as he glanced at his watch. And as the quartet discussed the next piece, Juliet felt a curious sense of disappointment that soon the night would be done.

'Perhaps we could play one of Mimi's favourites?' Louanna was suggesting, flicking through music sheets.

Juliet's gaze drifted to the table. Gio was asking Dante

why he hadn't brought a date to the wedding, but he declined to respond.

'And you?' Gio turned his attention to his eldest grandson, telling Sev he had a house, a home here, or surely he could stay at Dante's… 'And yet always you stay in a hotel.'

Sev put down his drink before responding. 'I might want to find company.'

'Then bring her along,' Gio retorted.

Only his voice seemed to be muted. And Juliet felt as if she'd stepped back into that soundproof booth. Because Sevandro Casadio was looking directly at her. For the briefest second it had felt as if he was addressing *her*, asking her a question…

She frowned, wondering if perhaps he had a musical request, or was impatient for the ensemble to resume. With one look he imparted the heat of a thousand stars, made her too aware of her painted lips. Turning her gaze, she looked to her music sheet, then to Louanna, who gave her a nod.

The music resumed, the night went on, and really nothing had happened—except Sevandro's one blistering look.

Juliet's heart was pounding and she wasn't quite sure why.

It was an idle glance, she told herself. He'd been bored, just looking over, avoiding his grandfather's questions. And yet she found she kept wanting to look back and reclaim that moment. To meet his gaze again…to feel whatever she had briefly felt that second when she'd become aware of her red lips, for she'd been too aware of her mouth, had suddenly known how it felt to be absolutely held by eyes too far away for her to know their colour yet. Somehow, they'd held her riveted and still.

Juliet resisted looking over again, scared she would blush, or fumble her music. Surely the night was drawing to a close…

Mimi stood. 'One more!'

She came over to the musicians and Juliet saw that Dante rolled his eyes.

'Ah, I know…' She gave them a smile. '"O Mio Babbino Caro…"'

The musicians tensed, and Dante whipped his head up, but Mimi was oblivious, waiting for the music to cue her in. But they knew it was an aria that had been played at Sevandro and Rosa's wedding, and later at her funeral, and it was on the forbidden list.

Gio would surely halt this, thought Juliet, but he was smiling at his bride, and now Juliet dared look at Sev. His expression was unreadable, almost impassive—if that word could be used to describe features carved from stone. But there was no emotion on display. He simply sat upright and very, very still.

What did they do?

The ensemble shared urgent glances, but Mimi was getting impatient, and Louanna made the decision to play, her cello leading them in.

Juliet didn't want to do it—she wanted to flee, watching in silent horror as Dante began to protest. But Sevandro gave a brief shake of his head to halt his brother.

With every stroke of her bow she felt as if she scraped it over his traumatised heart, but still he gave nothing away—not a single clue as to how he was feeling. He just sat through it, staring once at his brother, but apart from that he was clearly in his own head, alone.

Juliet wanted to put down her violin, but instead she played on.

She was torturing him.

To Juliet that was how it felt.

Sevandro didn't even flinch.

On the contrary, he applauded.

'Bravo,' he said as they concluded, and then applauded Mimi, before he stood and said he really must go.

He kissed Gio and Mimi…nodded in the direction of Dante.

Juliet did not get a second glance. She simply sat there, watching as he walked off while fighting the most ridiculous urge to run after him…

And she was fighting something else…something she didn't understand.

That company Sevandro had said he might want to find tonight…?

Juliet wanted it to be her.

CHAPTER TWO

'Juliet, this isn't what we agreed.'

It had been three months since Gio's wedding and Juliet was feeling even more behind with life… In an attempt to fix her finances and focus on her exams she'd responded to an ad on the noticeboard at the music school—free accommodation in return for a few light household duties.

Louanna had warned her she was making a mistake.

She'd been right!

'Anna, I said ages ago I wasn't available this weekend. I have a friend's wedding.' She shook her head. 'I'll be back in time to take the children to school on Monday.'

Juliet only had the hotel room for one night, but she badly needed her own space—this arrangement really wasn't working out.

She was flustered as she picked up her things. There could be no hasty exit with a violin case as well as her overnight bag, but at least her dress and shoes were already at the hotel, and Louanna had sorted out the music stands and storage of her back-up instrument.

Today the ensemble had another Casadio wedding to attend—and this one was going to be huge.

Juliet's instincts had been right. Susie was indeed pregnant. And on this sunny May day Susie and Dante were getting married.

It was such a relief to be out of Anna's and to walk into the heart of Lucca. From the day she'd arrived in the ancient city it had felt like home, and Juliet truly hoped that if work and visas worked out one day it would permanently be the case.

The hotel was old-world and elegant, and she felt a little underdressed in pale green cheesecloth and espadrilles, but then she realised the glamorous women and suited men might well be already dressed for Susie and Dante's wedding.

'Juliet Adams,' she said to the receptionist. 'I have an early check-in.' She couldn't help but ask, 'Are these people leaving for the wedding already?'

'Not yet.' The receptionist smiled. 'A few overseas wedding guests are meeting in the restaurant. It's an all-day event,' she explained as she tapped in Juliet's details. 'You have breakfast in the restaurant tomorrow. Oh, and I am to let the bride know when you arrive.'

Soon Juliet had her door key, an old-fashioned one, and she made her way to her room. She was just unpacking her bag when Susie arrived, dressed in a huge fluffy dressing gown, her hair all curled and pinned, delighted to see her friend.

'Oh, it's so good to see you. My sisters are driving me crazy.'

Juliet laughed, and hugged her, frowning when Susie handed her a pretty bag. 'What's this?'

'The underwear to go with the new dress that you wouldn't let us buy. Honestly, Juliet, you're part of the bridal party— you're my family here in Lucca.'

Juliet was touched. There was a unique loneliness to being in a foreign country when trouble hit, and that was possibly why Juliet had shared her financial woes and in turn Susie had admitted she was pregnant—oh, and then engaged, and now about to marry.

They sat on the bed and caught up. 'How was Dante with your family?' asked Juliet.

'They all seemed to get on. We'll see them back in London after our honeymoon.' She closed her eyes for a moment. 'The best man arrived very late last night.'

Juliet knew Susie meant Sev, though deliberately didn't react.

'I am a bit worried...' Susie admitted.

'Why?'

'You were there at Mimi and Gio's wedding. You've seen what they're like.'

'Not really...' Possibly the reason Juliet was so honest was that her very pale complexion flared red whenever she lied, but she attempted to lie now. 'I was too busy playing.'

'I'm surprised Dante asked him to be his best man,' Susie admitted. 'And perhaps more surprised that Sev agreed.'

So too was Juliet. She found she was biting her tongue in an effort not to delve, but Susie was anxious enough to fill her in.

'The one thing they agree on is that they both adore Gio. It would kill him if Sev wasn't there as best man. Even so...' Susie drew in a tense breath. 'Dante hasn't yet told Sev about the baby—that's why we've been keeping it quiet. Dante wanted his brother to hear it from him first, and he wanted to do it face to face.'

'But surely he'll be happy for Dante...?'

Juliet's voice faded when she thought of what Louanna had said. Usually she didn't probe, yet months on she still thought of that night and felt guilt-ridden when she recalled torturing him with her music.

'*Was* his wife pregnant when she died?'

'No.' Susie shook her head. 'Rosa wasn't pregnant. But...' She struggled to speak for a moment. 'When their engagement was announced Dante thought that she might be— The night before their wedding he suggested to Sev that Rosa might be trying to trap him. Dante's not exactly subtle. As you can imagine, it didn't go down very well.'

'No.'

'She wasn't pregnant. Dante got it all wrong. But he did have his reasons. There's more to it, but...' Susie's eyes filled with tears and she gave a helpless shake of her head. 'And now we're the ones marrying in haste.' She gave a mirthless laugh. 'Ironic, isn't it?'

'You two are crazy about each other,' Juliet pointed out. 'The baby's a bonus—not the reason for your wedding.'

They chatted more lightly, and Susie had cheered up by the time she left.

Juliet started to get ready—she had to be there well before the bride.

Pinning her hair up, and then applying neutral daytime make-up, she felt butterflies starting to flutter in her chest as she thought of the many guests that would be there today—and how important this was to her professionally.

She was about to slip on her dress, but then paused and took out the lingerie she'd been gifted, rather sure the delicate French lace wouldn't be enough support for her generous bust. She hadn't properly tried the bra on—she'd just been going along with things in the bridal boutique, and behind the curtain of the changing room she had barely done up the straps.

Juliet had only really guessed at her size—she'd always loathed bra shopping and her mother had been no help. Too busy with her new family and buying her own maternity bras.

Juliet could still hear her sigh.

'I never thought I'd be doing this again,' she'd said, flashing a look at her daughter.

Her father had said the same several times, when Juliet babysat for him and his new wife.

She'd felt the implication—*If only you'd kept your mouth shut.*

Some implications she might have imagined.

Others not.

'What did you think was going to happen, Juliet?' her mother had hissed. *'Of course you have to change schools.'*

And, no, she hadn't imagined her father's glare when he'd snapped, *'Why the hell do you think there's no money for violin lessons?'*

She did up the lacy bra, then pulled on the knickers and turned to the full-length mirror, still feeling as awkward as she'd been then. She looked at her pale body and rather fleshy bottom and stomach. The lace was so sheer she could see the pink of her areolae and nipples, and her hair was even redder *down there* and it showed.

Her phone rang and she saw it was Anna, but she was already nervous enough about playing and chose not to answer it.

She turned, about to reach for her own familiar underwear, but then hesitated and looked at her new dress. It had been a massive but necessary purchase. And because it was for work it wasn't as simple as just finding a black dress. She didn't like showing cleavage, especially when she was playing, and the arms had to be loose enough to allow movement, the skirt had to fall nicely when she sat...

She'd tried on several, and then the assistant had suggested this silky organza, way out of her price range. But the moment she'd slipped it on, Juliet had known it was perfect.

Now she felt the same, feeling the cool fabric sliding over her body, then doing up the concealed zip at the side. It looked better than she had remembered—the bias cut meant it fell beautifully, or was it the new bra that gave her a slight lift?

She slipped on her black shoes and took a seat in the dressing table chair. It was perfect. It didn't rise and show too much thigh.

She wasn't just being modest, worrying about cleavage

and flashing too much thigh or worse… They were the last things she needed to distract her when she was playing…

Sevandro Casadio had distracted her.

The butterflies were still there in her chest, but she was aware of new ones too, fluttering low in her stomach.

They weren't the same, though. They were really an entirely different species. Because they didn't dart like the ones in her chest…they were subtler than that.

He'd be there today.

She'd thought of that when she'd first tried on this dress. She'd thought of him so many times since that night.

And now, even before she'd seen him, he was already distracting her. Her mind was darting with hope that they might talk, that she would find another piece of the delicious Sev or Sevandro puzzle and finally know the colour of his eyes.

Juliet closed her own—but not before she saw her cheeks turn an unflattering red.

She was blushing at the mere thought.

It was hopeless.

Sevandro knotted the pale pink silk tie—*not* one he would have chosen for himself—and had a word with his reflection in the large antique mirror.

'Best behaviour!'

Just get through this day.

These next couple of days.

No distractions, and no burying himself in work or women—which were his usual escape routes of choice.

He wasn't just here for the wedding—he was in Lucca to tie up loose ends.

This morning he'd been to the winery to check things were running to plan. Always he had a plan.

Patting his breast pocket, he checked for the rings—but for just a moment his hand hovered over his unexamined heart.

Just the wedding to get through, then a few detatils to sort, then one more trip for the ten-year memorial, and then…

He would be done with Lucca.

Catching sight of his reflection, he pushed out a smile. But the mirror confirmed it was false.

'Come on,' he told himself.

But the best he could muster was the businesslike smile that he might use when he greeted an investor or chaired a meeting.

It would have to do.

He took the gated elevator to his brother's suite, nodding to a couple who wished him good morning and asked him to pass on their best wishes to Dante.

They were, Sev was certain, talking about him before the lift doors had even closed.

Sev knocked on Dante's door and entered.

'Everything's under control,' Sevandro informed his brother, and gave him a few updates.

But their conversation was so forced it was a relief when Gio arrived.

'You're looking very smart,' Sev said as he let him in. The Casadio men were all wearing dark grey suits and matching ties. 'Where's Mimi?'

'Doing some vocal exercises before we head to the winery,' Gio said, and then looked at Dante. 'I thought I would come to wish you well.'

It dawned on Sev that Mimi might have stayed in her suite to give Gio some time with his grandson. Perhaps he should do the same?

'I might head down to Reception,' Sev said. 'Check on the vehicles.'

'Good idea,' Gio agreed. 'I'll be down shortly. Wait for me there.'

Gio did want to speak to Dante alone.

Sev took the ancient lift down and found a seat by a large column in Reception, silently strumming his fingers on the leather sofa, just a little out of the way of all the activity, shaking his head when offered a drink.

He was trying not to consider what Gio might be saying now.

God, but his parents would have loved to be here today. Two social butterflies, they would have been in their element.

Closing his eyes, he breathed in deeply, refusing to go there. *Just get through today.*

There was the trill of a mobile phone, a slight scent of summer, and the feel of someone entering his space.

A cousin? An aunt? A family member of his late wife, perhaps?

Best behaviour, Sev reminded himself, feeling the indent of the sofa beside him as his company sat down, bracing himself to be told how he was feeling…how he must be missing Rosa today.

It wasn't that at all.

'Please, no…' someone said in English. 'Just leave me alone.'

She was speaking to herself, staring at her ringing phone, and she looked both gorgeous and familiar.

He watched her startle as she realised she wasn't on her own.

'Sorry…' She gave a nervous laugh and turned a shade more crimson than her reddish blonde hair. 'I didn't mean you.'

He said nothing, frowning a fraction, although not at the interruption. It was more that his slight frown was an invitation for her to explain. From Sev such an invitation was rare, but his recall of the stunning musician from Gio and Mimi's wedding was of someone sophisticated and poised, yet she was clearly flustered, blushing and clearly anxious now.

Why?

'My boss,' she explained, gesturing to her phone. 'She refuses to accept that I'm working today.'

'Your boss…?' he checked. 'Shouldn't she approve of you working on a Saturday?'

'No.' She shook her head. 'I have another live-in job.'

'I see…'

Juliet doubted that he did.

Furthermore, she doubted he wanted to hear about her dramas, so didn't elaborate. She would *never* have sat here if she'd seen him.

She assumed the conversation was over, gave an apologetic smile for disturbing him and looked away, back down to her phone. But she was still impossibly aware. Every nerve in her body had leapt to high alert, and now, for the first time, she was treated to his expensive scent—she hadn't been close enough before.

It did not disappoint. Subtle at first, spicy and peppery, but there was also a lower, woody note that made her breathe in a little more deeply, trying to define it. It was like night-scented tobacco plants after the rain…

Then he spoke. 'You were playing at Gio and Mimi's wedding.'

Somewhat stunned that he remembered her, even if she'd thought of him all too often, she turned and nodded.

He glanced down at her violin case. 'Are you playing this afternoon?'

'I am,' she agreed, and then, to save any possible embarrassment, quickly added, 'Though it's not just work. I'm also a friend of Susie's.'

'I won't be doing any speaking out of turn,' he said with an edge, clearly misconstruing her hurried warning.

'I didn't mean that.' She always left a conversation feeling like an incomplete Goldilocks, having said either too much or not enough. 'It's just better to say up front...given that I don't look like a wedding guest.' She gestured to her black dress. 'Somebody thought I was a guest at a funeral the other week.'

'Did they think you were the deceased's mistress?'

'Nothing as exciting. They did direct me to the viewing, though...'

He gave a soft laugh and she saw that his eyes were grey. But then she quickly looked away, simply pleased she now knew that much.

'So how do you know Susie?' he asked.

'We used to share a flat.'

'In England?'

'No, here in Lucca,' she explained. 'We hadn't met before that. I'm studying music.'

'Is your dreadful boss part of the ensemble?'

'No!' Juliet gave a small laugh, hesitant to explain, and positive that he was just doing his best man duty and being polite. 'It's all very boring.'

She had turned away again.

He glanced at the huge gold clock on the wall and wondered how long Gio's pep talk with Dante would last. What was being said?

She was now staring at her phone as if waiting for it to explode, and he realised he far preferred the distraction of their conversation to thinking about what was being said upstairs.

'Juliet,' he said, and she almost jumped at the use of her name. Two vertical lines appeared between her eyes and those lines were rare these days. 'You are allowed to turn it off.'

She had a beautiful unspoiled face. Her skin was as pale as porcelain—not just her face, but her bare arms and legs too. That was pleasantly unusual as well, and he wasn't thinking of olive-skinned beauties here—more those ghastly smelling spray tans.

'You could even block the number,' he added.

'That wouldn't be very sensible.' Her voice held a wry edge. 'I'm guessing you don't have a boss?'

'No,' he agreed. 'Well, I do have Sheikh Mahir. We're...' How best to describe that relationship? 'We're professionally intertwined, and he can be rather tricky at times.' Then he added, 'That's a polite way of putting it. And you're right— it wouldn't be very sensible to block him.'

He liked her gentle laugh.

Her phone bleeped again. 'Louanna,' she told him. 'The cellist. She messaged to say they'd soon be on their way, but now they're stopping for rosin.'

He frowned.

'For our bows. I'm sure she has plenty...she always does this...'

'Superstition?' he suggested.

'Maybe.'

And it dawned on her that Louanna might be nervous about today too.

It was then that the oddest thing happened. She realised she was no longer blushing. She took a breath and found it went all the way down to the bottom of her lungs, and that surprised her.

She'd thought she'd be blushing and dreadful if she spoke to him, and although she'd jumped out of her skin when she'd first seen him she felt more settled in his company now—if it was possible to feel 'settled' around someone as gorgeous as him.

Then she met his eyes and of course she was still a touch nervous—only not in the usual way.

They were more than grey. They were like a hail-filled

sky with little glints of black and hints of a silver lining, as if the winter sun was struggling to appear.

She did not jerk her eyes away.

Those *other* butterflies were gently fluttering.

And they were curious.

'How do you know my name?' she asked.

'Probably the same way you know mine—that wedding went for hours,' he pointed out. 'And Mimi put in a lot of requests.'

'She did…' Juliet smiled with fond affection. Mimi had, of course, got to know all her accompanists. 'It was a wonderful experience.' And his confidence must be catching, because now she felt not so much bold, just assured in his company. Enough to ask, 'Do you prefer to be called Sev or Sevandro?'

'I answer to both.'

She liked both.

'And what do you do?' She knew about Dante's dazzling career, and Sev knew a little of her own, but she wanted to know about him. Not rumours, or scattered pieces put together. She wanted to hear from the source. 'You live in Dubai?'

'Correct. And, with the help of Sheikh Mahir, I used to purchase hotels. Now, though, we're looking to build a rather large one from scratch.'

'How large?'

'Over a hundred storeys.'

'Wow!'

'More than looking,' he added. 'We're in the procurement stage—pre-construction.' Now he asked a question. 'Are you looking forward to today?'

'Very much so!' She nodded, but then she saw he'd cocked his head slightly to one side, as if he knew that wasn't the entire case.

'Well, I will be once we get there. We're all a bit nervous—this wedding is the biggest we've done...' She halted abruptly. 'I probably shouldn't be saying this to a member of the bridal party.'

'Susie clearly thinks you're up to it.'

'Yes,' she conceded. 'Hopefully she's not being biased.'

'We've all heard you, Juliet,' he said. 'And Mimi isn't backwards in coming forward. She's singing today, God help us.'

'What?' She gave a shocked gasp. 'Her voice is stunning.'

'Is *your* step-grandmother an opera singer?

'No.'

'That's why I get a pass to say it. She was also Gio's "housekeeper" for years.'

Juliet heard the quotation marks. Usually indiscretions unsettled her. They made her shrivel inside. And yet he spoke on, and she realised he wasn't being mean about Mimi's singing, or status, or anything like that.

He was reassuring her.

'I don't think our family are known for placating people. That includes Mimi,' he said. 'Her voice is incredible, and I know she takes it very seriously. If she wanted different accompaniment then she would have no qualms telling Susie.'

'Yes.' That helped—it helped a lot. 'She would.'

'So enjoy today.'

'Thank you.'

Juliet didn't understand how she could be in such stunning company and feeling so intensely attracted, yet somehow reassured, somehow starting to relax.

She hadn't felt any of these ways before.

These ways because there were many ways he made her feel.

It was just a conversation, one small part in his busy day, yet he gave her his full attention and it was like being placed under a gentle spell. She watched as he fiddled with his shirt collar, then checked his breast pocket.

'The rings,' he said. 'I'm getting like Louanna.'

It was a tiny joke, but it was one only they could understand. He too was nervous about today.

She wondered if Dante had told him about the baby yet, or if he was about to find out...

Then he saw her looking and she had to think of something to say.

'Your tie looks nice.'

'I'm not so sure—the bride chose it.'

Juliet was, for a nano-second, tempted to add that the bride had chosen her underwear, and she wasn't too sure about that either. Of course she didn't say that. It would be inappropriate and just a dreadful thing to say.

She settled for, 'Well, it looks very nice.'

'Do you want a coffee?' he offered as the eager waiter approached again.

'I'd better not. They'll be here for me soon.'

'A whisky to settle your nerves?'

'Gosh, no.' She smiled at his slight wickedness. 'Thank you, though. And for your company. I feel much better.'

Then she smiled at *him*.

She smiled from her plump pink lips right to her jade-green eyes, and for Sev it was as if her smile was a confirmation of what she'd just said.

There was no game, no flirtation, no attempt at seduction. Best of all there was no doubt as to its verity—it was a smile with no motive that came from such a rare place that, had his grandfather not called his name, Sev might, if he'd known how, have managed a real smile back.

One that said, *Thank you too for a nice moment on a hellish day.*

'Sev!' Gio called.

Sev didn't roll his eyes. Best behaviour and all that. But

nor did he rush to a stand. He had one more quick question for her.

'Do I wish you luck or is that forbidden?' He thought for a second. 'Should I say *Break a leg*?'

'All good wishes are welcome.'

'Good luck then,' he said. 'And please...' He glanced down at her deliciously pale legs for the briefest second. 'Don't break a leg...'

Then he looked back up to hear her soft laugh and he did indeed smile. A smile so natural it remained even as Gio called his name again. It was there, even as he did now roll his eyes.

'I have to go and check on the groom...make sure he gets there on time.'

'What are you smiling at?' Gio asked as he approached.

'It's a wedding,' Sev pointed out, as if it was completely normal for him to be walking through this hotel lobby, smiling, when it was far, far from that. 'I'll head up to Dante.'

'Try not to fight.'

'Gio...' He wished people would stop banging on about it. 'That was years ago.'

'Just hear what he has to say.'

'Shouldn't I be the one giving the pep talk?'

'Of course, but weddings can bring out emotions...'

'Please,' Sev teased lightly. 'We both know I don't have any.' Then he saw the concern in his grandfather's eyes. 'Gio,' Sev reassured him. 'I'll take care of him today.'

'You are brothers every day,' Gio said. 'Yet the two of you talk like strangers sitting on a park bench.' He gestured to the couch Sev had just come from. 'If anything, you chat more easily with strangers...'

Sevandro took the elevator up to Dante's suite and was greeted by an immaculate groom whose nerves seemed to have caught up with him—he was pale and pacing as Sev poured the obligatory drink.

'*Salute!*' he said, handing his brother a heavy glass. 'How was Gio's talk?'

'He offered me a partnership in the winery.'

'You knew that was coming.'

'Yeah…' Dante looked at him. 'Look, I know it holds no interest for you, but while Susie and I are on honeymoon can you try and get back there? It's been neglected for too long.'

'Come off it,' Sev said. 'I was there this morning; it looks as if every last leaf has been polished. The place is stunning.'

He knew what Dante meant, though. The place had been beautifully managed and exceptionally well run by Christos since the accident, but Gio had seemed to age overnight, and since the tragedy his attention to detail had been lacking.

'It's managed fine without us all these years—just enjoy your honeymoon, as well as your time in England.' He tried to say the right thing. 'I know our parents would have been proud—'

'I know.' Dante cut him off.

Gio was right. They spoke like strangers. After all, he'd never even properly met the bride. How the hell did he know if they'd have been proud? Then he thought of them fondly and looked at his brother. Dante was in love and, yes, Sev knew for a fact they'd be both proud and happy.

'They would be,' Sev said.

Dante nodded. 'Before we head down…' He put his hand in his pocket and took out a black velvet pouch, which he handed to Sev.

'What's this?' He opened it up and inside found a thin piece of paper, folded many times.

'Are we doing drugs before you go down?' he joked.

'Open it.' Dante wasn't joking. 'You know how after the crash I hired a search party…?'

Sev said nothing. He did not want to think of that time, especially today.

Opening the paper he saw a small dark ruby.

'It's from Mamma's eternity ring,' Dante told him. 'They found two. I've never known what to do with them.'

'Did you show them to Gio?'

'God, no. It would finish him. I kept one for a gift for Susie. I thought you might want the other...'

'Perhaps give her this one too? You could have earrings made?' he attempted, just to get rid of the tiny stone that shone with memories. But Dante shook his head. 'Okay.' He pocketed it, not knowing what to say, steadfastly refusing to feel—he couldn't afford to today. 'Should we head down?'

'There's still plenty of time.'

'Even so...'

It was awkward. He'd far rather be on that couch, talking with Juliet, than standing here in a strained silence.

Dante broke it. 'Sev, I have something else to tell you.' He took a breath. 'Susie and I are having a baby.'

Ah, so this was the real reason for his brother's nerves.

'In October.'

'Congratulations,' Sev said, and met Dante's eyes. 'I'm pleased for you both.'

'I wanted to tell you first, face to face, but...' Dante spread his palms and the small gesture spoke of the abyss between them. 'I haven't seen you.'

'No.' Sev said. 'It's good news.' He smiled and raised his glass, but it was clear Dante didn't believe that was it.

'Just say what you have to!' he invited.

'Meaning...?'

'Whatever it is you're going to say, whatever wry comment you're going to make—just get it over with now.'

'Oh, no.' Sev shook his head. 'I'm on my best behaviour.'

'Oh, please...' Dante was disbelieving.

'I am,' Sev insisted. 'I am going to be the perfect best man. No smart comments…no chatting up the bridesmaids.' He put a hand on his brother's shoulder. 'I don't want the groom to black my eye.'

Dante gave a low, almost-laugh as Sev gently referred to yesteryear, then he looked at his brother and the faded silver scar. 'I am pleased for you.' It was the truth. 'I know that you, Mr Divorce Attorney, must love Susie very much. I knew at Gio's wedding it must be serious.'

'How?'

'You've never dated anyone who lives here,' Sev pointed out—because, unlike himself, who had lovers everywhere, Dante only ever played well away from Lucca. His younger brother had always loathed the gossip here at home. And where the Casadio brothers were concerned there was always plenty. 'I knew if you were seeing someone here, then it must be serious. I'm happy for you, Dante, I really am.'

'Thank you.'

'Why so serious?' Sev checked, because his brother was still grey in the complexion and as close to tears as he'd seen him since the funerals. 'Dante…' Sev said. 'We fought ten years ago—move on from it. I have.' He spoke so assuredly Sev almost believed his own words. 'We're fine.'

They *almost* were.

Just as long as they didn't speak of that time.

As long as they remained in different countries and rarely got together.

'Today is your wedding day—let's not go over the past.'

It was everywhere, though.

It was there in the air they breathed, there as they drove in the car and passed the church, and the cemetery that housed Rosa's grave—which, to the scorn of many, Sev had never visited.

He did his level best to be there for his brother, trying not to compare the two wedding days, even managing a private joke as Mimi started to sing.

'Please, no...' Sev said, feeling his brother's silent laugh, as Mimi serenaded the groom. He knew Dante hated being sung to, because... Because they were brothers and he just knew.

Then Sev turned around and saw Susie approaching. And he was grateful that Dante had already told him about the baby because he'd have certainly found out now. She must be... He started to do the maths in his head, and then recalled looking at Rosa, whose pregnancy hadn't shown at all.

Stop, he told himself. *Don't compare, don't look back, just get through this day.*

'Your bride looks beautiful,' Sev told his brother, who now turned around.

'She does,' he said fondly.

And as she arrived by his side Sev saw there was so much love between them that, standing at the altar, he felt somewhat a spare part. Then he looked a little to the right, to the string quartet accompanying Mimi, and there was Juliet, playing her violin. Her eyes were closed and there was a slightly pained expression on her face. The same one he'd seen at Gio and Mimi's wedding, when she got into a particular piece. He'd been watching her that day too. How she swayed, how her left hand shook as she held a note...

There was tranquillity in the music, and the seemingly un-troubled way she made it. She was back to being the woman he had first seen play...sensual and poised. Her red hair was almost gold in the sun, and her skin was so pale he found his eyes looking up to check there was adequate shade.

When the music stopped he watched as she rested her vio-lin on her lap, her face flushed with pleasure as Mimi turned and thanked them. Then he watched as Juliet got her first proper glimpse of the bride, her mouth briefly gaping before breaking into a smile, and then she looked away from the bride and caught his eyes.

He gave her a small nod, to tell her just how perfectly she'd played.

Sevandro would never know how much that small gesture meant to her. Juliet had ached for it all her life—for that nod that told her she'd been heard and recognised. She was used to applause—it was part of her job—but to have that special nod was entirely different.

It was something she'd never known.

Not since she was twelve had there been someone there in the audience just for her.

Of course it was his brother's wedding, and from what she'd fathomed a difficult day for him, yet he made her feel special all through the proceedings. It felt as if he was looking out for her.

Of course he wasn't, Juliet told herself. He was best man, and it was his role to ensure things went smoothly.

As the guests mingled after the service with their aperitivos, and the quartet moved their equipment and instruments into the cellar, where the reception was being held, she saw him speaking with a waiter, and soon there were drinks and snacks waiting for them.

'Woo-hoo,' said Louanna, taking a long drink of sparkling water. 'For once we don't have to beg.'

It was a light tease, but all too often they were dashing to refill their own water bottles in the brief interludes.

'The cellar looks incredible,' she added, and Juliet too was taking in the scene.

It was one long table, dressed with incredibly tall candles. There were small posies of flowers, so as not to obstruct people's views, and the glass and silverware were stunning. It was a table prepared to enable conversation.

Like a ginormous family dinner, Juliet thought as they resumed playing and the guests drifted in to be seated.

The wedding feast commenced—and what a feast! Chefs from both Pearla's and the winery worked together and flamed huge cheese wheels to melt, tossing in fresh pasta beside the vast table, and it both looked and smelled incredible...

'We'd better get some of that when it's our turn to eat,' Louanna grumbled.

For now, they played, but that looked-out-for feeling remained with Juliet.

Occasionally she was aware of Sev glancing over.

Once, when she dashed to the ladies' room, he leant back in his chair as she passed. 'All okay?' he asked.

'Yes.'

He'd probably done the same with the others. She'd seen him speaking with all the staff. But this attention, this awareness of *one* other, was something she could not quite define.

When the guests started tapping their glasses for the bride and groom to kiss they obliged, and then there was a demand for Dante to speak.

'Grazie,' he said, thanking everyone for being there.

It was a very informal speech, more a call for people simply to enjoy, but then there were a few comments from guests about a *bambino*, and the secret was certainly out. As Susie stood, Dante kissed her, lightly touching her bump in a tender gesture that said there was nothing to hide, and everyone at the table applauded.

She found herself looking at Sev. His smile was perhaps a little tight, but he seemed relaxed in his seat. And then the guests urged him to speak.

Insisted.

Juliet felt her hands grip her violin a little more tightly. She felt nervous and unsure why. Perhaps because Susie had been so worried about the brothers? Yet it seemed unfounded… the day was going beautifully.

Was Sev thinking about his wife? she wondered as he stood. Was he thinking about his own wedding day and what Dante had said all those years ago?

It would seem not. He was relaxed and fluid as he spoke. Juliet's Italian was good, but it was a little hard to hear him with the guests laughing and chatting and teasing.

'Zio Sevandro!' someone called, and a few others joined in, all calling him 'Uncle' Sevandro.

He gave a smile, though not like the one she'd seen in the lobby. Juliet frowned. Had she not seen his smile this morning, she wouldn't have known this one was forced.

'There is a lot of good news today,' he went on.

He was flawless, thanking the right people, toasting the stunning bridesmaids, saying how nice it was to meet Susie and see Dante so happy, how proud his parents would have been.

He was interrupted by a guest. 'And being Zio…?' the guest insisted, asking for his take on being an uncle.

Sevandro paused for just a second and Juliet waited for him to be the smooth best man and say something about the baby, or that he was looking forward to being an uncle. But he turned to his grandfather.

'Gio…' He raised a glass to the old man, who was smiling and dabbing his eyes. 'Bisnonno!' He called him Great-Grandfather, and Gio both laughed and cried as Sev once again mentioned his parents and how they would have loved this day, would have welcomed Susie.

Oh, the Italians loved a good wedding—and news of a baby too! They were all delighted.

Was she the only one who'd noticed that pause? Oh, Sev was impeccable, yet this *was* hard for him—Juliet somehow knew that.

The thought was confirmed when, at the end of his speech, he looked over to her.

It was Juliet who nodded this time.

It felt—although perhaps it was ridiculous—as if they were in this together.

Of course not...

The party commenced, and as more modern means of music replaced them they put their instruments away. Then, exhausted yet elated, the musicians sat down to their very own feast.

'Caspita!' Ricco exclaimed as, instead of a warmed-up meal, as was so often the case at this kind of function, Cuoco came to the table and they were treated to the same melting cheese display as the guests.

'Ah...' Louanna said, with a slight edge. 'We're in Casadio land now.'

Sev didn't make his way over, and throughout their meal he didn't once look their way. But Juliet could see him at the bar, his back to her, talking to various guests.

His attention on her had surely been her imagination... going into overdrive.

Yet as their dessert was served she asked herself why. Because when it came to men there had been no imaginings before. A few awkward dates, a handful of awkward kisses and some frantic attempts to relax as hands that felt unwelcome moved from her waist—whatever their direction, they'd always felt wrong.

'You're quiet,' Louanna observed. 'Are you worrying about the instruments?'

'I might go and check on them.' Juliet nodded, pleased to have a reason to excuse herself. 'I'll see if they've found somewhere suitable to put them.'

They had moved them to a safer storeroom than the one first suggested. Where to store their instruments at functions was a constant problem—the area they'd first selected had turned into a bit of a throughfare—but the wedding organiser had found a storeroom at the back of the cellar.

With the instruments all safely housed, she could now relax and enjoy the night. But instead of heading back to the table, or even joining the party, she used the staff exit.

Well, she was almost staff, and she was taking a small break.

It was her private thoughts she wanted to examine.

To work out what was happening.

If anything *had* happened.

Stepping out into the dusky night, she took a breath of warm air, listening to the muffled laughter and music from the party. Then, as her eyes grew accustomed to the dark, she saw a silhouette and recognised the broad shoulders.

Sev's back was to her, his posture straight as he looked out to the hills, but there was something in his stance that told her he'd needed a break from the happy proceedings too.

This day was hard for him—Juliet was sure of it. But, more than that, she rather guessed he'd prefer this moment to be a private one.

She quickly turned—just as the door clattered closed behind her.

'Juliet?'

'Hello.' She smiled. 'I was just…'

'Escaping?'

'Yes,' she admitted. 'You?'

She didn't expect an honest answer, but he turned around and in the inky night their eyes met.

'I guess I'm escaping too,' he said.

CHAPTER THREE

SEVANDRO GESTURED FOR her to join him, and she walked over, taking in the view, the darkness of the valley in the near distance, and beyond the twinkling lights of Lucca.

'I was just checking on the instruments,' she explained.

'Sounds like having children.'

'It probably is a bit like that at times.'

He looked down at her, but she could not hold his gaze and moved her gaze back to the view. She'd come out here to think of him and the tumult he caused in her head—which had somehow faded now she was by his side.

'You've been working hard,' he said. 'The music was incredible.'

'Thank you.'

'Are you finished playing?'

'I think so—unless someone asks.'

'You never did tell me about your terrible boss.'

'No…' Juliet gave a soft laugh as together they walked over to a heavy stone bench that looked out over endless rows of vines. 'I took a live-in job…free accommodation in exchange for a few household chores, babysitting, walking the puppy…'

'Free accommodation?' he checked. 'In my industry you'd need a fleet of staff for those *few* chores.'

'I get that now. Before that I was working a couple of jobs but falling behind at music school, as well as in rehearsals and practice. I've got exams soon—and a big thing in August.' She tried to offer both sides. 'In fairness to Anna—my boss—I have been getting more bookings for weddings. My weekends aren't as free as they were, and I don't think she understands just how much I have to practise. It's not the same with a practice mute…'

'Could you move?'

'I think I'll have to.' That was the only answer. 'I need a soundproof room—preferably on Mars.'

'Mars sounds nice,' Sev agreed, and somehow she knew he was speaking of escaping this night.

She wasn't a nosey person, yet it felt right to acknowledge that she knew he was a widower. Right to ask, 'Has today been hard for you?'

'I keep being told it must be,' he said with a sardonic edge. 'As well as how much I must be missing Rosa.' He turned and met her waiting gaze, and when he spoke again that edge to his voice was gone. 'You're the first person to actually ask.'

'You don't have to answer.'

'Thank you,' he said, then added, 'I mean that.'

They sat in silence for a moment, but then he said, his voice low, but a touch lighter. 'If I don't answer you, does it mean I can't ask anything about you?'

'Of course not.' She smiled. 'Perhaps let's answer only the questions we want to?'

'Sounds good to me,' Sev said. 'So, what happens in August?'

For Juliet it was the nicest question he could have asked. 'I'm going to be playing in the concert hall for five nights. It's an opera. I'm playing first violin.'

'Does that mean solo?'

'No!'

She liked it that he'd asked, that his eyes didn't glaze over as she told him about the different arrangements, how her dream was a permanent chair in an orchestra.

'Dante and Susie are coming to the opening night,' she told him—and his eyes still didn't glaze over. Instead they held hers steadily, and he was so receptive he made it easy to share the importance of her friends being there. 'It will make it extra-special. Don't tell them that, though,' she added. 'I don't want to add pressure.'

'Why would it add pressure?'

'If they knew how much it meant,' she told him. 'I've never had someone in the audience before.'

'Your family?'

'No.' She shook her head. 'They're busy, busy. You know how it is?'

'I don't...'

'Oh, I'm so sorry!'

Gosh, how insensitive of her, when his parents were dead.

But he smiled at her sudden anguish. 'When I was growing up my parents were always in the front row—much to my horror at times,' he elaborated. 'My mother liked to make an entrance and then she'd applaud just for me, and blow kisses.'

'Ouch!' She laughed. 'Did you play an instrument?'

'No.'

'Act?'

'I'm talking about little school plays. Thankfully we went on to boarding school in Milan, or she'd have been embarrassing me through my teenage years too.'

He liked the softness of her laughter, and how it trailed away as if she understood how his parents were so greatly missed on this day. Then he reminded himself of his role as best man, and that his absence would soon be noticed.

As if to confirm it, in the distance his name was being called.

'I should get back.'

'And me. Louanna will be sending out a search party.'

They made no move to go, though.

And despite his promises to himself to behave on this day, now, at the eleventh hour, he caved. He wanted her tonight.

Sevandro stared into eyes that glittered and he liked the way she gazed back at him—as if anticipating the offer. But first there were clarifications to be made.

'So...' He resumed their conversation with different intent. 'No parents at your performances...what about boyfriends?' he checked, moving things along, aware that he had to get back inside and trying to gauge what this gorgeous violinist who had made today somewhat bearable expected from her lovers. 'Partners?'

'Gosh, no.' She shook her head. 'Nothing like that. I've never...' She shrugged. 'Well, what with my studies and...'

He assumed that, like him, she did not have the time or the desire for a serious relationship—but she was back to blushing, and his hand came to her burning cheek to let her know she did not have to apologise for preferring casual sex—certainly not to him!

'I guess with all that practice each day...' he said.

'And classes,' she added. 'There isn't time for dating.'

'Good—because I don't do all that.'

'I know you don't.'

She did know that—and right now it suited her.

Dreadful dates? They could bypass all that. They'd just go to bed.

And right now it didn't matter if that was it...

It was so much more than she'd ever had.

She wanted his skill and she wanted to be intimate with this man who had thrilled her on sight.

'You're staying at the hotel?' he checked.

She nodded.

'I'll sort out a key,' he told her. 'But now I should go.'

Juliet frowned, expecting a kiss.

Usually she felt a little fearful at this part…never quite wanting the kiss that was to come.

This was the complete reversal of that. He just stared. And her lips ached as if they needed the weight of his. And she had never stared at another so intently…

Then she heard his name being called once more, and she could have wept.

'They can wait,' Sevandro said, and she felt a flutter of relief as his mouth came down and lightly grazed her own. 'First I have to know your kiss.'

And she got to know his.

It was bliss, light and yet sexy, as if she were being brushed by velvet, and yet it set off a delicious reaction, from her tingling lips to her toes. As his hand slid behind her head she was shaking—but with pleasure. His mouth exerted more pressure and her lips parted to the reward of his tongue.

This was how every kiss should be.

It was slow, unhurried, and she closed her eyes and wondered why she'd been so reluctant in the past—why she'd fought not to pull away, and yet with Sev she instinctively moved closer.

She put her arms up and wrapped them around his neck. He kissed her harder. But what brought her undoing was the sound he made in her mouth…almost a sigh, akin to a moan. A sound more beautiful than any her violin could make.

His lips on hers were no longer soft, but thorough and delicious, and she kissed him back, their tongues mingling and her body all atremble as his hand came to her waist and he drew her closer.

Sev did not generally sit necking on a bench, and he hadn't intended to kiss her here, but this was a delight. And, while he was aware he had to go inside and resume his best man duties, he knew there was so much pleasure that awaited and this taste would sustain him.

He took her hand and moved it to where he ached, groaning at her teasing as she moved it to his thigh. His mouth explored her pale neck and he kissed away the throaty noises she made, knowing he must go.

But first he had one more question.

'Why did you deny me?'

'Deny you?'

'That night, why did you deny me?'

'Deny…?' she said again.

He heard the bewilderment, felt the pause in her body. He was about to insist she knew what he meant—and then it was he who stilled.

It was Sev who halted this tryst.

He went over her words, felt her hand still on his thigh…

She hadn't denied him that night.

He was starting to realise Juliet hadn't known that, when he'd told Gio he might find company for the night, his look had invited *her*… She had flicked her gaze away, and at the time he'd thought he was being given a very sophisticated no.

But she was a different woman with her violin.

The real Juliet did not know this game.

She didn't know anything!

'When you say you've never dated?' he checked. 'Are you telling me that you've never slept with anyone?'

'Yes. But I know my mind, Sev. It doesn't change anything between us.'

'Of course it changes things.' He dropped all contact. 'What the hell, Juliet? You are not into one-nighters.'

'You don't know that.'

'I do know that,' Sev said. 'Because I've already offered you that.'

He saw the furrow form between her brows.

'At Gio and Mimi's wedding.'

'We didn't so much as speak...' she started—and then her lips closed.

Juliet swallowed as she looked back with hindsight.

That look that had caused her heart to race...that moment when she had felt as if he spoke directly to her, as if he had a request...

Well, he had.

Just not the musical kind.

'Did you really think I was just going to finish playing and go to your bed?'

'If you so chose.' He took a breath. 'Don't you see? It's the same tonight.'

'No!'

She wouldn't have it. It wasn't the same. They'd connected, they'd spoken, they were talking now!

'Sev...' Juliet was struggling, trying to regroup from the bliss of their kiss and the promise of the night and then the plunge into rejection. 'I know we're not going anywhere, but I do know what I want.'

'*Do* you?' he checked, a little less gently, perhaps tartly. 'Because I don't do slow and tender, and I don't make love.'

'I'm not asking for love. I'm not expecting to be treated as if it's our wedding night. And I never said I wanted "slow and tender".'

'That,' he snapped, 'shows how little you know.'

'Why does my being a virgin scare you off?'

'Oh, I'm not scared, Juliet. I'm more concerned that we'd have got into that room and I'd have taken you against the wall...' He quickly shut that thought down. 'Juliet, what do you want for your first time?'

She stared angrily back at him. 'Preferably someone who turns me on.'

He gave a small laugh at her smart answer, because there could be no denying their ridiculous attraction, and he was kinder when he spoke again.

'Be honest, Juliet, in an ideal world, what would you want from your first lover?'

'I don't want to answer that one,' Juliet said. After all, that was the agreement they'd made.

'You do *not* want to cut your teeth on me.'

'Please don't tell me what I do and don't want.'

She stood and smoothed down her dress and he stood too. 'Your hair...'

He put a hand to her head to smooth it, and he was so nice as he sent her on her way. But then she answered his question—not to satisfy his curiosity, just to remember how she'd once thought.

'I do want more for my first time. I don't mean endless love—but, yes, red roses and such...and to be wined and dined...to dance and...' She halted.

'Go on.'

'I want someone who knows parts of me that no one else does, and gives me parts of himself...'

He was right, damn him.

'What else?' he asked.

'Picnics in sunflowers.'

'Picnics are muddy and itchy.'

'It's my dream, Sev.'

'Hold on to it,' he told her, and then he gave a soft laugh. 'Picnics? Oh, Juliet, you really did pick the wrong guy.'

'So you keep telling me.' She sniffed. 'I'm going back inside.'

She nipped to the ladies' and sorted out her hair and splashed her face, then headed back to the wedding. It was a gorgeous night, utterly perfect, and yet seeing Susie and Dante dancing, and all the other couples—some together for ever, some just together for this night—she felt out of step with the world.

'Come on,' Ricco said, and so they danced. Because they liked music and that was that.

It would have been nice to make Sev a little bit jealous, but there was no chance of that, because Gabriel came to grab his hand and Ricco was back dancing with the one he'd be with tonight.

She caught Sev's eyes and rolled her own, then got back to life without him.

'Juliet!' Susie was high on hormones and love. 'Thank you…'

'I've loved every minute,' Juliet said. 'It's been wonderful.'

It really was a brilliant wedding, and she danced some more, and then sat with Louanna, debating whether to play some music as the night wound up.

'There's a fire pit outside,' Louanna said.

'I can't take my violin by a fire.'

'Use Ricco's old spare?' she suggested, then paused. 'God, they could at least be discreet.'

'Who?'

'"Sevandro and Ella,' she said. 'She's *married*!'

'They're just talking,' Juliet snapped, more than a little fed up with Louanna's well-voiced opinions—though it did sting a little to see Sev in conversation with a stunning caramel blonde. 'Let's get the instruments.'

Sev saw Juliet heading outside—or rather was aware of her no matter how he tried not to notice.

That kiss still lingered in his mind, and also their conversation, and the music she'd made…

All the good parts of today, the gentler parts of today, had been because of her.

Damn.

He really hadn't handled things well—but then again, since Rosa's death he hadn't been one for sitting outside at night and looking at the view, or talking and making out on a bench.

And he wasn't one for virgins.

'Am I boring you, Sev?' Ella said.

'I'm sorry…' He pulled his mind back to the conversation.

'It's okay. I know today is hard for you.'

Juliet had *asked* if today was hard for him, rather than assumed it was. Ridiculously, he had wanted to discuss it with her, but he had closed off that escape hatch years ago.

'You must miss Rosa today…'

He chose not to respond to Ella's assumptions, and instead asked after her husband and young family.

'They're doing well. Of course we're busy…both working.'

'You took over the practice?' he checked. 'How is your father?' he asked.

Because there was a part of him that still wanted to speak to the older Dr Romero. A part that did want to know if his suspicions—Dante's too—had been right.

If there had ever been a baby.

'I was thinking of maybe visiting him,' Sevandro said. 'Just to catch up.'

'He'd have loved that, Sevandro, but he's not so well.' Ella told him about her father's dementia. 'It's so hard to lose a little more of him each day, and visitors just confuse him.'

'I'm very sorry to hear that.'

'He adored both you and Dante. The sons he never had.'

'Give him my best.'

'I will.'

As Ella slipped away he got back to duties, arranging the wedding car, and everyone stopped to wave off the happy couple.

'Give England my love,' he heard Juliet call as they climbed into the car.

And then she got back to the fire, playing her violin like a fiddle, and making people happy with the music she made.

The music was happy—the musician not so much.

Oh, it had been wonderful, and she loved nothing more than playing with friends like this, but she wanted to go back to the hotel and lick the wounds of her rejection.

Juliet saw him leave.

Not a moment after the bride and groom had gone, Sev signalled for a vehicle and without so much as a backward glance left the reception.

The party carried on, and so did the music, but after an hour or so Juliet gave in, returning Ricco's violin, collecting her own, and then climbing into one of the waiting cars.

It was a lonely ride back to the hotel—and Juliet was more than used to it.

Not so much returning to a luxurious hotel, more the wired feeling from performing. But tonight it was heightened. Or was it that she was still wired from that kiss? Or that delicious time spent on the bench, simply talking?

She stepped into the gorgeous foyer, almost drooping—not with weariness, but with dejection—and a head full of faded long-ago dreams of men who dated you and the shining star of one who didn't do that at all.

'Allow me.'

The doorman spoke in Italian, and so lost in her thoughts was Juliet that it took her a second longer than usual to translate as he reached for her violin case.

'I shall have it delivered to your room.'

'No need,' Juliet responded. 'I can manage.'

She walked off, past the sofa where they had spoken this morning, wistful and a bit misty-eyed as she waited for the elevator. She would like to get to her room and cry, Juliet decided. Although she was unsure if she was embarrassed at practically handing herself to him, or simply sad that he'd turned her down.

There was no sense of feeling relieved that nothing had happened.

Turning the old-fashioned key, in the equally old-fashioned lock, she realised the simple fact was she was tired of being considered an old-fashioned girl.

Juliet had wanted him so.

The lights were on as she stepped into her room, but instead of putting her violin case down she stood holding it, a little stunned, staring at the floral arrangement—deep red roses wrapped in gold paper—that had been placed on the dressing table.

Oh.

They must be from Susie, she told herself. Because she was nice like that.

Her heart started thumping as she put down her violin, then walked over and picked up a cream envelope with spiky black writing on it: *Juliet.*

She almost tore the envelope in her haste to get to the card, expecting her hopes to be dashed, and let out a sob when instead hope was renewed.

Before making love, at the very least he should send flowers...

   Sevandro

Her breath was rapid and shallow, making her a little dizzy as she reread the card and then looked back inside the envelope. She took out a little flat numbered card and saw it was a lift pass.

And with those flowers he took her back to something

that had never been, to her dreams for her first time, how it might be, should be…

Could still be.

She inhaled the scent of the roses and marvelled at how he'd got hold of them at this hour. She didn't know—she just knew that it was the single most romantic thing he could have done.

It made tonight special…

She walked into the bathroom and wondered how to prepare. She took in the shower, the deep bath, her tiny make-up bag… There was no time. She wanted every minute of this fading night to be spent with him. So she freshened up quickly, added a little lip gloss, then took down her hair and quickly brushed it.

Her nerves crept up as she used the card to access the elevator and it slowly creaked its way up. Oh, so badly she wanted to do this—to spend a night with Sev—but as she exited the elevator and stood at the door she didn't know *how* to do this. How to knock on his door and say, *Hi, I'm here…*

Hating herself for being so pathetic, she turned to go, summoning back the lift, hearing it groan as it wearily returned.

'Juliet…?' Sev was peering out through the door.

'I think I've got the wrong floor,' she lied.

'This is my floor,' he told her. 'And the only way to get here is the private access card.'

'Oh.'

'No problem.' His jacket was off, his tie unknotted, and he looked more delectable every time she saw him.

'Goodnight, then,' he said.

'Is this really your floor?' she asked.

Sevandro nodded.

God, he thought, she was nervous.

Usually it didn't endear him to a woman, but then again,

he'd never taken such time with a woman before. He rather guessed she'd hate herself tomorrow if she left now. And he'd regret it too. She was sexy as hell and just didn't know it. He'd felt her desire on the bench—perhaps because she knew it couldn't really go anywhere.

'It's okay,' Sev told her as she walked back to his door. 'It's a first for me too.' He took her in his arms. 'I've never slept with a virgin.'

There were questions in her eyes that he would not be answering. He did not want to discuss a long-ago wedding night that had been tense rather than tender.

It had not come close to this.

Tonight was no longer about distraction—and for him sex was usually that: an escape or a need fulfilled. He had lovers he could call—beautiful women who, like himself, did not want to tangle emotions.

This wasn't like that.

First, though, she had to relax.

'I have to make some calls,' he told her.

'I'll go…'

'No, I meant if you want to have a bath… I have to call my PA in Dubai.'

He led her into his vast suite. The doors were open to the balcony and that massive moon was still hovering, as if it had followed them from the vineyard. She'd seemed so much bolder there.

'I arranged this for you.' He opened up a door and she looked at all the candles and the steaming water.

'You did this?'

'The maid did it. I'm sorry I can't wine and dine you, but Italian weddings…'

She laughed, and it was nice to see her relax just a touch.

Sevandro had thought a bath might be good for both of them, and though he had since decided she might feel better alone he did not want that bathroom door closed. Very deliberately he would maintain the contact.

'We could have breakfast tomorrow,' he said as she went into the bathroom.

Hopefully she wouldn't still be a virgin by then, Juliet thought as she slipped into the bathroom.

She was about to close the door, but then he called out, 'I didn't know Susie's sisters were twins.'

'Yes.'

She kept on trying to close the door, but he had more to say.

'They didn't like all the attention being on Susie.'

'No.' She smiled, undoing her zip. She'd noticed the same.

'Do you have brothers and sisters?'

'Half-brothers and sisters.' It was nice to talk as she took off her dress and stood dressed only in French lace. 'All much younger. My parents got divorced.'

'How old were you?'

'Twelve when they broke up.'

He wasn't listening now.

'Helene?' he said. 'Thanks for getting back to me…sorry to call you at this hour…'

He rattled on about Sheikh Mahir and Juliet took off her underwear and slid into the bath and lay there, worried now rather than nervous. Leaning over, she looked at her phone and found out it must be three in the morning in Dubai.

Now she had a question of her own.

'Sev?' she asked when he'd ended his call.

'What?' he replied, coming to the bathroom door holding a drink.

'Do I smell?'

He laughed. 'Why do you ask?'

'Well, putting me in the bath…pretending you had to call Dubai…'

'I did have to call to Dubai. But to be honest I thought you needed a bath to relax. I'm not one for...'

'What?'

He came over and sat on the edge of the bath. He picked up her hand. 'Oh, Juliet...' He kissed her fingers, mimicking being chaste. 'I'm not one for feeling my way slowly...'

'It's nice, though,' she said.

Especially when he stopped faking being chaste and put down his glass, focussing on her hand and sucking on one finger. Then he paused, his silver-black eyes looking at her.

'Your underwear is very sexy.'

'The bride bought it for me.' She could tell him that now. 'Like your tie.'

'Seriously?'

She nodded.

'Why?'

'She just did.'

'I cannot think of a single occasion when anyone would buy me underwear.' He thought about it. 'And I would never buy it for anyone...'

'You don't buy your lovers sexy lingerie?'

'God, no, I don't do gifts.' He kissed up her arm. 'You lucked out again,' he said, kissing her neck. 'You got a mean billionaire.'

'You're not mean...'

No man with a mouth so soft on her neck could be called mean.

'Selfish, then.'

His hand came to her gorgeous breast, floating in the soapy water. Pulling back a little, he looked at her, huge black pupils with just a dash of green at the edges and her hair all curly from the steam.

And when he kissed her softly, Sev knew he'd never before come close to this moment. Feeling her tentative mouth, he made allowances for it, didn't try to hasten her with his tongue.

He'd never kissed like this—had never wanted or even needed to take the time to reassure a woman.

But Juliet suited his mood now, and as his tongue slipped into her warm mouth his hand moved between them, stroking the side of one generous breast. Her hardening nipple, despite the warm water, felt like a reward.

His hands, his mouth, felt incredible.

'I've wanted you since this morning,' he told her in a low, gravelly voice that made her feel both weak and wanting.

She started to unbutton his shirt, exposing the fan of black hair on his chest and flat mahogany nipples. He was just so male, so sexy...

He sat on the edge of the bath, so tall. Then he shrugged off his shirt and lowered his head, taking one breast in his mouth as his hand slid lower.

'You might fall in...'

'I don't care.' His tone was emphatic.

His hand was between her thighs, his fingers where none had ever been, and then his mouth left her breast, as if he preferred to look right at her.

Her hand moved to his shoulder, and then to the back of his head, and she stared right at him, closing her eyes at the slight stab and stretch of his fingers before they moved back to soft strokes.

Strokes that were more insistent.

'I don't think I can come,' she told him. 'Why don't we...?'

'Shh...' he said, concentrating on the feel of her, beneath the soapy water.

Then her hand came to caress his face.

Her warm, tender touch was almost too much for his black, icy heart, and yet he found he coveted it.

He looked right at her, feeling her come alive under his hand, seeing the flush on her cheeks and the slight sheen of tears in her eyes. He breathed in. He wasn't just turned on as he watched her come to orgasm, feeling her thighs grip him and her intimate beat—he felt something scarcer...felt a deeper contact being made, someone being with another. Caring...

'Sev...'

She closed her eyes, folded a little in the middle. He leant forward and she rested her head on his chest, his dark hair against her cheek, and his hand moved up to her waist as the pulses faded.

'I didn't think...' She was struggling to get her breath. 'I didn't think I was capable...'

Nor had he.

For ever he'd been numb.

Well, at least for a decade.

But now, as they lay on the bed, naked and kissing and aching for each other, touching each other, stroking each other...

'Let me...'

She was nipping at his nipple, then asking if it was nice.

'Yes.'

Her hand was on his stomach now and, nervous but bold, she slid it down. They lay face to face but he was looking down, watching her stroke him.

'I should put something on,' he suggested, as her fingers were moistened with his silver.

But they were both watching, and her breasts were warm, damp...just so nice to explore with his hands and with his mouth.

He was about to hook her leg over him and drive in, but...

He had to take it slow.

He liked her hand on his back as he reached over to the bedside table, rummaging for a condom, knocking the contents off but not caring.

He liked how she slid her hands between his thighs as he briefly faced away from her.

He rolled onto his back. 'Put it on me.'

'You do it.'

She watched him for a moment and then she took over, her slender fingers rolling it slowly down. She looked at Sev and leant over and kissed him. He pulled her head down and kissed her back hard, his jaw a little rougher now, and that giddy feeling was back as he flipped her and kissed her, removing a pillow from beneath her head.

The feel of him over her was delicious, and so was the scratchy feel of his thighs between her legs as he positioned himself. He was focusing on her neck, and then he moved up onto one forearm, holding himself at the centre of new pleasure.

'Sev…'

She was so ready she was almost begging. As he pushed in she waited for the hurt and pain, but it was more just a new and blissful sensation.

'Oh…'

The room went a little dark, but then there was nothing but pleasure, and the ragged moans from him made her curl inside.

'Juliet…' he said, almost as if he was apologising, and then he started to move.

She was so oiled and ready, so in tune from their long games in the bath, that it was new but not scary.

'Okay?'

He looked down from over her and their gazes locked. She nodded to say that she was okay and he moved deeper.

'It's perfect.'

She searched for his mouth and kissed him as he took her, her hands finding the planes of his back and moving down to his torso.

She lifted her knees and then wrapped her legs around him. He was moving faster, and she tasted his shoulder, his chest, wanting this never to end. But she could feel heat spreading, and there was the same warm feeling she'd had in the bath, except there were no little beats of pleasure, just a build-up of tension.

She started to moan, as if seeking escape. Then he stilled, and a zip of electricity seemed to shoot along her spine as she heard him moan and release. It was the headiest pleasure, her face on fire, her throat tight, but nothing like the tension and the intensity of her orgasm as he came inside her.

His head came down beside her own, and then he lifted a little and moved within her again, where she was so tender, before collapsing on her.

Juliet had nothing with which to compare, but she simply knew, as she lay there warm with pleasure, that somehow she could only have been found by him. As if since he'd laid his sexy eyes upon her that first night they'd been building to his, and now she lay sated and breathless as he moved from within her.

Sev sorted himself and then covered them. He waited for the moment to arrive when he wished she were gone, or for that numb feeling to return, but his new lover didn't allow for that. She was lying over on his side of the bed, her hair on his chest, and clearly delighted.

'That was magical,' Juliet said. 'Honestly, how did I survive without that?'

She leant over him to get some water and he felt her hair trailing over his face. It didn't annoy him.

'Sev...?' She was suddenly very still over him. 'You didn't take anything, did you?'

'What?'

He glanced over, saw the little sliver of paper and couldn't resist a little tease.

'Dante gave it to me before the service.'

'Dante?'

He laughed and reached over. 'It's a precious stone.' Unwrapping it carefully, he showed her the contents. 'A ruby.'

'Oh.'

'From my mother's eternity ring.'

His smile dimmed. He'd almost refused to look at it when Dante had given it to him—really, he'd given it only a mere glance—but now he held the little stone up to the light.

'Dante had it recovered from the accident site.'

'Now I feel terrible...'

'No need.' He folded the ruby back inside the paper and into its pouch, then put the little package in the drawer 'There's nothing terrible about tonight.'

CHAPTER FOUR

'I WAS RIGHT,' Juliet said, lying with her head on his chest, tethered by his arms.

It was just as well, because she felt so relaxed and floaty that she thought if he let go she might just float away.

'About what?'

'My first time was perfect.' She thought for a moment. 'Well, I didn't get a picnic…' She both felt and heard his low laugh. 'Or a dance. But apart from that…'

There was another thing she'd asked for, to share pieces of themselves only with each other, and perhaps that was why she asked now, 'Was your first time this romantic?'

'No!' He half laughed, but then lay still, thinking back to a version of himself he had long since forgotten.

For so long it had felt as if his bastioned life had started after the accident, or the fight with his brother, or his marriage. But this rare togetherness with another person, the curiosity rather than nosiness behind her question, meant his perpetual guard didn't shoot up. Her gentle silence allowed him to think.

'It wasn't like this, but perhaps it was a bit romantic.'

'Was it her first time too?'

He shook his head. 'She was older…a tourist.'

Juliet's questions still didn't feel invasive, even if it was something he had never discussed with anyone. Even if it was a topic that might be best not discussed as you lay with another woman. There was an honest element to her questions, and the agreement they'd made that they didn't have to answer—it made it easier for him to explore the past.

'She was staying at Forte dei Marmi…'

He told her about the sandy beaches, the jet-set tourists and luxury hotels…

'She was there for a few weeks. It suited us both…' He thought back. 'I was never in love, or anything like that, but I thought she was incredible. We both knew it was short-lived.'

'A holiday romance?'

'For her. I wasn't on holiday—I was working. For me, it was more a short indulgence.'

He thought back to lighter days. He'd always been serious, and held back from getting overly involved, but that long, hot summer was a world away from the brief interludes he allowed himself now.

'I was probably better company then.'

'I like your company now,' she told him. 'And I can see the appeal of short, intense relationships. It doesn't have to be for ever to be wonderful.'

Her words struck within him, making him think of long-ago days when he'd never given his heart or made promises he'd never keep.

'You're right…' He looked down, saw they were loosely holding hands. 'It doesn't have to be for ever to be…'

He couldn't say it. He didn't do 'wonderful' and never had. He'd always been a bit of a lone wolf, and more cynical than most, but there was something about lying here with her, the day he'd been dreading since his brother had told him about it now safely over.

'To be incredible,' he said.

Incredible because for more than a decade all his emotion had been locked in a vault, and tonight he had allowed himself to feel, to make love, to hold and caress and just escape into her charms and her scent. To get to know her some more.

For Sev, *that* was sheer indulgence.

'How old were you?' she asked.

'That, I am not answering.'

'You were old enough to work, though?'

'Work experience.'

'No-o-o…' She moaned and covered her face with her hands.

He leant forward and peeled them from her face. 'That was the same as most of my relationships.'

'With holidaymakers?'

'Yes.' He hadn't ever really thought about it, but now, looking back, he saw it. 'We could be close, but there was an expiry date. I could adore them, but know it wasn't going to last. It worked both ways—both of us knew the terms.'

She didn't seem shocked. 'Actually, it sounds perfect.'

'I think you might have more heart than me.'

'No…' She lay still. 'I wanted this—honestly. I really don't have time for a relationship. I have the most important months of my life coming up. I need to concentrate on that.'

'Why did you wait?' he asked. 'And don't give me all that nonsense about being too busy.'

'It's true, though,' she said. 'Well, in part… I told you my parents broke up when I was twelve, then both married again. I was always being roped in for babysitting and then I was working to pay for my music lessons.'

'They didn't pay for them?'

'Things changed after the divorce. School…their finances…' There was a stretch of quiet. 'We don't get on. Of course we never actually *say* that, but…' She trailed off, as if she was skipping past something. 'Then I went to university and I honestly thought my life would start then—well, dating and such. But…' She stopped again. 'You've never been shy, I assume?'

'Shy?' He thought about it. 'If you mean timid, then no. But I wouldn't say that about you either. You perform, you dance, you have friends…' He shook his head. 'Being busy is an excuse.'

'We can't all dive into bed with a single look.' Juliet thumped his chest, but then sighed.

They lay quietly and Sev wanted to know more—he wanted to get to the bit she'd glossed over. But that wasn't fair. They'd agreed not to press each other.

It was still there, though, that desire to talk…to open up to her.

They dozed, and she awoke lying on her stomach, felt herself being watched.

She smiled right into his eyes.

'You're not shy,' he told her.

'I'm not shy with you,' she admitted. 'Or maybe it's my casual lover persona?'

'Do you want breakfast? We could have it here or go down.'

'I'm not sure… I think the hotel restaurant might be a bit public. I'm not slinking about, but…' She rolled her eyes. 'I'd prefer it if Susie didn't know about last night.'

'Fair enough.'

'She'd be arranging double dates.'

'God, no,' he laughed.

'Oh, yes. And, knowing Susie, she'd have us seated together at the christening.'

His smile faded.

'I was joking, Sev.'

'I know that… You and Susie?' he asked. 'You're very close?'

'We are.' She leant up on her elbow. 'Though I shan't say anything to her about this. We're not *that* close. I don't normally open up to people.'

'I believe you.'

'And, given I don't discuss my sex life—or lack of it...' She looked right at him. 'I don't like to get too involved with anyone either.' She pressed her lips together for a second before continuing. 'Believe me, I shan't be saying anything about...'

She gestured to the rumpled bed.

'I don't mind,' he told her.

He put a hand up to her gorgeous hair.

No, he decided, she wasn't shy. It was something more.

And if he wanted more of those pieces of her then he should give her some of his own.

Some of those things no other person knew.

'Yes,' he said suddenly, and watched her slight frown. 'In answer to your earlier question, yesterday was hard for me. Thank you for being there.'

She smiled, and he looked at the jade-green eyes that were so patient, and he felt he was on the edge of telling her something not a single soul new—answering the second assumption all those others had made, that he'd missed Rosa yesterday.

'As to the other... No.'

She gave a tiny nod, the same one they'd shared a couple of times yesterday, and he knew she was just understanding that this was hard, and offering support.

'I didn't miss Rosa yesterday. I am sad that she died, but our marriage wasn't as good as everyone believes.'

'I'm so sorry...it must be hell whenever you come back here.'

'Yes.'

'Do you see her family?'

'They were there last night. They're always there. They own a small winery next to ours.'

He inhaled deeply. *Enough.* He looked over, wanting something in return.

'Who hurt you?' he asked.

'No one.'

But he knew that was lie.

He thought she was about to say she didn't want to answer that question, but then, with the sky outside starting to lighten, she did.

'I'm the one who caused the hurt. I broke up my parents' marriage.'

He waited rather than respond.

'My father was head of music at my school.'

'High school?' he checked. 'Or do you call it senior school?'

'Senior.' She nodded. 'At the end of my first year there was some gossip about him and another teacher. I just ignored it. But after the summer the rumours got worse. My mother kept asking me what was wrong. She was worried, I guess. I was in my room, crying a lot, trying to hide it. She insisted I tell her. She said that she loved me, that she was concerned, and that I could tell her anything. So eventually I did.' She shrugged. 'She's never forgiven me for it.'

'And your father?'

'He's never forgiven me either. They don't say it, but I know they blame me.'

'For what?'

'The divorce…the change in circumstances. I'm quite sure they both wish I'd just shut the hell up. Anyway, they both married again and had new families.' She took a big breath. 'You don't need to hear all this.'

'I asked to hear it.'

'You did…' She looked pensive for a moment. 'Would you have said anything? If you'd found out your father was cheating?'

'I wouldn't have had to, the way people talk here. My mother would've known about it before he made it home.' Then he thought for a moment. 'I don't know,' he admitted.

She closed her eyes in relief at his honest answer—relief that he hadn't just dashed in and said she'd been right. Instead, he seemed to be considering it—and then he told her something about himself.

'I've never really shared what's on my mind. Dante was always the more emotional one.' He laughed. 'At my *nonna*'s funeral he asked me when she was coming back. I said she was dead, and he said, "I know that, but when is she coming back…?" So I told him—never. I got told off for upsetting him.'

He was quiet then, as if he was really considering her question. She could almost feel him thinking.

'No, I don't think I would have told my mother,' he said at last. 'But that's more a reflection on me…' He squeezed her arm. 'I would hate it, though, if you were mine…to think of you in bed crying and unable to come to me.'

'My mother said I could tell her anything. And then, when I did, she took her love away. And you're right—it hurt.' She nodded. 'Everything was taken away. Truly, I wish I'd never found out. Certainly I wish I'd never said anything.'

'You got through it, though.'

'Maybe…'

'Of course you did. You're here, aren't you…?'

Sex was their reward for sharing, and soon they lost themselves in each other.

She missed breakfast in the restaurant and it was inching past her check-out time as they lay there, breathless.

'I should go,' Juliet said. 'I have to check out.'

'Have a shower,' he suggested. 'I'll get your stuff brought up here so you don't have to rush off.'

She didn't want to rush off.

She liked it here an awful lot.

Sex had always seemed to her like a hurdle to be jumped over. She'd never thought of *after*. She rather wished it had been awful and awkward... Not really, but it might be easier to leave if it hadn't been so wonderful.

If *he* hadn't been so wonderful.

'You okay?' he checked.

'Perfect.'

'No regrets?'

'None.' She shook her head, and her smile stayed in place, but she had to force it just a little, and there was a slight amendment taking place in her head.

She would deal with that later.

She dashed to his bathroom and bypassed the petals still strewn in the bath. She jumped in the shower, trying not to examine the thought that had occurred to her. After all, how could you possibly regret enjoying a lover too much? How could you regret your first time being so wonderful?

She found a new toothbrush in the little basket of goodies, and a bamboo comb, but her eyes lingered on his silver comb and heavy razor. She reached out for a heavy glass bottle, removing the stopper and almost folding at the delicious hit of his cologne. She breathed in the peppery, woody scent she'd first met in the lobby, and then later, so intimately, with her face in his neck, on his chest...

Don't think of that now.

She went to replace the stopper, but then ran it across her wrist. She'd think of him later, Juliet decided. Breathe him in when she was alone. Then she stared at herself and saw that her lips were plump from the attention. She also saw the slight panic flaring in her green eyes at the prospect of non-chalantly saying goodbye.

One night, she reminded herself, dabbing the stopper on her neck and somehow calming down, telling herself it was just as well their time was limited.

He could become very easy to fall for.

And far too hard to let go.

She wrapped herself in a towel and headed out, ready to put on last night's clothes. But all her things had been brought up from her room—her violin, even her flowers.

She went through her overnight bag and found the cheese-cloth dress she'd arrived in—not that he'd seen it.

'The real me,' she said, snapping on her regular bra and smiling as he pulled a sulky face. Then she put on her dress and combed her hair, before sitting on the bed where he lay and pulling on her espadrilles.

'Do you want to do something today?'

Her hand paused for a second, then resumed tying the straps as she answered, 'I don't know...' She looked over as she carried on fastening her footwear.

'I could sort out your boss...'

'It would take more than charm.'

She was tense at the prospect of saying goodbye...tense at the thought of returning to Anna's.

Just tense.

He looked at her as she stood and walked over to the long mirror and leant forward, coiling her long red hair and tying it on top of her head in one practised movement.

The dress was the colour of sea glass and it brought out the red of her hair, and he watched as she did up a couple of buttons at the front.

'You could maybe try and talk to Anna...'

She didn't realise he was watching her, and he saw her roll her eyes a little, as if to ask what the hell he would know.

'I saw that.'

She caught his eye and the tension left her and she actually smiled—but she was clearly still certain he couldn't help.

'You don't play an instrument.'

'True.'

'And am I right in assuming it's not a house-share set-up at your place in Dubai, Sevandro?' she asked, with a twist of light sarcasm.

'I don't share my space with anyone.' His response was equally dry. 'I have a penthouse apartment looking out over the Persian Gulf.'

For a brief second he saw her there, pale on his coffee-coloured silk sheets, the glittering ocean behind her.

'But it's all soundproofed. I could have an entire orchestra playing and no one would hear a thing.'

'Exactly. And we don't all have PAs to arrange our schedules.'

She was smiling and teasing him through the mirror. And he'd been right, Sev decided. She wasn't shy—just nervous about reaching out. But once that contact had been made it was like watching a flower open.

'Do you want to go to the beach?' he offered.

'The beach? I don't have anything to swim in.'

'We can get something there. There are some nice boutiques. Besides, I still haven't wined and dined you, and nor have we danced. How about a little intense romance?'

'Like you used to know?' She laughed, but then it faded. 'When do you leave?'

It was perhaps an odd question, but she needed to know—needed a timeline to give to her heart.

'When do you go back to Dubai?'

'Tomorrow. Leave your things here, then I can drop you back at Anna's later tonight.'

That sounded doable, she told herself. And she wasn't going to fall any further in a day.

Except she looked to where he lay and felt as if he were beckoning her towards a slightly more perilous path. But she discounted the silent alert, glancing at the rumpled sheets where he lay, in the bed he'd taken her in.

'I'd love to go to the beach.'

CHAPTER FIVE

THERE WAS NOTHING WORSE, Juliet decided, than choosing a bikini in a high-end boutique. Especially when you had big breasts, a tiny assistant, and the sexiest man alive kept making dreadful suggestions.

'What about this one?'

'I'm too pale to wear white.'

She shunned his suggestion and grabbed a nice navy-blue—but 'safe' was not always 'nice'.

'The sun will soon be setting on our romantic day,' he warned from the other side of the curtain as she stood in the changing room, hating it. 'Let me see.'

She peeled back the curtain and there he stood—in what looked like black boxers, really, only ones for swimming. And of course with that body he was beach-ready.

He glanced over. 'I still think the white one.'

She put it on once more, to prove a point, sure she'd look like a milk bottle. But instead… The white was so white it brought out the scrap of colour in her skin.

'I'll get this one,' she said, about to close the curtain to take it off.

'Just put your dress on over it.'

He came over and dealt with the exclusive label that hung from the top, his fingers light on the side of her ribs. It felt as deep as a thorough kiss.

'And this one,' he said, flicking out the label on the bikini bottom, the heat of his hand on the small of her back.

'Will we...?' She closed her eyes, stopping herself from asking if they might skip the beach and go directly to bed—not because she didn't want the bed, but because she wanted this day too. 'I might need sunblock.'

They walked out, she with her boring underwear in her bag, and then he told her he was getting factor one million sunblock for her and to wait there.

Juliet would have liked a moment to examine last night, to just go over all the bliss, but there would be many days and nights for that, so she wandered off and then stared into a window at a cream dress that would, if it were black, be the perfect concert dress. It was utterly gorgeous...

'Why are you gazing at a wedding dress as if you have to have it *now*?' His hand came to her shoulder. 'That's not intense, Juliet. That's scary...'

'I didn't know...' She laughed and looked up, and sure enough it was a bridal boutique. 'That's my perfect concert dress. Well, apart from the colour. And the scoop neck is a bit low.'

'Try it on.'

'No.

'Go on...' he insisted.

'No. Because you'll buy it for me, like you bought the bikini, and—'

'Juliet.' He cut that thought off at the neck before it had even formed. 'I told you I don't buy gifts. The bikini was necessary. And believe me, I am not buying you a dress from a bridal shop—just try it on.'

He made the impossible easier, by just walking in, and then she had to take off her new bikini top, and then the assistant told her the 'perfect dress' was actually not only too small, but not even a complete dress.

'This is just a base,' she explained to Sevandro, almost apologetically. 'We were about to dress the window...'

'No...' Juliet shook her head. 'It's gorgeous as it is.' She gazed into the mirror. It was very plain, and that was what she liked. 'Well, it is a little low...' She looked over to Sev. 'And the sleeves...' She explained all the factors she had to take into consideration for a concert dress. 'I'd have to have three-quarter sleeves, and the shoulders are a bit...' She ran a hand over the seams and tried to decide on a word. 'Pointy.'

'Pointy?' The assistant's lips pulled just a fraction. She was clearly thinking her a little diva, and not really understanding that she was discussing her requirements for work.

They had gelato for a very late breakfast, in a cone as they walked to the promenade.

'You should get something specially made,' he told her.

'I'm saving for a violin first,' she explained, as they stepped onto the golden beach and walked to the very nice loungers. 'Well, it's the one I play, but I'm renting it at the moment.'

'Just get a dress!' He looked at her. 'I'd be terrible at being poor...'

He was so bad he was good, and he made her laugh rather than feel embarrassed to strip down to her bikini on a gorgeous beach, and he slathered her in so much sun cream, and moved the umbrellas to the nth degree.

She felt...

Protected.

Factor fifty plus, plus, plus.

For the first time since she was twelve years old and it had all fallen away she felt looked after.

'It's beautiful here.' She rolled onto her stomach and looked at the gorgeous resort behind them. 'But I think this is a private beach...'

'It is.' He yawned. 'I used to work here. And then I bought it.'

'Is this where you...?' She put out a leg and lightly kicked him. 'Your first lover?'

'No,' he said. 'That hotel's a little further along the promenade. But this is the first hotel I owned, or at least part-owned, with Sheikh Mahir.'

'Wow...' She blinked. 'What's he like?'

'He's okay.' He put his arm up over his head, his eyes closed against the morning sun. 'We argue, but for the most part we get on.'

'What do you argue about?'

He smiled and gave a soft half-laugh, because he'd never really discussed it or pondered it. These were not the sort of questions his family or anyone really asked.

And even if they did?

He wasn't sure he'd answer.

The regular rules didn't seem to apply today. It was as if he and Juliet had a different operating manual—an access-all-areas code. Even if some of those areas perhaps weren't that interesting...

'Mahir likes to think his son, Adal, works harder than he does. I went to school with him. He hasn't changed at all.'

'Do you get on with Adal?'

'Not lately. This latest project—the new hotel—there isn't the scope to carry someone or pretend that the golden son is pulling his weight.'

'You've told them that?'

'Yes.' He breathed out heavily and then closed his eyes, surprised to have shared as much.

'And?' she asked.

He smiled at her curiosity and her impatience to know the result.

'They're still sulking.'

* * *

It was nice to just lie together and enjoy the sound of the ocean and occasional conversation. To just lie there and let her eyes drift over him.

His body was magnificent, and she stuck out a leg and held it near his.

'I'm so pale...'

Especially next to his skin, which seemed to soak in the Mediterranean sun and darken in the bright light.

Then her calf dusted his lower thigh and he caught her leg and held it there. And then they were not thinking of skin.

They ventured into the water, and it was a little cooler than his skin and whole lot warmer than she'd braced herself for.

'Do you go to the beach in Dubai?' she asked as they waded out.

'No.'

'Do you go in the pool?'

'No.' He shook his head, pulled her into him. 'I do have a yacht. It's all for work, though.'

He crossed his eyes and made her laugh.

'If I want people to pay for, design, build and furnish my beautiful hotel, I have to chat them up.'

He kissed her then, as he would have liked to on the beach, right there in the water. He tasted her sunblock and didn't care. His tongue was coaxing hers to tangle with his, to move in his mouth and suggest all the things they wanted to do.

'We should get you into the shade,' he said, his hands holding her waist as she sizzled beneath him. 'You are very red.'

It wasn't from the sun.

And they remained in the sea, jumping small waves and messing about as he told her about the Dubai skyline, and the incredible night-life.

'It's not all clubs and bars—there is a beautiful classi-

cal music scene. It's an exciting country, full of ambition—
you'd love it.'

'I don't know,' she said as they lay back in the water. 'I
love Lucca.'

They lay on their backs and floated like otters. He reached
for her hand and held on and she knew this was just fleet-
ing, and possibly he was just the best flirt, good at making
her feel relaxed and nice, but she loved his charming ways
and how, as they drifted, still they spoke.

'How long will you be here?' he asked.

'For good, I hope,' she said, squinting at the high sun. 'I'll
apply for residency in a couple of years, so long as work is
going okay. I hope things are going well by then. I'll have the
quartet, maybe a chair in an orchestra or regular substitute
work.' She laughed at herself. 'I'll give you a discreet wave
if I see you on the walls with some gorgeous date.'

'You won't see me,' Sev said, and then his voice was serious. 'This goes no further...?'

'Of course.'

'Once the memorial service is out of the way I'm not coming back here.'

The warm sea suddenly felt like ice, and she knew what
she was being told was serious indeed.

'I have a property here, which I'm putting on the market,
and there are a couple of things I'd hoped to sort...' He didn't
elaborate. 'That may not be possible now, but I want things
in the best order they can be.'

He had a plan.

Sevandro really was preparing to leave.

'For good?' she checked, and stood up in the water. 'What
about Gio?'

'Of course I'll come if there's an emergency, but no more

family events, or Christmases, or the million and one other reasons to return.'

'What about...?' she started, then shook her head.

They were sharing what they chose to and not probing. They were close because both knew that this connection was something short-lived and fragile, something both would respect.

'Do Dante and Susie know?'

'I think they have an idea.'

She thought about that pause yesterday, during his speech, how his smile had faded when she'd mentioned the christening. It hadn't been the mention of double dates that had caused that reaction.

They went back to the beach and dried off as her mind caught up with all that he'd said, all that she'd seen.

'You're not coming back to see the baby?'

'No.'

She didn't like that answer. She didn't like his cold decision. But his future wasn't her business. This wasn't about agreeing with each other, it was about being there for each other for a little while.

'They can visit me in Dubai if they want to.'

He was almost the scowling man she'd first seen, she thought.

'Dante doesn't want us to be close.'

'What about Gio and Mimi?'

'We can meet in Rome.' He pulled on his linen shirt. 'Gio will hopefully live another twenty years, but I can't keep coming back.' He looked over. 'Same as yours...' he said. 'Not all families work.'

And soon the most wonderful day—apart from that bit— ended with seafood and limoncello spritzers for her, still water for him, and sexy music pulsing from a dancefloor.

And as they danced to the pulsing beat she kept waiting

for a hotel to appear, or a bed—something to blot out what he'd said.

He was never coming back.

Oh, make that maybe once.

This really was all they'd have.

It was a winding drive home, and Juliet felt her eyes grow heavy.

'Sleep,' he told her.

'No, it's rude.'

Not only that—she didn't want to miss a moment.

'We haven't sorted out your boss…' he said.

'I'll sort her…' She gave a weary sigh. 'I'm going to get up earlier each day to fit the chores in, and I'll use the rooms at school for practice.'

'Aren't you already doing that?'

'Yes,' she agreed, leaning her head on the window, wishing they could turn the car around and go back. 'But once my exams are done…'

She didn't finish her sentence, and as she dozed Sev glanced over a couple of times, seeing her there, sandy and her limbs pink, as the streetlights flashed.

Thinking.

About leaving.

About coming home for the last time.

About her.

They passed through Casadio land—row after row of vines. Some planted when his parents had been born…others when he and Dante had.

They passed the entrance to the winery…passed Villa Casadio, where Christos lived.

Then they passed the De Santis winery, where Rosa's family still lived, and again he glanced over to where Juliet slept.

Her legs were stretched out, her head in an awkward position, and he reached out an arm and moved her a little, then reclined her seat. He let her sleep, resisting the urge to wake her, to tell her about his doubts about Rosa's pregnancy that lived only in his head.

He drove past the church where they'd married...where Rosa now lay.

Where he'd sworn on her grave never to share his doubts with another person. To let her rest, lie in peace...

There was no peace for him, though.

She felt the motion of the car change, or perhaps there were lights, or the sound of the indicator blinking, but she knew the end of their time was here.

Her subconscious tried to be kind and pull her back to sleep.

She never wanted this day to end.

'Juliet?'

She stirred and gave a nod. She knew they were at Anna's, and knew she had to somehow brace herself for goodbye.

'Come on.'

She was still half asleep and not wanting to wake up as he offered his hand and she stepped out of the car.

'I was really asleep!' She laughed, leaning on him more than she ever had so far. She frowned. 'We need to get my things from the hotel...' She was fuzzy from too much sun and too little sleep and the company of Sevandro. 'Wait—this isn't Anna's...'

This definitely wasn't Anna's. There were some gates that he opened, and then he took her hand and led her through a neglected garden and up some stone stairs.

Even neglected it was way beyond Anna's garden...

Sevandro...or was it Sev—she still hadn't made up her mind which name she preferred—was pressing a code into the panel next to a large front door. The lock clicked and he pushed the heavy door open and led her inside.

'Where are we?' Juliet asked as he flicked a switch and a beautiful and very large hall came into the light.

'Welcome to Mars.'

CHAPTER SIX

'OH, MY...'

The house was stunning.

Cold and empty, yet beautiful indeed, its floors were marble and the ceilings high, and she could have happily lingered just in the hall. But she followed him and found herself in a vast room—again empty, except for an elegant chandelier that he turned on and dimmed. Little beams of light danced around the vacant space and she walked to the massive fireplace, where the mantelpiece was higher than herself.

'It's going on the market,' Sevandro explained.

'It's yours?'

He nodded.

'But why stay in hotels if you have this?' She winced. 'Or was this where you and Rosa lived?'

'No.' He shook his head. 'Rosa took one look and hated it—we never spent a single night here. She wanted Villa Casadio.'

'Where's that?'

He didn't answer straight away, just walked on, and although she would have loved to linger she followed him out, gazed into room after empty room.

'Look at this library!'

Juliet's enthusiasm, even at three in the morning, with the place cold and bare, was a stark contrast to Rosa's reac-

tion. Though it wasn't Rosa's view he was comparing it to—
it was his. The first time he'd seen the property he'd been
composed and impassive with the realtor, but inside he had
felt as Juliet now did.

She wasn't following him around any more. She was exploring back in the main hall, standing at the bottom of the
spiral staircase gazing up, her mouth open.

'If we go down one level...' he started,

But Juliet was already making her way up.

She paused. 'Can I?'

'Of course.'

'Sevandro, it is beautiful.'

She peered into a bathroom, tried to turn on the light, but
had to rely on the moon shining in through frosted windows
onto huge mirrors illuminating a central clawfoot bath.

'Oh, my...'

'I had a domestic team come in last week to get it ready
to go on the market. There's still more to do. A *lot* more to
do,' he added. 'Still, it's probably better than I remember it.'

Far better—he hadn't set foot in the place since he'd come
to visit Gio at Christmas, and even then it had been a cursory look around, as he'd decided to put it on the market. It
had been freezing then, neglected and dusty, but he rather
thought she would have loved it even so.

'The realtor suggests I get a few rooms styled.'

'Why? Anyone can see it's gorgeous. But you need a piano
in the lounge...' She gave him her opinion. 'And navy silk
couches.'

'Maybe... The main bedroom has all the original furnishings. I like it, but the realtor said it's a disaster.'

He attempted to turn on the lights there, but again they
didn't work.

It didn't matter.

'It's beautiful.' She walked around the large shadowy

space, touching a chaise and then walking over to the velvety bed. 'Why would the realtor call it a disaster?'

'I think it's a love or hate thing. It's red,' he told her. 'Very red. The carpets, the bedding, the walls. And when the drapes are hung, they are red too.' He watched her sitting on the bed and walked over. 'So, what do you say?'

'What do I say? That it's stunning and that I cannot believe you stay in hotels rather than here. And that this…' she sank back '…is the best bed ever.'

She wasn't even flirting. She was so tired, and the sleep in the car had served only to remind her how exhausted she was.

'I don't know what else to say. I love it.'

'I meant what do you say about staying here?'

In the shadowy light he saw her immediate frown, and it surprised him that it hadn't entered her head why he had brought her here. Her reaction to his home was pure, he knew.

'Living here for a while?' he went on.

'In your home?'

'It's never been my home. And don't worry—I'm not asking you to move in with me.' He laughed at the notion. 'But you do need some space, and these are important months for you. I won't be here—it's going to be empty. Maybe you could just come here to practise?'

It was tempting…so tempting. But it was just too generous.

As well, there was a deeper truth: she was developing more than a crush on him. It scared her how much she liked him. A man who was about to turn his back on his family… a man who was close to no one.

'I don't think so.'

He lay down too, and they stared up at the ceiling, then wriggled and got comfortable, just lay side by side.

'No, it's too…'

'What?'

'Too much.'

'It's just sitting here empty. You can tell Susie and Dante that we spoke at the wedding…that I need someone to open up and such while tradesmen come through.' He shrugged. 'I probably do need someone.'

'What about when you're here?'

'I shan't be here. I'll try to fly in and out for the memorial, but I'm not even sure I'll have time for that. The pace at work is crazy—and that's before we've even signed off on the project. After that, it will be worse.'

'Why, though?' She stared. 'We agreed on one night only.'

'We did. You don't have time for a relationship and I don't want one. But it is good talking to you. Having…' He hesitated, as if he didn't know what to call it. 'This.'

'Yes…'

'I'm not just selling the house,' he admitted. 'I have some loose ends to tie up—things I need to sort out. Hopefully I can clear the air with Dante…leave things the best I can. Who knows? They might come and see me in Dubai.'

'What sort of things?'

'You know that Dante and I fought?'

She nodded.

'Dante asked if Rosa was pregnant—insinuating it was a trap, a grab for our land—there's lots of history between our two wineries. I didn't want to hear it.'

'Of course not.'

'I told him he was wrong.' He turned and looked at her then. 'However, that wasn't true. Rosa had indeed told me she was having my baby…'

'That's why you married?

'Yes.'

'Had you been together for long?'

'We never dated,' he said. 'It was just one night. I had just found out I'd got the loan from Mahir... I was supposed to be celebrating with my family.' He turned and stared up at the ceiling now rather than at her. 'I'm sure you don't want the details.'

'I do.'

It was an odd admission, yet lying here in the semi-darkness, at the end of such a glorious night and day, she somehow knew this was the only chance she'd get to hear them. It was like collecting tiny pearls scattered on the floor, each one a treasure, and she wanted all the precious pearls.

'If you want to tell me, of course.'

'I went to the De Santis winery. I thought we were meeting there—I'm not sure if the message was relayed wrong. Anyway, Rosa came over. She'd seen my car arrive, and she didn't know what I was celebrating.' He shrugged. 'Things just happened...'

Juliet swallowed. She understood how.

'That night I was careless, and when she told me she was pregnant, that her mother had already worked it out, there was no question I'd do the right thing.'

'No question?' she checked.

'Some questions,' he admitted in the still pre-dawn. 'But I kept them to myself.' He looked over. 'I'd never expected to marry.'

'Why?'

'I don't know,' he admitted. 'It just wasn't something I could envisage. You?' he asked, perhaps needing a break from his own thoughts.

'I used to want to...' she nodded. 'When I was younger. But then...' She paused. 'I think my father's affair messed me up.'

'Or your mother turning off her love like a tap when she didn't like what you had to say.'

His summing up was cold, even a bit brutal, but possibly it was required, because it cleared the mists around that time a fraction.

'Maybe.' She actually smiled. 'You can be very direct.'

'I know.' He half laughed. 'So can my brother. The night before I got married, when he tried to suggest it was a trap, I didn't appreciate it. I think most people had guessed it was a shotgun marriage, but I wasn't going to confirm it. It didn't seem like the best start for us, and I didn't want our child knowing we'd only married for their sake.' He took a breath. 'So I told him to go to hell and we fought.'

She nodded.

'Rosa lost the baby just after the wedding. At least that's what she told me.'

Juliet frowned. 'I don't know what you mean...'

'I think I got so angry with Dante because I was already starting to have doubts that she was pregnant myself.'

'You think she lied?'

'I do. But I don't know for sure. I was about to go looking for answers when the accident happened.'

Was this the 'more' that Susie had been unable to talk about? Juliet wondered.

'Does Dante know any of this?'

'No. After her funeral he apologised—said he'd clearly got it wrong...'

'You never told your family she was expecting?'

'No. Rosa didn't want anyone apart from her parents to know she was pregnant until well after the wedding. After the miscarriage she said we could try again.' He gave a mirthless laugh. 'Even though we'd never tried in the first place.'

Juliet sat up on the bed, really thinking about all he'd said. 'So they all think you married for love?'

'They do,' he agreed. 'I've never wanted to fall in love and marry. I didn't then, and certainly not now. But when I messed up I knew I had to do the right thing. On a selfish level, having a wife and baby suited my career. Sheikh Mahir is very family orientated. We're partners now, but I was new to him then. He was very pleased I was settling down.'

'Were you upset when Rosa told you she'd lost the baby?'

He looked at her for the longest moment, and then nodded. When she heard him swallow, Juliet guessed why he didn't speak.

'I'm sorry.' She blew out a breath. 'I get it now,' she told him. 'I get why you hate coming back to Lucca. Can you talk to Dante? Tell him he was right?'

'I still don't know for sure, though, and it seems unfair on Rosa to speculate when she isn't here to state her case. I was thinking of speaking to her doctor. He stitched me and Dante up that night of the fight, and he said a couple of things that have always stayed with me.'

'Such as...?'

'My hand was swollen and he said, "Your bride isn't going to be pleased if you can't put your ring on." Then he asked how Rosa was. I didn't think anything of it at the time, but when I look back he was asking as if he hadn't seen her for a while.'

'What else?'

'It was small things... He asked if I had any questions for him. I thought he was talking about my hand. But maybe he was inviting me to speak about something else?'

'Could you try asking him now?'

'It's too late. I spoke to his daughter at the wedding reception—not about this, but I asked after him. She told me he has dementia, so that window is now closed.' He shrugged. 'Don't worry about it.' He pulled her close. 'Forget about it now.'

He wanted to get back to the way they'd been, and so too did Juliet—she didn't want them to end on this low. But what he'd told her was important.

'I think I'd tell Dante,' she said.

'Well, you would say that, wouldn't you?'

Was he referring to her telling her mother about her father's affair? Surely not.

'But look at the trouble telling tales got you into last time.'
He was!

'Sevandro!' She was jolted—utterly shocked. 'You can't say that!'

But he had. And she was so shocked that she laughed. And the fact that he *could* joke, and she *could* laugh about something so dreadful, was a revelation in itself,

'Spiona!' he called her.

That meant tattletale. They had a sort of wrestle as he said it, and it was the most inappropriate fun she had ever had. And as they play-fought it was as if she was banishing the sting of that day, making a new memory of it that would always make her laugh.

She ended up on his stomach, legs astride him, and she knew there wasn't another person on this planet who could have teased her like that, who could have taken the most painful dark part of her and soothed it.

'So,' he said, with a smile that melted her. 'Are you going to be my housekeeper?'

Was she?

'No strings,' he told her. 'You know. I don't do all that.'

'I know.' She said, and then paused. 'Strings are my speciality, though.'

He gave a half-laugh at her reference to her violin, but she saw that he didn't get what she was trying to say. Juliet didn't know how to say it, but knew she had to try. She was exploring the boundaries of her own heart as she looked at the only man she'd ever been with...the only man she'd ever wanted to be with. But there were conditions.

'I can't be your lover in Lucca.'

'I'm not asking you to be a kept woman.'

'I understand that.'

'If I come back for the memorial I'll stay in a hotel—no problem.' He gave her a smile. 'Unless you want me?'

His hands slid up her outer thighs, warm and firm, then back down, and then they moved over the soft, sensitive skin of her inner thighs and she saw the arrogance in his smile.

He knew there was no question she would want him.

'Sev.' She put her hand over his, stopped his sensual stealth and looked right into his eyes. 'If you leave now and meet someone tomorrow, that's fine.' She swallowed, because that wasn't quite true. 'It might hurt, but that's fine. We shan't have this again.' She removed his hand from her thigh.

'I don't know what you mean.'

'If you come back for the memorial and there's been someone else...' She shook her head.

'Hold on... You want us to act like a couple, yet we'll be continents apart and not see each other for months—not see anyone—all because of one night?' He laughed at the ridiculousness of it, pulling back his hands of his own accord, clearly not used to such demands. 'I told you: I don't do relationships.'

'I'm just letting you know. And if I do stay here, and I meet someone, I'll move out.'

He frowned.

'I assume you won't want me bringing men back here?'

She watched his lips tighten, and his eyes darkened as they met hers. Possibly he'd got where she was coming from.

'They're two separate issues.'

He was sulking, and he looked so sexy, but then he gave a small smile, undoing the buttons on her dress, untying the strings of the bikini beneath.

Toying with her naked breasts, he came up with a possible solution. 'You could come to Dubai now and then...'

He moved up onto his elbows and blew on a nipple.

'I don't have time,' she pointed out, closing her eyes as his mouth took it in, feeling weak, and yet certain, alight with so many different responses to him. 'You know that.'

'We'll have to make time.' He came up from her wet breast and looked at her. 'Look, I really can't come back here. And I'm not talking about family now. Work is about to kick off...'

But then perhaps he remembered her exams, and the reasons she needed to retreat from the world, because he cursed and lay back down.

'I don't *do* the couple thing.'

He was seriously pissed off.

'I'm not demanding anything, Sev,' Juliet told him. 'Just letting you know.'

He lay silent and she sat up, her thighs warm from their day on the beach, loose against his loins. They were both firmly in their corners, but united in their turn-on.

'Okay...' he half relented. 'I shan't lay a finger on you again if there's been anyone else.'

'Excellent,' she said. 'And if I meet anyone—'

'Please...' He gave a low laugh as his hand returned, pulling at the ties of her bikini bottom this time, playing with the titian curls there, then slipping his hand down and feeling her oiled and warm. 'I don't think there'll be an issue there.'

Oh, she wanted to give a smart reply—to tell him not to be so certain. Yet she knew it would be pointless, and she knew, even if they ended things today, it would take a lot of time to get over him.

She also knew, even as he stroked inside her, even as he withdrew his fingers and gave his attention to the swollen knot of nerves there, that she was much too into him.

'Nice?' he asked needlessly, as she moaned, and he told her with his hand that no one could ever please her the way he did.

'I want...'

Her thighs were shaking, and she gave a frustrated sob as he ceased in his attention, left her on the edge. And there she remained, hovering for a moment, as he unbelted himself, then tugged at the buttons on his shirt, exposing his chest as he rolled on a condom.

'What do you want?' he asked, guiding her on to him.

'This,' she said, trying to focus simply on the sheer pleasure their bodies made, moving on him.

He pulled her head down and they were kissing, her breasts flattening on his chest and his hands moving her, her cheek beside his.

'Move in...' he said, his voice husky, his fingers digging into her hips and grinding her down on him. 'There'll be more of this.'

She nodded, perhaps unseen, but it was as if she was re-assuring herself. There would be more of this...

The want, the desire, was all new to her, so deep and acute, and even before he was gone she was missing him already.

'Don't cry.'

She heard his words and knew that she must be crying.

'Cry, then,' he said. 'It's been tough for you.'

His voice was ragged. Perhaps he thought she was simply relieved that her housing and financial woes were gone.

She was crying for other reasons, though. For making love while trying not to lose her heart...

He was stroking her bottom, and she realised she was moving now of her own accord. Or were they both moving as one? There were strings, invisible threads lacing them, pulling her closer, opening her up, tightening her centre.

The sound he made as he released was a perfect note— *her* perfect note—and it had her tightening and pulsing as he shot inside.

Her face was on his cheek as she drew in a breath, waiting to come back down to earth.

Normality should be pinging in now, Juliet thought.

'I'm going to miss you,' he told her.

And she felt her lips pinch on tears as she wondered why he got to say it while she dared not.

It was starting to get light, and they both knew they had to get her things from the hotel.

As they rearranged their clothes he spoke.

'Take some time. Think it through before you tell Anna you're leaving.'

'I've already said yes.'

'Never believe or be held to what's said during sex,' he told her. 'Think about what you really want.'

He was businesslike now, as he wrote down the entrance code.

'I'll need your phone number.'

They went through a few things as daylight started to filter in and the room was tinged red, then they headed down the stairs.

'Listen, if it sells quickly, I won't hand it over till your exams are done. Is that fair?' he asked.

'More than fair.'

She watched him look around, perhaps realising that it might sell fast and that possibly he might never see the place again. She felt a flutter of panic—because he really was closing things down here.

'When do you fly?' she asked at the hotel, as her things were loaded into the car.

'Midday. I'll have breakfast with Mimi and Gio. Do you think I can get them to come and see me in Dubai?'

'Good luck with that!' She laughed.

He drove her to Anna's and it was still only six a.m. as he pulled up.

'This was great,' Sevandro said. 'I didn't expect to have such a nice weekend. You?'

'I hoped to,' she admitted. 'Though it did exceed all expectations.'

They shared a smile—their smile, the one that repeated their words back to each other—but no kiss.

'We'll keep it between us?' she checked. 'Especially with me moving in?'

'Sure. Anyway, I'll be in Dubai.'

'Yes.'

'But I'll hopefully see you after the memorial,' he said, because three months of abstinence was rather a big commitment for him to make.

And she got that.

'I'll hopefully see you, too.'

She felt like a different person as she walked up the driveway to Anna's. Dawn was breaking and little birds were chirping. She turned to wave, or rather to hold up her violin, but he had already gone.

Get used to that feeling, Juliet told herself. *One day soon Sevandro will be gone for ever.*

CHAPTER SEVEN

MARS WAS GORGEOUS at this time of year!

Or at least the version of Mars Sev had given her.

Anna hadn't been best pleased when Juliet had told her she was leaving, but soon she had begun moving her things and was now installed in the beautiful home.

In the week it had taken to work her notice, Sevandro had arranged for a lot to be done.

The dust sheets had gone, the windows had all been cleaned, drapes had been hung and there was a large grey velvet couch in the lounge, with a few occasional tables. The lights all worked now, and there were towels and new linen.

The room she loved the most, though, was the main bedroom.

It was incredible.

It wasn't just red, as Sevandro had described, but a blushing crimson—from the walls to the carpets, from the drapes to the bedding—with just the occasional splash of gold around the mirrors and on handles and such.

'How is it?'

He called her on the very first night she was there—although perhaps that was to check on things at the house, rather than to check on her.

'Gorgeous…' She sighed. 'Peaceful! I can't believe I'm in the middle of Lucca—I feel like I'm out in the country.'

She looked around the crimson bedroom, examining it

again now she'd turned on the side lights. It was the most
sensual room on earth—like a womb or something. All red,
even this huge plump bed, also dressed in crimson.

'It should be too much.'

'What should?'

'The flagrant use of crimson.'

'Is that how to tell me you're in my bed, without telling
me you're in my bed?' he grumbled.

But she laughed. 'It's my favourite room,' she told him.

And not just because it was beautiful. Because it was the
room where they'd made love, where she'd cried as she came
to him. The room where they'd spoken so intimately...

Her music flourished, and at the end of each day she filled her
schedule with little triumphant ticks, but it worried her that a
day only truly became a gold star one when Sevandro called.

More often than not it was Helene, his PA, who called to
inform her of tradesmen arriving, or photographers, or gardeners and so on. But every now and then there was the bliss
of his voice for a few moments—a giddy high, followed by
the comedown of silence when he rang off. And then a few
moments when she sat quietly acknowledging the rapid beat
of her own heart at the mere sound of his voice, the lift it
gave her night or day.

It unsettled her.

Even if she hadn't made all the right choices, and it felt
lonely at times, Juliet was used to relying only on herself and
providing for herself. It wasn't so much the fact that she was
staying in his property that unnerved her—she knew it was
temporary, and was simply grateful for the chance to give
her all to her music in these important months—it was her
deepening feelings for Sevandro that unsettled her.

She could ignore her feelings as she wrestled with her
exam pieces or attended rehearsals and caught up with

friends. But at the end of their brief phone calls, or at night when she fell into bed, there were moments of silence where she did her best to ignore what her heart was telling her.

You like him too much.

Of course she did, Juliet would reason. She wouldn't have slept with him otherwise.

You're in too deep.

No. Thank you, heart, for the unnecessary warning, but I know what I'm doing...

Susie and Dante returned, and they had a quick catch-up, but Susie was busy juggling her new apprenticeship at Pearla's, and Dante being half in Milan and half in Lucca, as well as being pregnant.

But she brought lunch over to Juliet one day, and they sat on the portico looking out on the garden that was starting to take shape as the gardeners cut back the overgrowth.

'Wow,' Susie said, 'when did that fountain appear?'

'Last week.' Juliet smiled. 'Tomorrow they're filling the swimming pool.'

Susie completely believed that she and Sev had simply come to an arrangement about the house. The thought of her and Sev in a relationship of any sort had obviously been instantly dismissed. It was clearly easier to believe she was just the temporary housekeeper.

'Does it disturb your practice?' Susie asked. 'All these workmen?'

'No.' Juliet shook her head. 'And it's nice knowing they don't care about my noise. There's a basement room if it gets too much—it looks like it was a dance studio. I take myself down there sometimes, but for the most part...'

For the most part life was perfect. All the problems she'd had were gone. But nature did indeed love a void, and now she had a whole new set of concerns.

'Sev has asked Gio and Mimi if they would consider Christmas in Dubai,' Susie told her. 'Dante doesn't think Sev's ever coming back.'

Juliet chewed on a fat strawberry and tried to think what she might have said if she and Sev hadn't shared so much—if she didn't know so much.

'Well, he'll be coming back here to see the baby.'

'I don't think so…' Susie sighed. 'He told Dante that he doesn't know if he'll even be able to get back for the memorial.'

'Surely…?'

Juliet halted herself in her delving and asking for more details, but surely Susie had it wrong. She tried to keep her question vague, and not reveal the panic at the thought of not even seeing him one final time.

'It's the ten-year memorial, isn't it?'

'Yes,' Susie confirmed. 'But he's busy with work, apparently. How cold is that?'

Juliet didn't ask Sev about it when they spoke—didn't ask him to confirm if he was coming home one last time.

Perhaps she was too scared of his answer and having to face her feelings. It felt safer and certainly more sensible to focus on her music…to utilise this golden opportunity.

Occasionally she called him—usually regarding the house, or the garden. But on the eve of her first exam it was for a very personal reason that Juliet rang him, bracing herself to get his voicemail, unsure if she was right to interfere.

'Ready for your exam?' he asked.

'I hope so. What are you doing?'

'Looking at a gap in the skyline.'

'The one you and Sheikh Mahir are hoping to fill?'

He'd told her a little about the dazzling complex that he was aiming to get off the ground.

'It sounds incredible,' she said.

'I'll send you a picture.'

He did, and she stared at the beautiful Dubai skyline he gazed upon tonight.

'Did you get it?' he asked.

'Yes...'

He wanted to know what she thought—wanted to know if he should be thinking the way he was.

'What do you think?' he pressed.

'It's stunning,' she said. 'Are you outside now?'

'Yes—just having a drink on the balcony... We're hoping to sign off on it all soon.'

'How soon?'

'A few weeks...then life gets even busier.'

She guessed that meant no trips to Lucca—not even for the memorial. He was shifting his base to Dubai completely, and she felt teary all of a sudden, nervous about what she had to say.

'Sev, the reason I called... Look, I don't know if I should say anything...'

'Is Susie asking awkward questions?'

'No, she's delighted that I've got somewhere to stay and that your home's being taken care of.' She took a breath. 'I went to the doctor a couple of weeks ago.'

'You're okay?'

She heard the cautious note in his voice and it was merited, given what had happened with Rosa, and how careful they'd been.

'Absolutely fine,' she told him.

Should she tell him she'd gone on the Pill? That she ached for it to be the day of the memorial, a few weeks from now? That she so badly wanted it to be a day he actually dreaded?

How selfish was that?

'So, what are you telling me?' he asked.

'I think the doctor was the lady you were talking to at the wedding.'

'Ella?' he checked.

'I think so... Is she the daughter of the doctor you were telling me about?' She heard only silence. 'Could you maybe speak with her about Rosa?'

'She wasn't practising ten years ago.'

Juliet was flustered. 'I guess not... It was just a thought... maybe there are old notes?'

'Yes.'

He was still a bit terse, but Juliet knew he was thinking about what she'd said. The silence was a long one, and she wondered if she shouldn't have said anything, just let it go.

'I'll let you get back to your skyline,' she told him.

'Good luck tomorrow.'

Sevandro did get back to the skyline, but his thoughts were of home. Not so much of the past, but the present.

Telling Juliet about Rosa had changed things—she was the first person he'd opened up to...the first person to hear his doubts about the baby.

For a decade he'd thought it best to leave things alone, but her gentle enquiry today had matched his own thoughts, her call a quiet confirmation of what he'd felt on Dante's wedding night.

He needed to know.

And not just for himself.

He thought of the grief that came around each and every year—the hollow feeling when he didn't know if he was thinking of a child who'd be almost ten or a wife who'd lied. Rather than take to whisky, he always made sure he worked impossibly late as the date approached, and in the days after, burying himself in work rather than dealing with the past.

No more.

* * *

Sevandro didn't call to check how her exam had gone.

Nor did he call the next day.

Or the next.

Weeks were flying...summer was fading.

And of course it wasn't a romance—because there were no texts, few calls... In truth, there was nothing.

To celebrate her final exam she and Susie decided on a catch-up lunch at Pearla's. Such an extravagance would have been unthinkable a few short weeks ago, but things were going well. So well that for the first time in ages Juliet had bought new clothes that had nothing to do with work—a navy linen dress that buttoned up the front and was smart enough for auditions and lunch with a friend.

'Oh, it's so good to see you!' Susie hugged her.

'It's brilliant to be out,' Juliet admitted. 'It feels like I've been shut away.'

'You have been.'

'Susie!' Everyone in the kitchen seemed to cry out in unison as they entered. 'We miss you.'

'I miss you too,' she said. 'I'll come over for a chat in a minute.'

First, though, they took their seats.

'Have you finished up here?' Juliet checked, knowing that Susie had wanted to do a few more weeks at the restaurant before she went on maternity leave.

'I spoke to Cuoco yesterday and told him I have to stop.'

'Everything's okay?'

'Of course! We're just so busy, with Dante between here and Milan and the winery... I'll be back next year, once the baby's here.' She patted her very nice bump. 'How were the exams?'

'I think they went okay... Well, I know a couple of them went really well.'

'And rehearsals?'

'They start next week,' Juliet said, then crossed her fingers. 'I'm practising loads.'

'You'll be wonderful—we can't wait.'

It wasn't just that Juliet's accommodation was sorted and her exams were over. Bookings for the ensemble were picking up, the weeks and months ahead were starting to be filled in, and she was starting to believe that she might be able to support herself in the town she loved with her music.

They chatted about everything and nothing, and it was so lovely to catch up.

Juliet was adamant that they went halves. 'Susie, please,' she said. 'I am finally making headway, and I don't want you paying for everything when we're out.'

'I wouldn't have said Pearla's in that case.'

'Then I wouldn't have had the best truffle carbonara!' Juliet beamed. 'And you do get a staff discount!'

'True!'

'Now I have to dash. I need to pay the rent.'

'Sev's *charging* you?'

'No!' She laughed. 'For my violin.'

'He's out with Dante right now...'

'Sorry?' Juliet was sure she'd misheard.

'Sev's home. Well, he's in his usual hotel,' Susie said. 'He flew in yesterday, apparently, and asked Dante if they could catch up.'

'That's nice...'

Juliet didn't know what else to say, or even how she felt. Sev was here in Lucca and she didn't even know.

They said goodbye, but just before Susie went to talk to her colleagues she changed her mind. 'Oh, I forgot...'

'What?'

'Gio's decided to go all out for the memorial.'

'Oh.' She thought about how Sev was already dreading it, and then was startled as Susie spoke on.

'Can you guys play?'

'Us?'

'Of course. Gio won't hear of anyone else.'

She told her the date and Juliet didn't quite know what to say.

'Do you already have a booking?' asked Susie. 'Or…?'

'I'm not sure…' She honestly didn't know what to do. 'Let me check with Louanna—she deals with that side of things.'

Louanna would jump at the chance, and of course the prospect should be churning her up as she walked. But instead the fact that Sev was here in Lucca was her biggest issue now.

Sevandro was here and she hadn't even known.

She took out her phone—not to call him, but to see if there had been any attempt by him to contact her.

'Look where you're going,' a deeply sexy voice said.

And then she felt his hand on her elbow and she wanted to turn and collapse with relief into his arms.

But that would be pathetic—and, more than that, she didn't know who or what they were any more.

'Sev!' She snapped on a smile. 'I didn't know you were back,' she said. 'Susie mentioned it—we just had lunch.'

'What are you up to?' he asked.

'I need to get some rosin…pay my violin rent…'

'Will it take long?'

'No.'

'I'll come with you.'

She really wanted the calm and dark of Signor's to help her collect her thoughts.

'This is my favourite place in the world,' she told Sev.

She smiled, and pushed open the door, hit by the gorgeous scents of wood and varnish.

'Juliet?' a voice called. 'I'll be with you soon.'

'Is it a shop?' asked Sev.

'A workshop, really. He's a luthier. He does all the repairs and makes instruments too.'

Sevandro had never even glanced in the window, but now he was here he looked at this rather odd place that seemed to belong in another century.

He looked at the sign above the counter.

A table, a chair, a bowl of fruit and a violin; what else does a man need to be happy?

Albert Einstein

'I'd need a bit more than that,' he quipped, for Juliet's ears, but a very old man came out and shot him a look, then smiled for the lovely Juliet.

They spoke for ever about her exams, and how well the ensemble were doing.

'We even took a booking for Christmas,' she told him.

And then he asked her about the opera she was rehearsing for.

She had a life here, thought Sev. A good one. And on this day especially he simply could not envisage ever having his own here.

His head was pounding, the scent of varnish too much, and after all that he had found out yesterday, and Dante's reaction today, he had bile churning in his stomach.

Sev glanced at his watch. His flight left soon…

Juliet could almost feel his impatience, and even Signor noted it for he gave her a glance. But finally her rent was paid and they were heading back to the house.

Juliet wondered if he'd even have dropped in had they not crossed paths.

'You'll see a lot of changes,' she said as they arrived at the gates. 'The garden's—'

'I haven't got time for a tour,' he told her. 'I have to fly at five.'

'You should have said. I could have gone to Signor's another time.'

'I don't expect you to drop everything just because I show up.'

'So what exactly *do* you expect, Sev?' Juliet asked, surprising herself with her own boldness.

But his sudden appearance was unsettling. Her exams were done, her life was moving in the right direction, and she did not want an uncertain relationship destabilising that. If she was even allowed to call it a relationship.

'I get that we've made no real commitment…but to not even tell me you're back in the country…'

She looked at him, wanting to be able to say just how much she'd missed him, wanting to do all the normal things a lover might do—only his sudden appearance and his lack of communication with her only proved how far apart they were. Clearly she didn't factor into his days in the way he did hers.

'Imagine if you bumped into me in Dubai and I hadn't so much as told you I was there.'

'I'd be delighted.'

'Really?' she retorted disbelievingly.

'Juliet, you had your final exam yesterday. I didn't want to interfere with that.'

'I didn't realise you were so thoughtful.'

He gave a black smile. 'I assume that's you being sarcastic?'

'Yes,' she admitted, then closed her eyes, hating this row, trying to push aside her insecurities.

She opened her eyes and met his, almost scared by the relief she felt to be held in his gaze, and she registered properly, right then, how much she'd missed him. Every single day. The only reprieve had been when she was lost in her music.

'Look, it's good that you're here,' she told him.

'For eight more minutes.'

'It won't take long. I was going to call... I've got something to ask you. It's a bit awkward.'

'I don't *do* awkward,' he said.

'You'll just have to say if it's an issue.'

She knew he most certainly would.

'Of course.'

'Gio has asked us to play at the memorial.'

'What?' His voice was like the crack of a whip.

'I think it's going to be a bit of an event...'

'What the hell's Gio doing?' His jaw gritted. 'I don't even know if I'll be there.'

'So I heard.'

'What do you want, Juliet?' He came over to her, his eyes more black than silver. 'Should Helene send you my itinerary? Do I have to relay to you some half-conversation I've had with my brother?'

Sevandro halted. His anger was not aimed at Juliet. He had known it would be foolish to come here, and the reason for his visit was not one he'd intended to share with her—at least not face to face.

Yet here they were.

'Look, take the booking,' he said, trying to keep his voice even. 'It's no problem for me.'

He paused, about to say he'd always hoped she'd be there, but it sounded too much.

'I assumed you'd be there anyway,' he said. 'You've been at every recent family event, after all.'

'Assumed?'

He watched her eyes narrow at his choice of word, felt

her anger as she approached, and he liked the way she contained herself, how her lips pressed together, how she did not evade the issues.

God, he admired that a lot.

'The last time I performed for your family,' she said tartly, 'we weren't sleeping together.'

And when he should do the sensible thing—tell her why he was here, and about all the hell of the past two days—instead he caved, reverted to ways of old. Because it was so much easier to reach for her, to hold her hips and bring her closer.

'How about now?' he said.

There was no question as to what he was suggesting.

She could feel that he was angry and turned on as he kissed her, but so too was she.

This deep, hard kiss, thorough and intense, with his hands pulling her in, his energy drawing her into his vortex, was a kiss such as she'd never known.

His jaw was rough on her skin and his hands were between them, undoing the belt of her dress, lifting the skirt. She felt a lick of excitement, as if the craving of recent weeks was about to be banished.

But as abruptly as it had started he halted things, pressed their foreheads together, his breathing ragged.

'I ought to go.'

He must go.

There was no way he could stay.

He'd done far too much of using sex as a quick anaesthetic, and he'd sworn to do better by her.

'I really do have to go.'

'Do you?'

'I don't think me dropping in for angry sex is a good idea,' he said.

'Angry?'

'Yes. Not with you,' he added. 'But there's no tenderness in me today, and I think you'd regret it.'

'Maybe…'

She nodded, suddenly confused. Because she wanted him so badly and somehow he was taking care of her. Because, yes, she might well have regretted it about ten minutes from now, when he walked out through the door. But still there was this strain and desire and ache between them…this longing, still there.

'I don't know,' she admitted.

'I'm trying to be better.'

'Better?'

She could feel her heart hammering, hear his ragged breath, and she knew she'd just glimpsed the escape of rapid sex. She understood now what he'd been inviting her to partake in that first night.

Sex.

Pure escape.

With Sevandro the thought didn't scare her, and yet he'd closed that door to them—chosen a path he generally ignored.

And then he told her why he was here.

'I had lunch with Ella yesterday.'

'The doctor?'

He nodded. 'After we spoke, I called her.'

They were standing together, but no longer entwined. Her dress slipped back down and the dark passion of before was replaced by the pain of real conversation.

'I told her that I had doubts about Rosa's pregnancy. She seemed reluctant to discuss it…reminded me of her oath… but then she asked how it was affecting me. And the truth is that it *is* affecting me—even more so of late.' He took a breath. 'Do you remember you asked me if I was upset when Rosa lost the baby?'

Juliet barely nodded, but her eyes must have told him that absolutely she did, and also recalled how he'd nodded, but said no more.

Now he did say more.

'I was devastated. The baby was the reason we'd married, and though it sounds a shaky reason, I was determined to make it work. Now, when each anniversary rolls around, I don't know if I'm mourning or...'

She nodded. 'I know the memorial's approaching—'

'I'm talking about the anniversary of Rosa's miscarriage!'

Juliet's breath hitched as he interrupted angrily, though she knew his anger wasn't with her.

'Every year I think of what we might have had, or how old our child would be—and then I remind myself that I don't know if it even existed, if I even have anything to grieve.' His eyes flashed like flint, revealing a glimpse of the turmoil he wrestled with. 'When Rosa died I told myself to leave it... that knowing the truth wouldn't change anything.'

'But it does?' she offered.

'Ella seemed to understand why I needed to know and said that she would give it some thought. She called me back and said she would talk to me next time I was home. I explained I was up to my neck in work, and asked could we do it over the phone, but she wanted to speak face to face. There was really no way I could get out of work, without letting a lot of people down, but neither could I wait until the memorial.'

'I get that...'

'So Helene shuffled things about and I flew back. I got in at eleven yesterday and met Ella for lunch. She said she'd looked through Rosa's records but there was nothing she could tell me.'

'I'm sorry.'

'No,' he said. 'Maybe you had to be there to get what she meant.'

His face was pale, and she watched his throat as he swallowed, then looked back into his silver-grey eyes.

'There was no confidence to break because there were no records of any pregnancy or miscarriage. Rosa didn't see any doctor at the practice in the whole year before she died.'

'Sev...' Her mind darted for another explanation. 'Could she have seen a different doctor?'

'No.' He shook his head. 'I was told Dr Romero had taken care of her. I was in Dubai when she lost the baby, so her mother took her to hospital. She told me Dr Romero had said she should rest at their home, so they could take care of her. Lies...all lies.'

'I'm so sorry. Are you...?' What could she say? 'Are you okay?'

'I've been better. I was supposed to fly back yesterday, but I knew I needed to speak to Dante, and I needed a bit of space before that. So I had Helene move things around again and went to the hotel. Believe me, I wouldn't have been great company last night.'

'I don't need you to be great company...'

She halted, her thoughts all tumbled. She didn't think now was the time to reveal that she just needed his company. Just that. Wanted him good or bad. She pushed those thoughts aside and tried to focus on all he'd told her.

'You didn't have to be on your own.'

He gave her a look that said he didn't quite believe that.

'How did it go with Dante?' she asked.

'I don't know. He was quiet...'

'Perhaps it just needs to sink in.'

'Or perhaps there's nothing left to say. I think we're as close as we're ever going to be. There's too much water under the bridge for us to go back to how we were.'

'Could you stay a bit longer?'

She wasn't asking for herself—well, maybe a bit—but she hated it that he was glancing at his watch when there was still so much here for him to sort out.

'Just a couple of days? It might give Dante a chance to get his head around it.'

'I can't.' Perhaps he saw the flash of doubt in her eyes. 'It was hard enough to get these two days off.'

'Can't you tell Sheikh Mahir…?'

'It's not about Mahir—or Adal.' He looked at her. 'I work fourteen or sixteen-hour days. It's how my life is. And I don't get to jump off the hamster wheel without letting an awful lot of people down. It's like you,' he said, 'in exam mode.'

'That was temporary, though.'

Oh, there would always be practice, and her life would always be busy, but she couldn't imagine living at his permanent frenetic pace.

'I come up for air now and then.'

'I can't for a couple of weeks—but I will be back for the memorial.' He gave her a lighter kiss, a goodbye kiss. 'I wish I'd come here last night.'

Juliet was silent. She wished he'd been here too. Not just for sex but to be with each other, to be there for each other.

'You could come to Dubai,' he said. 'For a few days…'

He was so nonchalant about it—clearly thought nothing of flying her around the world.

'What? You'll pop me on your private jet?' She tried to keep her voice light.

'God, no—ghastly things. Mahir has one. I refuse to use it.' He smiled, 'You'd have to slum it in first class.'

'But will you be able to take any days off?'

'Probably not,' he admitted. 'But we could work something out.' He headed for the door. 'Think about it.'

* * *

She could not stop thinking about it.

He'd left her with a glimmer of hope.

He was all she thought about.

Even her music offered no escape.

Then again, Mozart's *Apollo et Hyacinthus* was so emotional—about youth, death, jealousy and betrayal—that instead of crying she just poured all her feelings into rehearsal...

CHAPTER EIGHT

HIS CALLS WERE RARE, but they still made it a gold star day, and her reliance on them still troubled her.

'How are the rehearsals going?' he asked one evening.

'Intense.'

She lay there on the crimson bed. In a couple of days he should be here—though according to Susie it was doubtful he'd even come.

According to her heart, he had to.

But then he'd be gone again.

'Am I interrupting?'

'No...'

She yearned for these moments.

They never referred to his brief trip to Lucca, but she wished he would. They were simply polite and a little formal.

Maybe there had been other women for him?

Perhaps that was why he had stopped kissing her when he had, and all these anguished thoughts were pointless ones. He'd return and not lay a finger on her—as agreed.

'How's work?' she asked. 'I looked at the photos.'

He'd sent her images of a scaled-down version of the new structure and it made her stresses about rehearsals seem small.

'It's incredible,' she told him. 'Well, it will be...'

'We're in the final stages of pre-construction,' he said.

She made herself ask. 'You *are* coming to the memorial?'

'Yes. Dante called and told me that Rosa's family are all going to be there, so he probably thinks I won't show, given what I've told him. He said that Gio would never have invited them if he knew.'

'Will you tell him?'

'Maybe someday, but not now. I'm sure you don't want to see the De Santises and the Casadios all kicking off at the cathedral…'

'No…' He always made her smile.

'Gio wants speeches—I've told him no. You were right. You don't need to hear me giving a speech about how I miss Rosa.'

'I don't care what you say.' Juliet sat up. 'And I do get how tricky it is. Please don't worry about me.'

'I've told Gio no speeches, but I'll do a reading at the cathedral.'

'I won't be at the cathedral. I'm staying back and setting up the instruments at the house. I think everyone else is going, though.'

'It's going to be big,' he agreed. 'I just want it over and done with. I'll come from the airport that morning and head straight for the cathedral. Then I'll stay for an hour or so at the drinks.'

'What if your flight's delayed?'

'Fantastic! Then I'll skip all that and spend the little time I have in Lucca sorting out your "first time" list. I still haven't wined and dined you, after all.'

'We had dinner in Forte dei Marmi and we danced.'

She smiled as they returned to personal conversation…as he soothed her fears. It would seem they were still on. And she didn't care right now if it was just for one more night.

'Oh, no,' he said. 'You're going to be fully wined and dined.'

'Good! But can I change my list?'

'Of course.'

'I don't want a picnic.'

'Believe me, you don't have to worry about that happening. I don't want one either.'

'I thought maybe…'

'What?'

'You haven't called much.'

'I'm trying to let you focus on your rehearsals. I know how important the opera is, and I don't want to land all my stuff on you.'

'There hasn't been someone else for you?'

'Why would you think that?'

'Because you came back and we didn't… I know you were doing the right thing—I mean, not just dropping in for sex, or whatever…'

'It wasn't just me doing the right thing.'

'No?'

'I didn't have any protection with me.'

'If you'd told me that then you'd have discovered that I've gone on the Pill.'

'Damn,' he cursed. And then he laughed. A low laugh, so seductive it was as if his breath was on her ear. 'I wish you were here…'

'I do too.' She was on fire just hearing his voice.

'Do you?'

'Oh, yes…' She tried to rein herself in. 'But it's impossible. I know that…' She let out a sliver of her heart. 'I can't wait to see you.'

'And you shall—in about thirty-six hours.'

'Yes.'

'And we can do all the things we haven't yet done. And perhaps we can talk. You know…ask each other questions we don't have to answer, but can if we want to.'

She took a shaky breath. Was she about to be told it was all too much effort for too little reward? Or…?

'I hope you get some decent practice in,' he said now.

'I will.'

'And I shouldn't say this, but I'm glad you'll be there. Even if it's going to be a hellish day, I'm pleased you'll be there.'

Was she just a diversion?

Something to look forward to for getting through the memorial?

It didn't feel that way.

She wandered around the house, knowing she wouldn't be there soon, loving every wall.

She thought of all the time he'd given her, even while they were apart.

This summer, even when she was without him, she had felt as if he'd been right by her side.

She'd hoped perhaps he'd change his flight and arrive in Lucca the night before the memorial.

He didn't.

Walking along the walls, listening to the church bells calling the congregation to the service, she heard a text land on her phone. It told her he was on his way to the cathedral.

She didn't know whether to send him a thumbs-up or a heart. So she sent both, watching the little pink heart zip off to his inbox while trying hard to hold on to her own.

Letting herself in at the staff entrance at Gio and Mimi's, she smiled as Cuoco came out of the kitchen in his chef's whites.

'You're not going to the service?' she asked.

'I am,' he said, seeming a little flustered as he looked around the kitchen, which had dishes laid out and covered, and notes hanging and timers ticking. 'Me and my team are all coming back straight after communion, but Gio wants us all to be there until then. There may be a little bit of chaos when the guests arrive, but I think we're ready to go.'

'Can I help?'

'No.' He shook his head. 'Don't touch anything.'

'I shan't!'

'*You* get to just sit and play,' he grumbled, being cheeky about her easy job today.

But then he took the cover from one of the beautiful plates and held it out to her.

'*Ricciarelli!*' She groaned when she saw the little Tuscan almond biscuits, so delicate and pretty. 'You're forgiven,' she said, sinking her teeth into one. The orangey tang as it melted on her tongue was sublime. 'I promise I'll only touch these,' Juliet said.

'You seem much happier,' he said.

'Yes…'

And it wasn't just because she would see Sev today. It was as if the pause he'd allowed them had meant she could catch up. Even if they said goodbye tomorrow, it had still been wonderful. That looked-after or looked-out-for feeling had stayed with her since Susie and Dante's wedding day.

It felt a little odd to be alone as she set up the instruments, though it had happened a few times, and it felt very odd to be alone in the home Sev had grown up in.

After collecting some of their equipment from the under-stairs cupboard, she walked through to the dining room and out to the portico.

It was too hot to be playing outside, really, and she wasn't thinking of her fair skin, but more of the instruments. She'd brought her old faithful violin, rather than the beautiful one, as had the others.

She carried things through, bit by bit, trying not to look at the floral displays and memorial portraits. But every time she passed it felt as if eyes were upon her.

She was being ridiculous. And almost to prove it, Juliet turned around to be met by the eyes of Rosa.

And, yes, it would take a better woman than her not to be curious, so she walked over and really *looked* at the other woman.

Oh, she had been gorgeous, with black eyes and beautiful black hair, and she was smiling, so happy and alive. Juliet understood that Sev couldn't be cross with her, that he still wanted to protect her even in death, because it was so cruel that she was gone.

Had she loved him so much that she'd been willing to lie?

It stung to look at Rosa, so she moved on to the portrait of Sev's parents. His father had been as dark-haired as his sons, and she thought he was wearing the cufflinks Dante had worn on his wedding day. Their mother had been blonde, her smile subtle, almost curious, and Juliet thought of her blowing kisses to her son in his school play, embarrassing him a little.

It was a fond thought. It made her eyes fill. And then Juliet heard the hitch of her breath—for it suddenly felt as if she knew...

Knew what?

That you love him.

No. Juliet shook her head as if to clear it, tried to deny what was being said in her head and in her rapidly beating heart. *I don't.*

Then she looked at Rosa, whose smile seemed a little mocking now.

Of course you do.

And then it was as if the golden feeling he triggered inside her had received its hallmark and was stamped right there, under the dark eyes of Rosa.

She loved Sevandro Casadio.

Juliet walked briskly from the dining room, her eyes a little misty, her face one burning blush, scared to fully admit, even to herself, how deep her feelings ran.

Her hands were shaking as she turned the key to the storeroom and stepped into the dark space. She leant against the wall, as if escaping the scrutiny of his parents' and Rosa's gaze, wanting to hide in there for ever.

She'd thought playing here today would be okay…that she could hold on to her feelings until he'd gone.

She was so wrapped up in her own realisation that she didn't even hear the front door, only footsteps, and she panicked that guests were already starting to arrive when she hadn't even set up.

Then she heard a male voice.

'Go and lie down.'

It was Dante.

Susie's voice when it came sounded strained and teary. 'I can't just disappear…'

'Go and have a rest in my old room. They won't be back for a while yet. Gio's going to be busy greeting people…you can have an hour. I'll be up soon. I'll arrange a drink…maybe something light to eat…'

She heard Susie's footsteps on the stairs, clipping above her, and then Dante calling for a maid.

'They're all at the service,' Susie called back.

It was a little awkward. Juliet would have stepped out straight away, except she could feel her damp cheeks. Of course she'd escaped to the cupboard to cry, to weep alone.

She wiped her tears, and was about to locate the light, when she heard Susie's footsteps as she came back down the stairs.

'Dante, maybe try to talk to him?'

'Susie, let's not do this today.'

'Then when? The baby's due in six weeks.'

'And your blood pressure is high. The doctor said to keep things calm. Go and lie down.'

Juliet screwed her eyes closed, wishing to God she'd stepped out sooner as this rather private discussion took place.

If it had been just about work, then overhearing things wouldn't have mattered.

It wasn't about work, though.

And it mattered very much.

'You can't clear the air unless you tell him.'

Susie was teary again. Juliet put her hands over her ears, because she didn't want to hear this.

'It was *once*!' Susie snapped. 'You slept with her once, and it was long before they were a couple. Rosa tried to trap you too—'

Her voice halted abruptly as the bell at the main entrance rang.

Never, ever, wish to be a fly on the wall.

Juliet stood in the darkness, her heart hammering. Not in fear of being caught, but in dread at what she'd heard.

Oh, she'd known on the day of the wedding that Susie had been holding back, but she truly hadn't wanted or needed to know—still didn't.

Only now she did.

Dante had slept with Rosa. And from the sound of it she'd told *him* she was pregnant too.

She'd stumbled into a secret—just as she had when she'd found out about her father—and she wanted never to have found out. To reach into her mind, into all her senses, and somehow erase what she had heard.

But it was indelibly there.

People were arriving. She could hear Cuoco shouting orders and the waiters getting busy. Almost on autopilot she found the light and dragged Louanna's cello out of the storeroom.

No one noticed when she emerged. If they did, no doubt they assumed that she had arrived with the catering staff.

'They'll be about fifteen minutes,' Dante informed her, coming over to help.

She tried to act as she would have done if she hadn't been here all along…ask the right questions. 'How was the service?' she asked.

'It was…' Dante thought for a moment. 'Tough.'

'Where's Susie?' Juliet asked—as if she didn't know. 'Still at the cathedral?'

'She's having a rest.'

Louanna and the others soon arrived, and as the catering staff took care of the last details the groundsmen opened the gates on the walls as they did their final tune-up.

Before the guests had even arrived, they commenced their playing. And Gio's choice to have the ensemble in the grounds was right for the ambience, if not the instruments, for as they walked along the walls it was as if the music invited the guests in.

The music was ambient, apart from a couple of more sombre selections, and when she saw Sev arrive her heart soared. She fought not to put her instrument down and go over, but then her heart plummeted when she recalled what she now knew. Instead of smiling to him or attempting to meet his eyes she focused on the score ahead and the sounds the group made rather than look up. But of course she could not entirely look away. He was shaking people's hands, thanking them for being there, and then he was standing with a tearful couple, and something told her they were Rosa's parents.

He was doing this for Gio.

And for his late wife.

Sevandro was the strongest person she knew.

She looked at both brothers, standing talking, and knew that if Dante told him it would surely finish them…

So it was time to forget what she'd overheard.

They commenced Pachelbel's *Canon*. Louanna played the same sombre notes on her cello over and over as the other strings played their own separate parts. Yet it was the cello that made the piece so achingly beautiful.

Dante and Rosa had once slept together.

Like the notes Louanna played, the words repeated in Juliet's head, over and over.

It didn't shock her—but knowing the secret scared her. She was terrified of blurting it out in the same way she had with her mother.

Yet how did she keep it?

How did she lie in bed with someone she loved while holding on to a secret?

Two secrets…

After all, he didn't know the depth of her feelings…

Sev could see that Juliet was struggling—so too was he. He would far prefer her to be by his side today. He was exhausted from playing the grieving widower, yet of course he would never bring a casual date to such an occasion.

They needed to work out what they were.

He didn't want to add pressure. He was more than aware that she was staying in his house, and he did not want the home advantage.

Nor to mess up her rehearsals.

He did not quite know what to offer or to say.

He just knew that it could not continue like this.

Susie followed his gaze. 'The music's lovely…'

'Yes.'

Sev took a breath. The sun felt too bright, but he offered a small smile for his grandfather, who had made his way over.

'It is all beautiful, yes?'

No.

'Sevandro, Rosa's parents are here. You have to make a speech.'

'I told you no speeches, Gio.'

But Gio was very old school. 'Do the right thing.'

Gio made his own speech, talking about his son and his beautiful wife and their gorgeous daughter-in-law. Then he called for Sevandro...

Juliet glanced over, saw the set of his features and knew he'd been landed with this. And she really didn't want to hear it, or make it worse.

'Louanna, I need to...'

'Go.' She nodded. 'There are headache tablets in my bag...'

They worked together a lot, knew when the other was off kilter and covered for each other—and anyway it was just the speeches...

Bloody speeches.

She was angry as she punched out two headache tablets and gulped water. Everything was spoiled. She didn't know how to get through tonight.

But as she went to go back she saw Sevandro going into a room. The same one he had that first night.

She stood there, thinking how she'd wanted to go after him that first day. The pull towards him had existed even then.

Don't tell him...

She said it over and over as she crossed the entrance hall.

Don't tell him...

She repeated it in her head as she pushed open the door.

'Sevandro!'

'Come here.'

His kiss was dark and passionate. His scent was familiar and the effect instant. She was undoing him even as he peeled down her knickers, and she hadn't known anything could be this desperate or instant.

His back was to the door and he was almost kneeling, but he was still too tall so he lifted her instead.

This wasn't how it was supposed to be. Tonight she was meant to be wined, dined and romanced. But the power of him stoked her own, and she wouldn't change a thing.

'Never again,' he said, his voice hoarse with suppressed anger. 'I'm out of here.'

She could feel his fingers digging into the flesh on her hips and knew she was moaning. She was grateful when his hand came to her mouth and she could sob into his palm as she came, and the groan he gave as he released himself into her shattered her again.

They were in a library, she realised as she looked over his shoulder. And although she should be blushing as he let her down, tumbled and shaken by the strength of their unleashed desire, she felt calmer...

'Okay?' he checked, and she nodded.

'Yes.'

'I didn't say much.'

'I don't need to know much.'

She didn't. And he didn't need to know what she'd over-heard earlier.

They didn't kiss, or say how nice it was to see each other again, or that they were looking forward to tonight.

That was separate from this.

'I ought to get back,' she said.

CHAPTER NINE

IT WAS DUSKY as she walked to the house.

The night she had longed for was finally here.

Her and Sev. Together and alone.

No flights to catch—at least until the morning—and no place they needed to be.

Now she walked along the gorgeous familiar streets towards the house she adored and the man she wanted to be with.

She'd felt a little emboldened after their encounter in the library, as if it had proved she could get through and not tell him.

But that had been a temporary escape, Juliet knew…

Tonight was about discovery…finding out more about what the other wanted, what was at the forefront of their minds.

She didn't know how she'd meet his eyes. In fact she felt sick to her stomach as she climbed the stone steps.

She was utterly relieved when he opened the door and she stepped inside, and he took her straight in his arms so she could bury her head in his chest.

'I know it was hellish,' he said. 'I should have thought…'

'It was fine…' She took a breath of him. 'Interesting at times.'

'Very,' he said. 'But it's the last one. I've told Gio no more. Forget about them all now…'

How could she?

They were his family, and she knew more than he.

But she pulled herself back and smiled when she saw he'd changed.

'You're all dressed up,' she said, glad to have something to focus on other than the secret she held. She ran her hand along the sleeve of his immaculate suit, a lighter grey than the one he'd worn for the memorial. 'Are we going out?'

'You'll see,' he said. 'Go and get ready.'

'Sev!' She laughed. 'I assumed we'd stay in. I haven't even thought about what to wear.'

'Your bath is ready.'

'Have you had a maid come in?' she teased walking up the spiral stairs. 'Should I expect petals floating on the surface?'

Oh, there was more than that. There were candles lit all around, and fragrant bubbly water, and a glass of Casadio wine.

It was all so perfect.

If only she hadn't heard what she had.

Juliet trailed her hand through the water. 'It looks gorgeous...'

'Enjoy,' Sev said. 'Are you okay?'

'Perfect.'

'Do we need to discuss what happened earlier today?'

'No.'

She was fine with what had happened in the library—had loved it, in fact. It had been far easier than being here, not knowing what to say.

She looked up and smiled, and thought she'd never given him a false smile before. She hoped the candlelight masked it.

'How long have I got?'

'As long as you need.'

'I need a hint before I get ready,' she said. 'Where are we going?'

'Somewhere we can talk.'

Damn.

'You're sure you're okay?'

'Of course.'

She stripped off and sat on the edge of the bath in a panic. Somehow she had to hold back from this man who drew her in closer than she'd been to any other.

She felt twelve years old again, with her mother asking why she was in such a mood. Only this was worse—far worse. She was twenty-five years old, and even if Sev might not want her love it was there, and she knew a secret that could destroy his fledgling relationship with his brother.

Spiona.

Tattletale.

That dawn he had called her that it had helped, and they'd laughed, and he'd been able to tease. But she just couldn't see them getting to do that over this.

What should she do?

Learn your lesson. Leave well alone.

Yes, she decided.

So Juliet climbed into the bath and lay there, and it was so perfect she felt some of the tension seep out of her.

Looking around, she saw the twinkling candles and had a sip of wine.

Why would she let something that had happened years ago spoil their night? It was between the two brothers.

Stay out of it, Juliet.

Yes.

She could do this.

Breathing deeply, she closed her eyes, and then she breathed in again and pulled up from the bath and wrapped herself in a towel.

'That was quick,' he said as she came into the crimson bedroom.

'It was gorgeous.' She smiled, feeling a little more like

her old self and confident with her choice. She frowned at a large white box on the bed. 'What's that?'

'A gift. I was going to lay it on the bed.'

'What is it?' she asked.

But almost the second she opened it Juliet knew. Soft, silky black velvet spilled out of layers of white tissue paper.

'This is…' She couldn't believe it. 'I thought you didn't buy your dates gifts?'

She was laughing, overwhelmed as she took the beautiful dress out of the box.

'Any alterations it needs can be done. It might be a little big.'

She hung it on the huge antique wardrobe and then found her lacy underwear—the only sexy ones she had. He took them, and she held on to his shoulder as he pulled delicate lace over her still damp skin.

'They're setting up for us downstairs,' he told her as she put her arms through the bra straps and he did up the hooks. He ran a hand down her spine, then turned her around and stroked one aching nipple with the back of his index finger. 'Do you want to do make-up?'

'No.'

'Not those red lips you wore that night?'

She went to the dressing table and put up her hair, and then she painted on those too-dark red lips. She didn't have to hide her eyes—this was just about them.

The dress was perfect.

It went on over her head, and she slid her arms in as he pulled the skirt down.

Then he led her to one of the many large mirrors.

'I love it.'

The scoop neck was higher than on the cream version she'd tried on, and this time her arms lifted easily. There were no pointy bits on the shoulders—he'd got every detail right.

'Oh, I can't believe you did this.' She smiled at him.

'You're going to play beautifully in it.'

'I hope so.'

They went down to dinner. Given the lack of furniture, she wondered where they would eat, but they went out into the late summer night in the cut back garden, with the fountain flowing, stars popping out.

'They want to see you in that dress too,' he said.

And so they sat, a little formal and awkward with the waiters there, but it was so nice to sit opposite him. To talk with him face to face about little things, nice things.

'Thank you,' he said at last, as the lightest lemon tart was served. 'We'll be fine now.'

Finally they were alone.

'How are the rehearsals?' he asked.

'They're going really well.'

'And the ensemble?'

She nodded. 'I think I might be able to call myself a professional musician for real soon.' She took a breath. 'I don't know how I'd have got there without this place.'

'You'd have got there.' He took her hand. 'You are going to be incredible,' he told her. 'I'm just sorry that I can't be there—and not only because I don't do double dates with my brother.'

'Perish the thought…'

She gave a little shiver and the real world impinged, just in a quick flash, with all the problems that awaited.

'Why don't you come to Dubai for a few days?' he asked her. 'We can talk about things there. I'll be working, but it will be easier than here.'

She asked the question she was dreading his answer to. 'You're really never coming back, are you?'

'I don't know,' he told her. 'I think things are better than they have been. The memorial went as well as it could have.'

And perhaps it was a culmination of the events of the day, or just a glimpse of what lay ahead, but her eyes filled with tears.

He took her hand. 'Stop,' he said.

And, yes, they did need to talk, she thought. But it had been such a wrenching day—surely they deserved to simply enjoy this beautiful night and each other.

'We haven't danced yet,' he said.

He opened an app on his phone and music filtered through the garden.

He stood and held out his hand. 'Please?'

Back in his arms, she was in bliss. She would always be happy there.

'It's nice music…' he said.

'Yes…' Juliet wound her arms around his neck. 'I used to play that piece.' Then she stilled and listened. 'Is that me?'

'Gorgeous, isn't it?' he told her.

'You've got my demo tape.'

'I've had it for quite some time.'

And now she was shaking inside as they danced, his hand on her back, her head on his chest, and he told her he found her music relaxing.

'I like watching you play,' he told her. 'I like listening too.'

He kissed her then, on the garden dance floor, until even the private garden would not do. Their lips were waxy with lipstick, and she loved his mouth dark and reddened.

Together they took the spiral staircase and then went into the crimson room, where they closed the door even though there was no one around.

'I've missed you,' she said, and they kissed, soft and slow.

'Undress me, then,' he told her.

And, while she wanted their clothes to somehow melt away, and to be naked beneath the covers, there was a different bliss to be had in this.

She wasn't sure she could stand still and steady if he was undressing her. Just stand the way he did as she removed his jacket and went to place the garment over an occasional chair.

He took it from her and dropped it to the floor.

Juliet was nervous—not because of him, more because she didn't quite understand what was required here.

'Your tie is…'

He smiled as she struggled with the knot, and she wished he'd kiss her, or that she could kiss the olive skin of his neck, but instead she went to deal with the buttons of his shirt.

'Cuffs first.'

'I don't know how cufflinks work.'

'That's fine,' he said, in a way that told her they had all the time in the world.

Only she could feel the energy in the air…could see his erection straining the fabric of his trousers as she dealt with the silver cufflinks. Even his hands were stunning—long-fingered, with neat nails.

'What about your watch? Should I take it off?'

'Please.'

How could removing a watch be a turn-on? How could exposing the veins of his inner wrist make her own skin thrum with desire and her mouth want to lower and kiss his pulse?

Now on to his shirt, and that button by his throat. A very sexy throat. She would have liked to tell him, but pressed her lips closed.

He made her feel light-headed as the fabric parted to reveal the dark mat of his chest hair and her impatient hands tugged the fabric up.

'Perhaps undo my belt?' he suggested.

'You're not being much help.'

'Very well,' he said, and kicked off his shoes and removed his socks. Then he stood still. 'Take your time.'

She was one burning blush as she dealt with his belt and

the top of his trousers, trying not to notice the bulge of him. Her nostrils filled with his smoky scent as she undid the last buttons, then peeled off his shirt down long muscled arms.

He took her hand and placed it on his chest, and she felt him warm beneath her palm. She wished her heart was as steady as his. Her eyes were drawn to his flat, dark nipples, and she drew her flattened palm back and stroked one.

Sev closed his eyes. Her slow perusal was a heady turn-on. And then he felt the wet of her mouth and her tongue tasting his nipple…

And he ached, his restraint becoming unbearable as her mouth moved to his neck.

'Juliet!'

She undid him and pushed down the dark trousers, struggled with the silk boxers and then freed him. She should finish the task, but she was too fascinated, watching as he stepped out of his clothes.

And there was Sevandro, made naked by herself, his narrow hips, strong thighs, black silky hair. She touched the back of her finger to his erection and then ran it along the base, turning her hand and feeling the velvety skin with loose fingers.

'Lift your arms,' he instructed.

'I don't want to,' she said, but she did so.

With practised ease he divested her of her dress, then he unhooked her bra with those skilled fingers. She felt the drop of her bust as he slid the straps down, and in a second she'd stepped out of her knickers.

'Nothing to stop us now,' he said.

And as they hit the bed there was so much lust in the eyes that searched her skin, although his touch was gentle on her breasts.

She didn't have to avoid his gaze any longer. His focus was intently on her, but in a pleasurable way, and there was nowhere to hide in his bed.

He kissed her so softly that it teased, and made her ache for more as his naked body weighted her down from the hips. But from the waist up there was still soft distance. He was up on one forearm and his mouth was tender, his hand stroking her face. There was no trace of the dark passion that had joined them this afternoon…his kiss was sublime.

'I've been waiting for this night,' he told her. 'Waiting for this,' he said, as he slid in unsheathed.

There was a catch in her breath as he filled her…a moan from him as he slid into her tight, oiled space, stretching her. And still he hovered above her as they joined intimately below, watching her.

'I've missed you,' she admitted, saying what she hadn't been able to the last time they'd made love.

'I know.'

He lowered his head and she heard his sigh of satisfaction as he moved within her, as if savouring the sensation, and she savoured it too—the feel of him deep inside her, moving within her, her body curling and arching, her legs wrapping around his.

'I really…' She wanted to say again that she'd missed him, but that didn't quite fit. Why did she cry when he was inside her? Why as he moved faster did she feel as if he were shaking out her secrets? 'I really missed you.'

'I'm here,' he told her, and he shifted, angling himself and delivering a pleasure so deep it made her cry out, had her saying his name.

'Sev…' She was a little frantic, the short word not enough. 'Sevandro…'

She could feel herself tighten, her neck arching back under the deep kiss of him on her throat, and now he was moving faster within her, each thrust a warning, urging her to complete.

'Juliet…' he warned her, and the growl of his tone told her he was close.

She pressed her lips together, unsure of the words she might spill as he swelled within her. As she watched his face contort, heard the groan of his release, she felt a flood of warmth and couldn't hold back. She just gave in to the endless sensations he delivered, her intimate pulses her only response.

He felt every flicker of her orgasm, deepening and prolonging his own, and he pulsed into her, then rested his full weight on the warm, flushed body beneath him.

He lifted his head and they stared at each other.

'I missed you too—a lot,' he told her, still inside her. 'Too many nights.'

She nodded. 'For me too.'

He pulled out and they lay together, and it was the closest he had felt to complete.

'We need to do something about that,' he said, as they lay sated and on the edge of sleep.

'How, though?' she asked.

And there was a tiny note of panic as she tried not to think of the oceans between them, or the closer problems they might have to face, not wanting the real world to impinge.

'Shh,' he said, as if was refusing to break their bliss. 'Let me sort it.'

And this was another moment of bliss.

To fall asleep in his arms and simply leave the impossible to him.

CHAPTER TEN

HIS ALARM WAS UNWELCOME. Pulling Juliet up from where she lay in his arms in a blissful sleep. Then those arms freed her to turn it off, and she lay in that gorgeous place between being awake and asleep, just enjoying the fact that he was here...

And going back.

'What time do you have to go?' she asked.

'Soon,' he said, and kissed her shoulder.

She lay still as he climbed out of bed. She sank back into sleep as he went to shower, but soon came the realisation that their one perfect night was over.

So perfect, she thought, wishing he didn't have to leave just yet. *Perfect apart from...*

There was a feeling of dread she couldn't place, but then, even before she'd opened her eyes, she remembered what she'd overheard.

Dante and Rosa.

She took a breath, tried to recover in herself the woman who'd been able to shut it all out last night, but it was right there in the forefront of her mind as Sev came back into the bedroom.

'I'll make coffee,' she said.

'No time,' he told her, opening up his case. 'Dante and Susie are coming to your opening night, yes?'

'Yes,' she said.

'Then there are four more performances?'

'Yes.'

She lay on her back, watching as he dressed, trying not to think about yesterday and get back to focusing on now.

'How about, after the performances you come to Dubai for a few days?'

She stared at him. When she wanted to nod and say yes, there was just this missed beat where she wondered how she could hold in the secret for days.

'Yes,' she said, but knew he'd seen her hesitation.

'When?' he asked. 'I'm trying to sort a couple of things out with work...with here.'

He sat on a chair to do up his laces but he looked at her as he did so, his hair blacker than normal from the shower and his eyes not leaving her face.

'When?' he asked again.

'I'll have to check.' She was trying to react normally, but there was nothing normal about the secret she held. 'If we've got any bookings or...'

'Check, then.'

She knew she couldn't lie for 'a few days'—and that would mean telling him what she'd learned. And she didn't know how, or even if she should. She wanted time to think about what to do, and bit on her lip as she picked up her phone.

'I thought you were just joking when you asked me before.'

'No.' He shook his head. 'I am deadly serious. Juliet, I'm trying to carve some time out for us. I get that you're building your career and that your life is here—but mine isn't.'

His eyes never left her face and she felt as if there was nowhere to hide. 'I can't see myself coming back here—not for months—so I'm asking if you want to come to Dubai for a few days. If we can't even manage that...'

There was no way forward for them.

She got that.

But they were so in tune and so honest with each other that of course he knew when she was not.

'Juliet, what's going on?'

She felt like an archer, scrambling for arrows to keep him back—a defeated archer, because she had no arrows and no response except a pale, 'Nothing...'

'Nothing?' he checked. 'Or is it that you would prefer not to answer? Because from the start we gave each other that option.'

They had, and she nodded.

'What does that mean?' he snapped, annoyed now and clearly not wanting to play any games. 'Can you look at me?'

She tried to, but his grey eyes were like a stormy sky, and she could see he was holding anger—who could blame him for that?

'Is there nothing wrong, or is it that you'd prefer not to answer? Which one is it.'

'I'd prefer not to answer.'

'Fair enough.' He pulled on his jacket. 'I'd better go.'

And he really didn't play games. Because there was no shared little kiss to pretend things were fine—he just took up his suitcase and wheeled it to the door.

She sat with the crimson sheet around her, recalling her decision never to tell him.

But then the thought that had helped her last night appeared again. Something that had happened so long ago shouldn't be ruining things now—and yet it was.

'Sev...'

His hand was on the door handle, and he paused.

'What?' His shoulders were tense, jaw gritted, but he half turned.

'There is something wrong, but I don't know how to tell you.'

'You just say it.' He turned around. 'What's going on?'

'I found out something,' she said. 'I overheard it...it's about you.'

Sort of. But it was going to devastate him, she knew.

'Am I supposed to be sleeping with Ella, just because we went out to lunch?' He shook his head. 'I know how people talk.'

'It's nothing like that.'

'Juliet?'

'Not so much about you…but about Dante and Rosa.'

'For God's sake!' He let out a half-laugh. 'It's just gossip.'

She shook her head, and something must have told him this might be real, because she watched the colour leach from his face.

'Something happened between them before the two of you were married. Long before.'

'Juliet, Dante has never dated anyone from Lucca. I told you…'

Then he swallowed—the same way he had when he'd told her there had been no baby.

'Who told you this?'

'No one told me. I overheard it. Dante thought Rosa was trying to trap you because the same thing had happened with him.'

'When did you hear this?' he asked. 'Who…?'

'Please don't ask. I wasn't meant to hear it; I wish I never had. I'm only telling you this because—' She stopped.

'Because…?' he persisted.

But he didn't need her declaring her love even as she hammered him with this news. And so, she bypassed the real reason and gave him the one that loving him would lead to.

'I think it's better that you hear it from me. If he ever tells you…'

'Why would he tell me?' he barked. 'If it's been more than a decade since he and Rosa…?' He briefly halted, but there was so much fury the unsaid word still hung there. 'Why would he bother to bring it up now?'

'I shouldn't have said anything...' She gulped. 'I've made it worse.'

'Worse?' He shook his head. 'You've made it easier for me to leave.' He flicked his hand, perhaps in the direction of the family home, or maybe Dante's. *'Bastard.'*

'Sevandro!' She jumped out of the bed as he reached for his case. 'Don't rush off.'

'I've got a plane to catch.' He shrugged her off. 'And now I can stop being guilted into doing the right thing by my family and by Rosa's family. I'm done. I'm out of here. For good this time.' He glanced over his shoulder. 'I might see you in Dubai if you can spare a couple of days.'

Juliet was too upset to cry—if it was possible to be such a thing.

She just sat in the crimson bed, holding her knees and waiting for the sky to fall. The genie was out—and, worse, she was the one who had let it out.

She thought of her parents—the fights, the rows—and of changing schools, losing her home, losing friends.

She cast her eyes around the crimson room, then climbed from the bed, peering out of the window as if expecting to see a convoy of flashing lights and emergency vehicles on the ancient streets. But there was gorgeous Lucca, bathed in a golden light, the tower and its holm oaks standing steady, oblivious of the changes surely to come.

Surely?

Yes. Everything she loved was about to be taken away.

Again.

'Corso Garibaldi...' Sev said to his driver.

A loaded catapult, he asked to be taken to Dante's address. He knew damn well where Juliet would have heard the secret. No doubt Dante had told Susie, and Susie...

Susie.

Pregnant and asleep, she would not need him pounding at the door...

'Ferma la macchina,' he ordered the car to halt.

The driver stopped the car and the world that had been spinning since Juliet had told him came back into focus— only with the twenty-twenty vision of hindsight.

Dante had been trying to talk to him. Not just on the eve of his and Rosa's wedding but in the weeks before...

As bloody as their fight had been, he'd always thought they ought to have been able to move past it...as brothers should.

'I'll be back in a bit,' Sevandro said, and got out of the vehicle.

He really was out of here, he decided. After today he would never be back. And so now he walked along the walls for one last time, and looked out to the mountains that had taken his parents and wife, and loathed the scoffing noise he made when he thought of Rosa.

But it was too hard to go there, so he loathed instead his smart Alec comment about seeing Juliet in Dubai if she could spare him a few days...

And then he gave up thinking and sat on a bench and stared out at the verdant hills that looked so peaceful but had taken so much.

Perhaps it was better to leave without a fight, so to speak.

He would never be back here—in that moment he was sure.

And so there were things to be taken care of before he left.

His flight would be taking off minus one first class passenger, he thought, when he left the little store in the centre of Lucca, having taken care of Juliet in the best way he could think of in such a raw state.

He was about to call Helene to arrange a new flight when he saw a flash of purple and stopped outside a florist's, looking at the citrus colours and blushing pinks.

There was no scoffing noise now when he thought of his late wife.

No more putting off what he had for more than a decade.

He'd never known what to say.

And as he stood at her grave he still wasn't sure.

Rosa De Santis

'You wanted to keep your family name,' he said aloud, placing down the flowers.

In Italy some women kept their own name, some took their husband's. It hadn't troubled him either way back then.

Now it did. Now that the red mist of anger was fading, he could see the influence her parents had had on her, and knew that Rosa would never have come up with that plan alone.

He spent some time there at the grave, his bile when he thought of his late wife gone. Seeing things so much more clearly now.

'What do you want me to do?' he asked, but of course was met with silence.

He thought of Rosa's fears, how she'd cared so much what others would think.

'Don't worry…'

He made her a promise he would keep. It was the best he could do for her.

'Dei morti parla bene…'

Of the dead, speak well.

He always had.

'I shall continue to do so.' This would stay with him. 'Rest now,' he said.

Peace made—at least with Rosa—he flew away from the hell and chaos of home,

And yet there wasn't the usual relief he felt when leaving.

Flying above the clouds, he kept going over and over things—not the past, and not Dante, not even his time with Rosa, or any of that.

Her words.

Juliet's.

'I'm only telling you this because...'

Was it love?

And if it was love, then where did they start?

Even in Dubai he worked ridiculous hours—had commitments from early morning till late at night. If the contracts all went ahead every minute of his next two years would be accounted for. How could he even consider plucking her from her blossoming career to a lonely ex-pat life there?

He couldn't.

He wouldn't do that to her.

He thought back to last night, their bodies still locked together, the closest he'd felt with another person, their souls searching for answers, for more time together and less lonely nights, and recalled the slight panic in her voice when she'd asked, *'How, though?'*

'Signor Casadio?'

He turned at the flight attendant's voice, realised they had landed without him even noticing.

'We're disembarking.'

Usually he was the first off the plane.

Today he would be almost the last.

Because Sevandro sat there on the Tarmac in Dubai, not sure where home was.

Letting himself into his apartment, he opened up the safe and took out the little stone Dante had given him. He held it up to the light, thought of his brother as a little boy in the jeweller's, always in trouble, always the charmer, always led by emotion.

He took out his phone.

'Dante.'

'Hey,' Dante said. 'You're back in Dubai?'

'I am.'

Sevandro waited for his brother to mention the memorial yesterday, or the conversation they'd had the other week when he'd told Dante he'd been right.

He was met with silence.

Now he understood why Dante found it so difficult to talk.

'How's Susie?' he asked.

'She's okay,' Dante replied.

And Sevandro found that he frowned, because he did still know his brother—at least a bit—and there was something not right with his tone.

'Just a few weeks to go, yes?' he said.

'Yes.'

'Is everything okay?'

'Of course.'

'Because you know you can...'

He paused. Of course Dante would not be able to tell him anything, or confide any fears about his wife. The secret his brother had kept had forced a wedge between them, and Sevandro could see things more clearly now.

Thank God he hadn't gone around there with all guns blazing. Instead, from the safety of Dubai, he offered better words.

'I'm always here if you need to talk.'

'I know.'

But instead they had a bland conversation, just as they had for the last decade—he asked about Gio, and the winery, and Dante asked him how the house sale was coming along.

'I saw the gardens have been done—it looks incredible.'

'I'm not so sure,' Sev admitted.

He didn't like how it felt now that the light shone in. He'd liked the dark space where he and Juliet had...

'Are you going to have it styled?' Dante asked.

'Probably.'

They spoke for a few more moments.

Just the same conversation they'd been having for a decade. Perhaps it was a bit easier than it had been, but really they still spoke as if they were strangers on a bench in a park.

Now he knew why.

Then he called Juliet.

'I'm sorry,' she said immediately. 'I shouldn't have said anything.'

'Stop,' he told her. 'You have nothing to be sorry for.'

'I am sorry, though. I called Louanna and there's a spare room in the apartment. The guys are going to help me move my things today.'

'Why would you do that?'

'Because we both agreed that my staying here was only meant to be until after my exams, and because I know that you're going to resent me for telling you what I heard.'

'Resent you?' he checked. 'I don't do that.'

'Maybe not, but it will change things.'

'What things?'

'Everything.'

'Change can be good,' he pointed out.

She gave a small disbelieving snort. 'I hate change! Anyway, I've got performances next week to prepare for. I can rehearse with Louanna.'

Sevandro thought what best to say. He did not want to add pressure, and the half-baked plans he had in his head would help no one.

He needed to think things through properly.

'Nothing has to change for now. You're not to let anything mess up this week,' he told her. 'Go and practise…go to your rehearsals. You certainly don't have to move out.'

'I think I do.'

'Is that what you want?'

'Yes. It is. Are you at work?'

'No. I'll go in tomorrow. I'm just thinking a few things through.'

'Did you say anything to Dante?'

'I just spoke to him,' Sevandro said.

Hearing her tense breath, he knew his decision to call Dante first had been the right one. At least he could put her at ease there.

'We didn't talk about anything much.'

'Will you ever talk to him about it?'

He evoked their agreement. 'I'd prefer not to answer that one.'

'Fair enough.'

'But I can say for certain that I won't be doing anything before the operas, so don't worry about seeing them at the weekend.'

'Okay…'

She didn't sound sure.

'Sevandro, I didn't tell you just to unburden myself.'

'I know that.'

'I wanted you to hear it from me. If Dante does ever talk to you—'

'He won't.' Sevandro shook his head. 'I'm pretty certain we're past all that. Can I ask you something?' he said, and heard her inhale. 'Actually, two things.'

'Sure.'

'When I asked about you coming to visit me here you were hesitant. Is it because you don't want to prolong things between us?' He walked through to the bedroom and saw the coffee silk sheets had been replaced by russet-coloured ones…the colour of her most intimate hair that only he had explored. 'Or was it because of what you'd found out?'

There was a long pause. 'The latter.'

'That's good to know.'

He could invite her to come now, tell her the offer was still there. But suggesting a few days in Dubai to celebrate the end of her exams and opera performances sounded not enough— it sounded vague, and not like any plan he would make.

And as for a lifetime here…

He looked at the gap in the skyline, knew full well the commitment it would take to fill it. He'd been heavily debating the same with Sheikh Mahir in recent weeks.

'What was the other thing?' she asked.

'Do you know how brave you are? After all you went through with your family, it must have been awful to overhear what you did. I am sorry you had to find out and be the one to tell me.'

'No, no,' she said. 'That's just it. I *wanted* it to be me.'

He didn't quite understand why she said that, but now Juliet had a question for him.

'Rosa…' He heard the tension in her voice. 'I feel as if I've made your memories of her worse…'

'It's okay,' he said, touched that in the midst of this she would think of a woman she'd never met. 'I've been thinking of Rosa too.'

He closed his eyes, stunned that he could share such a deep thought with her—that on this too bright day, when colours were too vivid and the world too sharp, he could somehow confide in her.

'I didn't go straight to the airport; I sat on the walls for a couple of hours. I realised it was Rosa's family. They always wanted the land…the wineries merged. There are feuds that go way back.' He could see it so clearly now. 'After the accident, when the wills were read, I remember how furious they were when they found out that my father hadn't owned a single vine. The winery was always in Gio's name. Even after her death they were thinking of how they could benefit from her.'

'Poor Rosa,' said Juliet, and then went quiet. 'Do you think she was worried you'd find out there never was a baby?'

'I was already finding out,' he said, and he held that un-examined heart that this morning had felt as if were being stabbed under a gentler inspection now. 'I would have got her away from them… I think she knew that.'

'You'd have been fine with a loveless marriage?'

'I would have been back then. I told you—I'm a selfish bastard.'

'You're not.' Then she asked him the same question he'd asked of himself. 'What if you'd found out she'd slept with Dante?'

'We'd have divorced, but I still would have got her away from her family. Well, that's what I told her this morning. I went to the cemetery and took flowers. I said what I did on the day I put her in the ground—that she can rest. And I think she can now.'

'That's nice.'

'Now, I've got a lot of work to do,' he told her. 'So, if I'm quiet for a while that's why. For now, stop worrying about my family—and good luck with the move and the operas.'

'Thank you.'

'Do *not* break a leg…'

She managed a shaky laugh.

'Juliet, it's going to be okay.'

It could never be okay…

He hadn't said when they'd see each other again, and nor had he repeated his invitation to her to spend those few days with him in Dubai.

She had an awful feeling she'd been let down gently.

That Sevandro had said goodbye.

On the evening before her big performance she sat with Susie at a pavement café, sipping Limoncello spritz as Susie topped up her sparkling water.

'How is it being back at Louanna's?' Susie asked.

'It's working out well, I think.' Juliet nodded. 'We're rehearsing a lot.' It helped take her mind off things...though not quite. 'I need it. I just can't...'

'Can't what?'

'I feel a bit wooden,' Juliet admitted. 'Technically, I'm playing okay. And while it's good to have Louanna pushing me, I do miss Sev's place...' She shrugged, refusing to think about the gorgeous home and its owner. 'I liked practising there. I could get into my music more.'

'Well, I doubt you could now.' Susie tore apart her *panettone*. 'Sev's getting it styled.'

'Oh?'

She picked out an ice cube from her glass and sucked on it, trying not to react, trying not to think of the gorgeous house with strangers coming in, and trying not to ask questions about Dante and Sevandro.

'He's not coming back,' Susie said.

Her ice cube crunched as she bit it, and she saw Susie's blue eyes sparkling with unshed tears.

'Apparently he took flowers to Rosa's grave...and what with his speech at the memorial...'

'I didn't hear it,' Juliet said, oh-so-nonchalantly, her face burning as she thought of them in the library. And then, breaking her own rules, she pushed for a little more information. 'What did he say?'

'Just how much his parents had enjoyed life... Rosa too. How she'd been on her way to Fashion Week...how they all knew that *la vita è bella*. Life is beautiful.' Susie sighed. 'Who says that at a memorial service?'

'Life *is* beautiful, though,' Juliet said, and couldn't help but smile, pleased that Sevandro had said that. She was proud that he'd stood up and respectfully said he would not play the game any longer.

'I was hoping that things might be sorted between Sev and Dante for the baby arriving. The wedding went so well. But really...' Susie took a breath. 'It's not all Sev. Dante shuts down too.'

'It's between them.'

'Yes.' Susie nodded. 'They were so close, though, and they both lost so much.' She picked up a serviette and blew her nose. 'Gosh, I'm teary.'

She looked tired, Juliet thought, and she felt worried. It wasn't her sixth sense kicking in, as it had when she'd first thought Susie was pregnant—she'd overheard her and Dante, after all, and knew her blood pressure was high.

She tried to ask in a roundabout way, but she wasn't very good at delving, and as they said goodbye Susie still hadn't told her of any concerns.

'We'll see you tomorrow night,' Susie said as they hugged each other goodbye. 'You're going to be fabulous; I know it.'

Oh, Juliet wasn't so sure...

It wasn't the best pre-opening night. She tried to sleep, but kept checking her phone, wishing her parents would message and wish her luck.

Not really.

She was lying to herself.

She kept checking her phone in the hope that Sevandro would call and she was trying to resist calling him, aching to hear his deep voice, feel the sense of calm he brought whenever he was near.

'You look dreadful,' Louanna informed her when she came into the kitchen the next morning.

'Thanks! I'm going to get some coffee...buy some more rosin.' She rolled her eyes. 'We've certainly been going through it.'

Louanna had been pushing her to practise, which was

good, but at times she could see the little frown lines on Louanna's face as she played. Could feel her worried glances.

Juliet wasn't playing well.

She was holding back, scared to put her heart into it for fear she'd completely break down.

She walked into the little shop that was her favourite place in the world. Well, it used to be. The crimson bed was now her favourite—but she was trying not to think of all that.

'*Signor!*' Juliet called. '*Sono io, Juliet...*'

'I won't be long,' Signor said from the workroom, and Juliet told him there was no rush.

It was lovely and dark, and so peaceful in here, and she wandered around, looking at the beautiful instruments.

'Are you ready for tonight?' he asked as he came out.

'I hope so.'

'Nervous?'

'A bit,' she nodded. 'Maybe not enough?'

'It's a beautiful piece, though rather dark at times.'

'Yes,' she said—because 'dark' was how she felt when she practised and she was scared to go there, to let loose her already off-kilter emotions and really pour herself into the piece. 'I'll get there. I just need some more rosin—and also to pay my rent.'

'No.' Signor frowned. 'That is your violin now.'

'It's not. I know my rent's due next week.'

'But it isn't,' he said.

And then the world seemed to stop when she was told her friend had paid her account in full.

'My friend?'

She thought of Susie, who kept trying to press gifts on her. But no, Susie wouldn't even know where this place was. Surely it wasn't...?

'He doesn't agree with my sign.' Signor laughed. 'We agreed to disagree.'

She glanced at the familiar Einstein quote and recalled what he'd said. No, that would never be enough for him.

'Sevandro was here?'

'*Si.*'

He went to fetch a leather folder and took out a ledger. Juliet stared at the figures and then saw his black spiky signature.

Yes, Sevandro had paid her account.

Yes, the violin was beautiful, and everything she had once wished for.

But really she was simply relieved to have an excuse to call him. She stepped out into the sun, almost folding in relief at the sound of his voice.

'Juliet?'

'It's too much,' she said. 'I just went to pay my violin rent and...'

'You weren't supposed to find out until next week!' He laughed. 'I hope I haven't messed up your pre-performance calm.'

'I'm not calm.' She took a breath. 'Maybe I am. I don't know... But I can't accept this.'

'Then donate it to a charity shop,' he teased. 'Or post it to me here. Of course you can accept it. How are the rehearsals going?'

'Not great,' she admitted. 'I feel...'

'What?'

'Like a fraud.'

'Fake it, then.' He laughed again, and so did she. 'You can do it.'

'I'm not so sure.'

'I know you can.'

For a sliver of time she felt their closeness again, felt warmed by his voice, felt emboldened and back on their beautiful Mars—but then he told her he had to go.

'I have to go into a meeting now. Don't break a leg.'

'Sevandro, wait,' she said. 'I can't take it.'

'It's already yours,' he said. 'It always was.'

He closed his eyes as his private phone rang again, telling himself to stay back...to give her the space she needed.

Certainly she did not need to know what he was dealing with here.

Helene came in. *They're waiting*, she mouthed, and he nodded, about to turn off his phone. But then Dante's name flashed on the screen...

Given the nature of his meeting, he had every reason to let it go to voicemail, and yet for whatever reason he quickly took the call.

'Dante, hey. I can't—'

'Sev.'

Brothers know.

Not everything—not every detail of each other's lives— but brothers who were close knew, and the husk in Dante's voice was reminiscent of a day long ago, and immediately Sevandro knew something was very wrong.

'It's okay,' Sev said to his brother, shaking his head at Sheikh Mahir, who had come into his office, and turning his back. 'What's going on?'

'Susie went into labour last night. They've tried to slow things down, but they think the baby will be born soon.'

'What else have they said?' he asked, and then listened as his brother brought him up to speed.

'Are her family coming?'

'They don't know. I'm going to call them later. Susie is quite upset, but she doesn't want anyone to know yet. I'll tell Gio and Mimi when we know more.'

It dawned on Sev that his brother had called only him.

An older brother was still required at times.

'She's going to be fine,' he responded with certainty. 'Both of them are.'

'You don't know that!'

Sev heard the sneer…knew Dante was scared.

'I believe that—as must you when you're with Susie.'

'Yes.' Dante took a steadying breath.

'Don't let her see you're worried.'

'Okay.'

'Juliet doesn't know?' he asked.

'Juliet?' Dante's voice was bewildered. 'I've just told you we haven't…' Dante paused, obviously remembering they had the opera tonight. 'We're supposed to be going to her opening night.'

'Maybe let her know you won't be there?'

'She won't even notice—it's a sell-out.'

Sev closed his eyes. Of course Juliet would notice. He thought of her looking up to the empty box and finding nobody there for her. Though of course Dante had far more on his mind right now and wasn't really thinking about cancelled plans.

'Sev?' Dante's voice broke into his thoughts. 'The other week, when you told me that Rosa had never been pregnant…'

'Don't worry about that now.'

'Let me speak,' Dante said. 'I need to say this. I'm going to be a father soon and I want…'

Sev closed his eyes and thought back to her words.

'I'm only telling you this because…'

Thank you, Juliet.

Now he understood why she'd said what she had about wanting to be the one who told him. So he'd be prepared for a moment such as this. So he'd know what to say when his brother finally reached out to him.

Dante cleared his throat, clearly determined to do this.

'I didn't know how to react. Or what to say. I've wanted to talk to you, but I've been worried about Susie. She thinks I should tell—'

'Dante,' Sev cut in. 'It's okay.'

'It's not, though...'

'But it is,' Sev said.

'No, there's something I need to tell you.'

'I already know.'

'You don't...'

It was a conversation that brothers never wanted to have, but the distance and the silence between them was killing them.

'Dante, I know about you and Rosa.' There was silence. 'I *know*.'

'How?'

'Doesn't matter.'

'How long have you known?'

'That doesn't matter either. It's time to move on. You're going to be a father soon. I'm going to be an uncle. Things are very different now. Go and be with Susie. If it helps, tell her that we're fine. Call if you need me, or call Helene to get hold of me.'

He could hear the shake in his brother's breathing, the same sound he'd heard in it at their parents' funeral, and Sev said now what he hadn't been able to then.

'Ti sono vicino.'

It meant, *I'm close to you*, or *I'm right here*.

And if he was going to be there for his brother, then Dante needed to be there for him too.

'Before you go back to Susie can you do one thing for me?'

'What?'

Sev looked at the time. Even if he left now there wasn't a hope of him getting to the concert, but he couldn't bear the thought of Juliet looking up to see an empty space.

She needed to prepare for that in private...

'Can you let Juliet know you won't make it tonight?'

'Sure.'

'She'll understand, but...'

'I'll call her now.'

'Thanks,' Sev said. 'Then get back to Susie.'

He sat for a moment, then buzzed Helene.

'Sheikh Mahir is getting impatient,' she told him.

'Could you ask him...?' He stopped, and thought of the board sitting there, waiting. He knew Mahir would not appreciate being asked to come to Sev's office. 'Could you arrange a private room, and advise the Sheikh I need to speak with him?'

Things were not going to plan.

Or rather things were happening rather ahead of schedule.

He'd wanted her performances to be over...for his work situation to be in better order...for him and Dante to...

That last one was already taken care of.

He opened the privacy drawer on his desk, and seeing the little gift he'd had made didn't jolt him, or look like a foreign object. He picked it up and saw the diamonds glinting and the one tiny ruby.

The perfect plan would have to wait.

Juliet needed him now.

It was time to deal with the *other* because...

He was certain.

Juliet had told him because she loved him.

CHAPTER ELEVEN

FLOWERS WERE BAD luck before a performance.

But Sev knew she wasn't superstitious, and so all through the morning and into the afternoon she desperately hoped for some.

She ached for more than his call this morning. She wanted Sev's reassurance...for him to tell her she'd got this.

She'd laid out her dress, and was checking she had everything she needed for tonight, when her phone rang.

It was, though, the wrong Casadio...

'Of course I understand.' Juliet was touched that Dante had thought to call her when he was so worried for Susie and the baby. 'Please give her my love.'

Yes, she was touched, and worried—she felt all of those things—but she felt so lonely as she sat on the bed in her old apartment.

She opened her bedside drawer, where she'd put her copy of the ledger, just to see his signature. That little piece of him...

But now, she read it properly—not the monetary sum... she dared to look at the date.

He'd paid this the morning he'd left.

And, thanks to Signor's meticulous record-keeping, even the time was noted.

He must have gone there before he got the flowers for Rosa's grave, or maybe the other way round...

It didn't really matter who'd come first.

He'd been saying goodbye to Rosa.

And there was but one other realisation she could come to—at nine twenty-seven that same morning he'd been saying goodbye to her.

The floodgates opened then—horrible tears that she'd held back not just since he'd left, but since the morning of the service, when she'd realised fully that she was in love with him.

Maybe she wasn't meant for love, Juliet thought, frantic with tears. Possibly it would have been better never to have met him than to be so raw and tender now, with her soul in agony.

She was gulping, crying more than she had at the age of twelve—because this hurt more than it had when she was little.

Really, she'd been alone since then.

And she'd got through it.

She was still here. Even if there was no one to see her... even if he was gone.

She was here.

She could do this alone—just as she always had.

And she was not quite alone.

She thought of Susie and Dante, who had such a wonderful reason not to be there tonight, and then ran a hand over the gorgeous violin that Sev had bought for her. It had felt like too much at the time, yet it felt like a comfort now.

Their time together had been wonderful, and beautiful, and everything she had ever wanted.

She would play tonight.

Enjoy tonight.

Pour all her troubles into her beautiful violin.

There was a knock on her door and Louanna came in with a glass of water. 'I'm heading off. See you there?'

'Yes.'

'You're okay?'

'I am now.'

Right now she had the biggest performance of her life—and, yes, the show must go on.

She slid on her new underwear.

It was gorgeous, but a little more *her*—silky, but plain, with not a bow or a shred of lace.

Then she did a light make-up—mostly to cover her complexion, which was a little blotchy from crying. Almost as a warning to herself that her crying jag had to be over, she put a little mascara on, and some lipstick, and then pinned her hair back from her face, but left it loose down her back.

The dress was heavenly, and as she looked in the mirror Juliet felt like a real musician.

'Come on,' she said to her gorgeous violin—the one Sev had bought for her, though she decided not to think about that right now...not with mascara on. 'You too,' she said, and took her spare and most trusty back-up. 'Just in case.'

Lucca was so beautiful as she walked to the *concerto* hall. It was the only place she knew where it was normal to walk in a velvet gown, carrying your instruments, and people smiled and wished her good luck with no real idea who she was. It was enough that she was on her way to make music in a town where it was revered.

Backstage was tiny and crowded—and the most exciting place on the planet.

This planet.

Mars was possibly her favourite other planet—but she wasn't allowing her head to go there tonight.

And then it was time for the orchestra to file out, and she took her place. She could see the hall filling up, glanced up and saw the empty box, but then quickly looked away.

Soon the buzz of the audience was drowned out by the wonderful sound of an orchestra tuning up.

She was here. She had made it. Even if there was no one to see her.

Then the conductor entered to applause, and the orchestra were invited to stand and take their own applause. It was a gorgeous tradition—to look out to the people you would play for, to invite them to share in this night.

She tried not to look up again to where Susie and Dante would have been, but foolishly she did—and then she saw him. Yes, it was dark, and, yes, he looked a lot like his brother... But she would know him anywhere.

It was impossible. She'd spoken to him just a few hours ago. And, having tracked his plane that dreadful morning, she was quite an expert in flying times from Dubai.

But he was here.

Somehow.

And even if she couldn't see him properly, she knew he was looking straight at her.

And then his head moved in that small nod of encouragement, and she wished to God she hadn't worn mascara.

Or perhaps it was a blessing that she had, because it forced her to blink and snap out of the gentle spell he'd placed her under and take her seat.

Juliet was magnificent.

She didn't look up at him once.

He could see her head moving as she gave in to the music, and while he didn't like opera—or rather he didn't *love* it— tonight he decided he did.

Of course he'd never tell Mimi. She'd sing him to death.

At the interval a fruit platter and some herbal tea were placed by a table at his side. Given this should have been Susie's seat, Sev realised he was being served her order. Thankfully Dante had ordered whisky and dark chocolate.

The second act commenced, and even while eating chocolate-dipped strawberries he conceded that he might come to agree with the old luthier's sign. Einstein, with a few modifications, might just be right. A velvet chair, and chocolate-dipped fruit, and a violin—so long as it was being played by Juliet.

He could watch her every night for the rest of his life.

In fact, he very much hoped that he would...

Be calm, Juliet told herself as she headed for the stage door. *He's here because of Dante.*

Probably he felt sorry for her.

But she was delighted, and she couldn't hide it when she stepped out. 'You! I never imagined...'

'You were incredible,' He told her. 'I can't believe I might have missed it. What an opening night!'

One kiss, she told herself as he pulled her into his arms.

She was weak for his mouth. His kiss was so delicious she had to stop and put down her violins so she could focus on the sheer pleasure of it.

They were going to sleep together. She knew that as their tongues reunited and his hands roamed the black velvet. There was a desirous energy to their kiss, and his mouth was so insistent. Their necks craned to be closer, nearer. He was stroking one velvety breast...

This kiss was far from a greeting.

But if she slept with him then she'd have to start getting over him again.

'I am not being your Lucca lover,' she said, peeling back. 'Any news?'

'Loads,' he told her. 'Come on.'

They walked down the cobbled lanes, holding a violin case

each and holding hands. She was wired, and happy, and simply refusing to let trouble spoil it. She licked her lips and his peppery scent was in her nostrils again.

'Okay...' she conceded as they headed for his house. 'Just tonight.'

'That was easy,' he said, and they both started to laugh.

'How on earth did you get here? You were in Dubai when I called.'

'I spoke to Sheikh Mahir...explained the emergency.'

'Was he okay about it?'

He made a wavering gesture with his hands. 'Not at first... But he's very much a family man, and he gave me a loan of his private jet to get here fast.'

'Ghastly things!' she teased. 'But wonderful when your brother needs you and there's a baby on the way!'

He gave her a very strange look.

'Juliet, I didn't fly back because of the baby.'

'Of course you did!' She laughed. 'You and Dante can both deny it all you like, but you love each other really.'

'I guess... But I'm not overly involved.' He gave a short, incredulous laugh. 'Juliet...'

But they were at the gates to the house—and, no, they were not having this discussion in the street.

'Inside.'

He pushed the door open, and as Juliet walked into the entrance hall she felt her nose twitch with annoyance—because, yes, it had been styled.

It looked fabulous.

Dammit.

So did the lounge. The grey sofa was gone and there were two large navy silk ones, and beautiful rugs like those she might have mentioned. There was even a piano...

'You liked my suggestions, then?'

'I did.'

She almost wished she'd never seen the house come to life like this. Now she'd remember it for ever, stunning and gorgeous and with all the things she loved in it.

'It's perfect.' She gave a slight sniff. 'You didn't waste much time.'

'No. I got Helene on to it the day you moved out.'

'The same day!'

'I was actually relieved that you moved out…'

The chances of her being his Lucca lover tonight were rapidly diminishing, she thought, and she was about to tell him that.

'We have a lot to discuss,' he went on. 'Maybe a few rows. This way you don't get to storm off so easily.'

'Why would I storm off?'

'Hopefully I've negated any need to, because I've been in some serious talks with Mahir,' he told her. 'I knew I couldn't ask you to come and live in Dubai.'

'Live there!' Her mouth gaped. 'Sevandro, I haven't even been.'

'I've been asking you to come.'

'For a few days!'

'To see if you like it. Juliet, I knew I couldn't ask you to give up your career, and I know you love it here…'

She was back in that audio booth again…or maybe it was Mars. Because she could hear his voice, and she was looking into silver-black eyes, but he was telling her about pulling back from billion-dollar contracts. Not pulling out. Just stepping back.

'When did you decide all this?' she asked.

'On the Tarmac in Dubai.'

'And you didn't think to discuss it with me!' Her mouth

gaped. 'Aren't we supposed to be able to tell each other any-thing?'

'We have our little amendment,' he reminded her.

'But I've been missing you. I was on the floor crying over you this afternoon.'

'You still made the performance,' he pointed out. 'I didn't want to mess up your preparations for the *concertos*, nor to discuss things with you till I at least had…'

'A plan?'

'I guess…'

She saw he was being very honest.

'My life was not geared up for two, Juliet,' he said. 'There wasn't anything to discuss until I'd sorted things out. How could I ask you to come to Dubai with the hours I work? And what if you wanted to live here…?'

She swallowed, realising what he meant.

Lucca was her home.

She'd built a life she loved here; her career was just tak-ing off.

'We could have spoken about it,' she said.

'We are going to talk about it,' he affirmed. 'I have no plane to catch, no alarm to set, and I have forty-eight hours.'

At first she laughed, because he spoke as if he had man-aged to carve out an entire month to focus on them. But then her laughter faded. She knew how big this was for him, and realised how much he respected her career—how he'd worked to bring the very best of himself to the negotiating table.

'So, this plan…' She was shaking a little. 'Sevandro, I would live anywhere with you.'

'I know that,' he said, and then he led her to one of the gorgeous navy couches, where he sat down and then pulled her onto his knee. 'And I knew if I was asking you to do that for me, then I had to be prepared to offer you the same.' He looked right into her eyes. 'I would live anywhere with *you*!'

Her breath hitched. 'Even here?'

'Yes.' He nodded. 'I can say that in all honesty now. Even here. I always chose not to examine my past, but with your help I have now, and I'm okay with things. I can live here—so long as it's with you.'

'You mean it?'

'I more than mean it. This is your home, and I can't wait to share it with you.'

'What about Dante and…?'

'We're fine. I am so grateful to you for telling me. I know why you did it. Because it was better I heard it from someone who has my heart in mind.'

'And I do.'

'Dante called this morning. He was about to confess, but thanks to you he didn't have to. I told him I already knew.'

He gave her a kiss that told her of his relief and gratitude.

'Thanks to you, I didn't say something I would later regret.'

'That's good.'

'We all know everything now!' he said. 'Thanks to my little *spiona*.'

Sev, or Sevandro, was so many things. He said what no other ever could, and he went to places in her heart no one else could touch, and he turned the impossible into a smile.

'I landed to the news that I'm an uncle. Dante and Susie have a little boy—Eduardo…'

Juliet felt as if she was spinning with happiness, and yet she sat still held in his arms.

'I'm an *uncle*.'

He rolled his eyes, but she knew he was both pleased and proud.

'And Mahir's fine. The agreement I've been trying to broker is that I will hand over more to his son. It was all very tense, but then I told him about you…about the opera opening night, and nobody being there for you. He came with me to the airport and we talked a few things out.' He pulled her to him. 'Juliet, *you* were the emergency he lent me his jet for. Dante and Susie were meant to be there, but when I found out they couldn't...'

'Seeing you up there,' she told him. 'It meant everything. And I didn't even know you loved me then.'

'*I* knew,' he said. 'I was getting things in order, while you did what you needed to.'

'You know I love you.'

'Of course—you were looking at wedding dresses the morning after you lost your virginity.'

'I was not.' She thought back, blushing all over again. 'No, I was not.'

'You soon will be.'

She gave an excited nod, and she thought this must be love because neither had to ask.

It was just happening!

'We'll get a ring later. This is to celebrate your first official first chair performance tonight.'

He took a little black box from his pocket, and she knew she really was being looked after.

The brooch was exquisite—a tiny silver violin, encrusted with diamonds. Her eyes were too blurry at first, but as she lifted it from the box she saw one dark stone...one little ruby for the bridge.

She knew it was from his mother's ring.

'I'll treasure it for ever,' she told him staring deep into his eyes.

'As I shall treasure you.'

He would take the greatest care of her heart.

EPILOGUE

SHE WAS TINY. With little knots of red hair and huge navy eyes that were attempting to focus as she stared up at her father. Her chin trembled, her sweet rosebud mouth quivered, and Juliet looked up to Sev.

'You're okay,' he told their daughter, whose chin stopped wobbling as she got back to attempting to examine his face. 'It's all just a bit new.'

It was a whole new world.

From her hospital bed, Juliet looked out at the stunning skyline. The Dubai sky looked as if it were on fire. The sunset was spectacular, lighting the buildings red, orange and gold. And there was the new father's work in progress—it was going to be stunning.

They'd hoped to have their baby in Lucca—but of course Sevandro had stepped *back*, not *down*, and Juliet loved it here too. He'd been right—there was a wonderful music scene in Dubai, and she was a substitute in an orchestra here as well as at home.

Home was Lucca.

Dante was running the winery now, and still trying to reel his older brother in. Lately he seemed to be succeeding...

'Soon you'll meet the rest of your family,' Sevandro told his daughter, then tore his eyes from their tiny baby. 'I can tell them to come tomorrow?'

'No need. I can't wait for them all to meet her.'

'Girls are easier,' Sevandro had said, delighted when he'd found out he was having a daughter and was not going to have to worry about all the stuff boys got up to. 'You don't worry about them as much...'

She and Susie had shared a glance, and Dante had rolled his eyes.

'She'll have you wrapped around her little finger,' he'd told his brother.

And now they'd messaged that they'd arrived, and Juliet took her beautiful daughter from her very calm husband.

He'd been incredible through the birth, even when it hadn't quite gone to plan!

Nothing about this journey had fazed him.

Well, if it had, it hadn't showed.

Yet.

'Are we going to tell them her name?' she asked.

'Yes!'

In they came. Susie first, her eyes brimming when she saw the newest Casadio, and Gio all smiles and tears too. Dante was holding Eduardo, who had dark curls and huge brown eyes. He peered at his cousin, then swooped in for a kiss, as almost all two-year-olds would.

'Gently...' Susie said, then swooped in too, and asked for a cuddle. 'Oh, she's perfect... How was it?'

'Worth it,' Juliet said.

'You weren't planning a Caesarean, though?' Susie checked.

'No!'

She was still a bit dazed, but so thrilled to have the people who loved them the most here on this day.

'Are your parents...?' Gio started, but Mimi stopped him.

'Gio, get Eduardo.'

Sevandro did it, picking his nephew up and making a fuss of him as Juliet looked out of the window for a moment, wishing her own family could have been like this.

She looked at the brothers. Dante was asking how it had all gone and Sevandro was nodding, explaining that she'd just needed to be born, and that perhaps she'd been a little flat when she came out, but she was perfect now.

'Good,' Dante said, and came over and looked at his niece. 'You scared your daddy,' he said quietly to the baby.

Brothers *do* know.

'She scared Mummy too,' Juliet admitted, then looked down at the little pink face and the one tiny hand peeking out. She was absolutely worth all the fright in the delivery room.

'Do we have a name?' Susie asked.

Sev looked over to her—just making sure—but they had discussed it at length. Even though Sevandro had frowned when she'd first suggested it.

'We do,' he agreed, taking the baby. 'Mimi,' he said.

Juliet looked at her, smiling in the background, staying well back...

'Sorry?' Mimi said. 'I am listening. I was just looking at her curls...'

'Her name is Mimi,' Sevandro clarified.

'After the opera?' Mimi checked.

'After you.'

They had thought about his mother's name, or his grand-mother's, and had gone around in circles with old-fashioned names and more modern ones.

Juliet had kept going back to one, and finally she'd said, 'I know she and Gio have only recently married, but she's been in your lives for a long time...supporting you all, loving Gio.'

'It will go to her head,' Sev had warned with a smile.

'Good.'

And now there was no attempt to stay back. Mimi came over and scooped up her tiny namesake and started to sing to her.

'What have you done?' Dante said to Sev, and they shared a small eye-roll.

They were back to being brothers.

When Juliet got tired, Sev had no compunction in shooing the happy lot out.

'Are you okay?' he asked her.

'A bit tired...but yes.'

He sat on the bed and they had a small kiss, and a very big gaze at little Mimi, who was getting hungry...or needed changing...or whatever it was that made her squeak and wriggle.

'She's so pretty...' Juliet was fascinated, touching her slender fingers. 'I think she's going to play the violin...look at her chin wobbling...'

Sevandro didn't say anything. If he had it might have come out a bit hoarse.

Of course he loved little Mimi, but it was at that moment that she took his heart and melted him, and also terrified him, and all the other things love did.

'God...' He breathed out sharply and put his head right down next to hers, breathing in her new baby smell. 'Never scare me like that again.'

'Girls are easier, huh?' Juliet checked. 'She's fine.'

'Yes...' He looked up, checked in. 'You?'

She nodded. 'You?'

'Completely.'

* * * * *

MILLS & BOON ®

Coming next month

RUSH TO THE ALTAR
Abby Green

As if being prompted by a rogue devil inside herself, she blurted out, 'I couldn't help overhearing your conversation with your solicitor earlier.'

Corti's mouth tipped up on one side, and that tiny sign of humour added about another 1,000 percent to his appeal. For a second Lili felt dizzy.

'What was it you heard exactly?' He folded his arms now, but that only drew attention to the corded muscles of his forearms.

Lili swallowed. 'About how you have to marry and have an heir if you want to keep this villa.'

'And this is interesting enough for you to bring it up...why?'

The night breeze skated over Lili's bare skin, making it prickle into goose bumps. She was very aware that she was wearing just a swimsuit and a tiny towelling robe, her wet hair streaming down her back. The sense of daring fizzled away. She was being ridiculous.

She shook her head. 'It was nothing. I shouldn't have mentioned it.'

'But you did.'

There was a charge between them now. Something that felt almost tangible. 'Yes, I did.'

Continue reading

RUSH TO THE ALTAR
Abby Green

Available next month
millsandboon.co.uk

COMING SOON!

We really hope you enjoyed reading this book.
If you're looking for more romance
be sure to head to the shops when
new books are available on

Thursday 22nd May

To see which titles are coming soon, please visit

millsandboon.co.uk/nextmonth

MILLS & BOON

FOUR BRAND NEW BOOKS FROM
MILLS & BOON MODERN

The same great stories you love, a stylish new look!

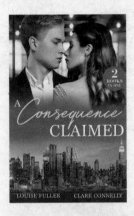

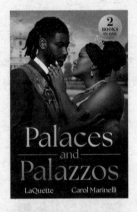

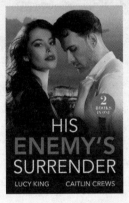

OUT NOW

afterglow BOOKS

Afterglow Books is a trend-led, trope-filled list of books with diverse, authentic and relatable characters, a wide array of voices and representations, plus real world trials and tribulations. Featuring all the tropes you could possibly want (think small-town settings, fake relationships, grumpy vs sunshine, enemies to lovers) and all with a generous dose of spice in every story.

♪ @millsandboonuk
◎ @millsandboonuk
afterglowbooks.co.uk

#AfterglowBooks

For all the latest book news, exclusive content and giveaways scan the QR code below to sign up to the Afterglow newsletter:

SCAN ME

afterglow BOOKS

 International

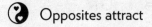 Opposites attract

Spicy

Workplace romance

Forbidden love

Spicy

OUT NOW

Two stories published every month. Discover more at:
Afterglowbooks.co.uk

LET'S TALK

Romance

For exclusive extracts, competitions
and special offers, find us online:

f MillsandBoon

X @MillsandBoon

⊙ @MillsandBoonUK

♪ @MillsandBoonUK

Get in touch on 01413 063 232

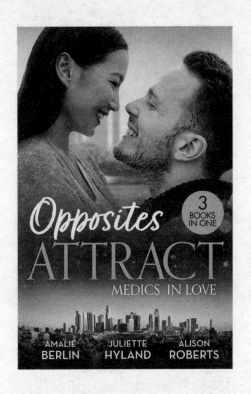

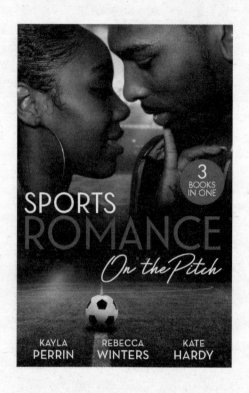